HARD
EVIDENCE

HARD EVIDENCE

JOHN T. LESCROART

DONALD I. FINE, INC.

New York

Library of Congress Cataloging-in-Publication Data

Lescroart, John T.
Hard evidence / John T. Lescroart.
p. cm.
ISBN 1-55611-344-7
PS3562.E78H36   1993
813'.54—dc20   92-54457
                                                CIP

Manufactured in the United States of America

10 9 8 7 6 5 4 3 2

Designed by Irving Perkins Associates

This book is dedicated to my wife, Lisa, who is always there; and to Nishion Matosian, aka Don Matheson—Marine, cop, bartender, actor —always the best man.

ACKNOWLEDGMENTS

For the initial inspiration and the continuing education, I'd like to thank Joel T. Kornfeld and Al Giannini, respectively.

A host of other knowledgeable and helpful people assisted in the making of this book. Among them are several attorneys from the San Francisco district attorney's office: Jim Costello, Susan Eto, Jerry Norman and Bill Fazio. From Davis, thanks to attorney Steve Shaffer. The substantial liberties I have taken herein with assistant district attorneys in San Francisco are the purist of fiction and the result bears no resemblance to these or any other members of a very professional, efficient, and forthcoming prosecutorial team.

Nonlegal contributions were no less important: San Francisco coroner Dr. Boyd Stephens was extremely gracious with his valuable time. No less so were Tristan Brighty, Mike Hamilburg, Joanie Socola, Dr. Phil Girard, Mark Detzer and Bob Eisele. All contributed importantly to the finished work.

Finally, I'd like to thank my two young children, Justine and Jack, for their wonderful attitudes and behavior for most of the time I spent completing this endeavor.

If there are any technical errors, they are solely the fault of the author.

HARD EVIDENCE

Every year if not every day we have to wager our salvation upon some prophecy based on imperfect knowledge.

—Oliver Wendell Holmes, Jr.

PART I

1

Dismas Hardy walked hip-deep in green ice water, his rubber-gloved hands on the fins of a six-foot white shark.

Outside in the world, it was nearly two o'clock of an early summer morning, but here at the Steinhart there was no time. The overhead light reflected off the institutional green walls, clammy with distilled sea-sweat. Somewhere, out of the room, a motor throbbed dully.

The only noise in Hardy's world was the steady slush and suck of the water curling behind him as he walked around and around, alone in the circular pool.

Pico Morales had called around seven to ask if he felt like doing some walking. When Pico called, it meant that some fishing boat had landed a great white shark and had contacted the Aquarium. The sharks bred just off the Farallons, and the Steinhart—or Pico, its curator—wanted a live one badly. The problem was that the beasts became so traumatized, or wounded, or both, after they were caught, that none survived. Too exhausted to move on their own, they had to be walked through the water so that they could breathe.

It was Hardy's third and last hour-long shift tonight. He'd been spelled by a couple of other volunteers earlier, and Pico was due any minute, so Hardy just walked, unthinking, putting down one foot after another, dragging and pulling the half-dead monster along with him.

On his first break, he'd stripped off his wetsuit, changed and walked over to the Little Shamrock for a Guinness or two. Hardy's brother-in-law, Frannie's brother Moses McGuire, had been off. Lynne Leish was working her normal Sunday shift behind the rail, and Hardy had taken his drink to the back and sat, speaking to no one.

On his next break, he'd gone out and climbed a fence into the Japanese Tea Garden. Sitting on a footbridge, he listened to the orchestrated trickle of the artificial stream that flowed between the

3

bonsais and pagodas. The fog had been in, and it hadn't made the evening any warmer.

Hardy wasn't paying attention when Pico came in. Suddenly there he was at the side of the pool, his huge bulk straining his wetsuit to its limit. Pico had a large black drooping mustache that got wet every time he brought the steaming cup to his lips. "Hey, Diz."

Hardy, willing his legs forward, looked up and grunted.

"How's the baby?"

Hardy kept moving. "Don't know."

Pico rested his cup on the edge of the pool and slid in. He shivered as the cold water came under his suit. Next time Hardy came around, Pico grabbed the shark and goosed its belly. "Let it go," he said.

Hardy walked another two steps, then released the fins. The shark turned ninety degrees and took a nosedive into the tiles on the bottom of the tank.

Pico sighed. Hardy leaned his elbows up against the rim of the pool. "Lack of family structure," Pico said. "That's what does it."

"What does what?" Hardy was breathing hard.

"I don't think they have much will to live, these guys. You know, abandoned at birth, left to fend for themselves. Probably turn to drugs, run with a bad crowd, eat junk food. Time we get 'em, they're just plum licked."

Hardy nodded. "Good theory."

Pico, in the bottoms of his wetsuit, his enormous stomach protruding like a tumor, sat on the lip of the tank, sipping coffee and brandy. Hardy was out of the pool. The shark hung still in the water, its nose on the bottom. Without saying anything, Pico handed his mug to Hardy.

"We're doing something wrong, Peek."

Pico nodded. "Follow that reasoning, Diz. You're onto something."

"They do keep dying, don't they?"

"I think this one OD'd. Probably mainlining." He grabbed the mug back. "Fucking shark drug addicts."

"Lack of family structure," Hardy said.

"Yeah." Pico plopped in and walked over to the shark. "Want to help hoist this sucker out and stroll through his guts? Further the cause of science?"

Hardy emptied Pico's coffee mug, sighed and brought the gurney over. Pico had tied a rope around the shark's tail and slung it over a pulley in the ceiling. Suddenly, the tail twitched and Pico jumped back as if stung. "Spasmodic crackhead shark rapists!"

"You sure it's just a spasm?" Hardy didn't want to cut the thing up if it wasn't dead yet.

"It isn't the cha-cha, Diz. Pull on that thing, will you?"

Hardy pulled and the shark came out of the water, slow and heavy. Hardy guided it onto the gurney. He waited while Pico hauled himself out of the pool.

"I am reminded of a poem," Hardy said. "Winter and spring, summer and fall, you look like a basketball."

Pico ignored him and reached for his coffee mug. "Need I take this abuse from someone who steals my coffee?"

"There was coffee in that?"

"And a little brandy. Cuts the aftertaste."

They flipped the shark on its back. Pico went into his office and came out a minute later with a scalpel. He traced a line up the shark's belly to its gills, laying open the stomach cavity. Slicing a strip of flesh, he held it up to Hardy. "Want some sushi?"

The tank gurgled. Hardy leaned over the gurney, careful not to block the light, while Pico cut. He reached into the stomach and began pulling things out—two or three small fish, a piece of driftwood, a rubber ball, a tin can.

"Junk food," Pico muttered.

"Leave out the food part," Hardy said.

Pico reached back in and brought out something that looked like a starfish. He pulled it up, looking at it quizzically.

"What's that?" Hardy asked.

"I don't know. It looks—" Then, as though he'd been bit, Pico screamed, jumping back, throwing the object to the floor.

Hardy walked over to look.

Partially digested and covered with slime, it was still recognizable for what it was—a human hand, severed at the wrist, the first finger missing, and on the pinkie, a sea-green jade ring.

2

Hardy expected that the guys in blue would be first on the scene. He would likely know them from the Shamrock, where the police dropped in frequently enough to keep the presence alive. Sometimes your Irish bar will get a little rowdy and it helped to have the heat appear casually to remind patrons that a certain minimum standard of decorous behavior would be maintained.

For the better part of nine years, Hardy had been the daytime bartender at the Little Shamrock. He'd only been back in the D.A.'s office for four months now, since Rebecca had been born and he and Frannie had gotten married.

Hardy and his onetime boss, current friend, partner and brother-in-law Moses McGuire were both reasonable hands with the shillelagh of Kentucky ash that hung behind the bar under the cash register. McGuire, Doctor of Philosophy, in his cups himself, had twice thrown people through the front window of the Shamrock. Most other times, the forced exit was, Old West fashion, through the swinging double doors. Neither Hardy nor Moses was quick on the 86—no good publican was—but both of them had needed assistance from the beat cops from time to time. The Shamrock wasn't a "cop bar," but the guys from Park Station had trouble paying for drinks if they stopped in during off hours.

Hardy stood just inside the front entrance to the Aquarium. The black and white pulled up, the searchlight on the car scanning the front of the building. From the street to the entrance was a twenty-yard expanse of open cement at 2:15 of a pitch-dark morning. Hardy didn't blame them for the caution. He stepped outside.

They walked back behind the tanks in the damp hallway. Bathed in a faint greenish overhead light, the two cops followed Hardy amid the burps and gurglings of the Aquarium. He did know them—Dan Soper

6

and Bobby Varela, a fullback and a sprinter. Hardy thought the three of them made a parade: the give of leather, slap of holster, clomp of heavy shoes, jingle of cuffs and keys—beat cops weren't dressed for ambush. It reminded Hardy of his days on the force, walking a beat with Abe Glitsky.

He had been a different guy back then. Now he felt older, almost protective of these cops. The beat was the beginning.

They came into what Hardy called the walking room. Pico had changed into a turtleneck and sportcoat, though he still wore his swim trunks. He stared emptily straight ahead, sitting on the edge of the pool next to the gurney that held the shark.

"Find anything else?" Hardy asked.

Pico let himself off the pool's lip, withering Hardy with a look. After the introductions, Varela walked over to the hand, still lying where Pico had thrown it. "That what it looks like?"

"That's what it is," Hardy said.

"Where'd you get this shark?" Soper asked. "Hey, Bobby!" Varela was poking at the hand with a pencil. "Leave it, would you?"

Pico told Soper how the shark had come to the Steinhart. Soper wanted to know the fishing boat's name, captain, time of capture, all that. Hardy walked over to Varela, who was still hunched over, and stood over him.

"Pretty weird, huh?"

Varela looked back over his shoulder, straightening. "Naw, we get these three, four times a week."

"I wonder if the guy drowned?"

Varela couldn't seem to take his eyes off the thing. "You'd hope so, wouldn't you? How'd you like to have been alive instead?"

Soper had passed them, going into Pico's office to use the telephone. Pico came over. "He's getting some crime-lab people down here. No way am I putting my hand in that guy again."

Varela shivered. "I don't blame you." He walked back to the shark and gingerly lifted the incision along its stomach with his pencil. "Can't see much."

"There's more in there," Pico said. "We'd just started."

Varela stepped back. "Dan's right. I think we'll just wait."

Hardy stared down at the hand. "I wonder who it was," he said.

"Oh, we'll find out soon enough," Varela said.

Pico leaned back against the pool. "How can you be sure?" he said. "It could be anybody."

"Yeah, but we've got one major clue."

"What's that?" Pico asked.

Hardy turned. "Let me guess," he said. "Fingerprints."

3

Hardy lifted his red-rimmed eyes from the folder he was studying. It was three-thirty in the afternoon, and last night had been a long one, ending around sunrise. He'd driven home from the Steinhart, changed into a new brown suit, looked in at Frannie curled up in their bed, at Rebecca sleeping in the new room he'd built onto the back of his house, and headed downtown where he now worked as an assistant district attorney on the third floor of the Hall of Justice on Seventh and Bryant.

The job wasn't going very well. The case he was laboring over now, like the others he was currently prosecuting, came from the lower rungs of the criminal ladder. This one involved a prostitute who'd been caught by an undercover cop posing as a tourist wandering around Union Square. The girl—Esme Aiella—was twenty-two, black, two priors. She was out on $500 bail and was, even now as Hardy read, probably out hustling.

Hardy was wondering what purpose this all served. Or the bust of a city employee, Derek Graham, who sold lids of marijuana on the side. Hardy had known guys like Derek in college, and very few of them went on to become ringleaders in, say, the Medellin cartel. Derek had three kids, lived in the Mission and was trying to make ends meet so his wife could stay home with the kids.

Still, this was Hardy's job now—nailing the petty malefactors, the lowlifes, the unlucky or the foolish. This wasn't the high drama of the passionate crime, the romance of big deals gone crooked, beautiful people desperately denying their libidos, their greed, their shallowness. No, this was down below the stage lights, where the denizens lived on the slimy border of the law, slipping over the line, not even seeing it, trying to get a little money, a little power, a little edge, maybe even some release, some *fun* in a life story that wasn't ever going to make it past the footlights. Mostly, Hardy thought, it was sad.

9

Hardy had thought, perhaps unrealistically, that coming back to work as an assistant district attorney he wouldn't have to deal with this level again. He was, after all, nearly forty now, and he'd done his apprenticeship with the D.A. ten years ago. Back when he started, he'd had to work through the issue of whether he could morally prosecute the so-called victimless crimes—hookers, casual dopers. Somewhere in his heart, he believed that these crimes weren't as real as the ones that hurt people. He tended to believe that if grown-ups wanted to get laid or get high or get dead by jumping off the Golden Gate bridge, society should let them. God knows, it had enough truly bad things to correct. Why waste the time on this pettiness?

But this, he knew, wasn't a good attitude. His job was to prosecute people who broke the law. Whether they had done anything he considered wrong was moot.

And he was a new hire, only brought on because he'd left with a few friends, like Chief Assistant D.A. Art Drysdale. Also, he suspected, although he didn't know for certain, that his ex-father-in-law, Superior Court Judge Andy Fowler, had put in a good word for him.

He hadn't actively practiced law in ten years. He'd been a bartender, was still part owner of the Shamrock, and he really couldn't expect guys who'd made a linear career of criminal law to step aside while the new guy got the hot cases.

Of course, even if he were doing murders—the fun stuff—the majority of them were NHI cases—"no humans involved." It was a pretty apt term. Lowlifes killing each other for reasons that would be laughable—they were laughable—if they weren't so tragic. . . .

This morning, Hardy had run into Arnie Tiano and Elizabeth Pullios in the hallway, laughing so hard their sides hurt:

". . . so this poor son of a bitch, the victim, Leon, he's trying to get some hubcaps back on this car in the middle of the day. It's his car. Red, you know, an old Ford. So the perp, Germaine, sees him, comes out and asks what he thinks he's doing messing with his, Germaine's, car, which in truth is parked around the corner. Looks a lot like Leon's car, I guess. Same model, red and all. But Germaine is so loaded he can't see that well, and Leon says fuck off, it's my car, which it is. So Germaine goes inside and comes out with a gun, and Leon says, "What you gonna do, shoot me?" and Germaine says, "Yeah," and pumps four shots into him."

Pullios howls. "Get out of here!"

"Swear to God, I mean, there's ten witnesses hanging around the curb and this guy just blows Leon away, walks back inside and takes a nap, which is what he's doing when we get there."

Both Arnie and Elizabeth laughing, laughing, laughing.

But it beat bartending.

Not that there was anything wrong with bartending. Working behind the rail was an uncomplicated and stress-free life. He'd taken pride in the way he mixed drinks, getting along with everybody, sleepwalking.

Then suddenly it wasn't enough. Wasn't nearly enough. After he'd broken his routine, once trying to help the Cochrans, once trying to save his own life, he realized that he'd changed. Survival wasn't enough. He'd fallen in love. His new wife now had a baby that he'd treat as his own even if it wasn't.

There was a future again, not a succession of days in half a Guinness haze. It surprised him how good it felt.

The time behind the bar had begun to weigh heavily. The regulars, the pickups at the bar, the stupid Irish fights over darts or whether Jameson was better than that Protestant piss Bushmills. It was all the same ol' same ol', the alcohol discussions laden with a profundity that never stood the scrutiny of the next sunrise.

So it was back to the law, to a real job, to something he cared about to go with the new life he was building.

Frannie was pregnant again, too.

4

The coroner's office was in the same building Hardy worked in, on the ground floor. To wheel the gurneys in, there was easy access from the parking lot. The public could enter without being frisked, without going through the detector at the back door to the Hall of Justice.

Hardy was sitting on one of the yellow plastic chairs in the outer office. It was four-thirty and he was meeting Esme's attorney at five in his office, so he took a break and decided to go check on the hand.

The receptionist was one of those rare marvels of civil service. Sixto was about twenty-five, wore a tie and slacks, combed his hair, spoke English politely and with some grammatical precision. A miracle.

"I don't think they've found anything yet, Mr. Hardy," he said. "It hasn't been a good day. Mondays never are."

"Bad weekend?"

Sixto nodded. "Two homicides. This drive-by stuff. What gets into people?" There wasn't any answer to that and Sixto didn't expect one. "So I doubt if they've gotten to anything with the hand, but I'll keep on it, okay? I'll let you know."

Hardy thanked him and got up. Outside the door, in the June fog, he stopped to take in the parking lot, the freeway blocking the horizon to his right, which was starting to sound like rush hour. Walking toward him from the back door were Detective Sergeant Abe Glitsky and Chief A.D.A. Art Drysdale.

"Guys," Hardy said, nodding.

The guys were not in good humor. Coming abreast of him, Drysdale said, "We don't want to talk about it."

"The hand?"

Glitsky, as big, black and mean looking as the lanky, white Drysdale seemed benign, snapped, "What hand?" He reached behind Hardy and pulled at the door.

"We're not talking," Drysdale said.

12

They were walking in the door. "That's what I like," Hardy said, "the free and easy flow of information, the genial give and take of ideas . . ."

The door had closed on him. Hardy stood a moment, shrugged, and went up to meet Esme's attorney.

Aaron Jaans crossed spit-shined shoes over his well-creased pants, showing a bit of the red garter that held black socks halfway up his calf. The thought crossed Hardy's mind that Jaans might be Esme's pimp as well as her attorney. Hardy didn't have any moral problem about prosecuting pimps. He hated pimps.

"I guess the basic problem here is the priors," Hardy said. "Esme doesn't seem to be getting the message."

Jaans leaned onto the back legs of the chair across from Hardy's desk. He pulled the cuff of his pants down over the distracting garter. The lawyer had a broad, elastic, dark black face, high forehead, aquiline nose, straight hair starting to go a little gray. There was still a trace of a rogue British accent from somewhere.

"She's a working girl, Mr. Hardy, and you and I both know that you can arrest her every other day and she's still going to go on the street when she's out."

"Not if she's in jail she won't."

Jaans rolled his eyes, but quickly, deciding against too much histrionics. "In jail?"

"We've got felony grand theft here. Four hundred and sixteen dollars. That's jail."

Jaans leaned forward again, elbows on his knees. "Mr. Hardy, you and I know that no judge wants this kind of rap going to trial. Clogs the docket horrible. It also ties up your vice witness for the better part of a day or two, gets him off the street and what good is he doing? You start taking all these people to trial . . . well, you know this as well as I do."

Hardy was getting a little tired of the civics lesson. He shuffled the folder in front of him, pretended to be reading. "The offer," he said, "is felony probation, ninety days in jail or a five-thousand-dollar fine."

"Are you serious?"

Hardy nodded. "Yep."

"Is there some new policy going down?"

Hardy shook his head.

"Where's my client going to get five thousand dollars? Do you think she's going to go out and get a job typing somewhere? Managing a McDonald's? She won't do that. She has no skills, Mr. Hardy. You know what she'll do, don't you? She'll have to be on her back for a month to make that kind of money. Do you want that?"

"I'm sure her pimp could get her that money in two and a half seconds. But she's not talking about her pimp. She says she doesn't have a pimp. So, I ask myself, how can we get a handle on this pimp, close up his shop?"

Jaans took a breath. "You know, Mr. Hardy, some of these pimps are not nice men, I grant you, but they do provide protection for their girls, abortions if they need them, that kind of thing."

"They're keeping their assets productive, that's all. Simple business."

"You know how long a lone girl on the street is going to last?"

"You're telling me that pimps are solid citizens, is that it?"

Jaans turned his palms up. "They provide a service."

Hardy leaned forward, fingers laced, elbows on his desk. "What they do, Mr. Jaans, what pimps do," he paused, "as you and I *both* know, is take these ignorant, poor, sad, really helpless women and keep them degraded, stoned, and on their backs until their looks go at twenty-five. After which their life span, due to needles and disease and just generally getting the shit beaten out of them, is about six months." Hardy took a breath, calming himself down. "So maybe this five thousand will make Esme decide to give up her pimp, and then maybe I can have a little fun."

Jaans nodded. He uncrossed his legs, stood up and reached his hand over the desk. Hardy, surprised, got up himself, hesitated, then decided to take it. "I'll convey your offer to my client," Jaans said.

He stopped at the door, turned, raised a finger to make a point, then decided against it and disappeared into the hallway.

Lou the Greek's was a restaurant and watering hole for cops and D.A.'s, across the street from the Hall of Justice. Lou was married to a Chinese woman who did the cooking, so the place served an eclectic menu of egg rolls, chow mein, shaslik, rice pilaf, hot and sour soup, baklava and fortune cookies. Occasionally Lou's special would be something like Kung Pao pita pockets or pot-sticker kabobs.

There were two bars, standing room only, at the front and back walls. Now, at five-thirty, the din was ferocious. An arm-wrestling contest was going on in the center of the room, twenty or thirty cops screaming, trying to get their bets in.

Drysdale and Glitsky huddled over an ancient Pong machine by the back door. Hardy pushed his way through the crowd. Drysdale was ahead, eight to six. Neither of the men looked up.

"Boo," Hardy said.

Glitsky looked up for an instant, but it was long enough for the blip to get by him. "Damn."

"Nine six," Drysdale said. "Gotta pay attention."

"Just play," Glitsky growled.

Hardy watched the blip move back and forth. Both of these guys were good, playing at the master level, and the blip really moved. Hardy went to the bar, elbowed his way in and ordered a pint of cranberry juice, lots of ice.

Back at the Pong game, Glitsky glowered in defeat. Drysdale sat back in his chair, legs crossed, savoring a beer. Hardy squatted, checking out the final score of eleven to six. "You owe me five bucks," Glitsky told him.

Drysdale sipped his beer. "He never beats me anyway. I wouldn't pay him."

"Can we talk about the hand?"

"What hand?"

Hardy looked at Drysdale. "What hand, he says."

Drysdale ran it down for Abe, who had spent the day interviewing family members of a murdered old man. The hand wasn't the most compelling item of the day for him.

"So who is it?" Glitsky asked when he'd finished.

Drysdale shrugged. "Some guy," he said. Then, to Hardy, "What's to talk about?"

"How about if he was killed?"

"How about it?"

"You think he was killed?" Glitsky asked.

"I think he's dead at least. How he got that way I don't know. I wondered if you'd heard anything."

"I heard a good new song the other day," Glitsky said.

Hardy turned to Drysdale. "I thought the coroner might have come up with something."

Drysdale frowned. "I doubt he's even looked at it."

"It sounded like Garth Brooks, but it could have been Merle Haggard. A lot of these country guys sound the same to me."

Hardy chewed some ice. "Yeah, well, if it does turn out to be a homicide, I wouldn't mind drawing the case."

"Homicide's a pretty long shot," Drysdale said. "Guy might have drowned, anything."

"I know. I just wanted to put the word in."

Drysdale thought about the proposal. "You haven't had a murder yet, have you, Diz?"

Hardy shook his head. "Not close."

"It could have been Randy Travis, though," Glitsky said. "Sometimes when he sings low he sounds a little like the Hag."

Drysdale appeared to think hard a minute. Glitsky was humming the first few bars of his song. Finally Drysdale looked at the last inch of beer in his glass and finished it off. "Sounds fair," he said to Hardy. "You found it. If it's a murder, it's your case."

Glitsky stopped humming. "Hardy makes the big time," he said, reining in his natural enthusiasm.

Hardy fished in his pocket and dropped a couple of quarters into the console in front of him. "Have another game," he said to Drysdale, "and this time let him win."

Hardy sat on the Navajo rug on the floor of his living room, way up at the front of the house. His adopted daughter Rebecca was in his lap, her tiny hand picking at the buttons of his shirt. In the fireplace, some oak burned. Outside, the coccoon of fog that wrapped the house was darkening by degrees. Up in the kitchen, he heard Frannie humming, doing the dishes from their dinner.

The room, like the rest of the house, had changed with Frannie's arrival. Previously, Hardy had lived almost exclusively in his back rooms—the kitchen, his bedroom, the office. His house was in the old Victorian "railroad" style, living room up front, a dining room, then a small utility room, all of which opened to the right off a long hallway that ended at the kitchen.

While Hardy had designed and built the back room for Rebecca, Frannie had painted and redecorated the front rooms, brightening them up in white with dusty rose accents. Hardy's nautical theme pieces, such as they were, were banished to his office. Now, on the mantel in place of the dusty old blowfish, was an exquisite caravan of Venetian blown-glass elephants. A framed DaVinci poster, a study of horses, graced the wall to the left of the fireplace. On the right, Frannie had filled the built-in bookshelves with hardcovers from Hardy's office—Barbara Tuchman, Hardy's complete Wambaugh collection, most of Steinbeck, Márquez, Jack London. Four new lamps filled the corners with light.

Hardy took it all in—the plants, the dark sheen of the cherry dining-room furniture, his baby girl. It seemed nearly impossible to him that all of this was so comfortable now, so right. Frannie came through the dining room and stood leaning against the doorpost. Her long red hair glinted in the light from the fire. She wore jeans and a Stanford sweatshirt, white Reeboks.

"You were so quiet," she said.

Hardy rested a flat palm against Rebecca's stomach, feeling the heart pumping. "I don't think I was home once this time of night when I was bartending."

"You miss it?"

"Bartending?" He shook his head. "No. It's funny. I used to think I was addicted to it—you know, the noise and the action. Now I'm sitting here, the fire pops and that's plenty."

She came over and sat down Indian style across from him. She ran a finger up her daughter's leg, left her hand there. "Aren't you tired? Did you sleep at all last night?"

Hardy shrugged. "As Mr. Zevon says, I'll sleep when I'm dead."

Frannie didn't like hearing that. Rebecca's biological father, Eddie Cochran—Frannie's husband—had been killed just about a year ago.

Hardy sensed it. He put his hand over hers. "In truth, I am severely fatigued."

As Frannie got up to pull the curtains over the bay window, the doorbell rang. "We don't want any," Hardy said.

"I know." Frannie went to the door.

Jeff Elliot knew news when he saw it, and if a human hand turning up in a shark's belly didn't deserve more than a graph on the back page, he'd eat his press card.

He knew that a good percentage of all the great stories—Watergate, Lincoln Savings, Pete Rose—had begun as tiny drops in the vast pool of information that came to a paper every day. And what made those drops congeal to a trickle that became a flood had been the reporters who viewed the news as their canvas. News happened, sure, but what made the news a *story* was what excited him. You couldn't make things up, but you could manufacture interest, an angle, a hook.

That's what made a good reporter. And Jeff knew he had the gift—his bosses just hadn't seen it yet.

So things weren't moving as quickly for him as he'd hoped. In college in Wisconsin, he'd been the editor of the paper, then three years at the Akron *Clarion,* and finally his big break, the San Francisco *Chronicle.* But now he'd been on the coast for seven months, and he was amazed that even here in the big city, so little came in via the police incidence reports—the IRs—that was even remotely sexy.

And that's what he'd been doing—the lowest dog work, checking over the IRs, looking for a lead, a grabber, a story. And then, today, finally, the hand.

He balanced his crutches against the doorway to ring the bell. Almost immediately, the door opened to a very pretty red-haired woman in a Stanford sweatshirt. The house smelled of oak and baking bread. He gave his little waif grin.

"I'm sorry to bother you," he said, "but is this where Dismas Hardy lives? I'm Jeff Elliot with the *Chronicle* and I'd just like to ask him a few questions."

"It's interesting you should ask that," Hardy said. "It came up just today downtown."

"What came up, the homicide question?"

They'd moved into the dining room, and Frannie had poured a black and tan—Guinness and ale in two layers—for her husband. The reporter, really not much more than a kid with a pair of bad legs, had a cup of coffee. Frannie, pregnant, had a glass of water and sat quietly nursing Rebecca, listening.

"Well, the odds are good that whoever it is, he's probably recently dead. It could be a straight drowning, but we had to consider the fact that somebody killed this guy and dumped him in the ocean."

The reporter had his dictaphone on the table between them.

"But," Hardy said, "we're still a long way from knowing that. I don't believe the coroner's even had a chance to examine the thing yet. At least he hadn't by the time I left the office."

"Is that normal?"

"Well, if there was a body to go with it, he'd have done something I'm sure. But we haven't got anything from Missing Persons, at least not yet. They're checking other jurisdictions I'm sure." Hardy shrugged. "It's a process, that's all. They'll get to it."

Frannie finished nursing and went to the back of the house to put down the sleeping infant. When she got back, Dismas had finished his beer and she could tell by his look that he was fading. He hadn't slept, after all, in two days.

They were talking about Pico Morales pulling out the hand, back at the Aquarium. Frannie went around behind Dismas, massaged his shoulders and cleared her throat. "I'm afraid this news conference had got to come to an end. I've got a tired man here who's too macho to admit it."

"Oh gosh!" Jeff Elliot looked at his watch, flicked off the tape machine. "I'm sorry, I didn't mean to keep you. I've got to get this story written and filed, anyway."

"I'm afraid it's not much new as a story."

"I don't know. I've just got a feeling about this one. It's somebody's hand, for gosh sake."

Hardy nodded. "You got a card? I'll let you know if we find something."

5

D.A. CALLS MYSTERY HAND A HOMICIDE
by Jeffrey Elliot
Chronicle Staff Writer

An assistant district attorney conceded last night that the grisly find on Sunday of a human hand wearing a jade ring was a homicide.

The hand was discovered in the stomach of a great white shark—the same animal featured in the movie *Jaws*—that had been delivered alive to the Steinhart Aquarium over the weekend.

Assistant District Attorney Dismas Hardy, who coincidentally had been present at the aquarium when the hand was discovered, said the D.A.'s office was looking into the matter. "Somebody killed this guy and dumped him in the ocean," Hardy said.

To date, there are no leads on the victim's identity. Hardy acknowledged that authorities were checking with other jurisdictions in the area.

Although the coroner has not yet performed any tests on the hand, Hardy appeared confident that the victim would soon be identified and an investigation into the probable murder begun.

"It's a process," Hardy said. "They'll get there."

CHRISTOPHER LOCKE WAS FIFTY-TWO YEARS OLD and the first African-American ever elected district attorney of the City and County of San Francisco. Locke thought his job essentially took place in the rarefied air of policy. He lobbied hard for the death penalty, for example. He determined whether there would be a crackdown on graffiti prosecutions, on gay bashing in the Mission district; he worked with the police department on coordinating the work of the Gang Task Force. He went to a lot of lunches, spoke both inside the city and around the state on issues involving law enforcement.

Locke's longtime ally and best friend (to the extent it was possible to have one) was Art Drysdale, with whom he entrusted much of the day-to-day running of the office. Art was fair and firm, too outspoken to be a political rival, a good administrator and even better lawyer. The last thing Locke had time for, or wanted to do, was interact with his junior staff.

But here he was this Tuesday morning awaiting the arrival of Dismas Hardy, four months in the office. Hardy's file lay next to the *Chronicle,* open on his desk in front of him.

It didn't seem to Locke to be much of an article, but it had evidently been enough to prompt a call from some homicide lieutenant to the police chief himself, Dan Rigby, who in turn had deemed it important enough to call Locke at home before he'd had his coffee. Then, fifteen minutes later, he'd gotten another call from John Strout, the coroner, asking what the hell this homicide business was all about.

Drysdale had thought he'd just run down and tell Hardy to button it, but Locke had promised Rigby he'd handle the matter personally, so here he was.

Dorothy buzzed, and a minute later Hardy let himself through the door. Locke remembered him from when he'd welcomed him to the office—a formality about which Locke was punctilious. At the time, Locke had briefly wondered how Drysdale had found an opening on the staff for a male Caucasian.

Hardy wasn't a kid by any means. This was his second time around with the D.A. He should know better.

"Don't sit down, Hardy. This won't take long." Locke busied himself for a moment with Hardy's file. Without looking up, he said, "I notice you've got seventeen specially assigned prelims"—preliminary hearings—"you're supposed to be prosecuting."

"Yes, sir, that's about right."

"That's exactly right, according to your file. Am I missing something?"

"I hadn't counted them."

"Perhaps prelim work isn't worthy of your time."

Hardy stood in the classic at-ease position. "This is about the article." It wasn't a question.

"That's right. It's about the article."

"The quote was out of context."

"It happens all the time. I'm wondering why you found it proper to be discussing this matter with the press at all."

"I found the hand. I thought the reporter was going for something a little more human interest."

"It doesn't appear he was. It appears you got yourself sandbagged."

"Yes, sir, it does."

"So I've instructed Mr. Drysdale to send a little more prelim work your way. The way we do it, we like to have our attorneys work on the cases they get assigned, is that clear?"

"Yes, sir."

"And Mr. Drysdale will be doing the assigning."

"Yes, sir."

"And it would be good policy and a good habit to acquire if you prefaced any remarks you ever make to a reporter with the words 'This is off the record.' Understood?"

Hardy nodded and agreed until he was dismissed.

Though Hardy didn't like him, Aaron Jaans was a decent, even well-respected, attorney. In response to what he considered Hardy's outrageous offer he had requested that they talk to a judge in superior court rather than municipal court, before there was even a preliminary hearing to determine whether Hardy's offer would be made to stick. As a courtesy, Hardy had complied with the request.

Now they were in Judge Andy Fowler's courtroom and Esme Aiella stood before the bench, next to Aaron Jaans. She was wearing a skin-tight blue tube that began an inch above her nipples and ended four inches below her crotch. Her hair had been straightened and dyed a shade of red that did not occur in nature.

"Ms. Aiella," the judge was saying, "the facts of this case seem to speak for themselves, but before I make any ruling whatever, I want to hear from you that you are not interested in reducing grand theft, the charge against you, from a felony to a misdemeanor."

Esme stood silent, her hand to her mouth.

"Ms. Aiella!"

"I don't believe you asked her a question, Your Honor."

Fowler glared at Aaron Jaans, threw a glance at Dismas Hardy, who was standing to Jaans' right, then spoke again, looking directly at Esme. "Ms. Aiella, the court directs you to speak up. Can you hear me clearly?"

The woman nodded.

"Would you please use words? Can you hear me clearly?"

"Yes, sir."

"Your Honor, my client—"

Fowler held up his palm. "Mr. Jaans, I am speaking to your client directly, is that clear?" Without waiting for a response, the judge continued. "Now, Ms. Aiella, you are in a bad situation here. I must tell you that the charge of grand theft is very serious. If you are convicted, there will not just be a fine, there is the possibility—the very real possibility—of going to prison. Do you understand?"

The hand came away from her mouth. "Yes, sir."

"Do you care about that?"

She shrugged. "It don't matter."

"Going to prison doesn't matter?"

Esme shrugged again.

Fowler looked over at Hardy. Clearly, it didn't matter. Lecturing, arguing or threatening wasn't going to make any difference. The judge's eyes roamed the back of the courtroom for a moment, then he brought down his gavel. He indicated that Hardy follow him to his chambers. "The court will take a brief recess."

"There's no hope," the judge said. It was a statement so atypical of Andrew Bryan Fowler that Hardy couldn't immediately reply. There was nothing about the judge that suggested he could ever think there was no hope. He looked, as always, terrific. His thick black hair was peppered with enough gray to suggest wisdom, but not at the expense of advanced age. As a teenager he'd modeled for the Sears catalog, and his tanned face still had those fine All-American lines. His gray-blue eyes were penetrating, chin strong, teeth perfect, nose straight.

Andy's handmade blue dress shirt was wrinkle-free, even under his robes, and the gold cufflinks customized with his initials, ABF, provided just the right tone for a judge.

The cufflinks were often visible as Fowler sat on the bench, his fingers templed at his lips, listening to an argument he would later recall nearly verbatim. The cufflinks added to what the Romans had called *gravitas*—the nearly indescribable quality that rendered a man's acts and judgments significant. On the bench, His Honor Andy Fowler possessed *gravitas* in spades.

Here, in his chambers or at home, it was different, but not so very different. Hardy hung out around the house in jeans and a sweatshirt —in his bartending days, he'd been happy in tennis shoes, old corduroys, t-shirts. Even now, in one of his three new suits, Hardy was aware of the knot of his tie at his Adam's apple. Andy, by contrast, would arrive at a Sunday barbeque in pressed khakis, tasseled cordovan loafers, dress shirt and blazer, sometimes with a tie. When Andy played tennis, which he did well and often at the Olympic Club, he wore whites. Hardy guessed he slept in tailored pajamas and wore a bathrobe and slippers to have his coffee alone in his kitchen.

Hardy picked the paperweight off the desk. It was a strange and beautiful piece of light-green jade, nearly translucent, oddly shaped, with sea birds and whales etched in light relief on the highly polished surface.

Fowler was hanging his robe in the corner. He turned around. "I don't like to do this to you, but even without this girl's cooperation, we're not going with felony grand theft on this."

"We're not? Why not?"

"Because this kind of entrapment will not wash in my department, Diz. Chris Locke knows this. Art Drysdale knows it. I don't know why they keep sending these turkeys up here to Superior Court."

The judge was getting to be infamous around the Hall for his views on entrapment. His popularity, once very high, had suffered for it, but he was opposed to putting people away for crimes he thought they wouldn't have committed without a push from the police.

"The woman," he said, "picks up a john in Union Square and they go to his hotel room. The television set in the room is, surprise, really a video camera, and when our boy goes out of the room to the bathroom, we get a lovely picture of Esme Aiella taking his wallet, which happens to contain just enough American dollars to constitute what the law calls grand theft." He shook his head in disgust. "Because I like you, I run a bluff like I just did. Who knows, maybe she'll give up her pimp. But she's not going to give up her pimp—there's no way. So now this goes back to what it is—a misdemeanor prostitution that should not take up time in my courtroom."

"She did steal the money, Andy."

"Diz, they all steal. Why do you think prostitution's illegal in the first place?"

"So we just fine her and forget it?"

Fowler's shoulders sagged. "Every single day of the year we fine 'em and forget 'em. There's just no hope," he repeated.

The heft and balance of the paperweight felt incredibly good. Hardy sat down with it, passing it back and forth in his hands. The judge walked to one of the two windows behind his desk and crossed his hands behind his back.

Hardy got up, put the paperweight back in its spot and went and stood next to the man who'd been his father-in-law for five years. "Andy, are you all right?"

The judge sighed. "Sure, I'm fine." He flicked his smile back on. "See?"

Fowler didn't talk about there being no hope, but if he didn't want to talk at the moment, Hardy wasn't going to push it. "So what about next time with Esme Aiella? Don't we ever get the hammer?"

The judge stared at nothing out his grimy window. "Cure her, you mean?" His laugh was more a bitter snort. Fowler parted the shades of his window as if looking for something. Not seeing it, he moved back to his desk, into his red leather chair. "A girl like Esme, all the girls like Esme, they're turning tricks because nothing matters anyway. Their pimp is their father. He beats them and sleeps with them."

"You think Esme's father was sleeping with her?"

Fowler reached for the paperweight now himself, nodding. "Or her brother, or uncle, or all of the above. Women in the trade, they were broken in at home. And on the flip side, if their daddy was screwing them, even if they don't go into it full-time, they'll turn a trick or two. It's cheap psychology, but it's in every profile."

Hardy knew it was true. He remembered the interview he'd read where some reporter had asked a prostitute whether she had been abused as a child. And the woman had laughed. That was her response—laughter that the guy could be so dumb as to even ask that question. "Honey," she'd replied, "not 'abused.' Fucked, hit, messed with, and that's everybody I know. Every single girl in the trade."

"So there's no hope," Hardy said.

"I wouldn't hold my breath." The judge absently cupped the paperweight in his hand, bouncing it with a dull thump on the desktop.

A minute had passed. Fowler continued to tap the paperweight against the desk. Then, as if they'd been talking about it all along, he said. "Yeah, something's eating me, I suppose." He put the jade down, swiveled in his chair. "I'm not myself, Diz. I feel like an old clock who's run out of spring."

"How's long's it been since you've had a vacation?"

Fowler snorted. "A real vacation? A year ago August. But I just spent last weekend in the Sierras, put some miles on the hiking boots, didn't see a soul." Fowler put the paperweight down. "Here I am back in civilization and it doesn't seem to have helped a bit."

Hardy nodded. "Couple of years ago, I was feeling the same way, so I went on the wagon and flew down to Cabo for two weeks."

"Did that make you feel better?"

"Not at all."

Fowler smiled. "Well, that's a big help. Thanks."

"It did pass, though. Other stuff came up."

"Yeah, I know. The problem is, life keeps going on while you're waiting for that other stuff." Suddenly, almost with a jolt, the judge straightened up. "Oh, listen to me. A little case of the blues and His Honor becomes maudlin."

"His Honor's allowed to get down just like anybody else. You getting out at all? Having any fun? Want to come over and see my new family, have some dinner?"

"I don't think so, Diz, but thanks. I'd keep seeing you with Jane, thinking about what might have been." Hardy's first marriage, to the judge's daughter, had ended in divorce. "If you want to play some squash though, I'd be happy to whip you at the Olympic." Fowler was up now, going back to his robes.

Hardy reached over and picked up the paperweight again. "Deal," he said. Then, "Where'd you get this thing?"

Fowler turned. "What—?" But seeing what, his face darkened, uncontrolled for a second. "Why don't you take it?" he said.

Hardy went to put it down. "No, I can't—"

"Diz, take the damn thing. Put it in your pocket. I don't want to see it anymore."

"Andy—"

"Come on, Diz, let's pack it up. I've got a courtroom waiting for my august presence." He brushed by in a swish of robes. Stopping at the door, he held it open for Hardy. "I'll call you when I get a court. For squash."

True to his word, Locke saw that Hardy got more prelims. Five new special assignments were in his box when he got back from court. He sighed, pulled the paperweight from his pocket and picked up the telephone. The files could wait.

Jane Fowler worked as a buyer for I. Magnin. She was getting ready to go out to lunch, but she took his call. He hadn't talked to her since his marriage to Frannie—which he thought was understandable. The idea of platonic friendship with an ex-spouse made them both un-comfortable, and the last time they'd seen each other, before Hardy and Frannie had gotten engaged, they slept together, which also didn't make things easier.

Hardy and Jane had loved each other for several years. They had had a lot of good times, then had endured the death of their son together. But after that, Hardy had lost faith in everything, and if a marriage needed anything, it was faith.

So they'd gotten divorced. Then, after nearly a decade's separation, they'd reconnected for a few months, long enough for them both to realize that another try at marriage wouldn't work. They wanted different things out of life now, and if they were still attracted to one another, Hardy thought it would be bad luck to confuse that with what he had with Frannie.

Jane sounded as she always did—refined and composed. Shades of her father.

"I'm glad you called," she said. "I've missed you. It's okay to miss you a little, isn't it? Are you all right? Is everything okay?"

Hardy laughed. "I'm fine, Jane. Everything's peachy with me, but I just got out of a meeting with your dad. Have you seen him recently?"

"I know," she said, "I almost called you about it last week, but I didn't know how you'd feel about that. I didn't want to make you uncomfortable."

"You can call me, Jane. What's going on with Andy?"

"I don't really know. I'm really a little worried. He asked me over to his house for dinner last week and he was so distracted or depressed. Slower. I thought maybe he was just showing his age finally."

"He wasn't any slower from the bench. It was only back in chambers, on his own time."

"I thought he might have had a small stroke or something."

"Did you ask him?"

Jane laughed. "You know Daddy. The Great Deny-er. He's picking at his food, hardly talking, and I ask him if he's all right, and of course he's just fine, couldn't be better. And then he got drunk."

"Andy got drunk?"

"You remember the time you and Moses drank a watermelon full of gin? The answer is no, you don't remember anything about it."

"I remember the hangover."

"Okay, that, but up till the last time I saw Daddy, I'd never seen anybody so drunk since then."

Hardy whistled. The watermelon drunk had become part of Moses and Hardy lore. If Andy Fowler had gotten that drunk, he was not himself. Something was seriously wrong.

"Did he give you any idea what was bothering him?"

"No. He just said he deserved a little fun in his life. What was the matter with a judge being human too? Then he started drinking cognac, talking about Mom and when I was a baby and all the decisions he'd made not to have fun while he got to be a lawyer and a judge and now his life was almost over . . . Anyway, finally he just got all slurry and I put him to bed." The line was silent for a second. "I'm glad you noticed something, too. It wasn't just me."

"No. I don't think it was just you. Anyway, I'm here to help if something comes up. Just so you know. Maybe I'll play some squash with him, feel him out a little."

There was another pause. "Thanks for calling," she said. "We're still friends?"

"We're still friends. We're always friends, Jane."

After they hung up, Hardy took the jade paperweight out of his pocket and put it on his desk. Why would Andy have just given him—hell, not just given, demanded he take—such a beautiful piece?

Well, enough about Andy Fowler, he thought. Time to go to work. He reached for the new case folders and pulled them in front of him. He opened the first one—a DUI, driving under the influence, the influence in this case being alcohol. Eleventh offense. Level of point nine, which last year wasn't illegal. Hardy closed the file, squared the small stack on the middle of his desk, put the paperweight on top of it and decided to go to lunch.

6

Art Drysdale was juggling baseballs in his office. In his youth, he'd played a couple of weeks as a utility man for the San Francisco Giants, capping a five-year career in professional baseball before turning to the law. Now he coached a Police Athletic League teenage baseball team and played a little B-League men's softball at nights.

He liked juggling. He could do it blindfolded if he had to. It also tended to disarm anyone watching him, such as Dismas Hardy, who was standing in the doorway in the early afternoon.

"Pretty great stuff you threw me there," Hardy said. "There's even one guy who might have done something wrong, as opposed to illegal."

Art kept juggling, not looking at the balls. "Illegal is wrong. D.A.'s Handbook, Chapter One."

"I like the woman who didn't use her pooper scooper. We ought to really throw the book at her."

"Doggy doo on the street." Drysdale gathered the balls in, held them in one huge hand. "Heck of a nuisance. We've got to enforce those leash laws. Next thing you know packs of wild hounds are destroying our society."

Hardy came in and sat down. "But seriously, Art—"

"No, but seriously, Diz." He moved forward in his chair. "You are not making friends here. Friends is how we like to do it. I scratch your back, you scratch mine. It's a big office, what with the police and the D.A. and the coroner all here in one big happy building. Now, in one swell foop you have pissed off Rigby, Strout and Locke. This is not good politics."

"Politics is not—"

Drysdale held up a hand and three baseballs. "I know you've been out of the desk-job environment a while now, but any office, I don't care where, call it what you want, there is politics. Cooperation gets

29

things done. You alienate the chiefs of three departments, I guaran-goddamn-tee you, you will not have job satisfaction."

"I don't suppose it matters that everything the reporter said was taken out of context?"

"Oh, that matters. You still got your job, so it matters that much. But it's close. I'd go mend some fences if I were you. Work hard, impress people with your enthusiasm to get convictions on your cases, like that."

Hardy stood up. "This gives a whole new meaning to helping clean up the streets, you know."

Drysdale allowed himself a smile. "Maybe the hand'll turn into something." The baseballs flew back up into the air.

Hardy stopped in the doorway. "Maybe the hand'll turn into something."

Drysdale nodded, his attention split at best. "Could happen," he said. "Could happen."

At four o'clock, Hardy called it quits and went over to Lou the Greek's.

It had been a long afternoon. John Strout, the coroner, was a courtly Southern gentleman who accepted Hardy's apology with apparent sincerity, although Sixto's clipped and formal greeting at the desk indicated there had been some harsh feelings earlier in the day.

The chief of police, John Rigby, wasn't available, so Hardy scheduled an appointment with him for the next afternoon. The police sergeant who served as Rigby's secretary took the opportunity to gently remind Hardy that homicides were usually determined by police work, after which they were passed up to the D.A.'s office.

Hardy tried to cheer himself with the argument that he had very quickly passed through the just-another-face-in-the-crowd stage at work. Everyone in the building seemed to know who he was. It wasn't much consolation.

He wrote a memo to Locke that he threw in the wastebasket. There wasn't any fence to mend with Locke. He figured he'd either get a good conviction record and move up, or not get one and move out. There was a fine line between kissing ass and mending fences.

At Lou's, Hardy sat alone at the bar, spinning the jade paperweight. He was nursing a black and tan when a tall, very attractive woman pulled up the stool next to him. Hardy had never spoken to her before, but he knew who she was. She put a hand on his shoulder, leaned close and told him not to let the bastards get him down.

He dropped the jade into his pocket as she flashed him a mouthful of teeth and extended the hand that had been on his shoulder. "Elizabeth Pullios. You're Dismas Hardy."

"Guilty." Hardy took the warm, firm hand. "Which seems to be today's magic word."

Pullios might not be the best-looking woman in the D.A.'s office, Hardy thought, but she thought she was and so occasionally really could be. Perhaps five foot eight, with shoulder-length chestnut hair that shone even in the dim light at Lou's, she had a big nose, a generous mouth, deep-set eyes and high cheekbones. She wore a brush of tasteful makeup, just enough to set off the angles and highlight the eyes.

"Guilty is every day's magic word," she said. She signaled Lou behind the bar for a drink, then came back to Hardy. "Ruffled the brass feathers, huh? Art told me about it."

"Art told me about it, too."

"You get reamed?"

Hardy managed a wry smile. "I can still sit down. But I think I'll pass on talking to reporters for a while."

"No, don't," she said. Her drink arrived, a double Scotch mist from the looks of it, and she drank half of it in a gulp. "Don't stop talking to anybody. They're just trying to bust your balls. Talk to anybody you can use."

"Who's trying to bust my balls?"

"Locke and Art. You're new and that's what they do. Find out what you're made of. They play the bureaucrat game 'cause it's their control mechanism. Which sometimes is good for some people, but if you want some kick-ass cases, don't let 'em stop you. If you're good in front of a jury, everything's forgiven, believe me."

It was coming back to Hardy, the story on Elizabeth Pullios. She was known as a ballbreaker in her own right. She delighted in prosecuting—did it with a singular passion. It was said, more than half truthfully, that she favored the death penalty for car theft, pickpocketing, purse-snatching. She had been married during her first few years as a D.A. to a guy in the office, and when he accepted a better job in private practice on the *defense* side, she had divorced him. She couldn't live with a defense attorney, she said. They were the scum of the earth—worse, almost, than defendants.

Now the word was she'd have you if you were good enough.

So Hardy was forewarned. He figured he could talk to her safely

enough. He was, after all, in love with Frannie. "I'm afraid this reporter Elliot kind of used me instead of vice versa," he said.

She shrugged that off. "Look, that's what reporters do. But they
also can keep a case hot. A lot of us have been known to leak stuff—
just don't let your name out."

"That message was pretty clear."

Pullios finished her drink and signaled Lou again. "Buy you another?" she asked.

Hardy wasn't half through his first, but an old-hand bartender like
himself could nurse a couple of brews along for as long as he needed.
"Did Art ask you to talk to me?"

"No, but he told me you were frustrated about your work. I put a
little together and I hate to see new guys get shafted. It's bad for all of
us." The round of drinks came. Hardy and Pullios clicked glasses. "To
the good guys," she said. "That's us, Hardy, remember that. That's
always us."

Hardy was out of Lou's before five. There was a steady cool breeze
coming off the Bay and it threw some grit up into his face and eyes as
he walked down the alley next to the Hall of Justice.

Detective Sergeant Abraham Glitsky was sitting on the hood of
Hardy's Suzuki Samurai. "If you're going home I could use a drop-
off," he said. "My city-owned vehicle is once again on the blink. Why
is there never enough money to keep things working?"

"I've got a better one—what accounts for your jolly high spirits
lately?"

Glitsky slid off the car, letting out a breath. "I know," he said. Hardy
passed by him and unlocked the passenger door. "Too many dead
guys, I guess. You go see enough bodies a day, you smile less. It's a
proven fact."

It brought Hardy up short. His desire to get interesting cases—
murders—tended in some way to reduce their horror, especially after
his chat with Elizabeth Pullios. But most of the time on his job he was
in "suspect" mode, where he had a perpetrator he was trying to convict. It was easy to forget that half of Glitsky's job was concerned with
victims—families, friends, mourning.

Hardy got in his seat and started the engine. Glitsky shook his head.
"One of the weekend drive-bys was a kid about Isaac's age." Isaac was
the eldest of Glitsky's three children, a twelve-year-old. "Even looked
a little like him, except for the hole in his forehead."

Even after a few months on the job, Hardy hadn't developed a taste for cop humor. He didn't know if he wanted to—it rarely made anyone laugh.

They rode in silence for a minute, heading west into the sun. Finally Hardy said, "I'm waiting."

"For what?"

"Your two cents' worth."

Glitsky squinted into the sunset. "And I'd love to give it, as I know you're often in need of my counsel and advice. But I don't have a clue what you're talking about."

"The hand being a homicide."

"That was you, huh? I was afraid it was you."

"You didn't see it?"

Glitsky shook his head. "I didn't get to the paper today. But some guys were talking about this jerkoff D.A."

"Yeah. That was me."

"Well, look at the bright side like I always do. Maybe it was a homicide, maybe you'll get the case, win it, get a big conviction, become D.A., run for governor, win that—"

"Here's your stop," Hardy said. "You need a lift in the morning?"

"I'll bet it's a woman," Frannie said.

"Not Andy Fowler."

"You wait and see. It's a woman. The paperweight was a gift from a woman that he isn't seeing anymore. She broke up with him and suddenly he couldn't bear to see it anymore. It reminded him too much of her and she'd broken his heart."

"I knew I shouldn't let you stay home all day. You've gotten addicted to the soaps, haven't you?"

"Dismas."

"My finely honed prosecutorial skills have wheedled the truth from you at last."

"Jesus," Frannie said, "I have never watched a soap opera in my life and you know it."

"I'm not so sure anymore," Hardy said. "The soaring language— 'Andy couldn't bear it. She'd broken his heart.' And all that from a piece of jade." He looked across the table at his wife. Her green eyes looked nearly black in the candlelight.

They were in the dining room, finishing up a meal of filet mignon with béarnaise sauce, new potatoes, and string beans that Frannie had cooked in olive oil and garlic. Hardy was half through a bottle of good California cabernet.

"Okay, Sherlock, but I've known Andy for fifteen years, and he doesn't have girlfriends."

"That you have known about."

"You'd think I would have gotten some inkling once or twice."

"Maybe he just keeps that separate. Especially from Jane. Maybe Jane would be hurt."

"Why would Jane be hurt?"

"I don't know. Her mother's memory."

Hardy shook his head. "Not after all this time. I'm sure she'd want her dad to have some love life."

"I'm not so sure of that. Maybe he just thinks it's better to be discrete. I mean, he is a public figure. If he went through a succession of women . . ."

"Now it's a succession. The guy didn't keep a harem, Frannie."

"He might have. How would you know?"

"I know him."

Frannie smiled. "You wait."

Hardy moved the last morsel of his rare filet around in the remainder of the sauce. "I'll wait," he said. "This is very bad for my cholesterol, you know."

"I notice you're struggling with it. How did Jane sound?"

Hardy swallowed his food, took a sip of wine. "Jane was all right." He reached across and covered Frannie's hand with his own. "Jane's okay, and we don't have any secrets, you and me, right?"

"Right."

"Come around here."

She pulled away, still smiling. "No."

"Would you please come around here?" Hardy pushed his chair back, and Frannie came around the table and sat on his lap.

"Since you asked so nice," she said. She put her arms around his neck and kissed him thoroughly for the better part of a minute.

Hardy stood up, carrying her, and walked through the kitchen into the bedroom.

7

The *Chronicle* building was at Fifth and Mission, about six blocks from the Hall of Justice. Hardy walked through the morning fog, which did a lot more than chill the air, and while Tony Bennett might not care, he was probably one of the very few who didn't. Hardy gave away a few bucks in change to some homeless people who sat against the buildings on Third, wrapped in newspapers or old blankets, shivering. By the time he got to the *Chronicle,* his bones felt brittle and old.

Jeff Elliot anchored one of the newer desks in a cavernous room that smelled like an old school. His crutches were propped against the desk, all too visible. Propped as in prop, Hardy thought. He was turned to face a video terminal and was talking on the telephone when Hardy got to his desk.

"All of this is off the record," he began.

Elliot turned, saw Hardy, held up a finger and continued talking into the mouthpiece.

Hardy continued right on. "When I got into work this morning, I wasn't as mad as I was yesterday, but pretty close. Did I mention this is off the record?"

Elliot muttered something into the telephone, hung up and turned squarely to face Hardy. He didn't look so young nor so friendly as he had at Hardy's house two days earlier. His face, still boyish, looked sallow and wan, as though he hadn't slept in a couple of days. The dishwater hair hung lank and long, over the ears. His tie was loosened at his throat, although his shirt was fresh.

"Mr. Hardy," he said, sticking out his hand over the desk.

Hardy ignored the hand. "Off the record. Everything I ever say to you again. Completely and absolutely off the record. Is that clear?"

Elliot, to his credit, didn't bluff much, though he did try his sheepish grin. "My editor wouldn't run the story without a source. You didn't tell me not to use your name."

Hardy held up a hand. "I don't care about your politics. There's enough where I work."

Elliot shrugged. "I needed the—"

Hardy stopped him. "You could have accomplished the same thing being straight with me. I'm a pretty reasonable guy, but I am truly a bad enemy."

Elliot was sitting farther back, eyes wide. "If that's a threat," he said, then stopped.

To his surprise, Hardy noticed Elliot's hands were shaking on the desk. The boy was scared. Something in Hardy wanted to go for the jugular, but he had liked Elliot at his house and the shaking hands made him lose the stomach for it.

He sat down, put his arms and elbows on the desk. "It's no threat. It's a tip, that's all. Don't make enemies you don't need to. This is the big city. People play for keeps, even nice guys like me." Hardy flashed him a grin. "Now I'd like you to do me a favor."

Elliot came slowly back forward. "If I can. I guess I owe you one."

"That's the right guess," Hardy said.

"Owen Nash." Jeff Elliot's voice was thick with excitement.

"Where are you now?" Hardy, at his desk, pushed away one of the case folders and swirled on his chair to look out the window. Gray on gray. He had asked Elliot to go to Missing Persons and check to see if either a large woman or a man—someone with a full-sized hand—had been reported missing.

"I'm downstairs. The call just came in this morning."

"The timing's right," Hardy said. Missing Persons would not get involved with a person's disappearance until three days had passed.

"Right. Well, this was called in by a guy, wait a sec, a guy named Ken Farris, phone number, you got a pencil?"

Hardy took the number. "Owen Nash, and this number. Anything else?"

"They've got nine missing kids and three skipped or missing wives —all of them within the range of normal size. But Owen Nash is the only missing adult male this week. That's not so common. It's a real start."

"It's a start, maybe, and that's all it is, Jeff. And it's a big, big maybe."

"Still," Elliot said. "But why couldn't you just come down and ask around?"

Hardy sighed. Why get into it? "Politics," he said. "But it was a good idea. I wish it had been mine."

"So what do we do now?"

"You don't do anything. I start a little follow-up and you wait until I call you, got it? And I might not."

"But if there's a story?"

"It's yours. That's the deal."

Hardy hadn't intended to mention anything to anybody, but Drysdale poked his head in through his door the minute he hung up. "Just making the rounds," he said. "You better today?"

"They've got a missing adult male."

Drysdale frowned, leaning on the door. "Who does?"

"Missing Persons."

"Does this directly relate to one of the two dozen folders I see so prominently displayed on your desk?"

"Not even indirectly." Hardy smiled.

Drysdale let himself in the door and pulled it closed after him. "Diz, do yourself a favor, would you? Clear a few of these." He picked up part of the stack of files and dropped it on the middle of the desk. "Give me some numbers so I can point to your caseload and say, 'This guy's been a horse in the minors, let's give him a shot at the big time.'"

Hardy spun the jade paperweight, now doing its appointed task on his desk. "Okay, Art. Okay."

"Thank you." Drysdale started to go, but Hardy called him back. "Can you tell me anything about Elizabeth Pullios?"

"I can tell you a lot about her. Why?"

"She kind of gave me a pep talk yesterday, out of the blue."

"Maybe she thinks you're cute."

"I got the feeling she doesn't need to seek out men."

Drysdale nodded, leaning against the doorpost. He had his hands in his pockets, one leg crossed over the other, relaxation incarnate. "No, she does not need to seek out men."

"So what's her story? Why's she such a red-hot?"

Checking the hallway behind him, Drysdale pulled the door shut and straddled one of the chairs facing Hardy's desk, looking out the window at the gray behind him. He took a breath. "Her mother was raped and killed by a guy who'd been on parole three days. He'd been a model prisoner, in for rape. Served four years when they let him out for good behavior. I think it left her with an impression."

Hardy whistled.

"Well, I guess we're all motivated by something, but some of the staff thinks Pullios takes it a little far." Drysdale stood up and stretched. "Anyway, the fact remains, I want to put somebody away, I'd go with her every time. Don't get personal with her, though. She's very one-track."

Hardy held up his left hand, the one with Frannie's ring. "I'm a newlywed, Art. I'm not in the market."

"I wouldn't bet that's a big issue with her."

Hardy's first move after his superior left was to pick up the telephone and dial the number Jeff Elliot had given him—Ken Farris, the man who had reported the missing person, Owen Nash. A sultry-voiced receptionist got crisp and efficient when Hardy said he was from the D.A.'s office. He patched him through immediately.

"This is Ken Farris. Who am I talking to?"

Hardy told him. There was a pause.

"I don't understand. You're with the San Francisco district attorney's office? Is Owen in *jail*?"

The telephone beeped.

"If that's your call waiting—"

Farris cut him off. "We record all our phone calls here. Is that a problem?" He didn't wait for a response. "Look, I'm sorry, but what's the D.A. got to do with Owen being missing? Is he alive, please just tell me that?"

"I don't know that, Mr. Farris." He heard a deep exhalation—relief or frustration, he couldn't tell which, and didn't want to wait to find out. "What I'm calling about, how I'm involved here, has to do with a hand that turned up in a shark's belly."

Hardy could almost hear Farris's brain changing gears. "The one in the *Chronicle*? I read about that. What has *that* got to do with Owen?"

"Maybe nothing. Mr. Nash is a missing male, and the hand may be from an elderly male."

"What do you mean, might be? Did the paper have that? You think the hand might be *Owen's*?"

"I think it might be worth a look, that's all. There might be some bit of skin with something you'd recognize, the shape of a fingernail, something. The fingerprints are gone, but . . . ."

"Don't I remember something about a ring?"

Hardy nodded into the phone. "There was a jade ring on the little finger."

The phone beeped again. All their calls? Hardy thought.

Farris was curt. "Then it wasn't Owen. He wore a gold wedding band on his left hand, but no other jewelry. What hand was it?"

"It's a right hand."

"Well, it isn't Owen then. That's definite." Farris sighed again, letting out some more pressure. "Thank God."

Derek Graham had been a maintenance man in sewers for thirteen years. He was a forty-year-old Caucasian male supervisor with a wife and three children. As a tenured city employee, he was immune to just about anything that might threaten his job, but the political reality was that a white management person who lost his job in San Francisco would find it filled immediately by a member of any one of the myriad minority groups San Francisco called its own. Already, Hardy knew, the sharks were circling, and a righteous drug-bust conviction could put Derek not only in jail but on the street.

For while it was still only a $100 misdemeanor to smoke marijuana in San Francisco, possession of anything over an ounce was interpreted as intent to sell and that was a felony.

Derek's city-issued Chevrolet Caprice with its "Buy America" bumper sticker had a burned-out brake light. This turned out to be bad luck for Derek. He had just finished half a joint so he could get home a little relaxed and not snap at his kids when a patrol car pulled him over, the officer had smelled that smell and, with his olfactory evidence as probable cause, had searched the Caprice and found roughly eight ounces of sensimilla in the trunk.

This led to a search of Derek's house and discovery of the hydroponic garden in the basement. Derek was in a lot of trouble, and he was very worried about it.

"Look," he told Hardy, "I can't lose my job."

He was in Hardy's office with his court-appointed attorney, a young woman named Gina Roake. Ms. Roake hadn't said a word since introducing Derek to Hardy five minutes earlier. Hardy had addressed his remarks to her at first, but Derek kept butting in, so Hardy went to the horse's mouth.

"Losing your job isn't the half of it," he said.

Derek was six feet tall and weighed, Hardy figured, about one-

eighty-five. He had a handsome, clean-shaven face topped by a busi-
nessman's haircut. For this meeting, at which he wasn't particularly
welcome by either attorney, he'd chosen not to wear a tie. But in dress
slacks and a pressed button-down checkered shirt, he looked more
than presentable. He could have been applying for a job at a construction site.

"It's not like I've done anything criminal. Hell," he said to Hardy,
"you work for the city, what do you make?"

"Growing dope is criminal," Hardy answered, "and my salary is
irrelevant."

"I could look it up, but say it's forty-five." Derek continued without
pause. Hardy made $52,000 a year in his new job, and he let his
suspect go on. "You got kids?"

Hardy nodded.

"Well, then, you know. You can't make it on forty-five. Here I work
for the city fifteen years—"

"The file says thirteen."

"So split a hair. Thirteen. I work here thirteen years full-time and
my wife and I are trying to raise three kids right, so she can stay home
with 'em. Why have kids if you're not going to raise them yourself,
right? I got no record before this. I'm not whining, I'm just telling you
the truth."

"Raising your kids right includes marijuana horticulture?" Hardy
asked.

"My oldest kid is seven. The grass is a second job, that's all it
is."

There wasn't any doubt of that. Hardy made his fifty-two, but he
owned one quarter of the Little Shamrock and that brought in another grand or so a month, plus Frannie had a quarter-of-a-million-
dollar insurance policy from her first husband's death, which they
were saving for the kids' college. But at least if they really needed it, it
was there. Hardy knew what Derek was saying—it *was* hard to make it
on one salary in these times.

But Hardy, right now, was a prosecutor. He remembered Art Drysdale's words, *Illegal is wrong*. He said, "You should have thought of
that when you planted your garden." Not liking himself very much.

"Who am I hurting? Tell me that. I'm no dealer. I got eight guys I
off-load a key on."

Hardy held up a hand. "Now we're talking. Any of these people have
names?"

Derek just shook his head. "Come on, man, these are normal people like me and you. How old are you, forty? Tell me you didn't smoke a little weed in college."

Hardy couldn't tell him that. He didn't know many people of his generation, including many on the police force, who hadn't had a hit or two of marijuana at one time or another. To him it was a nonissue. But, here he was, playing at—no, being—the law.

Suddenly he turned and spoke directly to Ms. Roake. "Could we have a conference, please?" He looked pointedly at Derek. "There's a reason the court appoints an attorney. The coffee shop's down on one."

When he'd gone, Hardy closed the file. "Ms. Roake. Gina, may I call you Gina? What does he want?"

"He doesn't want to lose his job, I think."

"Is there an automatic administrative removal on conviction? There's no question the plea is guilty, am I right?"

"The question is the charge." Gina gave him a tight little smile. "Misdemeanor, I don't think so, but if we're talking felony, he's fired." Gina seemed to be about twenty, although she must have been older. She bit her lower lip. "I really think he just wanted the money to help his family."

Hardy fairly snapped at her. "People rob banks and kill people all the time to get money for their families." Gina stiffened visibly, and Hardy backed off. "Look, I don't mean to jump all over you, but let's not play his game. The guy was growing a good amount of dope, and that's illegal. How about you think up some heavy misdemeanor that will satisfy me? I mean a good one. He pleads to that, pays a heavy fine, does some community service, I'll try to sell that to my boss, and your man keeps his job."

Gina's dark eyes brightened. "You'd do that?"

"He goes near marijuana again—even a little recreational joint— and we'll crucify him, clear?"

She nodded her head, holding her hands tightly together in her lap, as though she were congratulating herself. "Oh, yes, yes. That's wonderful."

She got up from the chair in a shush of nylons, shook Hardy's hand, thanking him, and went out the door before he could change his mind.

He'd just handed one to the defense. He wondered what Elizabeth

Pullios would say about that. On second thought, he didn't have to wonder—he knew what she'd say.

Thinking on that, he crossed his hands behind his head and looked up at the ceiling, brown water stains on the acoustic tile. "Wonderful," he said.

8

On the way into work Hardy had told Glitsky that his wife was coming downtown to meet him for lunch. Now his friend Abe was sitting in the snack bar, holding Rebecca, Frannie across from him laughing at something.

Frannie's face, her laughter, still had the power to make him forget the bad things life could dish out—it was more amazing to him that she could laugh at all. Only a little over a year before, someone had shot her husband in the head, leaving her a twenty-five-year-old pregnant widow drenched in the gall of that sorrow.

He stood a moment, one step into the employees' lunchroom, and took in the sight—Frannie's glowing face, the life in it.

Somehow, Hardy, who had known his own tragedy when he'd lost his infant son years before, and Frannie had gotten together, and suddenly the backward-looking emptiness had changed its direction and its essence. Now they were together; they looked ahead.

Hardly slid in next to Frannie and kissed her.

"John Strout is a funny guy," Glitsky said. "I was just telling Frannie."

"When did you see our fine coroner?"

"I see him too much as it is, but this morning I thought I'd do you a little legwork."

"Abe does a great Southern accent," Frannie said.

"Wha thenk y'all, ma'am. Jest tryn' ketch the good doctuh's flavuh, so to speak." Abe switched back to his own voice. "You may have got him mad, Diz, but he looked at the hand. I figured it would be easier for me to ask about it than you. Just routine. Is it a likely homicide or not?"

"And what'd he say?"

"He said the guy might have done some karate, maybe some board breaking. There were calcium deposits on the knuckle of the middle

43

finger and the little finger had two healed breaks. Oh, and the pad opposite the thumb was a little thick."

"That all?"

"That's a lot, Diz. Plus he did die recently. Rigor had come and gone, but Strout thought it was still a fresh hand."

"I love it when you guys talk shop," Frannie said.

Hardy took his wife's hand. "It's a glamorous profession. Nothing else could have lured me back." Then to Abe, "It wasn't a cadaver, then?"

Glitsky shook his head. "Strout's checked all the local med schools." He looked at Frannie. "Every couple years some med students steal a body and play some games. This doesn't look like one of them."

"So it's a homicide?" she said.

"A homicide's just an unnatural death," Abe said. Rebecca was starting to get restless and Glitsky moved her onto his other leg, bouncing her. "And we don't even have that officially until Strout says it is, and he won't say till he's positive, which means more tests to see if the hand is really fresh, which he thinks it is. Finally," Abe said, "even if it's a homicide, a homicide doth not a murder make, much as our man Dismas here might like to try one. We've still got three options on cause of death—suicide, accident and natural causes—before we get to murder."

Rebecca began to squirm some more and suddenly let out a real cry.

"Here, let me take her," Hardy said. He reached across the table and Abe passed the baby over. Immediately she snuggled up against his chest and closed her eyes.

"The magic touch," Frannie said. "I'll go get some lunch."

She got up, and the two men watched her for a second as she headed toward the steam tables. Hardy stroked a finger along his baby's cheek. "You want to do me another favor?" he asked.

"No."

"It's not much," Hardy continued, "a phone call."

Hardy cleared seven cases in the two hours after his lunch: three DUI's with priors, a shoplifting with priors lowered to a misdemeanor for a plea, one possession of a loaded firearm by a felon, and two aggravated assaults—a purse snatching and a soccer father beating up his son's coach. None of these cases would have to go to trial and further clog the court system, and he was glad about that, but this plea bargaining was demoralizing and tiring.

Glitsky appeared in his doorway just as Hardy finished taking care of the weapons charge—his toughest case of the day. If you were convicted of carrying a gun without a license in San Francisco, you went to jail. So people facing time in the slammer tended to prefer a jury trial where they perceived they'd at least have a chance to get off. But in this case Hardy had persuaded the guy's attorney to plead nolo contendere and take weekend jail time. A sweet deal for both sides, all things considered.

Glitsky perched on the corner of the desk. "So who am I talking to?" he asked.

Most of the prosecutors shared a room with one of their colleagues, but since Hardy had come on as an assistant D.A., his roommate had been on maternity leave, which suited him fine.

Glitsky got up to close the door behind them and went and sat at the other desk. Hardy got through to Farris's office, then Glitsky punched in so Hardy could listen. The receptionist told Glitsky to hold, and they waited through five of the beeps that signified the call was being recorded.

Glitsky identified himself, referred to Hardy's earlier call and told Farris about the new information from the coroner. As soon as Glitsky said the word *karate,* they knew they were onto something.

Farris was silent a long moment. Then he quietly said, "Shit."

"Mr. Farris?"

Again an interval. "I'm here. Give me a minute, will you."

Glitsky waited, fingers drumming on the desk. Beep. Beep.

"It might not be Owen. Lots of men do karate."

"When did you see him last?"

"Friday around noon, lunchtime. He wasn't wearing a jade ring then, just the wedding band. At least, I suppose he had the band on. I would have noticed something different, I think."

"But Mr. Nash did practice karate?"

"He was a black belt. He started it a long time ago, when we were in Korea."

Glitsky's brows went up. He glanced at Hardy. "A bone in the little finger had been broken and healed twice," he said.

Farris swore again, waited. Glitsky whistled soundlessly. Beep.

"I think I'd better come up," Farris said.

*   *   *

Hardy almost forgot his appointment to apologize to the police chief, Dan Rigby. Glitsky was going down to Strout to see if he would be amenable to having Hardy around when Ken Farris arrived to inspect the hand. Frannie had called to tell him that at her next Ob/Gyn in a month they could expect to hear the new baby's heartbeat, and would Hardy try to get the time off so he could go with her? Did he want to know if it was going to be a boy or a girl? She wasn't so sure, herself, if she wanted to know. Also, she was so young the doctor didn't recommend an amnio, and she hadn't had one with Rebecca and she'd turned out fine. What did he think?

Hardy, answering her questions, enjoying her excitement, idly flipped his calendar page and saw the note: Rigby 4:00.

It was 3:55.

He got to the chief's office on the dot and waited outside for twenty-five minutes. He didn't want Farris to have come and gone by the time he got out, but he couldn't really push things too much here. The sergeant/secretary had made it clear yesterday that he was not one of Hardy's fans and by extension neither was the chief.

The intercom finally buzzed on the sergeant's desk. He looked over at Hardy and pointed a finger at the double doors.

Dan Rigby sat back in a leather chair, still talking on the telephone. He had a boxer's face, red and lined, and gray hair that was nowhere longer than a quarter inch. Hardy knew he often wore a business suit, but today he was in his officer's uniform. It was meant to be impressive.

Hardy stood on the Persian rug before his desk, trying to hit on a suitable opening. Rigby, listening into the telephone, scrutinized him as he walked in. Hardy waited another minute. Then Rigby hung up and squared his shoulders as though they caused him pain. "You used to be a cop, didn't you?"

"Yes, sir. I worked a beat about three years."

"Then went to the law, right?"

"Yes, sir." Here it comes, Hardy thought.

Rigby relaxed his shoulders, sunk back into his chair. "I often wondered about going the same way, though of course it's worked out well enough, I guess. But getting away from the police end of it—I suppose there just wasn't enough action anywhere else."

"The law's not so bad," Hardy said.

Rigby laughed hoarsely. "Naw, the law's all pleading and bullshit. The difference is most of the time we all know, we damn well know, who did it, but you guys, you lawyers, have got to prove it. Us, we know who did it, we catch 'em, our job's over, just about. So I figure the thing about this incident yesterday, you got your hats mixed up. You get good training as a cop here, and it sticks with you, you think like a cop. Even when you're over on the law side. Locke's got a hair up because I called him and he does hate to be bothered with his department. But you and I got no gripe. You get a murder out of this, or a suspect, you just do us all a favor and keep us informed. We'll go get the collar, and then you can do your job."

The phone rang again. Rigby picked up the receiver and listened for a moment. "I don't care what his constituency is, he does not get a police escort to . . ." Rigby looked up, surprised to see Hardy still there. He waved him out of the room and went back to his call.

Ken Farris stood next to the nearly leafless *ficus* by the window that looked out at the parking lot, his hands crossed behind his back.

He had just come from the cold room, looking at a barely recognizable thing that had four appendages—the index finger was missing—and he went instinctively to the window, as though for air, although the window was never opened.

Farris was a broad-shouldered, slim-waisted sixty. His light brown $750 suit was perfectly tailored, lined with tiny blue and gold pinstripes. The light yellow silk shirt was custom made; so was the tie. The alligator cowboy boots added an unnecessary two inches to his height.

Glitsky and Hardy sat on the hard yellow plastic couch in the visitor's room of the morgue. John Strout had pulled up a folding chair and sat slouched, his long legs crossed.

Farris turned around, fighting himself, still somewhat pale. "Well, that was a wasted exercise."

Strout reached into his pocket and extracted a small, plain cardboard box. "Maybe this will jog something." He held the box up and Farris came over and took it.

It was a jade ring—a snake biting its tail—with a filigreed surface. Hardy leaned forward for a better look; he'd only seen it on the hand. Farris held it awhile, then put it over the first knuckle of his ring finger.

"This wouldn't have fit Owen," he said. "He had bigger hands than me."

"The ring was on the pinky," Strout said.

Farris moved the ring over and slid it down onto his little finger. It was an easy fit. He removed it just as quickly. "Well, that still doesn't make it Owen."

"No, sir, it doesn't." Strout was agreeable, genial, professional. Hardy sat forward, arms resting on his knees.

Abe Glitsky sat back comfortably, watching, his legs crossed. He shifted slightly, enough to bring attention around to him. "You and Owen—Mr. Nash—were close, is that right?"

"Could we not say *were* just yet? He's been missing before."

"Long enough for you to call the police?"

"Once or twice, I suppose, but I didn't."

"What made you do it this time?"

Farris shook his head. "I honestly don't know. A feeling. Last time he ran off with no notice was maybe ten years ago. That much time, you figure a man's habits have changed. I can't fathom his just taking off anymore. Back then I could."

"Where did he go, that last time?"

Hardy spoke up. "What's all this running away?"

Farris looked around the room, found another folding chair, and moved it over next to Strout's. He put the ring in the box and handed it back to the coroner. Then he sat down heavily.

"Good questions. You think he might have gone back to the same place?" He shook his head. "No, no, I don't think so. Once he went to the Mardi Gras in New Orleans. But it turns out that time he took his daughter, Celine. So they were both gone, and we figured they'd taken off somewhere together. Back then, it was in character."

"But not now?" Hardy asked.

"He's mellowed. Or I thought he'd mellowed. You know how it is."

Glitsky was gentle. "Why don't you tell us how you mean it?"

Farris sat back. He took a deep breath and blew out a stream of air. "Time was, used to be every six months or so Owen would do something to make you hate him, or hate yourself. He was like this, this *force,* where he'd get a notion to go do something and goddamn if anything was going to stop him—not his friends, not his family, not his responsibilities.

"He had his devils, so I never got inclined to try and stop him. His wife, Eloise, died in a fire in their house back in the fifties. He couldn't get back in to save her, barely pulled out their child." Farris paused, remembering. "So he had this guilt over that. From time to time he didn't feel worthy of all his success and he'd duck out from under it, leave it all for me to run.

"Other times, just the opposite, he'd figure, 'Well, goddamn, here I am, the great Owen Nash, and if I want to go to Bali for a month, let the mortals handle it. They'll appreciate me more when I get back.'"

But Glitsky wanted to keep to his line of questioning. "So he went once to New Orleans, another time to Bali . . . ?"

"But that's just it. He didn't have a favorite place, at least one that he ran to. We've got this place together outside Taos, no phones, no heat, that's served us the last five or six years, but I was up there—flew up on Friday night—and he wasn't."

Strout pulled his long legs in under him and sat up straighter. "'Scuse me," he said quietly, "but it seems the only thing tyin' this here hand to Owen Nash is the karate."

Farris scanned the room. If he was looking for comfort, it was the wrong setting—the yellow vinyl couch, the institutional green walls. A near-dead plant and some artificial ones. "I don't know if he ever broke a finger. I doubt he'd say if he had."

"You mean doing karate, breaking a board, something like that?" Hardy asked.

Farris nodded. "That circus stuff, breaking boards, that's Owen. If he was showing off for some woman . . . hell, for anybody, he could break his whole hand and never mention it. One of his conceits was he didn't feel pain like the rest of us."

Hardy sat forward at the change of tone. This guy might love Owen Nash, but that wasn't all he felt.

"The little finger on this hand has two obviously healed breaks," Strout said, "that were never set."

"That sounds more like Owen."

Strout straightened up in his chair, laced his fingers and stuck his arms out until his knuckles cracked. "Well, gentlemen," he said, "this doesn't move me any further along in the line of identification. We could run a DNA scan, but without a sample of what we know to be Mr. Nash's tissue, it wouldn't prove anything."

Everyone sat in silence, all but Strout back in their seats. Farris still sat forward, eyes turned inward, trying to come up with something to settle the question. There was a knock on the door, and Sixto poked his head in. "There's a Celine Nash out here to see Mr. Farris."

* * *

The woman's startling blue eyes were red and puffed, dark circles under them as if she hadn't slept in several days. Her mascara had run over too much makeup. In a black suit, black nylons, black gloves —even black onyx earrings—she was elegantly turned out, but she'd run her hands through her ash-colored hair too often, and it straggled in uneven shanks to her shoulders.

She came forward and hugged Farris, choking back a sob, and he held her for half a minute, patting her back. "It's okay, honey, it's okay. We still don't know."

She pulled back slightly, took Farris's pocket handkerchief out and dabbed at her eyes. She briefly held herself to him again. Hardy saw her close her eyes as though gathering her strength. Then she turned to the other men. "Is one of you the coroner?"

Strout stepped forward. "Yes, ma'am."

"I'm sorry, but I thought Ken said . . ." She looked around as though lost. "I mean, when I heard coroner, I just assumed . . ."

"No, ma'am, we just don't know yet. You might see if you recognize this." Strout proffered the small ring box.

Celine stared at the ring for a moment. "What is this?"

"It was on the hand," Strout said.

She took it from the box, looking at him quizzically. "But Daddy didn't wear this ring. Ken, Daddy only wore Mom's ring, didn't he?"

"I already told them that."

The handkerchief went back to her eyes. She held it there a minute, applying some pressure. "Are you all right?" Hardy asked. He moved forward.

Celine had gone a little pale. She gave Hardy a half-smile, but her eyes went back to Strout. "Well, then, this couldn't be my father."

Glitsky, in his softest voice, asked her when the last time was she had seen her father. Her eyes narrowed for an instant, and Hardy thought he saw a flash of resistance, perhaps even fear. "Why? I'm sorry, but who are you?"

Farris broke in and introduced everyone, after which Glitsky explained, "He may have gotten the ring after you'd seen him."

She nodded, accepting that. "I don't remember exactly. Two weeks ago, maybe. But he didn't have this ring on then—he wouldn't have worn it anyway. This just isn't him."

Farris, up beside her, looked at it again and shrugged. "He wasn't much of a jewelry person."

"All right," Strout said. "It was worth a try. Thank y'all for your time."

After he'd escorted them to the door, Strout shambled back, hands in his pockets, to Hardy and Glitsky. "It might be Owen Nash," he said simply. "Off the record, of course, but it might be. I'll keep y'all informed."

9

The garage had Glitsky's car repaired and ready to go for him, so Hardy found himself walking alone though the parking lot at five-forty-five, ready to head for the Little Shamrock, where he was meeting Frannie. The fog, which had clung to downtown all day, had lifted, or moved west with the breeze off the Bay; the sky overhead was a cloudless evening blue.

Most of the staff at the Hall of Justice had gotten off at five, and the lot was about half empty. Two rows down from where Hardy was parked, Ken Farris sat in the driver's seat of a Chrysler LeBaron convertible with its top down. Hardy slowed down and finally stopped.

Farris was staring into the distance, arms crossed over his chest, unmoving. He might have been a statue. He'd left Strout's office with Celine Nash nearly forty-five minutes ago, and he was still in the parking lot? Maybe she had stayed and they had talked awhile. Still, Hardy found it odd. The man wasn't even blinking. Maybe he was sitting up, dead.

Hardy crossed a couple of rows of parking places. He got to within ten feet of the LeBaron before Farris moved. It was a slight shift, but Hardy knew he was in view now.

"I saw you sitting here so still," he said. "I wondered if you were all right."

The mask gave way to a self-deprecating smile. "Relative term, 'all right.' I guess I'm all right."

Hardy gave him half a wave and had started to walk away, when Farris called his name. He came back to the car. "You know, Celine mentioned something. I don't know. It might be relevant."

Hardy cocked his head. "You wouldn't be a lawyer, would you, Mr. Farris?"

A flash of teeth. "Why would you think that?"

"Well, defining 'all right' as a relative term. Something you might know as relevant. Those are lawyer words."

Farris stuck out a hand. "Good hunch. Call me Ken, would you. Stanford, '55. But I never practiced, other than being counsel for Owen."

"Full-time job?"

"And then some. Now I'm COO of Owen Industries. Owen's CEO. Electronics, components, looking into HDTV."

"I don't know what that is, HDTV."

"High-definition television. More dots on the screen. Better picture. The Japanese are miles ahead of us on it, but Owen liked it, so we're moving ahead."

"So what's your maybe-relevant information?"

"Celine just mentioned it to me. Owen had told her he was going out on the *Eloise* . . ."

"The *Eloise*?"

"Owen's sailboat. He was supposedly going out Saturday with May Shintaka—May Shinn she calls herself."

"His girlfriend?"

Farris made a face. "Something like that. More a mistress, I guess you'd say."

"He kept her, you mean? People really do that?"

Farris laughed without much humor. "Owen figured you paid for your women one way or the other. 'Cost of doin' bizness, Wheel'—he called me Wheel, like Ferris Wheel, spelled wrong of course—'cost of gettin' laid, same goddam thing. Might as well pay for it up front. No bullshit.' "

"It's an approach, I guess," Hardy said.

"Mr. Hardy . . ."

"Dismas." Then, at the squinted question. "Dismas, the good thief on Calvary."

"Okay, Dismas. It's not my approach, I've been married to my Betty twenty-five years. But Owen isn't like me or anybody else I know. He loved Eloise, his wife, and after she died he knew he wasn't going to love anybody else, so he wasn't looking for love and wasn't going to kid around about it. It might sound cold, but it was pretty honest."

"So this May Shinn . . . ?"

"He's been pretty steady with her since January, February, around in there."

"Did she go out on Owen's boat Saturday?"

"Celine says he was planning on it. That's all I know."

"If he did, our probabilities increase," Hardy said.

"Why do you say that? . . . oh, I see."

"Do you have a way to reach her, May Shinn? Find out right now."

The shadows had lengthened, the breeze had died. Farris dug into his wallet and pulled out a square of white paper. "Emergency numbers. I don't know why I never thought of May."

Hardy walked back beside him as Farris punched numbers into his car phone. He squinted at the paper. Next to May Shinn's name, he had just enough light and distance to make out the numbers, just enough time to memorize them.

He thought he'd also have enough time to swing by the Marina on his way out to the Avenues. It wasn't far out of the way. And if he could prove Owen had been on the ocean on Saturday, the day before a hand that might be his turned up inside a shark at the Steinhart, he thought he'd be on his way to having a case.

May Shintaka hadn't been home—or she hadn't answered her telephone. Ken Farris had gotten an answering machine and asked her to call him as soon as she could.

Now at full dusk, there was a traffic jam just outside the Marina Safeway. Hardy remembered. It was Wednesday, the night the Marina Safeway turned into a meat market, the yuppies picking up each other with clever lines about the freshness of the arugula or the relative merits of dried versus handmade pasta.

His Suzuki Samurai out of place in the row of Beemers and Miatas, Hardy waited in the line of traffic, feeling old—so much older than when he'd been a father the time before. He was really running late. He ought to call Frannie, or Moses, at the Shamrock. Let them know he was on his way.

Or else forget about stopping at the Marina. What did he expect to find on or around the *Eloise* that wouldn't be there in the morning? Except that he was already here. He'd call the Shamrock from a pay phone. Frannie would be with her brother—it wouldn't hurt the two of them to kill a little time together alone. He'd only be a minute or two looking at the boat.

The light changed and he got through it on the yellow, after which it was only two blocks to the Marina itself, two hundred craft along four long pontoons behind a jetty, the land side closed off with an eight-foot fence topped with barbed wire.

Hardy sometimes thought he must have been a sailor in an earlier life—he had a visceral reaction to anything nautical. He loved to fish, to scuba dive, to walk sharks—trying to will them to life as though he had a special bond with them.

Now the briny scent of the air pumped him up. Locke and Drysdale be damned—he felt in his bones he was onto something and he was going to pursue it.

The guardhouse was set in a manicured square of grass at the entrance to the boat area. Hardy knocked on the open door and walked in. The attendant was about nineteen, dressed in a green uniform with a name tag that read "Tom." He stood up at his desk behind a low counter. "Help you?"

To Hardy's right, he could see the boats through the picture window. Four strings of white Christmas lights glittered over the pontoons.

He showed the boy his D.A.'s badge, which was not issued by the office and not officially condoned. Hardy had gotten his at a uniform store down the peninsula and knew it could come in handy, especially with people who perhaps couldn't read but understood a badge. He asked the young man if they kept a log of boat departures.

"We tried that," he said, "but most of the people here like to come and go as they please. Still, we generally have some idea who's out."

"Is the *Eloise* here now?"

"Sure." Tom looked out the window and pointed. "She's that low forty-five-foot cruiser at the end of Two." In the fading light, the sailboat looked beautiful. "Last time she went out was Saturday."

"Saturday. Did Mr. Nash take her out?"

Tom shrugged. "I suppose so, but I didn't see him. She—the *Eloise* —was out when I came on."

"When was that?"

"Around noon. I work twelve to eight."

"Does somebody else come on then, after eight?"

"No. We close up till next morning at six. What's all this about? Is Mr. Nash in some trouble?"

Hardy gave him all he really had. "He's missing. It'd be helpful to know who saw him last."

Tom bit his cheek, thinking. "I don't think you'll have much luck here. José, the morning guy, said she was already out when he came on."

"At six in the morning?"

Tom shrugged, wanting to be helpful. Hardy could tell he was wrestling with something. "Sometimes José'll be a little late," he said finally. "But when that happens, he always stays late and makes up the time."

Hardy fought down a shiver of frustration. "What time did he stay till on Saturday?"

Tom got a little evasive. "I don't know exactly. Three, three-thirty, around there."

"So he wasn't here until seven or seven-thirty?"

Another shrug. "I don't know for sure. I wasn't here, either."

Hardy blew out a breath. "Okay, this isn't about José anyway. Could I take a look on board the *Eloise*?"

Grateful to abandon the discussion on Jose's tardiness, Tom bobbed his head. "Sure. It's pretty slow now anyway."

On their way out to the boat, Hardy learned that security wasn't all it could be at the Marina. Though Tom had a ring of master keys for the boats and a key for the gate that opened through the fence, the reality was that people slipped through with other parties all the time and owners forgot to close the gate behind them, or even to lock their boats. Theft wasn't rampant by any means, but neither was it unknown. But what could the attendants do? Tom and José tried, but they had no real authority. If the boat owners weren't going to follow their own rules, whose fault was that?

Up close, the *Eloise* was even more impressive than it had looked from the guardhouse. With a wide boom, Hardy thought maybe twelve to fourteen feet, it was berthed perpendicular to the main pontoon, too big to maneuver into any of the slips. Technically, the boat was a ketch—two poles, one fore and one aft. The steering wheel was sunk into the deck so the aft boom would clear the head of a standing pilot.

Casting off under motor power, even at only five knots, Hardy figured it wouldn't take three minutes on the straight shot to get out beyond the jetty.

"You mind if we go aboard a minute?"

It was already too dark to see much on the deck, not that Hardy was looking for anything specific. Tom, meanwhile, walked forward to the cabin door. "See, this is what I mean."

Hardy came up beside him.

"They leave the door unlocked. What are we supposed to do?"

"Anything get taken? Maybe you should check."

It was so easy Hardy almost felt guilty, but not enough to stop himself from following Tom down the ladder into the cabin.

The boy turned on the lights and stopped. "No, everything looks okay," he said.

Hardy thought *okay* was a bit of an understatement. They were in a stateroom that was easily as large as Hardy's living room. A zebra rug graced the polished hardwood floor. Original art—oils in heavy frames —hung along the walls. There was a black leather sofa and matching loveseat, an Eames chair or a good copy of one, a built-in entertainment center along an entire wall—two TVs, large speakers, VCR, tape deck, compact disc player.

Being aboard seemed to make Tom nervous—he fidgeted from foot to foot. "Maybe we better go back up, huh? Doesn't look like anything's gone."

But Hardy was moving forward. "Might as well be sure," he said lightly. He was at the galley—tile floor, gas stove, full-size refrigerator. A glimpse at the wet bar—Glenfiddich, Paradis Cognac, Maker's Mark Bourbon, top-shelf liquors.

He heard Tom coming up behind him and kept walking forward to where the bulkhead came down. A full bathroom, far too big to let it go as the "head." The master bedroom, up front, was as large as Rebecca's new room, the queen-size bed neatly made. Two desks, one a rolltop, an exercycle and some dumbbells, more expensive knick-knacks.

"This is something," Hardy said. Tom stood mutely behind him. "Are there rooms aft?"

Hardy ached to open a few drawers in the desks. Casually, he moved to the desk on the bed's right and pulled at the top drawer. It appeared to have nothing useful—paper clips, pens, standard desk stuff. The drawer on top to the side contained what look like sweatbands. Hardy reached in and felt around. Sweatbands. "Nothing here," he said, lightly as he could, closing the drawer.

Then around the bed, hoping Tom would stay another minute. The rolltop was closed up, but the front drawer slid open. Same story— nothing. Hardy pulled the side top drawer. "I don't know if we should . . . ," Tom said.

A quick glance down, the drawer open a couple of inches—inside, some maps, navigation stuff. He pushed it closed with his hip and turned around.

"You're right, good point." Mr. Agreeable. "Let the police get a warrant." Hardy turned around and walked quickly back through the galley and stateroom, past the steps leading up to the deck, past another bathroom off the aft hallway, to the first guest bedroom—double bed, dresser, television, a floating Holiday Inn.

"We really should go up," Tom said from the steps.

"Okay," Hardy, casual but determined, browsed the route back along the opposite hallway, passing through the second room, which was mirrored from floor to ceiling and equipped with most of a complete Nautilus set, a stair-climber, more free weights. Owen Nash took his workouts seriously.

Up on the deck, Tom took a minute to carefully lock the cabin door. Hardy asked, "How's a boat like this sail?"

Tom locked the door, double-checked it. "Well, it's not a hot rod. It's really for deep water."

"Could one man handle her?"

They were walking back up the pontoon to the office, Tom leading. "Oh sure. The sail's are on power if you need it. Mr. Nash went out alone a lot. Over to the Farallons and back. It's harder in a smaller boat, but he liked it."

"What's at the Farallons?" He asked about the small rock islands twenty miles off San Francisco's coast.

"I don't know," Tom said. "They say that's where the great whites breed—you know, the sharks. Maybe he was into them."

Bad pun, Hardy thought.

They were at the Purple Yet Wah, out in the Avenues on Clement. Moses McGuire was sucking on a crab claw. "Black bean sauce," he said. "I believe with black bean sauce on Dungeness crab we have reached the apex of modern civilization."

Frannie was glaring at Hardy, who was looking down at his plate.

"I hate it when you guys fight," Moses said. "Here I am talking about cultural issues, without which we would all soon be savages and—"

"Why don't you tell your friend Dismas that we had an understanding about telephones and being late." She stood up and threw down her napkin. "Excuse me, I'm going to the bathroom."

Hardy picked up his chopsticks. "I think I've already said I was sorry four times, now five. I'm still sorry. Six. Sorry sorry sorry sorry." Hardy put down his chopsticks. "Ten."

"Don't tell me," Moses said. "She thought you were dead."

"She always thinks I'm dead, or going to die."

"There is some justification there."

"There is no justification at all. I have not come close to dying. Being late doesn't mean you've necessarily died."

Moses rubbed his crab claw around in the sauce. "It did for Eddie." He held up his hand, stopping Hardy's response. "Uh uh uh. Here's an area where we could increase our sensitivity."

"Moses . . ."

"You could have called. Phones are nearly ubiquitous in our society." McGuire was the majority owner in the Shamrock Bar, but he also had a Ph.D. in philosophy from Cal Berkeley.

"You, too, huh?"

"She's my sister. I'm allowed to be on her side from time to time."

"I was working on a case. I'm a lawyer now, remember. I wasn't out running around with loose women. I wasn't narrowly avoiding death. I was working."

"You had an appointment with me and Frannie. A simple one-minute phone call and all would have been well."

"Okay, all *right,* next time I'll call. Big deal."

"Frannie's worried it's going to start happening all the time. As you say, you're a lawyer now. Well, that's the way lawyers are."

"Lawyers aren't any one way . . ."

Moses stabbed the last pot sticker and popped it into his mouth. "Excuse the generalization, but yes they are. Frannie wants you to be a daddy, not to work all the time. That's why the job looked so good, remember. Regular hours, interesting work. I can hear your words in my memory even as we speak."

"How late was I?"

Moses chewed. "One hour and forty-five minutes, which is plenty of time to work up a good head of worry. It's not Frannie's fault she worries. She loves you, Diz. She's carrying your baby. It's pretty natural, don't you think?"

"Well, I love her too."

"I am sure you do."

"Well . . . ?"

"Well," Moses repeated. "There you are."

Their white frame house was bracketed by two apartment buildings. Back in the mid-'80s, Hardy had been offered a sinful amount of money to sell to a developer so that a third five-story anonymous unit could rise where now his sixty-foot-deep green lawn was bisected by a stone walkway, a low picket fence, and a doll house with a small front porch and a bay window.

Before their marriage they had talked about moving—starting over with a place they could equally call their own. The problem was that although the house had been Hardy's for a decade, Frannie already loved it. One of Hardy's first actions after the wedding was to transfer half the title to Frannie's name—they didn't have a prenuptial agreement. Frannie's quarter-million-dollar insurance policy was both of theirs; Hardy figured the house put them on relatively equal footing.

Street parking was often a problem. With no garage, driveway, or back alley, you either got your spot by six o'clock or you had to walk. Now, at ten-fifteen, they couldn't find a space within three blocks. It was a mild, still night with no fog, and they strolled east on Clement, under the trees of Lincoln Park, back toward their house. Frannie leaned into her husband, her arm around his waist.

"Pinch me," she said.

"I know." Hardy tightened his arm across her shoulders.

"Would you have thought this?"

"I guess so. It's why I thought we ought to be married. But still . . ."

She stopped. Hardy took the cue and leaned over and kissed her. "What is it?" Frannie asked.

"Nothing. A little shiver. How often do you notice when everything is perfect? It's a little scary. I used to believe that's when things were most likely to go wrong."

"I think that's why I was so upset tonight. I'm just getting so I can accept that all this is happening, that it's not some dream I'm going to wake up from." She looked up into Hardy's face and pulled herself close against him. "I don't want to wake up from this," she said. "I want this to keep going on."

"It's going to, Frannie. I'm not going to let anything get in the way of this, promise."

Frannie nudged him with her hip. "Let's get home."

They paid the sitter, looked in on the slumbering baby. Hardy fed his fish while Frannie got ready for bed. In his office, his answering machine had calls from Jane and from Pico Morales, both of whom he could call in the morning.

He could hear the shower running in their bathroom. He picked up

his telephone and hit the numbers he'd memorized earlier that night
—May Shinn's. The phone rang four times, then picked up.

"Just leave a number, please, and I'll get right back to you." That
was the whole message. No trace of a Japanese accent. A deep, cul-
tured voice. Hardy hung up after the beep.

His desk was cleared. The green-shaded banker's lamp threw a soft
pool of light around the room. The dried blowfish pouted on the mantel of the office fireplace. Absently, Hardy crossed from the desk to the
mantel, straightened out the pipe rack—unused for over a year—and
grabbed three darts from the bull's-eye of the dartboard, where he'd
left them. Back at the line near his desk, he began throwing.

His dart game was off. In his first round, none of the three darts
landed in the 20, where he was aiming. A year before, that couldn't
have happened. If anyone had asked him, he would have said he was
semi-serious about darts. He still carried his custom set of twenty-
gram tungstens with him every day in his suit jacket's inside pocket.

But the reality was that new priorities had taken over. As he re-
trieved his first round, he heard the water shut off in the bathroom.
He was back at the line near his desk now: 20, 19, 18. There you go.

Then Frannie was in the doorway, barefoot, wearing the purple silk
baby-dolls Hardy had bought her for Christmas, the ones she hadn't
been able to wear until after Rebecca was born. A tiny dark spot
marked where a drop of her milk had leaked from her nipple.

Hardy crossed to her, went to his knees and lifted the hem of the
pajamas, burying his face against her.

10

FINANCIER MISSING IN "MYSTERY HAND" CASE
by Jeffrey Elliot
Chronicle Staff Writer

The case of the mystery hand found Sunday in the stomach of a great white shark at the Steinhart Aquarium took on a new dimension today as Bay Area financier Owen Nash was reported missing by Ken Farris, counsel and chief operating officer of Owen Industries of South San Francisco.

Mr. Farris reported that Nash was last seen Thursday evening by members of his personal staff at his mansion in Seacliff. On Friday, Mr. Nash failed to appear at a luncheon appointment. On Saturday, Nash reportedly was scheduled to go sailing with May Shinn, a friend. Neither Nash or Shinn has been heard from since then, although Nash's sailboat, the *Eloise,* remains at its berth in the Marina. It is unclear at this writing whether or not the boat was taken out over the weekend.

The police will not speculate on the possibility of foul play, although yesterday a representative of the district attorney's office gave strong credence to that possibility.

Farris reported that Nash's life had been threatened "half a dozen" times in the past five years over his mostly hostile takeover efforts of several Silicon Valley companies.

Strengthening the bond between Nash and the mystery hand is the fact that Nash was a black belt in karate. The hand has several unusual characteristics that can be associated with karate, among them calcium deposits and a somewhat overdeveloped "heel," or pad, at the side of the hand. San Francisco coroner John Strout, however, had no comment on the likelihood of the hand being that of Owen Nash and dismissed any possible identification at this time as "decidedly pre-mature."

"THE BOY BUSHWACKED ME," Farris said. "He was waiting at my house-boat when I got home, had already charmed the skirts off of my Betty."

Hardy, in his office at home, was beginning to admire Jeff Elliot's spunk. The reporter was nobody's little lost boy. Hardy had thought he'd scared him into some controllable space yesterday, but evidently he'd read that wrong. Hardy wasn't going to get Jeff Elliot off his story. It didn't look like anybody was.

"You never told me about the death threats."

"I never took them seriously anyway. People say things when they lose negotiations, you know."

"But you thought enough to mention them to Jeff."

"Not really." Hardy heard a rustling noise. "I've got the paper here in front of me, and I must admit it reads pretty dramatically, but all I did was answer a straight question—had anybody ever threatened Owen? I said, 'Sure, half a dozen times,' but it wasn't anything. At least, until I saw it here in print."

"You don't think it could be related?"

"I guess anything's possible. But as I said, this was all settled a long time ago. I think the last man who got bitter—Owen took him and his wife to Hawaii for a couple of weeks, wined and dined then, bought her a Mercedes, made him president of some division somewhere. The man made out like a bandit. 'Course, Owen made out better."

"Who was that?"

"It wasn't any real threat. I've told Owen I was gonna kill him twenty times myself, and half those times I meant it."

"Okay, but if Mr. Nash turns up dead, somebody's going to want that name."

"I still pray to God he's not dead."

Hardy sat still a moment, drumming his fingers on his desk, trying to decide whether or not to tell Farris what he knew. Hell, the man had been forthcoming with him. He said, "The *Eloise* did go out on Saturday." He told him about his visit to the Marina, his tour of the boat.

"But if the boat went out, and now is back, and the hand is Owen's . . ."

"Those are big ifs . . ."

"But you see what that means? It means May—"

"No . . . May or someone else. Maybe not May at all. Or May and some third party."

Farris was collecting himself. "You're right."

"A boat like that, it's not unknown to get used once for drugs, then abandoned."

"Drugs?"

"It's more common in Florida, or down south in San Diego, but it's happened here. Smugglers board the ship, kill whoever's on it, throw them overboard, load up their cargo, deliver it, dump the boat."

"Back at its own slip?"

"I'm not saying it's likely, but the boat being back doesn't say much about anything."

"I've got to find May," Farris said.

"Why don't you go by where she lives?"

"I don't know where she lives. Owen never told me that. Getting her phone number was a major concession."

"How about if they just ran away, like you were saying he might have done yesterday, except that it was Owen and May together, not just him?"

"I hate to think we're down to that."

"Why?"

"Well, I really think the running off—it's something Owen's outgrown. I just don't see him doing that anymore. If anything, he was more settled, less spontaneous, since he's been with May. She really calmed him down. I mean, for Owen, he seemed relatively at peace for the first time in his life. Since Eloise, anyway. Besides, they've gone away together before—and told nobody except me. But he did tell me."

"And this time he didn't."

"Nothing."

Hardy looked up as Frannie walked by the door to his office, holding Rebecca, singing quietly to her. He missed Farris's next sentence.

"I'm sorry, what was that?"

"I said it's getting more unlikely every day anyhow."

"How's that?"

"Well, I'm Owen's executor and I've also got power of attorney. It's Thursday now and nobody's seen him in a week. If he ran away, even with May, he'd need money, right? And he never carried much cash."

"So he'd use a credit card, and you'd have found out about that?"

"Right. I checked all his accounts this morning—so far there's been no activity."

Hardy wished he could say something about not giving up hope until they had some more information, something definite.

Farris cut that thought off. "He's dead, isn't he?"

The answer to that, a line from a comedy routine of the old, now-defunct Committee, a North Beach comedy troupe, was "Deader than hell, Bob."

Hardy wasn't even tempted.

Officer Patrick Resden was never going to make inspector. He was never going to make sergeant. He was fifty-one years old, a big, wheezy, friendly dog of a cop who was twenty years on the same beat.

Resden had taken the sergeant's exam five times in the early '70s. Hardy had helped Glitsky study for the sergeant's exam around the same time, but after a review of the first few chapters of the prep book, those "study sessions" had become the boys' night out—Jane and Flo, respectively, staying home while their husbands improved their minds and careers. What they had really improved was their tolerance for alcohol. They knew they'd drunk enough on any given night when a question in the prep book—any question—stumped them.

Hardy had known plant life—and definitely some of his fish—that was smart enough to pass the sergeant's exam on the second try, and Resden had flunked the thing five times.

But this did not mean he didn't have a place on the police force. He could follow simple instructions. He did not abuse his gun or his badge. Resden was a good beat cop—his heart was in the right place and he had a lot of experience helping people out, pulling kittens out of trees, busting neighborhood bullies.

One of whom—the defendant in this case—was named Jesus Samosa. It seemed that about two months ago, Officer Resden had had occasion to reprimand Samosa when he caught him about to spraypaint a sidewalk in front of the Mission Street BART station. Instead of getting a hard-on for him, Resden had simply confiscated the can of paint and let the boy go—he was only eighteen—with a warning.

Two days later, in the street in front of the same BART station, Samosa failed to stop at the sign on Mission. His maroon '69 Chevy got pulled over and Resden was the citing officer. This time, Resden gave Samosa a ticket—this was evidently very funny to the passengers in the Chevy, but again, Resden simply warned everyone and let them go their way.

Now, it turned out that Jesus Samosa worked at the Doggie Diner three blocks from the BART station. About a week after the stop-sign incident, Resden and his partner, Felice Wong, decided to take their lunch at this same Doggie Diner. Resden ordered his usual couple of double burgers, double cheeses—a special order. Felice was grabbing some napkins, with a clear view of the grill area, when Jesus, to the delight of his broiler mate, spit into the bun that he then placed on top of one of the double burgers.

Felice drew her gun, walked behind the counter, confiscated the burger for lab analysis and bagged Jesus Samosa on the spot.

Now *this* defendant, Hardy thought—this guy is going down. Hardy gave a moment's thought to ordering an HIV test—if the guy tested positive they might be able to charge him with attempted murder. On reflection, though, that might be a little extreme, even if an Elizabeth Pullios might go for it.

As it was, they had Jesus on a couple of health and safety-code violations, misdemeanor aggravated assault, profane language and re-sisting arrest. The maximum penalty if he got everything was forty-five days in the county jail and fines totaling $3,115.

If the defendant's attorney wanted to bargain, Hardy figured he would be a sport and knock the fines down to an even three grand.

After he'd talked to Ken Farris, Hardy had taken his yellow legal pad from his top drawer and wrote notes on everything he could remember relating to Owen Nash. It took him almost twenty minutes, filling two pages.

He then called Art Drysdale at his home, making it clear that he had taken no part in supplying Jeff Elliot with any information used in the *Chronicle* story. "But just between you and me, Art, my bones tell me the victim is Owen Nash. And if May Shinn is still alive, we may be looking at my murder case."

Once again, Drysdale counseled Hardy to cool his jets and wait for the police investigation to catch up. Hardy replied that of course he would do that.

He dialed Jane, but she hadn't been home—either out working early or spending the night in a strange place. Well, Hardy didn't know that and it was none of his business anyway. He'd left a message.

The morning light in Hardy's office at the Hall of Justice was especially flattering to Elizabeth Pullios. She wore a blue leather miniskirt —far enough down her leg by about an inch to still be professional if the term were loosely applied—with a tailored robin's-egg man's shirt made less conservative by the three-button gap at the top. A raisin-sized ruby on a thin gold chain hung to where her cleavage began. Her chestnut hair was loosely tied at the back of her neck. She knocked demurely at Hardy's door.

"Good work," she said.

He invited her in and she closed the door behind her.

"What is?"

She placed her rear end on the corner of Hardy's desk and pushed herself back so she could sit back with her legs crossed, showing and showing. Hardy pushed his chair back almost to the window, put his own feet up on the desk, crossed his hands behind his head and leaned against the glass. "What is?" he repeated.

"The *Chronicle* thing. Keeping it alive."

"Believe it or not, that wasn't me." But then he realized that it had in fact been him who had sent Elliot on the mission that took him to Missing Persons. "Not completely, anyway."

She waved that off. "Well, whatever, it's still on the burner. Who killed him?"

Hardy spent a couple of minutes on Owen Nash, Farris, May Shinn, the Silicon Valley connection. "The bottom line, though, is that we don't have an identified victim yet, so there's nowhere to go. I think we're going to need a body."

"Well"—she leaned toward Hardy, both palms resting flat on Hardy's desk, the ruby swinging out from the gap in her shirt—"not necessarily. You remember the Billionaire Boys Club case down in L.A.? They never found the body in that one. And you've got part of a body. Get some good pathologist—"

Hardy laughed. "Whoa. I don't think we're there yet. What about the ring?"

Pullios shrugged, mercifully straightening up. "The ring's a detail. Maybe his friend Farris was wrong, or lying. Maybe Nash only wore it sailing. Who knows?"

Hardy put his feet down and stood up. "That's just it. If nobody knows—"

She shook her head. "Dismas, this is too good. You've got to grab these when they come around, which, believe me, isn't often. Mega-rich victim, corporate intrigue, the paper's already on it. This could make a career."

Hardy remained casual, motioned to his stack of folders. "I think until I clear some of these, my career is on hold."

She slid off the desk, adjusting her skirt, which entailed leaning over again. If body language talked, Hardy thought, this woman was yelling from the rooftops. He didn't get it.

"Well, it's your decision," she said.

It was that rare San Francisco treasure, a truly warm day. Hardy had decided to walk down to Fifth and Mission without calling first. He wanted to be outside, and going to see Jeff Elliot was an excuse more than anything else.

Jane had reached Hardy during the morning, and the two of them were having lunch at noon at Il Fornaio. Hardy reasoned he could pass a pleasant hour until then, putting in some nonbillable time.

Now he stood in bright sunlight on the steps outside the *Chronicle* Building. Jeff Elliot hadn't been at his desk, and the guy who sat next to him told Hardy he thought Jeff had said something about going down to the Marina and did Hardy want to leave a message. He did.

Walking down Howard toward the Ferry Building and the Bay, hands in his pockets and tie loosened, Hardy drank in the smells of truck fumes and pork bao, of tar and roasting coffee. Whenever he passed an alley, about every half block, the heavy odors of urine and garbage would overlay the city smell, but even these were, in their own way, mnemonic and pleasant—Paris when he was in college, Saigon later. He found himself whistling, marveling at the new skyline with the Embarcadero torn down after the Big One, the World Series quake.

He decided to keep walking along the waterfront. Gulls sat on guano-stained pilings, occasionally lifting off with a squawk. Three or four of the docks were unfenced, and a few Orientals squatted fishing with long poles. The Sausalito ferry came in with a deafening honk of its horn, spewing out a carefree river of tourists. Hardy went with the current, letting it carry him inland with the flow. He turned uptown, noticed the time and hailed a cab to take him the last ten blocks.

11

Jane was in a banquette in the dining area behind the bar. There was a tulip glass of champagne on the table in front of her. She had cut her dark hair very short, but Jane always managed to look good. As a buyer for I. Magnin, she always hovered at or near the top of haute couture, six weeks ahead of everybody else. He leaned over and kissed her cheek.

"Ivoire de Balmain," he said. It was the perfume he'd always bought her on Christmas. He didn't think it was a coincidence she was wearing it now.

"You have a good nose." She kissed him again, quickly, on the lips. "It's good to see you."

"It is," he admitted.

He ordered a club soda and found out Jane was seeing a younger man, an architect named Chuck.

"Chuck, Chuck, bo-buck, bo-nano-bano, bo-fu . . ."

"Dismas." She put a shushing finger to his lips.

"I've always wanted to do that," he said.

"I'm sure you have." She gave him an amused look. "He's a wonderful guy."

"I'm sure he is. It's a wonderful song, too. You can't do it to Dismas, you know. Dismas, Dismas, bo-bismas . . . it just doesn't scan." The club soda arrived.

"Club soda is a change," Jane said.

Hardy sipped. "Change is my life right now. If I have my old usual couple of beers for lunch, you can forget about the afternoon. I tried it a few times. Bad idea."

She sipped her champagne. "So you're really back at prosecuting?"

"I am."

"And you like it?"

He lifted his shoulders. "Sometimes. It's more b.s. than I remember, but it's all right."

They waded through another five minutes of small talk before they ordered—calamari for Hardy, a *quattro formaggio* calzone for Jane. Hardy broke down and decided to have some wine, so he and Jane ordered a half bottle of Pinot Grigio.

When the waiter had gone, Hardy said, "So you've seen your dad?"

She nodded. "You were right. There's definitely something."

"That's what I thought. Frannie says it's a woman."

Jane took that in, sipped at her champagne. "Why did she say that?"

Hardy told Jane about the jade paperweight, how Andy had demanded he take it. "Frannie said seeing it every day reminded him of his broken heart, so he had to give it away." He held up a hand. "Her words—she's more melodramatic than I am."

"I also think she's right."

"Did he say that?"

"He didn't deny it. I asked him point blank if he was all right, if something was bothering him."

"And what'd he say?"

"He said he'd just become more aware of mortality lately, that nothing lasts forever."

"This is not exactly headline stuff, Jane."

"I know. It just seemed evasive, the way Daddy's always been about his personal life. So I asked if something specific had triggered all those feelings, you know. He said a friend of his had died and he just had to accept it. I asked who, and he said I didn't know him, it didn't matter."

"He said you didn't know *him?*"

She shook her head. "But I don't think he meant that, meant it was a man."

It occurred to Hardy that, impossible as it might seem, Andy Fowler could be gay. In San Francisco, you never knew. "But if that's what he said . . . ?"

"No. There was a pause before he said that. Something, anyway. Then he patted my hand and thanked me for being concerned, but that he could work all this out himself, he was a big boy."

The food came, the wine ritual. Hardy dipped some fresh bread in a little bowl of olive oil on the table. Jane cut into her calzone and let the steam escape.

"What I think," she said, "is it might have been someone he's ashamed of being involved with, maybe the wife of one of his friends, something like that."

"And she broke it off?"

"Either that, or he couldn't go on with it anymore. Can't you just hear one of them saying it? 'We'll just have to pretend the other one died.' I can imagine Daddy taking that tack."

"Yeah, that flies."

"It's a problem when you've always been perfect. You can't even let your daughter see anything else. Even when I told him that whatever it was, I'd still love him."

"You told him that?"

"Of course. I would."

"No, not that you would. You told him you suspected it was something he might be ashamed of?"

"Not in so many words."

Hardy was thinking Andy Fowler didn't need so many words. He was a subtle and intelligent man, accustomed to dealing with nuance every day on the bench. He could imagine Jane's forthright approach scaring him off, driving him back further within himself, if that's where he was.

Hardy chewed on the delicious bread, filled his mouth with wine and sloshed it around. "Well, whatever it is, you think we can do anything to help him out? He talked about a vacation."

Jane half smiled. "Sure. Daddy's idea of a vacation is not bringing work home for the weekend. You know any women he might like?" But she tossed the idea away. "No. I can hardly see Daddy allowing himself to be set up."

"Maybe it's what he says—awareness of mortality. That can stop you."

Jane scratched at the tablecloth with a perfect coral fingernail. She and Hardy didn't need reminders of the lessons of mortality. Every time she thought of their son, Michael, who'd died in a crib accident ten years before, it stopped her again, as it had stopped her life, and Hardy's, back then. A tear came from one eye and she turned away.

Seeing it, or simply knowing, he reached over and covered her hand. "Let's leave it for now, Jane. Come back to it later," he said. "We'll think of something."

* * *

He missed the stud the first time and figured it must have been the wine.

After lunch, he'd stopped at a sporting goods store on Market and picked up the dart board he'd promised himself. Back at his office, he'd banged on the wall opposite his desk, listening for the hollow sound to give way to solid wood, locating the stud, or thinking he had.

The first stroke of the hammer drove the nail through drywall clear up to its head. Hardy was a good carpenter. Wood was one of his hobbies. It wasn't like him to miss a stud. He banged on the wall, thought he'd found the stud again, and this time was right.

Measuring off eight feet with a ruler from his desk, he put some tape down on the floor just under where his chair would normally be. Then he moved the chair back up, took out his leather case and fitted the blue flights onto the shafts of his darts. He stood up at his tape line and threw two bull's-eyes and a 20. Leaving the darts in place, he picked up his phone.

Judge Fowler had called in sick. That was odd. Judges never called in sick—their dockets were too full. A sick day inconvenienced too many people. Hardy tried his home, but no one was there either, not even an answering machine. He was tempted to call Jane again but why worry her?

Maybe Andy was simply taking a mental-health day. God knew, he worked hard enough to deserve it. Maybe after seeing Jane last night, he'd gotten drunk again and was hung over. In any case, if Andy Fowler wanted to take a day off, Hardy would not disturb him.

He looked at the still-large pile of case folders on the corner of his desk, wondering what unknown thrills lay in store for him in that mountain of paper. He considered going around to his darts and throwing a solo game of *301* to keep his eye up. He wondered if Jeff Elliot was back from the Marina or wherever he'd gone. He should call Frannie and see how Rebecca was doing.

Anything, he thought, but . . .

It wasn't a big enough room to pace in. He pulled his chair up to the desk and sat down, feeling lethargic and heavy. The wine. Blame it on the wine.

Elizabeth Pullios was still wearing the gold chain with the ruby, but that was all she was wearing. Christopher Locke, the district attorney, was lying with his hands crossed behind his head. He had a barrel chest covered with curls of black hair. His stomach was beginning to bulge, but it was a hard bulge. He had a pretty good body for an older guy, she thought. And as long as he let her be on top, his mobility wasn't much of an issue—she could control things, which was how she liked it.

She moved forward a little, adjusting her position. The D.A. moaned with pleasure. His black, broad-featured face broke into a grin. "My, don't we look smug," Pullios said. She tightened herself a little around him and he closed his eyes with the feel of it.

"I feel smug," Locke said. "Come down here."

She leaned down over him. He took one breast in each hand and pulled her face up to his. She took his tongue into her mouth and bit down on it gently, then pulled away.

"You are such a bitch," he said. Still smiling. She moved her hips again. He tried to come up to meet her face, but her hands were on his shoulders, forcing him down, grinning at him.

"I know, and you love it." She came down and licked the bottom of his ear, staying there, beginning to rock rhythmically.

"God, Pullios . . ."

She pulled away, halfway up. Her face now was set. She had found her angle, concentrating. Her hands cupped his head, tighter. He rose to meet her, feeling it build.

"Not yet, not yet . . ." She was breathing hard, her teeth clenched. "Okay, okay." She pounded down against him, now straightening up, arching, her head thrown back. "Now. *Now. Now.*" Grinding down into him as he let himself go, collapsing against his big chest, a low chuckle escaping from deep in her throat.

12

Turning south on Highway 1, Hardy was thinking that fate could be a beautiful thing.

The dunes with their sedge grasses obscured the view of the ocean, but with the top down on the Suzuki, Hardy could hear and smell it. The afternoon, now well along, was still warm. Dwarf cypresses on the east side of the road attested to the near-constant wind off the ocean, the evergreen branches flattened where they faced the beach, as though giants walked the land, stomping them to one side.

Where the highway turned inland at Fort Funston near the Olympic Club golf course, hang gliders filled the sky. Even on a windless, cloudless day, thermals up the cliffs at the shoreline provided decent lift. Hardy thought he might like to get into hang-gliding sometime. Take the wife and kids. Soar.

The fate that had saved him from his files had come in the guise of a call from Abe Glitsky, who'd been called down to Pacifica to view a body that had washed ashore. Calls from the SFPD to other local jurisdictions over the past few days had gotten the word out, and when the call came in, Abe had been in the office and volunteered to go down and have a look. He'd called Hardy from his squawk box, patched in.

The turnoff was just north of Devil's Slide, a two-mile stretch of Highway 1 where the curving roadway's shoulder disappeared at the edge of a three-hundred-foot cliff. Most of the time, the area was shrouded in fog, and it was the rare year that didn't see another verification of the fact that automobiles could not fly.

Hardy wound back on a rutted and unpaved roadway toward the city. Glitsky's car was parked in the dirt area at the bottom, along with a couple of Pacifica police cars. As Hardy was getting out of his car, an ambulance appeared on the road he'd just used.

The tide was out. Getting on four o'clock, there was still no wind at all, no fog. Maybe, Hardy thought, we're going to have our three days of summer.

He nodded to the ambulance guys, but was too anxious to wait for them. Crossing the soft sand, he got to harder ground and broke into a trot. The officials were knotted around a still green form about twenty yards from the line of surf.

Hardy nodded to Glitsky, who introduced him around. "Here's your victim," he said.

The body lay covered with a tarp, on its back. Hardy asked permission to look, and one of the Pacifica cops said go ahead. He pulled the tarp away and involuntarily stepped back.

Sand flies buzzed around the half-open mouth, the nose, the empty eye sockets, the thinning head of gray hair. Hardy was momentarily startled by the fact that the body wore jogging sweats identical to a pair he owned—except that the body's green sweatsuit had a large crescent-shaped tear in the right torso. There was also a ragged break in the lower left leg, with flesh showing beneath it. Two small clean holes—one in the chest and one just over the crotch—spoke for themselves. Forcing himself to take it all in, Hardy noticed the wedding band on the left hand. But, by far, the most arresting detail was the end of the right arm, a jagged and torn mess of tendon, bone and sickly greenish white flesh. Hardy knew what had happened to the hand.

The ambulance men had made their way across the beach with a stretcher. Hardy stepped away and let them move in.

"You get an ID?" he asked Glitsky.

Glitsky had a scar that ran through his lips, top to bottom; when he got thoughtful or tense, it seemed sometimes to almost glow white in his dark face. It was glowing now. He wasn't saying anything.

"Looks about the right age for Owen Nash," Hardy said.

Glitsky nodded, still thinking, looking off into the horizon. "That's why you're here," he said.

"Shot twice?" Hardy asked.

Glitsky nodded again. "Before the sharks got him. Small caliber, one exit wound out of two." Like a dog shaking off water, he came back to where they were. "Once in the heart, and whoever it was tried to shoot his dick off." He thought another moment. "Probably not in that order."

Hardy felt his balls tighten. Suddenly Glitsky spoke to the ambulance attendants who had opened the stretcher and were preparing to lift the body. "Excuse me a minute." He went over to the body, got down on one knee and picked up the left hand. "I'm going to take off this ring," he told the Pacifica cops.

He looked at it briefly, showed it to them, then brought it over to Hardy. "You see anything?" he asked.

It was a plain gold band. On the flat inside surface, there was a tiny stamp in the gold that said *10K*. Nothing else at first glance. Hardy faced away from the sun and held the ring up to catch the light, turning it slowly. "Here you go," he said. He brought it closer to his face. Worn down flush to the gold, invisible except at one angle, Hardy could make out some initials. *"E.N.* and some numbers—something looks like fifty-one."

"What was Nash's wife name?"

Hardy remembered mostly because of the boat. "Eloise. And fifty-one—sounds like a wedding date, doesn't it?"

Glitsky uttered an insincere "Absolutely brilliant" and held out his hand. Hardy dropped the ring in it. He put the ring in a zip-loc evidence bag and stuck the bag in his pocket. "So I can either check the prints, have Strout do some DNA testing this month at a cost of ten grand or call his attorney again. How do you vote?"

The body was on the stretcher, and the ambulance attendants began carrying it over the beach. Hardy, Glitsky and the other men fell into a rough line behind them, and the caravan trudged over the sand. Nobody said a word.

"The *Eloise* was out all day Saturday!" Jeff Elliot was excited.

"I knew that," Hardy said. He was at home, talking on the kitchen extension. He lived fifteen blocks from the beach, just north of Geary, and he'd seen no point in going downtown for ten minutes so that he could turn around and drive back home.

Twenty minutes after leaving Devil's Slide, he was cutting up some onions in his kitchen. When the spaghetti sauce was made, bubbling on the stove, he opened himself a beer and called Jeff Elliot.

"I thought you were keeping me up on the breaks in the case," Elliot said. "If you knew the boat had gone out—"

"We didn't even know it was Owen Nash, so what difference could his boat make? In fact, I would tend to agree with our good Dr. Strout," Hardy drawled, "that yo' conclusions were de-sahded-ly prematuah. All we knew was that a man was missing and the hand might show that it was used in karate. That's a long stretch for hard news."

There was silence on the other end. Then, "You got something, don't you?"

"Turns out," Hardy said laconically, "odds on you were right."

He told him about the body, which was on its way, or had just arrived at, the morgue—the hand bitten off, where the shots had gone.

"He was shot? Somebody killed him you mean?"

Hardy thought of where Glitsky thought the first bullet had gone. He felt he could rule out suicide. "Yeah," he said. "Somebody killed him."

"God, that's great!" Elliot nearly shouted. "That is just great!"

"The guy's dead," Hardy reminded him. He took a sip of his beer. "That's not so great."

"The story, I meant the story."

"I know what you meant. Listen, if you've got a file picture on Nash, you might bring it down with you, remove any doubt in case no one's identified him yet."

"Good idea!"

"Oh, and Jeff, if Mr. Farris or Celine Nash—Owen's daughter—is down at the morgue, try to rein in the enthusiasm a little, would you? I don't think they're going to be as happy about it as you are."

"No, I understand that. Of course."

Hardy rang off. "Of course," he said.

It was going to the front page in tomorrow's edition, Jeff's first front-page story. Not the main headline, but lower right, three columns, his byline—not too shabby.

Not only that, but the lead graphs had already gone out on the wire that night, and Jeff had received a followup call from the L.A. *Times*, la-di-da, and from Drew Bates over at KRON-TV, who wondered if he —Jeff—had anything more to give out on the Owen Nash murder. Imagine, TV coming to him! The L.A. *Times!*

He had left his forwarding number at night reception and now sat in the bowels of the building where he worked, checking the Nexis listing on Owen Nash. It was nine-thirty at night, and he'd been up since six, but he felt completely fresh. Parker Whitelaw, his editor— Christ, THE EDITOR—said he'd give him a sidebar on Nash they'd

run with the pickup on the back page of the first section, but he had
to have it done by eleven-thirty. Did Jeff think he could do it?

Jeff thought for a lead story and a sidebar he could stand on his
head and spit nickels, dance with Nureyev, run a ten-flat hundred. He
looked at the mute reminder, his crutches, leaning on his right
against the table. Well, the hell with them. He could get this done. He
had the raw data—now it was just putting it together. Piece of cake,
though there was more than he would have thought—and he had to
get it down to three hundred words maximum. Well, hit the high
spots.

Jeff had started the Nexis search at quarter to seven after getting
back from the morgue. Almost three hours, close to two hundred articles—some merely a mention at a society event, a few substantial
interviews, a cover story in '87 in Business Week. Owen Nash, from
the evidence here, had been a very major player. He'd been mentioned in one U.S. publication or another on an average of once every
six weeks or so for what seemed like the past twenty years.

Jeff looked away from the orange-tinted screen. He was having a
problem reconciling the Owen Nash in these articles to the body he'd
witnessed at the morgue.

He'd gotten there as a limo had been pulling up. Ken Farris and his
wife had recognized him immediately from the previous night, and
while they didn't seem all that happy to see Jeff, they were also too
distracted to make any real objection when the hawk-faced black inspector with the scar through his lips admitted them.

The other woman in the limo was Celine Nash, Owen's daughter.
She was much older than Jeff, probably near forty, but something
about her, even in grief, made him react. He didn't know if it was
posture, attitude or the shape of her, but he couldn't take his eyes off
her.

Stupid, really. A cripple like him stood no chance with most
women, much less a beauty of her class and caliber—if that powerful
a sexual draw could be called beauty—but he thought there couldn't
be any harm in letting it wash over him.

Until, of course, they saw Owen Nash. At the sight of him, everything else vanished. The assistant coroner had pulled back enough of
the sheet to show the face, and there was no question of identification. Celine sobbed once. Farris hung his head and pulled his wife
closer to him.

The inspector—Glitsky—had asked the formal question and the assistant was pushing the body back, when Celine told him to stop. She wanted to see her father one last time.

Nobody moved. The assistant coroner looked at Glitsky, who nodded, and the sheet came off, revealing Owen Nash, naked and blue, on the gurney.

First, of course, was the hand, or the lack of hand. The ragged stump without any cauterizing or sutures—one pink tendon extending two inches beyond the rest.

Jeff had seen pictures of the damage a shark bite could do to, for example, a surfboard, but he found that it did not prepare him for the sight of Nash's ribs opened by the slashing teeth, the wedge taken out of his lower leg.

Celine walked up to the body. Her eyes, he noticed, were dry in spite of the sob. Perhaps they glistened with shock. The coroner's assistant made a motion to come and steady her, but something in her bearing stopped him. The room became for an instant as silent and colorless as an old black-and-white snapshot—all the life, not just Owen's—leached out by the tension.

Celine put a hand on the body's chest, another on the thigh. It might have only been five seconds, but it seemed she stood there forever, unmoving, taking it in. Now a tear did fall. She leaned over and placed her lips against the center of his stomach.

Suddenly it was over. She nodded at the inspector, then turned around and walked past them all to the door and on out without looking back.

In the lobby, Ken and Betty thanked Glitsky. Celine was already in the limo. The evening light was startling—Jeff remembered walking out of matinees as a child, how the Saturday-afternoon light after the dark theater was so jarring, so unexpected. He'd felt that way, squinting against the setting sun.

He knew he should have asked someone more questions—the assistant, Glitsky, Ken or Betty—but he'd been too shaken. By the time he recovered, the limo had driven off. Glitsky had gone into the Hall of Justice. He couldn't bring himself to go back into the morgue.

He shook himself, pulling out of the memory. The orange screen still hummed in front of him. He looked at his watch and saw that he'd wasted twenty minutes. He had to get down to work.

There was, first, the business side. In 1953, Owen had borrowed $1500 from a G.I. loan program and put a down payment on a near-bankrupt television repair shop in South San Francisco. He began tinkering with used parts, and within two years had perfected and patented an improved insulation technique for the hot tubes of early TV. General Electric picked it up, and Owen was on his way. He diddled with vacuum tubes, invested in copper wiring, got into simple components before the microchip came along. By the time Silicon Valley exploded, he was ready for it.

Shares of Owen Industries, Inc., were trading on the New York Exchange for $17 a share, and Nash himself had controlled eight hundred thousand shares when he took the corporation public in 1974. Figuring three or four stock splits minimum, Nash's personal worth on stocks alone, at the time of the Business Week cover story, was close to $70 million.

His other assets were also substantial. Besides the $250,000 *Eloise* and his Seacliff mansion, he owned a house and more than a thousand acres of land in New Mexico, pied-à-terres in Hong Kong and Tokyo, a condominium in New York. According to Business Week he also held part or controlling interest in three hotels, ski resorts in Lake Tahoe and Utah, a restaurant on St. Bart's in the Caribbean. His one failure, as of five years ago, had been an airline, the Waikiki Express, which had made two round trips daily between Oahu and Los Angeles for sixteen months before it went bankrupt.

But the man hadn't spent all his time in boardrooms. The first mention of Owen Nash in any publication had nothing to do with business. In 1955 he was the first non-Oriental to break more than six one-inch pine boards on top of one another in a sanctioned karate exhibition. Jeff was tempted to get up from his chair and see if Archives had the picture referenced in the display, but decided against it. Time was getting short.

In 1958 Nash's house in Burlingame had burned to the ground. He managed to rescue his six-year-old daughter, Celine, but had nearly died himself trying to get back inside to pull his wife, Eloise, to safety.

After his wife's death, he bought his first sailboat and took it around the world, accompanied only by Celine. The papers picked up on the rugged outdoorsman life now—for a year in the 1960s he held the all-tackle world record for a black marlin he'd taken off the Australian Barrier Reef. As recently as last year he and Celine and a crew of three college kids had sailed a rented ketch to runner-up in the Newport–Cabo San Lucas race.

His forays into big-game hunting stirred more and more controversy over the years. Jeff Elliot thought the change of tone of the articles was interesting: when Nash bagged a polar bear in 1963 he was a man's man featured in Field & Stream; by 1978, taking a zebra in the Congo got him onto the Sierra Club's public-enemy list.

He didn't "give a good goddamn" (Forbes, "Ten CEOs Comment on Image," Sept. '86) about the public. He was one of the only western industrialists to attend the coronation of Bokassa; the Shah of Iran reportedly stayed aboard the *Eloise* in the Caribbean while the U.S. government was deciding how to handle him after he was deposed; Nash appalled the *Chronicle* reporter covering his trip to China in '83 by feasting, with his hosts, on the brains of monkeys who were brought live to the table.

He made Who's Who for the first time in 1975. He never re-married.

13

"I wish I made more money," Pico Morales said. "I wish I *had* more money. Anybody else, they would have more money."

His wife, Angela, put her hand over his. "English isn't even his first language," she said, "but he sure can conjugate the dickens out of 'to have money.'"

They were in the Hardys' dining room, sitting around the cherry table. After the spaghetti and a jug of red wine, Frannie had brought out an apple pie, and Pico had put away half of it.

"He is a man of many talents," Hardy said.

"Is there anything special about today and money?" Frannie asked.

"See? That's what I mean." Pico had a knife in his hand and was reaching again for the pie. "We don't think—I don't think—like a rich person. I think it's genetic."

"He thought sharks dying was genetic, too," Hardy said.

"No, that was lack of family structure."

"What would you do if you had money," Angela asked, "besides maybe eat more?"

Pico had no guilt about his size. He patted his stomach and smiled at his wife. "What I would do, given this news tonight about Owen Nash that the rest of the world doesn't know yet, is go out and invest everything I owned in stock in his company."

Hardy shook his head. "That stock is going to dive, Peek."

"I *know*. So you sell short, make a short-term bundle, buy back in."

"How do you know when it's going to turn around so you buy back at the right time?" Frannie asked.

"You don't for sure," Pico said, "but that's the nature of stocks."

"Either that, hon, or they go the other way tomorrow and take off because Nash was mismanaging his company and now they can fly. Then you lose everything." Angela patted his hand again. "Like every other time we have had hot tips on the stock market. Have another piece of pie."

"I'm interested in what you meant when you said anybody else would have had more money. When?" Hardy had pushed his chair onto its back legs and was leaning into them, thumbs hooked in his front pockets.

"Today. The last few days. We should already have an agent, be cooking up a book deal, movie rights, something. We're the ones who found the hand. We should be famous by now."

"Fame's an elusive thing," Hardy admitted.

"Okay, laugh at me." Pico consoled himself with a mouthful of pie. "But you wait—somebody's going to make a fortune off this somehow and then where will we be?"

"We'll be right here," Frannie said. "I'm kind of immobilized for a while anyway."

"Don't you like where you are, Peek? I mean, curator of the Steinhart Aquarium is not exactly an entry-level position."

"I just feel like we're all missing an opportunity here."

"Probably," Hardy said. Angela agreed. So did Frannie.

Pico ate some more pie.

May Shinn's apartment was on Hyde, directly across the street from a boutique French deli. The cable-car tracks passed under the window, but this time of night, the cars weren't running.

There was hardwood in the foyer, an immediate sense of almost ascetic order—a hint of sandalwood? The streetlights outside threw into gauzy relief the one room where she sat in front of her corner shrine, across the room from a low couch with a modern end table and a coffee table. Hardwood glistened around the sides of the throw rug. Along one wall was a high cabinet—thin and elegant lines, glass fronted. Another wall held Japanese prints above a low chair and a futon.

The entranceway itself was an eight-foot circle. Older San Francisco apartments often had turrets, alcoves, arches and moldings that no modern unit could afford. Another rug, two feet wide, was in the center of the circle. A hand-carved cherry bench, the wood warm, highly polished but not over-lacquered, hugged the side. Close to ten feet long, it was built to the curve of the wall, apparently and impossibly seamless. It would cost a fortune, and that's if you knew the artist, if he could get the matched cherry, if there was the time.

The wall in the foyer had an ivory rice-paper finish. Three John Lennon lithographs, which didn't look like prints, hung at viewer's height. The light itself came in five-track beams from a central point overhead. Three of the beams were directed at the Lennons, the other two at ancient Japanese woodcuts on either side of the door leading to the kitchen.

There was another longish block of cherry with a slight ridge down its middle on the floor by the open entrance to the living room.

May had bathed after forcing herself to eat some rice with cold fish left over from Friday night. She had combed back her long black hair and pinned it, then sat on her hard, low platform bed for a long while, still undressed, unaware of time's passing.

When it was dark, she began picking out what she would take with her. Not much. Two suitcases perhaps. She had to decide. Would too little cause someone to notice? What did business people take on a trip to Japan? On the other hand, she didn't want to tip her hand that she was not coming back by taking too much. She walked around the apartment, taking things down, then putting them back up, unable to decide. Everything was expensive, hard to replace, precious to her. She'd designed her living space that way.

She went to her shrine and lit a candle. It was not a shrine to any god particularly, just a raised block of polished cherry with a pillow in front of it. There was a white candle, a soapstone incense burner, a knife and, tonight, a plain white piece of bond paper, five by seven inches, with a man's scrawl on one side of it.

She had gotten out the piece of paper after reading the *Chronicle* article about Owen Nash that mentioned her, already tying her to him. The paper was a further tie—a handwritten addendum to Owen's will leaving $2 million to May Shintaka.

She didn't know if it was legal or not. It was dated a month ago, May 23, and was written in ink and signed. Owen had told her that's all she needed.

"Maybe I'll die on the way home," he'd told her, "before I get the Wheel to get it done right. This way, even if its disputed, after taxes you ought to get at least half a million."

She'd told him she didn't want it, and he'd laughed his big laugh and said that's what was so great about it. He knew she didn't want it. But he'd folded it once and put it in her jewelry box. Every time he came by, he checked to make sure it was still there.

She wondered if he had told Ken Farris—the mysterious Wheel—

about it. Sometimes she wondered if the Wheel really existed, but there he was in the *Chronicle* article today. She wondered why Owen had never had them meet.

No, she didn't. She knew why. It came with her profession. You didn't meet friends of your clients. In fact, what you did together couldn't survive outside of its strict boundaries, although Owen had promised her it could.

But it never had. And now, could she go and present this little scribbling to the Wheel, Owen's financial protector? He would laugh at her, or worse. Perhaps she would do it later. But later might be too late. All the money might be gone, and none left for her.

But she had never expected the money, had never wanted to believe any of Owen's promises. He'd even told her, in other contexts, "A promise is just a tool, Shinn. You need to promise something, you promise. Later you need to not remember your promise, you don't remember."

He'd said that before he'd changed, of course, before something had really happened betwen them. And yet . . .

It broke her heart, that heart she'd hardened and decided to keep to herself forever. She was kneeling back on the pillow, and a tear fell and landed on her polished thigh. Should she pick up the knife? Should she burn the piece of paper? What could she take with her to Japan and where would she stay when she got there?

PART II

14

Elizabeth Pullios found out about it first in Jeff Elliot's *Chronicle* story. Owen Nash was a righteous homicide, and probably, she thought, a murder. Also, its position there on the front page changed her opinion about the case.

While Dismas Hardy was stirring up the kettle she had been all for him—it never hurt for a rookie to get some heavy trial experience, and there were only a few ways a new person ever got to try a homicide. One was getting what they called a skull case—an old murder with some new evidence. Another way was when one of the regulars, like Pullios herself, would hand off a slam-dunk conviction to one of the rising stars, leaving herself time to try a more challenging case. Once in a while one of the regulars would go on vacation and everyone else would be full up, so a case would fall to the next level. But that was about it.

She had thought that Hardy's interest in the mystery hand fell more or less under the umbrella of skull cases. Interesting stuff maybe, but not grist for her. There were four, and only four, homicide assistant district attorneys in the City and County of San Francisco. None of these people would hand off a publicity case. If Hardy had hit the jackpot, Pullios felt as though he'd done it by playing what was rightfully her dollar.

She dressed in her red power suit and sauntered into the Homicide Detail on the Fourth Floor at seven-forty-five on Friday morning. No one sat at the outside desk, and she walked through into the open area for the inspectors' desks, all twelve of them. The lieutenant's office was closed up, dark inside. Over by the windows, Martin Branstetter was doing some paperwork. Carl Griffin and Jerry Block were having coffee and some donuts at Griffin's desk, talking sports.

"Hi, guys." All the homicide cops liked Pullios. They liked her because when they went to the trouble to arrest a suspect and provide

89

her with witnesses she generally saw to it the person went away, and often for a long time. "Anybody got a fuck for me?" Her smile lit up the office. Branstetter looked up from his report.

When she was speaking to these guys, she called all suspects "fucks." She knew, as all of them knew, that anybody who got all the way to arrested was guilty. They had done something bad enough to eliminate them from society forever. Therefore, she would start the process of making them nonpeople. They were fucks, starting here in Homicide. And fuck them.

"Slow night, Bets." Griffin put his donut down.

"So who's got the Nash thing?" She held up her folded newspaper. "Front-page stuff."

The cops looked at each other and shrugged. "Sounds exciting." Griffin was more interested in his donut. It wasn't his case. End of story. "I must have missed it."

"I think Glitsky might have gone down there," Block said. "You can look on his desk."

It was on top of the stack of papers on the corner of Abe Glitsky's desk. There wasn't much more than the manila folder with the name NASH in caps on the tab. Inside, Glitsky had started writing up the incident report, but hadn't gotten far. There were no photos yet, either from the discovery scene or the coroner's office.

Pullios closed up the folder, took a post-it and wrote a note asking Glitsky to call her as soon as he got in.

Hardy, awakened by Rebecca at five-thirty, had gone out running in the clear and already balmy dawn. Down Geary out to the beach, south to Lincoln, then inside Golden Gate Park back to 25th, and home. A four-mile circle he'd been trying to keep up since getting sedentary in March.

Now, near eight, he sat in his green jogging suit, taking his time over Frannie's great coffee. She sat across the kitchen table from him, glancing at sections of the paper when she wasn't fiddling with the baby, who was strapped into a baby seat on the table between them.

"And this was a baby shark," he said. "Imagine what a twenty-footer would do."

"I think they made a movie about that."

Hardy made a face at her as the doorbell rang, followed by the sound of the front door opening. "Don't get up, commoners," Glitsky called out, "I'll just let myself in."

The sergeant wore a white shirt and solid brown tie, khaki slacks, cordovan wing tips, tan sports coat. Entering the kitchen, he stopped. "Taking fashion tips from dead guys?"

"Hi, Abe," Frannie said.

Hardy pointed to the stove. "Water's hot."

Glitsky knew where the tea was and got out a bag, dropped it into a cup, came over to the table. He looked again at Hardy. "Oftentimes, I'll go see a body and the next day decide to wear exactly what it had on."

Hardy shrugged. "It was next up in my drawer. Am I supposed to throw it away?"

"If anybody ever asks if your husband is superstitious, Frannie, you should tell them no."

Hardy explained it to her. "Owen Nash was found in some sweats just like these. Abe thinks the streets are infested with sharks that are going to start a feeding frenzy over people in green sweats." Hardy lifted the front of his sweatshirt away from his body. "Besides, this is different. There aren't any holes in this one."

"Major difference." Abe nodded and sipped his tea. "So tell me everything you know."

Hardy and Glitsky went back into the office, where Hardy had the notes he'd taken after talking with Ken Farris. Abe sat at the desk while Hardy threw darts.

"Who's this guy in Santa Clara? Silicon Valley."

"I don't know. Farris said he'd tell me if we needed it."

"I need it."

"Yeah, I thought you would."

Glitsky kept reading, taking a couple of notes of his own. "He went out with this May Shinn on Saturday?"

Hardy pulled darts from the board—two bull's-eyes and a 1. He was throwing pretty well, a good sign. "We don't know that for sure. Farris says he was planning on it."

"But no one's talked to her?"

"Right. That's her number there at the bottom. You're welcome to give her a try."

Glitsky did. He held the receiver for a minute, then hung up. Hardy sat at the corner of the desk. "You didn't want to leave a message? Ask her to call you?"

"I'd love to, but nobody answered."

"No, there's a machine. I heard it."

Glitsky thought a minute, then dialed again. "Okay, last time was four, I'll give it ten."

The sun reflected off the hardwood floors onto the bookcase. Hardy walked over and opened the window, a reasonable action only about ten days a year. The view to his north, up to Twin Peaks and the Sutro Tower, was blocked from his office by Rebecca's room, but overhead, the sky was clear. Hardy could see Oakland easily. The air smelled like grass, even out here in the concrete avenues.

"Nope," Abe said behind him. "Ten rings. This listed? Where's she live? Where's your phone book?"

She wasn't listed. Without going into it too closely, Hardy said he'd gotten the number from Farris. "So she's home, I'd guess," Abe said. "At least she unplugged her machine in the last couple days, right? You going to work today dressed like that?"

Hardy allowed as he would probably take a shower and get dressed, and moved toward his bedroom, Abe following. "You know," he said, "I wouldn't get too red hot about this."

"Why not?"

"Well, the body turns up yesterday, but Nash was probably dead on Sunday, we go on that, right?"

"Yeah."

"Okay, today's Friday. One week, assuming he went down on Saturday."

"And after four days . . ." Hardy knew what Abe was saying, understood the statistics. If you didn't have a suspect within four days of a murder, the odds were enormous that you'd never get one.

"All I'm saying is don't get your hopes up."

Hardy stripped off his shirt. "Okay," he said. "But you've got Mr. Silicon Valley and you got May Shinn if you can find her."

"If she didn't go swimming with Owen Nash."

"Then who unplugged her answering machine?"

"I know, I know. I'm an investigator. I'll investigate. I also thought we'd check out the boat."

"No, the boat's clean." Hardy told Abe about his visit on Wednesday night.

"You brought along a forensic team, did you?"

Hardy shut up and went to take his shower.

*　*　*

The case of *The People v. Rane Brown* was not going to be an easy one.

Back in late March, at around ten at night, two officers in a squad car cruising under the freeway heard a man calling for help. Turning into the lot, they saw one man down on the ground and another man going through his pockets. When he saw the cops, the suspect took off. The man on the ground was yelling, "Stop him! That's the guy!" The officers followed the running man as he turned into one alley, then another, a dead end. Getting out of their car, they proceeded cautiously down the alley, guns drawn, flashlights out, until they came upon a man crouched between two dumpsters.

This man turned out to be Rane Brown, a 5'8", 135-pound, nineteen-year-old black male with four priors for mugging and purse snatching. When apprehended by the officers, he was wearing a black tank top and black pants that matched the clothes of the man who'd run from the scene. The officers found a .38 Smith & Wesson handgun under the dumpster next to Rane. The gun was registered to a Denise Watrous in San Jose.

What made the case especially difficult was that when the officers returned to the scene, the purported victim had disappeared, having evidently decided that the hassle of pursuing justice in this imperfect world was simply not worth the trouble.

But there was Rane Brown in custody, and the police didn't particularly want to let him go and mug someone else.

So Hardy was in Department 11 with Judge Nancy Fiedler this Friday morning, trying to prove a robbery and knowing that he didn't have a prayer of winning.

Which is what transpired. After a fairly stern lecture by Judge Fiedler on the advisability of producing some evidence before wasting the court's time on this minor and unprovable transgression, she had granted the motion to dismiss and Rane Brown was a free man.

Hardy and the two arresting officers had been waiting by the elevator when Rane and his attorney came up and joined them. Everybody headed to the first floor, and Rane was in high spirits.

"Man, you give me a turn when you walk in that courtroom," he said to Hardy.

"Why's that, Rane?"

"You know, the man here"—he cocked his head toward his attorney —"he tole me you ain't got no witnesses, no victim, like that. So I be thinkin' everything's cool and you walk in and I thinkin' *you* the victim." He smiled, broken teeth in a pocked face. "I mean, you get it? You look just like the man I rob."

Hardy stared at Rane a moment, letting it sink in. He saw the two cops that had arrested him, one on either side of him. Hardy allowed himself a small smile.

"You're telling me I look like the victim you just got let off for?"

Rane was bobbing his head. "Exactly, man, exactly." He just couldn't believe the resemblance.

Hardy looked from one officer to the other. "If I'm not mistaken," he said, "we just got ourselves a confession." The elevator door opened and Hardy stepped out, blocking the way. "Take this guy back upstairs and book him."

"The boat was out when you got in? And what time was that?"

José and Glitsky sat on hard plastic chairs by the doorway to the Gateway Marina guardhouse. José was about twenty-five years old, thin and sinewy. He wore new tennis shoes with his green uniform, a shirt open at the neck. The day had heated up. Even here, right on the water, it was over eighty degrees.

"I got here six-thirty, quarter to seven, and the *Eloise*, she was already gone."

"And nobody signed her out?"

"No. They 'spose to, but . . ." He shrugged.

"Were there any calls on the intercom, anything like that?"

"You remember Saturday? It was like nothing, maybe two boats, three go out. If anything had happen, I remember." José stood up and got a logbook from the counter. "Here, look at this. Air temp forty-eight, wind north northeast at thirty-five. Small craft up from the night before."

"So nobody was going out? What about the other boats? The ones that went out?"

José tapped the book. "These I write down." He ran a finger over the page until he got where he wanted. "The *Wave Dancer,* she goes out at ten-thirty, back at two. Then *Blue Baby,* she just clear the jetty" —pronounced "yetty"—"then turn aroun' and come back in, like one-fifteen. *Rough Rider* leaves about the same as *Blue Baby,* like one-thirty. They no come back in on my shift."

Not bad, Glitsky thought. Every new witness didn't double his work, it squared it. Here were only three boats to check, and maybe he could leave out the *Blue Baby*. Possibly one of them had seen the *Eloise*. If

Saturday had been a day like today, clear and calm . . . He didn't want to think about it. He started writing down names.

A uniformed officer appeared in the doorway. "Sergeant, the lab team is pulling up."

As soon as he'd left Hardy's that morning Glitsky had arranged to have the *Eloise* placed under the guard of a couple of officers. He stopped off downtown for an easily obtained search warrant, not even dropping into his office. After he and Forensics had gone over the *Eloise,* a prospect about which he entertained no great hopes—they'd cordon it off with crime-scene tape. But the boat was the place to start —it was more than probable that Nash had at the very least been dead on the boat and dumped from it. From there, he'd see where the trails led.

José was next to him as he greeted the team at the gate to the slips, and the six men walked out in the glaring sun to the end of Dock Two. José opened the cabin for them, then Glitsky dismissed him.

Abe went below, taking a moment to let his eyes adjust to the relative darkness. As the room became visible, one of the forensic team on the ladder behind him whistled at the layout.

They went to work.

It was a tough call because they were looking for anything and nothing. Two men were on deck above, starting at the bow and coming back. Glitsky and two other guys were below, but there wasn't much evident there either. No sign of any struggle.

Glitsky started in the main cabin, just poking around, looking. He wasn't a forensics man. He would let them go over the fabrics and rugs and smooth surfaces. Whatever he was looking for would have to be obvious. But not too obvious, he thought, or Hardy would have seen it.

All of the cabinets were secured, both in the main cabin and in the adjoining galley. He opened each one, moved a few things around, closed it back up. Moseying back to the master suite, he noted the made bed. He considered calling back to remind his guys to bring the sheets in, but thought better of it. They would do that automatically.

To the right of the bed there was a wooden desk, shaped to the bulkhead, its surface cleared. He tried one of the side drawers and found it locked. The center drawer, however, slid open easily, and, with it open, the other drawers came free.

But it was slim pickings. The gutter to the center drawer contained pens and paper clips, several books of matches from various restaurants, a couple of keys on a ring that Abe assumed fitted this desk, rubberbands and a handball from the Olympic Club. The flat back part of the drawer appeared to be completely empty, but reaching his hand back, Glitsky found two stale, crumbling cigars. The top side drawer, the slimmer one, was filled with lots of different colored sweatbands, which seemed to go with the exercycle and dumbbells on the other side of the bed. The bottom side drawer was empty.

On the other side of the bed was a rolltop desk, its cover down. He rolled back the oak top. There were probably twenty-five cubbyholes above the desk's surface, most of them containing pieces of paper, some of them rolled up, some folded over. A general catchall. Glitsky pulled out a piece at random and found a shopping list. Eggs, cheese, spinach, orange juice. Sunday brunch, he decided. Another paper, also at random, read "W. re Taos/reschedule." That was all. Glitsky put the two pages back where he'd gotten them. Forensics would take them back downtown if they found any other evidence that Nash had been killed here.

The center drawer looked much like the other one—matches, cigars, pens and pencils, junk.

He pulled open the upper right drawer, expecting to find more headbands. At first glance this looked to be another functional drawer, but when Glitsky pulled the drawer out a little further, he saw a nickel-plated .25 Beretta 950 lying on top of what looked like a collection of folded-up navigational charts.

Just then one of the forensics men on deck called below. "Sergeant, you want to get up here? I think we got us some blood."

15

It was close to noon on what was already the hottest day of the year and, naturally, the air conditioners were on the blink. There were no windows in the courtrooms in San Francisco's Hall of Justice. Fans were set up on either side of the bench in Judge Andy Fowler's courtroom, Department 27, and they did move the air around. Unfortunately the temperature of the air getting moved was ninety-one degrees.

The whir of the fan blades also upped the decibel level. Nearly uniform in size, twenty-five by forty feet, with high ceilings and no soft surfaces except the minimal padding on the seats of jurors, judges and witnesses, courtrooms were, under the best conditions, loud and uncomfortable.

And today, under far less than optimal conditions, Andy Fowler was once again being forced, reluctantly, by the luck of the draw, into a role he hated—protector of suspect's rights.

He'd been a young man at the time of his appointment to the bench. He'd worked on Pat Brown's second gubernatorial campaign against Richard Nixon—more because he hated Nixon than loved Brown—and persuaded a goodly amount of his Olympic Club confreres, some of them Republicans, to donate to the cause. At the time, though not yet thirty, he'd already made partner in his firm, and he had put the word out that he would accept a judgeship if one came around, which, in due course, it did.

Though his politics rarely came up and hadn't radically changed in thirty years, this was the 1990s in San Francisco. Anywhere but in the Hall of Justice, a Kennedy-style liberal Democrat was considered right-wing. Actual conservatives, again excluding the Hall, were as rare in the city as a warm day.

Political San Francisco was a Balkanized unit of special interests, many on the so-called left—homosexuals, people of color, middle-

97

class white radicals . . . so political survival in the city was in large part a matter of pleasing enough of these groups to form a majority coalition on whatever issue happened to be the day's hot topic.

In reaction, the denizens of the Hall of Justice—the police department, the D.A.'s office, judges—had become a little Balkan republic of their own. It was tough, they said, to be for law and order, to serve blind justice, when first you had to take into account the trauma and/ or discrimination that had been visited on you and yours on account of skin color, gender, sexual preference, religious orientation, poor potty training, whatever.

And in this climate, until three years ago, Andy Fowler had been a popular judge. He knew it was true, because prosecutors went out of their way to tell him they loved getting cases in his department. Why? Well, he tried to be fair. He wasn't a wiseguy. He didn't throw things —erasers, pencils, paper clips—from the bench at attorneys, bailiffs or suspects. If someone needed waking up in the courtroom, he would politely ask the bailiff to shake that person. He had a sly humor and no political axe to grind. He was knowledgeable about the law. He was, in short, a good judge.

The first sign of change came in the case of *The People v. Randy Blakemore*. It seemed Mr. Blakemore was hanging out on Eddy Street one evening and saw an apparently drunk tourist stumbling along in a nice suit. Randy noticed a Rolex, a fat bulge in the tourist's back pocket, the gold chain around his neck. When the man fell into a doorway to rest, Randy moved in and had his hands on the Rolex when two other "homeless people" appeared with badges and guns. The tourist opened his eyes and uttered an extremely sober, "Boo, you're it," and Randy was taken downtown—one of seventeen arrests in a police program to get the word out on the street that tourists were a valued business in San Francisco and were not to be hassled.

Six other cases had already come up for PXs—preliminary hearings —in other departments when *Blakemore* came up in Andy Fowler's courtroom. Four of those men were awaiting trial and two had already been convicted and sent to jail. Andy Fowler took a look at Randy standing in the docket in his orange prison togs and told him it was his lucky day—this was as clear a case of entrapment as Judge Fowler had ever seen and though he had no doubt that Randy was a bad person who shouldn't be on the streets, on this particular charge he was going to walk.

Other judges reconsidered. Three of the four remaining prelims resulted the same way. Both of the felons already convicted were released on appeal. The last suspect had also mugged the "tourist" and fought the arresting officers, so he did go to trial, although the jury didn't convict. The other dozen or so arrestees had their charges dropped by an angry District Attorney Christopher Locke.

So Fowler's ruling had alienated Locke, the sixteen officers who'd taken part in the operation, Chief of Police Dan Rigby and the mayor, in whose brain the original germ of the idea had hatched in the first place.

For a short while Fowler became somewhat the darling of the media —the Sunday *Chronicle*'s Calendar/Style section did a piece on him, further alienating the Hall. Esquire liked his wardrobe. Rolling Stone asked his opinion on *Roe v. Wade*. People had a little squib on him in End-Notes, calling him a "crusading justice."

Fowler laughed it off as his allotted twenty minutes of fame, and most of it blew over after a while. But it did leave a bitter residue, especially on a young female D.A. named Elizabeth Pullios, who didn't like to lose and who'd been prosecuting Blakemore.

Now, on this sweltering morning, Fowler had listened to a half-hour of opening statements by Chief Assistant District Attorney Art Drysdale, making a rare personal appearance in a courtroom. The case was *The People v. Charles Hendrix et al.,* and Drysdale was here because Locke had asked him to be.

There were eight sitting judges in San Francisco, their cases assigned by one of their number, a rotating calendar judge, in Department 22, starting at nine-thirty every Monday morning. When *People v. Hendrix* went to Fowler, Locke knew he was in trouble—*Hendrix* was another entrapment. In this case, the SFPD had set up a phony fence, a warehouse to receive stolen goods. After word got out, they had videotaped twenty to thirty suspects a day, waiting for a big score or a connection to a major dope deal, before they'd make some arrests. This, Locke suspected, wasn't going to fly in Andy Fowler's courtroom.

". . . And I want to see prosecuting counsel in my chambers immediately."

Fowler, recovered from his illness of the previous day, left the bench and had his robe off before he left the courtroom. He told the bailiff to bring one of the fans into his office.

A minute later, Drysdale was knocking at his open door. "Your Honor."

The bailiff brushed by Drysdale with the fan and plugged it in so it blew across Fowler's desk.

"How many of these turkeys are we likely to be seeing here? Come in, Art. Sit down. Hot enough?"

Drysdale crossed a leg. "With all respect, Your Honor, I think a flat dismissal is out of line as a matter of law." Fowler's eyes narrowed, but Drysdale ignored the obvious signs, reaching into his briefcase. "I've got a brief here—"

"You've got a brief already? Before you knew my ruling?"

"Mr. Locke had an . . . intuition."

Fowler did not smile. "I'll bet he did." He laced his fingers and brought them up to his mouth. "Why don't you just give me the sense of it?"

Drysdale hadn't written a "memorandum of points and authorities" —a paper laying out current law based on past decisions in other courts, law-review articles, recognized lawbooks—in about eight years, and when Locke asked him to figure out a way to get by Fowler he thought this was as good a time as any to try one.

Entrapment was generally frowned upon in the 1st District Court of Appeal, San Francisco's district, but there was a lot of leeway granted police depending on how the sting was set up. In this case, *Hendrix,* and in the many others sure to follow from the phony warehouse, the police were not arresting the suspect at the scene. Rather, they were using information gathered by videotape at the scene to identify the suspect, after which they tailed him to see what he was up to. This approach had resulted in righteous convictions that held up under appeal in several states, and Drysdale laid it all out in a nutshell while Fowler sat back in his chair, eyes closed, letting the fan blow over him.

When Drysdale had finished, Fowler opened his eyes. "Let me tell you a story, Art. This kid is sitting on his front lawn, minding his own business, and one of his neighbors comes by and tells him there's a warehouse down the street paying top dollar for any goods brought to it, no questions asked. The neighbor shows him a roll he just got for a car stereo and two bicycles. Another neighbor comes by, flashes another wad of dough. This goes on for a week, and pretty soon our boy is thinking he'd be some kind of fool not to take advantage of this opportunity like all of his neighbors.

"See? There's two parts to stealing—taking and fencing—and both are risky, but now one half the risk is eliminated. So, and this is important"—Fowler leaned forward over his desk, out of the flow of air from the fan—"it is the *impetus* of this sting operation that causes our boy to go and commit a crime."

"Excuse me, Your Honor, but these people are already committing crimes. They're going to fence them somewhere."

"But by making it *easy* to fence them, Counselor, we are encouraging them to steal more."

Drysdale sat back. He knew Fowler's argument. He just didn't agree with it. But he was only the running footman. "Mr. Locke doesn't agree with you, Judge. Neither does Mr. Rigby."

Fowler allowed himself a tight smile. "Well, now, that's what makes this country great, isn't it?"

Drysdale leaned forward himself. "The cops have put in a lot of time and money on this already, Judge. So have we. We're taking these guys off the street—"

"Shooting them would also take them off the street, Art. And shooting them is also illegal."

"This isn't illegal."

Fowler finally sat back, breaking the eye contact. "You know, it's funny, but I'm the judge. It's my courtroom and if I say it's illegal, you and Mr. Locke and Mr. Rigby and anybody else will just have to live with it."

Now Drysdale sat back. He realized that he was sweating and wiped a hand across his forehead. "I'd like to at least leave the brief," he said.

"Fine, leave the brief. I'll read it if I get the chance."

"The son of a bitch! The arrogant, pompous, liberal son of a bitch!"

"Yes, sir." Drysdale stood by the window in Locke's office, hands held behind his back. The air conditioner seemed to be working better on the third floor.

"This was a righteous bust. We didn't take Hendrix in dumping the goods—we caught him in the act."

Drysdale turned around. "An act he would not have been drawn to commit had we not set up our fence."

"Oh bullshit!"

Art shrugged. "It's not my argument."

"Hendrix does this for a fucking *living*. He steals things. You know that as well as I do. He breaks into your house or my house or his fucking honor Andy Fowler's house and takes things that aren't fucking his. He is not coerced into doing this by finding a good place to unload it."

"Yes, sir, I know."

The warehouse was an ongoing operation that had been in business for about four months. The police department had already brought in over forty suspects and had collected some $2.5 million worth of contraband, a good portion of which they had returned to its owners. It was a successful tool that they felt was working. Arrests were up, convictions should follow. And Locke was damned if he was going to let some commie judge screw it up for everybody.

He sat down now, played drums with a pencil on his desk. *Shave and a haircut, six bits. Shave and a haircut, six bits.* "Who's on Calendar this month? Maybe we'll get lucky in another department."

"I think Leo Chomorro's taken up permanent residence."

"Poor bastard."

Art lifted his shoulders. "He asked for it. If he rides with us, maybe we can ease him out of there. Maybe he's ready."

"Find out, would you? Find out if he'll play, keep any of these away from Fowler. Rigby's going to have a shit-fit."

"Yes, sir," Art said.

Locke looked at his watch. "God, how could it be lunchtime already? I just got here. I've got an appointment in ten minutes, Art. You want to fill Rigby in? No, I'll do it. He's gonna shit! What are we going to do about Fowler?"

Drysdale shrugged. "He's a judge, Chris. He's in for the duration, I'm afraid."

Locke was moving around his desk, straightening his tie. "I'd like to get a crack at him, I'll tell you that. Son of a bitch could ruin my career."

Drysdale, who'd been around and seen it all, was about to tell his boss that Andy Fowler was an okay guy, good on a lot of other issues. It was just his interpretation of the law, nothing personal. But he bit his tongue—he knew better.

It *was* personal. If it didn't start personal, it got that way in a hurry. To the people who practiced it—even a seasoned veteran like Art Drysdale—everything about the law was personal. There were ego, careers, and lives wrapped up in every yea or nay, every objection sustained or overruled, every conviction, every reversal. If you didn't take it personally you didn't belong there.

Andy Fowler wasn't just interpreting the law. He was stepping on toes, big toes. Although he was loyal to Locke, Drysdale had always gotten along well with Fowler, and he hoped like hell the judge knew what he was doing. If he slipped up, he was going to get squished.

16

"You love this, don't you?" Frannie asked.

Hardy hadn't stopped grinning since he'd told the cops in the elevator to rebook Rane Brown. He had just told his wife the story. "It has its moments, I must admit."

"So who are you nailing this afternoon?"

Hardy looked at the folders on his desk, still a formidable pile. "The afternoon looms large before me," he said. He noticed Andy Fowler's jade paperweight and picked it up, cool and heavy in his hand. "Maybe I'll shoot some darts, eat lunch . . ." His feet were up on his desk, his tie loosened. Abe Glitsky appeared in his doorway, knocked once and sat down across the desk from him. "On the other hand, I'm sure Abe says hi. He just walked in."

"I'll let you go then."

"Okay, but guess what?"

"I know. Me, too."

"Okay." Saying they loved each other in code.

Glitsky had come directly to Hardy's office from the evidence-locker room. The telephone receiver wasn't out of Hardy's hand yet when Glitsky said, "As you astutely predicted, Diz, the *Eloise* was clean."

Hardy was tossing the jade from hand to hand. "Well, I didn't think—"

"Except for a gun, a slug, a bunch of blood, some other stuff."

Hardy put the jade down, swinging his feet to the floor. "I'm listening."

Glitsky filled him in. He had bagged the Beretta for evidence. You could still smell the cordite. He would bet a lot it was the murder weapon, although Ballistics would tell them for sure by Monday. On deck, they had found what looked like blood on the railing where Nash might have gone overboard. "Whoever shot him, whoever

104

brought the boat back in, must have washed down the deck, but they missed the rail."

"The gun registered?"

"I'm running it now. We'll know by tonight."

"Any word on May Shinn?"

"I was thinking you might have something there. Maybe Farris?"

Hardy shook his head, told him a little about how he'd spent his morning, about Rane Brown. Glitsky nodded. "You ever notice how just plain dumb these guys are?"

It had crossed Hardy's mind. "So what's my excuse to talk to Farris again? Maybe you want to talk to him. Till you give me a suspect, I'm not really in it."

Glitsky was firm. "You're in it, Diz. You already know the guy. Tell him we need Mr. Silicon and we haven't located Shinn. See what he'll tell you. He's probably handling disposition of the body, too. Although maybe the daughter . . . no, probably him."

"I'm on it," Hardy said.

Hardy passed on his lunch. It was too nice a day to stay cooped up, so Hardy called, got directions and made an appointment, then drove with the top off his Samurai around the Army Street curve down 101. He got his first view of the Bay as he passed Candlestick Park—remarkably blue, clear all the way down to San Jose, dotted with a few sailboats, some tankers. The Bay Bridge glittered silver a little behind him and the pencil line of the San Mateo Bridge ran over to Hayward. You could see it every day, Hardy thought, and the beauty still got to you.

He exited the freeway at South San Francisco and drove north and west through the industrial section. Owen Industries spread itself over nearly two acres of land at the foot of the San Bruno mountains, a bunch of white and green structures that looked like army barracks. Hardy was issued a guest pass at the guard station after he'd had his appointment confirmed. These folks were into security.

He drove a hundred yards between two rows of the low buildings, then turned left as instructed and came upon the corporate offices, which showed signs of an architect's hand. A well-kept lawn, a cobbled walkway bounded by a low hedge, a few mature pines, relieved the drab institutional feel of the rest of the place. A flag flew at half-mast. The corporate office building itself was fronted in brick and glass. It, like the surrounding compound, squatted at one story.

Inside, red-tiled floors, potted trees, wide halls with modern art tastefully framed, gave the place an air of muted elegance. An attractive young receptionist took Hardy back to Farris's office and explained that he would be back in a moment and in the meantime Hardy could wait here.

The door closed behind him and for a moment after turning around, Hardy was struck by an intimate familiarity.

The walls were painted lighter and the view outside the window was certainly different, but otherwise Farris's office was strikingly like Hardy's own at his house. There was a fireplace with its mantel, the seagoing knickknacks, even a blowfish on the green blotter that covered the desk. There was no green-shaded banker's lamp, but the file cabinets were wooden, the bookshelves contained business stuff but also some popular books. Finally, there was a dart board studded with two sets of what Hardy recognized as high-quality custom darts.

There were differences, of course. This room was twice the size and altogether brighter than Hardy's. The floor was of the same red tile that had been in the lobby, partially covered by three Navajo throw rugs and a couch.

Hardy walked to the desk, felt the grain of the wood, moved to the bookshelves, then to the dartboard. He removed three of the darts and stepped back to the corner of the desk.

After throwing all six darts, Hardy sat on one of the stiff-back wooden chairs, crossed one knee over the other and waited. In under a minute the door opened.

"Hardy. Dismas, how are you? Sorry to keep you waiting. Something came up." A somewhat forced smile in the handsome face. Again, impeccable clothes—a charcoal business suit—with the personal touch of cowboy boots. Hardy thought he looked exhausted. He went around his desk, arranged some papers and sat down. His eyes went around the room. "You've thrown my darts."

"That's an impressive bit of observation."

Farris brushed it off. "Party trick," he said, "like Owen breaking boards." He explained. "You're around Owen, you better have something you can do better than he can. I got good at details." He seemed to slump, remembering something.

"You all right?" Hardy asked.

"Yeah, I'll live. This is a bitch of a blow, though. I'm not much good pretending it isn't."

"You don't have to."

"With you, okay. But out there"—he motioned toward the door he'd just come through—"I set the tone. People out there see me panic, then it starts to spread, right? I just put the word out we're closing up for today. Maybe things'll look better on Monday."

Hardy gave it a minute, then thought he might as well get down to it. He briefed him on Glitsky's discoveries on the *Eloise,* which Farris took in without comment. Then he got the name, address and phone number of Mr. Silicon—Austin Brucker in Los Altos Hills. Finally he got around to May Shinn.

"I wanted to be clear on May, though. Wednesday when you called her, you left a message?"

Farris nodded. "That's right. You were right there."

"Yeah, I know. I'm a little confused, though, because Sergeant Glitsky tried to call her this morning and no one answered."

"How'd he get her number?"

Details, Hardy thought, this guy is into details. He lifted his shoulders an inch. "Cops have access to unlisted numbers." He hoped.

Farris accepted that. "But the machine didn't answer?"

"Ten rings."

"No, it picked up after two, three for me." He thought a minute. "Maybe it got to the end of the tape."

"You'd still get her answering message, wouldn't you?"

"I think you would."

The two men sat, putting it together. "She's alive then," Farris said. "She unplugged it."

"Would she have had a reason to kill Owen?"

"May?"

"Somebody did."

Farris shrugged again. "I don't know. I didn't know her. I wouldn't know her if she walked in here."

"But did Mr. Nash—?"

"Owen liked her." He paused. "A lot. More than a lot."

"So how about if he stopped liking her?"

"So what?"

"So might she have gone off, something like that?"

Farris shook his head. "I just don't have any idea. The last I knew, Owen liked her. But, I mean, the woman's a prostitute, right? She kills a john over his dumping her? Even if it's Owen, I don't see it. And I don't think he was dumping her."

"So where is she? Why hasn't she returned your calls?"

"I don't know. That's a good question."

Hardy finally had to let it go. "What are you doing about the body?" he asked.

Celine was going by the coroner's this afternoon to sign some papers. The autopsy was supposed to have been done this morning. So they planned to have the cremation Sunday morning, scattering his ashes over the Pacific that afternoon.

Farris looked hard out the window. He had a minimum view of the sun behind the low green buildings, some grass, a couple of pine trees. He put his hand to his eyes and pushed against them, then pinched the bridge of his nose.

Hardy stood and thanked him for his time. Farris got up from his chair, shook hands over the desk and apologized again. He wasn't himself. Sorry. Thanks for coming by.

Hardy turned back at the door. Farris had sat back down in his chair behind the wide expanse of the oak desk. He was staring out again into the evening shadow cast over the lawns and pine trees, the shade now reaching to his no-view window—a statue of grief.

The flight was on Japan Airlines at eight-fifteen.

It was four-fifteen, far too early to leave, yet she had phoned for the cab. What was she thinking of? May knew she would go mad sitting out at the airport for three hours, worrying that someone would stop her, knowing that she had to leave here, that this place, maybe America itself, was over for her.

Her bags were by the front door. She had decided to pack the Lennons, and the foyer looked bare without them. The sun shone in through the turret windows, which she'd opened due to the heat. The heat made her feel as though in some ways she was leaving a place she'd never been.

She wore a dark blue linen suit with dark hose, not the perfect outfit for this weather, but she thought it made her look more businesslike. Her hair was in a tight bun, her most severe look. She didn't want people coming up and talking to her.

When the doorbell rang, she was surprised. Normally, the drivers would honk out on the street. Nevertheless, she determined that she would tell the man she'd made a mistake; he could come back later if he wanted the fare.

Or maybe she wouldn't. Through the peephole, his looks scared her —a light-skinned black man with a nasty-looking scar through his lips, top to bottom. On the other hand, she wanted someone who wouldn't talk to her and this man looked like that type. She opened the door.

She was looking at a badge of some kind, the man identifying himself as Inspector Abe Glitsky of the San Francisco Police, Homicide. She stepped back as he asked if she was May Shintaka. "May I come in?" He sounded polite enough.

"Certainly."

He stood in the foyer. There was nothing she could do to keep him from noting the newly empty walls, obvious where the Lennons had been taken down. "I'm here about Owen Nash."

A nod. She turned and walked back into the living room. Now she was really hot and she took off her coat, draping it across the arm of the couch. She went to the turret window and heard the honk of the cab down below.

The sergeant took a few steps into the room, but stopped near the foyer. "Your shoes," she said. "Do you mind?" She motioned to a long, polished and ridged board that began next to the door. Her own pair of dark-blue pumps were already resting over the ridge.

Abe stepped out of his wing tips and placed them on the board. "Were you planning on going somewhere?" He motioned to the bags in the hallway.

She was coming back across the room. He seemed to fill up where he stood even more than Owen had, and Owen was a big man, had been a big man. "That's my cab down there now," she said. "But it's too early anyway. I should tell him."

Abe was nervous about letting her go down, but she'd left her bags as well as the jacket of her suit. She didn't take a purse. If she got in the cab, he'd be able to call the dispatcher and possibly stop her before she'd gone a mile.

The advantage was his now. She had invited him into her apartment. He hadn't needed to show a warrant, which in any event he didn't have.

As soon as he'd left Hardy, he decided he had to do some police work. He had the phone company run a reverse list on May's phone number and got her address, which was on his way home. He'd called back Elizabeth Pullios, but she was out with a witness and wasn't due to return to her office until Monday. He finished up his paperwork on the Nash incident report, grabbed an afternoon cup of tea and some peanut M&Ms downstairs, then went upstairs to the jail and interviewed a snitch who supposedly knew the name of the shooter in last weekend's drive-by. The information was worth checking, so he scheduled a videotape session for Monday.

Back at his desk, now getting on four o'clock, he called records and got a registration on the Beretta. The gun belonged to May Shintaka.

Nash's autopsy showed that the bullets that killed him were .25 caliber, and Glitsky figured he didn't have to wait for the formal ballistics report. He had her address, and for the moment at least, May Shinn was "it."

She didn't hop in the cab and make a run for it. He was standing in the turret, watching her say something into the passenger window. After she stepped back, the cab took off with a squeal of rubber.

Glitsky watched her close the door to the apartment, gently, holding the knob with one hand and fitting the door into the sill with the other, the way mothers sometimes did when their children were sleeping in the room they were closing off. Seeing her dark blue, low-heeled pumps and the tailored suit, he had to remind himself that according to all the information he had, this woman was a prostitute.

She was out of the shoes, then, turning away from the door. She came back into the living room. He found he couldn't make a guess as to her age and hit it within a decade. She could be anywhere from twenty-five to forty-five. She had, he thought, a very unusual face, the bones clearly defined, the skin smooth and stretched tight with the hair pulled back.

She walked over to the low couch, next to where she'd laid her jacket, and floated down onto it. She made some motion that he took to be an invitation to sit, which he did, feeling like a clod in his brown socks and his American sports coat.

"Would you like some tea?" she asked. "Please, take off your coat. It's too warm."

So far as Abe knew, he was the only male tea drinker on the force. He thought about declining, then realized he would enjoy watching May Shinn move around. "That would be nice," he said. He folded his coat over his end of the couch, thinking if she kept this up, he'd be stripped before long.

She walked into the kitchen, open from the living room, and he watched her back, the straight shoulders, tiny waist, womanly curve of her hips. Even barefoot, her ankles tapered, thin as a doe's.

She poured from a bottle of Evian into a kettle. "Owen's dead," she said.

"Yes, ma'am. Somebody killed him."

He kept watching her closely. She was taking down some cups, placing them on a tray. If her hands were shaking, the cups would betray her, but they didn't. She stood by the stove, turning full to face him. "I read that."

Glitsky sat forward on the couch, elbows on his knees. "The suit-cases," he said. "You were going somewhere."

"Japan. On business," she added, spooning tea into the cups.

"You have business over there?"

She nodded. "I buy art. I am a—a broker for different friends of mine."

"Do you go over there a lot?"

"Sometimes, yes. It depends."

Glitsky would have time to pursue that if he had to. He decided to move things along. "We found your gun on Mr. Nash's boat. On the *Eloise*."

"Yes, I kept it there."

"We're reasonably certain it's the gun that was used to kill him." She seemed to be waiting, immobilized. "When was the last time you saw him, Ms. Shinn?"

She turned back to the stove, touched the side of the kettle with a finger and decided it wasn't ready yet. "Friday night, no, Saturday morning, very early. He stayed here."

"In this apartment?"

"Yes."

"And then where did he go from here?"

"He said he was going sailing. He sailed many weekends."

"And did you go with him?"

"Most times, yes. But not Saturday."

"Why was that?"

She tried the kettle again, nodded, then poured the two cups. She brought the tray over and set it on the low table in front of them. "He had another appointment."

"Did he tell you who it was with?"

She shook her head. "No."

"Or what it was about?"

"He didn't say. He only said it was clearing the way for us."

"What does that mean, clearing the way for you?"

"I don't know. I think he needed to be alone. To think it out." She seemed to be searching for words, although not the way a foreigner would. She appeared to be a native speaker of English, but there was a hesitation, a pause. It threw Abe off—he couldn't decide when, if, she was editing, when she was telling the truth. "We were going to be married."

"You and Owen Nash were going to be married?"

"Yes." Keeping it simple and unadorned. The best kind of lie, Abe thought. And this, he was sure, was a lie. Owen Nash, internationally acclaimed tycoon and business leader, intimate of presidents and kings, did not marry his professional and well-paid love slave. Period.

"Had you set a date?"

"No," she said. She picked up one of the teacups and held it a second, then put it back down. "It is still too hot," she said. "We only decided, finally, last Friday. It was my ring."

"The snake ring? The one on his hand?"

"Yes, that one."

"Then you've known since Monday that he was dead?" Or since Saturday when you shot him, he was thinking. "Why didn't you call the police?"

She picked up the teacup again, perhaps stalling. "When it doesn't burn the fingers, it can't burn the mouth," she said. She handed him the cup.

It was strong, excellent green tea. Abe sipped it, not really understanding why you could drink hot tea on a hot day and feel cooler. "May, why didn't you call us, the police?"

"What could they do? He was already dead. I knew it was Owen. The rest didn't matter. It was his fate."

"It wasn't his natural fate, May. Somebody shot him."

"Monday I didn't know that. I only knew it was Owen's hand."

"What about today? Did you read the paper today? Or yesterday?"

"Yes."

Glitsky waited. "Just yes?"

May Shinn sipped at her own tea. Carefully she put the cup down. "What do you want me to say? My instinct, after all, was not to call the police. Whoever killed Owen will have to live with himself and that is punishment enough."

Abe put his cup down and walked back to the turret window. Across the street was another apartment house, the mirror image of this one. A cable car clanged by below. The sun was still fairly high, slanting toward him. There wasn't a cloud clear to the horizon.

From behind him. "Am I a suspect, Sergeant?"

Glitsky turned around. "Do you remember what you did last Saturday, during the day?"

"An alibi, is that right? I am a suspect, then."

"It's an open field at this point, but unless you have an alibi for Saturday, I'm afraid you're in it. Did you kill him?"

Just say no, he thought, I didn't do it. But she said, "I was here Saturday, all day."

"Alone?"

"Yes, alone. I was waiting for Owen to come back." A little short there, exasperated. Deny you did it, he thought again, just say the words. But she said, "I loved the man, Sergeant."

"Did you make any phone calls, order out for pizza? Did anybody see you?"

Finally it was getting to her. She sat on the front three inches of the couch, ramrod straight. "I got up late, around nine. Owen had left sometime around six. I took a long bath. I was nervous. Owen was doing something to make it so we could get married—deciding, I think, that he was going to go through with it. He thought best out on the water. I waited. I paced a lot. When he wasn't back by dark, I went to bed. I couldn't face anybody. I was crying. I thought he'd decided not to."

Glitsky put his jacket over his knees. "I think you might want to put your trip on hold," he said. "And maybe see about retaining a lawyer."

He thought about taking her downtown now, but knew that he'd be asking for repercussions if he did. It was premature. He really had no evidence. It had been a week since the gun had been fired, and even the most sophisticated laser analysis wouldn't show powder on the hands after that long. What May had told him was plausible, though pretty unlikely, and there was still plenty of legwork to try and verify her alibi or not, maybe neighbors hearing her walking around and so forth. If she agreed to put off going to Japan, there wasn't any risk of imminent flight, and he didn't really have any probable cause.

Plus, she being Oriental and he being half black, he didn't want to give anybody any ammunition to be able to accuse him of hassling her on racial grounds. She had invited him, without a warrant, into her apartment. It was bad luck to arrest somebody under those conditions. Now if she took flight, it would be a different story.

But she was standing, too. "All right," she said. "I understand."

Glitsky was picking up his shoes. "Can you get a refund on that ticket? If you can't, we may be able to help you."

She shook her head. "They should refund it. God knows I paid full price, they should."

So she'd bought the ticket recently, Abe thought. Probably since last Saturday. He hesitated. Strike two and a half. Tough call, but he was still an invited guest in her house, and she'd promised to stay around. He'd really prefer to have an indictment before he decided to arrest somebody on a murder charge.

He thought he'd bring his suspicions to Hardy and Hardy could decide whether they wanted to try to persuade the grand jury. But he doubted there was enough yet. Two and a half strikes didn't make an out.

He said goodbye and she closed the door, gently, behind him.

Abe didn't love himself for it, but it was too close and he thought with a little patience he could at least not have to worry over the weekend. He pulled his Plymouth away from the curb and made a point of turning west at the corner under the turret window. He drove three blocks, turned north again on Van Ness, left on Geary and back up to Union. He parked at the far end of May's block on her side of the street.

Even with the windows down, in the shade, it was hot. Fortunately, he didn't have long to wait.

A cab pulled up in front of the corner apartment building and honked its horn twice. Glitsky waited as May came out of the building. He let the driver load her suitcases into the trunk, let May get settled into the back seat before he pulled out into the street.

As the cab rounded the first corner, Abe turned on his red light and hit his siren. The cab, directly in front of him, pulled over immediately.

Abe came up to the window and flashed his badge. The driver asked what he'd done; Abe had him get out of the car, then asked him where this fare had asked to be taken.

"Down the airport," he said. "Goin' to Japan at eight o'clock."

Glitsky thanked the man, then opened the back door and looked in at May. "I'm sorry," he said, "but I'm afraid you're under arrest."

17

It was after five, but yesterday Hardy had gone home early after the beach, so today he felt compelled to check in after his visit with Farris instead of going directly home from the field. He parked under the freeway and stopped for a moment to admire the huge hole in the ground that now, after a year of political struggle, was the beginning of the new county jail.

Like everything else in San Francisco government, the decision to build a larger county jail had been arrived at after a fair and wide-ranging debate of other uses to which the alloted money should, in a perfect world, be put. Although the electorate had approved the bond measure that would provide the funds, the board of supervisors had at first leaned toward using this money to buy electronic bracelets to keep track of prisoners—Hardy grinned involuntarily whenever the thought crossed his mind—and using the remainder for AIDS research. This enlightened plan was discussed by the mayor, the board and various agencies for eleven months. Finally, over the threatened resignations of both Police Chief Dan Rigby and County Sheriff Herbert Montoya, the jail had been approved.

Hardy gazed down into the hole as the last of the workmen were wrapping it up for the day. He had a vision of five gang members in an old Ford cruising out to one of the projects to shoot whoever might be standing around, each of them wearing a Captain Video wrist bracelet to keep him from committing crimes because, see, if the cops knew where you were at all times, then it would be the same as being in jail, wouldn't it?

The first time he'd seen her she'd had mascara running down her face, hair witched out in shanks, so Hardy didn't immediately recognize Celine Nash, who was coming out of the coroner's office, on Hardy's left, thirty feet in front of him.

The ashen hair—or was it blonde?—was thick and combed straight

115

back, to just below her shoulders, looking like it had been professionally done about ten minutes before. She wore a peacock-blue leotard
on top that disappeared into a pair of designer blue jeans, cinched at
the waist with a red scarf. Watching the body approach him from the
side, he was almost preternaturally aware of its substance, the solid
thereness of a splendid female—the movement almost feline, the rock
of hip and jounce of breast. He stopped breathing.

Then she turned toward him, and he recognized her.

"Ms. Nash?" he said.

She was still ten feet away when she halted. Hardy introduced himself again, coming up to her.

"I'm sorry," she said, "there's been so many . . ." She let it trail
off. "Were you with the coroner?"

Hardy explained his connection, that he would be handling the
case when it got to the district attorney. "I just got back from seeing
Ken Farris. He told me you might be up here. He's pretty broken up."

"I imagine he is." Her eyes were light blue, almost gray. He thought
he might as well be invisible—the eyes looked past him, then came
back to him, waiting.

"I'm sorry about your father," he said, meaning it.

She nodded, without any time for him, or simply lost inside herself.

"Well, I'm keeping you." He took a step and she touched the sleeve
of his jacket, leaving her hand there, her eyes following an instant
later.

"I'm sorry," she said. "It's all this keeping up appearances."

Her hand was like a brand on his lower arm—he felt it through the
sleeve of his coat, a grip like steel. He caught her eyes, still distant;
her face a mask. He wondered if she might be in some kind of shock.

"Are you all right?"

She took a deep breath, then seemed to realize she had his arm. A
flush began at the top of her leotard. She let go of Hardy and brought
her hand to her neck, embarrassed. "It's one of the main traumas,
death of a parent," she said. "I guess I'm not prepared for it."

"I don't think we get prepared for it," Hardy said. "That's the
point."

"I do things . . . I don't know why." Letting go of her neck, she
brought the palm of her hand down across her breasts. The flush was
still on her chest. "Like I'm just going through motions, you know?
Doing what has to be done, but all this other stuff is going on inside
me."

"Would you like to take a break? Come up to the office? Go get a drink somewhere?"

"I don't drink, but it would be nice if . . ."

"We can go to my office then."

"No, you go ahead. I'll just . . . well, we could go to a bar, thanks. I could use the company."

Lou the Greek's would not have been an inspired choice under these conditions.

They were sitting on high stools around a small raised table at the front window of Sophie's, which after eight turned into a dinner club for the young and hip. But two blocks north of the Hall, if you wanted a quiet short one after work it wasn't a bad spot before the scene came alive.

Celine wore expensive Italian sandals and no socks. She crossed her legs on the high stool, showing off the pedicure, the toenails a light pink, the skin between her ankle and her jeans honey-toned— warm and smooth. She watched Hardy take the first sip of his Irish whiskey.

On the way over, in the warm dusk, she had again taken his arm. They hadn't said ten words. Now she said, "Thank you."

"For what?"

"For taking this time, that's all."

He didn't know what to say. He lifted his drink, clicked it against her glass of club soda and brought it to his lips. He found it hard to believe that two days before he'd been around this woman and had no reaction. He felt pretty sure it wasn't anything she was doing purposely, but he was acutely conscious of everywhere her skin showed— at her feet, above the leotard on her chest, her arms and neck. But why not? It had been a broiling day. He kind of wished he could be sitting there wearing a tank top, instead of his shirt and tie. He'd folded his coat over another stool at the table. "I've got time," he said at last.

"That's all I've got now, it seems."

"It's rough, isn't it?"

Now her eyes met his. "What I was saying before—that's the hardest part. The stuff going on inside."

"I know," Hardy said. He couldn't exactly say why, but he found himself telling her how after his son Michael had died by falling out of his crib, Hardy had made the decision that he would be strong and deal with it, the way adults dealt with things, right?

"It didn't work?"

"Oh, I made it maybe two months. You know, go to work, come home, eat, drink, wake up, do it again." Hardy paused, remembering. "You're not married, are you?"

"No. I was once."

"I don't know if it's better or not, having someone there. It broke me and my wife up."

Celine didn't say anything for a long time. The music in Sophie's changed, or at least Hardy became aware of it—some automatic stuff that he hated. The sun was almost down, hitting the tops of the taller buildings north of Market and a few up on Nob Hill.

"I almost wish there were somebody to break up with," she said at last. "Take it out on somebody else. But Daddy was my only family, so now what?" She tipped her glass and found it empty. "Do you think I could have a drink now? Something with gin in it?"

At the bar, Hardy ordered himself a second Bushmills and Celine a Bombay on the rocks. The bartender poured a three and a half count, a solid shot, close to a double. Hardy tipped him two bucks and asked him if he could lose the noise on the speakers.

Celine sipped at the gin and made a face. "I haven't had a drink in a couple of years," she said. "Daddy didn't like me to drink too much."

"He didn't too much like you to drink or he didn't like you to drink too much?"

She smiled, small and tentative, but there it was. "Both, I think." Her eyes settled on him again. "Sometimes I'd get a little out of control. You couldn't get a little out of control around Daddy."

"Why not?"

"Because if the daughter of Owen Nash is not in control, that means he's not in control of me." She took another sip of the gin, and this time it went down smoothly. "And if Owen Nash is in the picture, he's in control."

"He was that way?"

"God, what am I saying? I loved my father. I just miss him. I'm so mad at him."

"It's okay," Hardy said. "It happens."

"He was just such a . . . I mean, I was his only family, too, so it made sense he wanted me to be a good reflection of him."

"He saw you as his reflection?"

She shook her head, putting more movement in it. "No, not exactly, you know what I mean." She put her hand over his on the small table. "He wanted what was best for me . . . always."

"And that got to be a burden?"

"Sometimes," she admitted. She took a drink. "I'm sorry. I shouldn't get so worked up."

Hardy found himself covering her hand now. "Celine, look. This is one time you should be allowed to get worked up. You can let it go once in a while or it'll come out all at once, and you don't want that."

"But it wasn't so much of a burden. Look at all the good it's done me. I'm serious. Stuff I never would have done without Daddy."

"I believe you."

She shook her head. "He was just always so hard. Even when he was good, he was hard. He pushed people—I'm surprised Ken Farris didn't tell you. I mean, look at us, we're perfect examples. But it was worth it for what you got out of it."

"Which was what?"

She took her hand away and Hardy thought he'd offended her. "The main thing was being close to him. You got to be close to Daddy, which was the most alive you could be."

Hardy swirled his drink in the bottom of his glass. Outside, it was full dusk. A couple more people had come into Sophie's. "You know what I think?" he said. "I think you're allowed to have some mixed feelings right now. I wouldn't worry about it."

Celine put her hand back over Hardy's. "I'm sorry, I think I feel this gin already."

"You want some cheap advice? Go get a bottle of it, find somebody you can talk to and drink half of it. There's nothing more natural than being mad at somebody close when they die."

"I can't talk to anybody," she said. "Not about Daddy."

"You've just been talking about him to me for a half hour."

She tightened her hand over his one last time, then released it. "You're the D.A. This isn't personal for you. It's not the same thing."

"It's personal enough for me. This is my job, my case."

"But that's what it is, a case."

"It's also that, Celine. Somebody killed your father."

"And maybe it was me, right?"

"Don't be silly."

"You're investigating the murder, and now you get me to tell you I'm mad at him—"

"Celine . . ."

"Well, I was down in Santa Cruz the whole weekend. I was staying in a house with three of my friends. I couldn't have been up here . . ."

Hardy stood up and moved close in to her, pulling her head tight against him. The gin was hitting her, the panic on the rise as it loosened her up. "Stop it," he whispered. "Stop."

He felt her breathing slow down. A bare arm came up to his shoulder and held him, pulled him down to her. A second passed. Five. Her grip relaxed and he lifted himself away from her. Her blue-gray eyes had teared up. "I'm sorry," she said. "I'm a mess."

"You're okay," he said. "Come on, let's get out of here." She waited meekly by the door while he grabbed his coat, then took her arm. They walked out into the warm early night.

On the way back to the Hall, she told him about Owen's Saturday appointment on the *Eloise* with May Shinn.

"I know," Hardy said. "We're looking into that." He considered telling her about everything they'd found on board, but there was still police work to be done there, and all of that could wait. What Celine needed was some understanding and a little time to get used to her father having been murdered. Hardy didn't think an update on the investigation would do a thing for her piece of mind.

They got to her car—a silver BMW 350i—and she hugged Hardy briefly, apologizing again for her "scene." She told him he was a good man, then she was in her car, leaving him with the faint scent of gin, a memory of her body against his and the feeling that, without ever meaning to, he'd done something terribly wrong.

They were having pizza in the reporters' room on the third floor of the Hall of Justice, the same floor that contained the offices of the district attorney.

The room, befitting the esteem with which the police held the medium of print journalism, wasn't much. There was a green blackboard that kept up a running total of murders in San Francisco thus far that year (sixty-eight). There was a bulletin board tacked three deep with Christmas cards the press guys had received from their friends in the building, as well as the jails some of them had gone to reside in. The surface area of all three desks combined did not equal the expanse of oak on Ken Farris's desk in South San Francisco. There was also an old-fashioned school desk. Jeff Elliot sat in that one.

It wasn't bad pizza. Anchovies, pepperoni, sausage and mushroom. Cass Weinberg, an attractive gay woman of about thirty, had ordered it. She was with the *Bay Guardian* and didn't have much going on until later that Friday night, so she thought she'd bring in an extra large and schmooze with whoever might be hanging. Holding down the second "big" desk was Oscar Franco from the Spanish-language *La Hora.* Then there was Jim Blanchard from the Oakland *Tribune,* who'd been worried for the past eighteen months about his job ending when the paper went bankrupt.

"My theory," he was saying, "is that Elliot here did the guy himself. Otherwise how's he gonna get a story this good."

Cass picked it up. "You used to be a sailor, didn't you? Didn't you tell me that? In college?"

"He did," Blanchard said. "At college, in Lake Superior."

This was true. Before the multiple sclerosis had kicked in, Elliot had loved to sail, spent his summers under the canvas. He'd covered the America's Cup for his high-school newspaper as a special project. "Not in Lake Superior, on Lake Superior, anchovy breath," he said.

"In, on, doesn't matter. He finds out where Nash keeps his boat, scams his way aboard and kills the guy."

"Then I jump overboard and hand-feed his hand to the shark."

Blanchard popped pizza. "Exactly. That's the part that took guts."

Cass was judicious. "It could have happened. People nowadays do anything to get famous."

Jeff was in heaven. He would take all the razzing they were going to give him. He was one of them now.

Oscar Franco rolled his bassett eyes around the room. "How long you guys been in the business an' nobody even noticed the really big story today? Just me."

Cass looked at Blanchard. "That's the longest sentence he's ever said, isn't it?"

"You laugh," Franco said. "The big story is in Department Twenty-seven on the Charles Hendrix sting. Fowler threw out the case."

"Oh boy." Blanchard sat straight up.

"That man is a mensch," Cass said.

"What?" Jeff Elliot didn't like to miss a big story, no matter whose it was. "Judge Fowler? What did he do?"

Oscar explained it to him. Cass and Blanchard sat listening for a moment, then both of them asked him to slow up and start again while they took a few notes. Owen Nash was a good story, but this thing with Fowler might be the opening sally in a protracted war.

They were still into it when Jeff saw the cop—Glitsky, that was it—who'd been at the coroner's the night before, going toward the elevator. He left his pizza on the small desk, grabbed his crutches and said he had to run, hoping he'd catch the guy before the elevator got to the third floor.

Glitsky wasn't happy in the first place about having to stay around late on a Friday night booking somebody for murder, writing up a report on his conversation with her, the reasons for his arrest when there wasn't the hint of an indictment. But more, he'd finished all that, closing in on eight o'clock, still a chance to get out and have a nice dinner with Flo, when he went to his car downstairs and found out that, new tune-up or not, it wouldn't start.

"Officer." Now there was this reporter again.

The elevators weren't setting any land speed records and the temperature in the hallway was over eighty degrees.

Elliot came right up next to him. "Excuse me, Officer," he repeated.

Glitsky corrected him. "Sergeant," he said. "I look like I'm wearing a uniform?"

"Sorry. Sergeant. We met last night, briefly." Jeff introduced himself again. "At the coroner's. Owen Nash."

"That's right."

Elliot pushed on. "Well, we're on the third floor. I thought you might be seeing the D.A. about that, about something breaking?"

The one elevator in service after business hours arrived with a small *ding.* Glitsky stepped in and Elliot stuck with him. "I just did an hour-and-a-half's worth of IRs upstairs."

"So something's happening?"

Jeff thought this was a pretty scary man. "Something's always happening," he said. "That's why there's time—it keeps everything from happening at once."

The elevator doors closed—finally. "As to the third floor, that's where they give out keys to city vehicles, and my goddamn Plymouth has quit on me again, and all the other cars are out for the weekend, so I'm taking a cab home." Elliot didn't know it, but Glitsky swore about as often as he laughed out loud, maybe twice a year.

"Where do you live?" Jeff didn't miss a beat, and though he'd been planning on stopping back in at his office, he said, "I'm heading home now, I could drop you off."

Glitsky said he lived out on Lake, and Jeff only fibbed slightly, saying it was right on his way. The sergeant thawed a little. "That'd be nice. Where are you parked?"

They had reached the ground floor and the door opened, hitting them with a welcome shot of cooler air. "First slot out the back."

"You're lucky," Abe said.

Jeff grinned his winning grin. "No," he said. "Handicapped."

Except for the green gauzy glow of the fish tank, the lights were out. The bedroom window, facing east to the city's skyline, was wide open, but no air moved.

Hardy's wife was curled against him spoon fashion, and he was inside her, holding her to him at the waist. They were both sweating, at it now a long time, Hardy wanting to prove something.

"Diz."

He shushed her, trying not to hear her and break his own spell. He'd started with his eyes closed, she coming to him, feeling a distance there after the quiet dinner, the brooding in the living room.

"Diz."

He didn't want to hear her and buried his mouth into the back of her neck, under her hair. When he opened his eyes, he could make out the shape of her back in the dim light. Only her back. Any back. Anyone's he wanted it to be.

But he was closing in on it now, feeling the thrust of her—wanting to help him even if she was ready to quit, reaching down for him, arching herself backward. He pulled at her waist, up against him now, feeling the air now between them, closing the distance, hard up in her wetness. Harder then, pounding, losing her as he felt himself starting, finding it again and driving in again and again and again.

It was Celine's back. An angry Celine. And Hardy for some reason furious too, feeling her grip, the tight grip she had on him. And now he heard her, crying out, after she thought it was over, liking it rough, and the sound of her cry starting something at the base of his backbone, moving up.

He slapped her against him, as hard as he could, knowing he wasn't hurting her, crying out himself, his hands now up against Celine's breasts that were somehow wet, crushing them to her, crushing himself against Frannie's back, she pumping him, the sweet agony . . .

Finished now, he lay on his back, breathing hard. He felt the sweat cooling, the lightest warm breeze through the window. Frannie was on her side, leaning on her elbow, all up against him. She kissed his cheek. "I love you," she said. "Are you all right?"

"Sorry."

She kissed him again. "There's nothing to be sorry about. I liked that."

He pulled her to him and kissed her. She put her head down against his shoulder and started breathing regularly. In one minute she was asleep. Hardy lay with his eyes open, listening to the gurgling of the fish tank for almost an hour.

18

He woke up refreshed, his devils exorcised by spent lust and deep sleep. In the light of day, he thought it hadn't done him any harm to fantasize—it was natural once in a while. No need to whip himself over it.

Now he wasn't fantasizing. Frannie was in his here and now. He was cooking breakfast—french toast and sausages—in his black cast-iron pan, the only artifact he'd taken from his time with Jane. In the decade he'd lived alone, that pan had been one of the inviolate certainties in his world. He cleaned the pan with salt and paper towels, no water, no soap. After every use, he put a drop or two of oil in it and rubbed it in. No food stuck to that pan. It was a joy.

Taking a bite of a sausage link, he turned a piece of sliced sourdough bread over in the mixture of egg, milk and cinnamon—dipping it only for a second so it wouldn't get soggy—and forked it into the pan, where it hit with a satisfying hiss. Outside, the sun had come up hot again. Maybe they'd get an entire weekend of summer this year.

Frannie was dressed in hiking boots with white socks, khaki shorts and a Giants t-shirt, ready for the historical expedition to Martinez that she, Hardy and Moses had planned for the day. They were going to track down the elusive origin of the martini.

"Or is it the origin of the elusive martini?" Moses had asked. This had been last Wednesday night at Yet Wah.

"The martini itself is not elusive," Hardy had replied.

"But the *ideal* martini can be elusive." Two bartenders, Jesus, finally coming to an agreement. Frannie was smiling, remembering. She came back down the hall from the front door with the morning newspaper and laid it on the table in front of Rebecca, who was finger-painting with baby food on the tray of her high chair. Standing, opening to the front page, she grabbed a sausage and took the mug of coffee Hardy handed her.

"This Jeffrey Elliot's turning into a daily feature."

Hardy came over and stood with his arm around her.

SUSPECT ARRESTED IN OWEN NASH MURDER
by Jeffrey Elliot
Chronicle Staff Writer

Police yesterday arrested May Shinn, the alleged mistress of Owen Nash, for the murder of the local financier. According to the arresting officer, Sergeant Abraham Glitsky, Ms. Shinn had purchased a ticket to Japan after the discovery of Nash's body Thursday on a beach in Pacifica, and was attempting to leave the jurisdiction after she had agreed to remain in the city.

Although Glitsky refused to go into much detail regarding the evidence collected thus far, he did acknowledge that a search of Owen Nash's sailboat, the *Eloise,* had revealed traces of blood and a .25-caliber Beretta handgun registered to Ms. Shinn. Additionally, a slug, imbedded in the wall of boat, was recovered. The gun had been fired twice, and Nash's body contained two wounds. The ballistics department has not yet conclusively identified the gun as the murder weapon, although Glitsky conceded he thought the possibility "likely."

THE ARTICLE PICKED UP ON THE BACK PAGE, but Hardy was already at the telephone. "That's what I like," he said, "when I follow the comings and goings of my dear friends and professional colleagues by reading about them in the newspaper."

"What are you eating?" Glitsky asked. "It sounds great."

Hardy swallowed his sausage. "You forgot my phone number, Abe. I'll get it for you."

"On Friday night? Come on. I got done talking to Elliot around nine-thirty, ten. I thought I'd call you this morning."

"What were you doing talking to Elliot?"

"My car went out again. He was at the Hall. He gave me a lift home."

"What a guy," Hardy said.

"He seems like a good kid."

"I know he does. Nicest guy in the world. Is she out of jail?"

"I doubt it. I guess it depends who she calls. A good lawyer might find a judge to set some bail, get her out today."

"And when do I talk to her? Did she do it?"

After a minute Glitsky answered. "I don't know. She might have. No alibi. It's her gun. She was getting out of Dodge, and she bought her ticket to Japan after Nash was identified, after the paper had it."

"No alibi?"

"The famous I-was-home-alone-all-day. When's the last time you were home alone all day, no phone calls, no nothing? I didn't want her going to Japan."

"You think I ought to go down and see her?"

"Hey!" Frannie gave him the eye. "Martinez," she whispered. "The elusive martini, remember?"

In the normal course of events, there was a skeleton staff at the Hall on weekends. The D.A.'s office was officially closed. Courtrooms were not in use. Of course, there was still police work and people getting into and out of jail, which occupied the top floors until the new one in the back lot was completed. A clerk was on duty twenty-four hours a day to let people out if a bondsman met bail. Defense attorneys came and went. There were visitors.

Hardy had parked in his usual spot under the freeway, promising an unhappy Frannie he'd be home by noon for their foray into history. You didn't want to drink martinis before noon anyway, he had told her. She told him she wasn't going to drink martinis for seven or so months, and in any event, she had gone along with this idea just to be with her husband, brother and daughter and have a relaxing time together, which seemed to be becoming less of a priority for him day by day.

You thought you had trained yourself. You'd traveled far enough along your own rocky path to some inner peace that you had come to believe you couldn't go back—events would never control you again.

Then they took your clothes from you. They gave you a yellow gown that smelled like Lysol and put you in a small barred room with a sullen young black women and a toilet with no seat, the whole place, beneath the disinfectant, smelling like a sewer.

You threw away your phone calls on the man who'd been your lover's attorney. "You ever need help—I mean real help—and I'm not around, you just call on the Wheel. He's your man." He would come down and get her out. He was a lawyer and knew about these things. But he wasn't at the number Owen had given her. No one had answered, and now there was no one to call and she was alone.

You spent the night in fear, waking up sweating in the still heat, the smell of yourself, of the other woman who didn't talk, who sat on her mattress with her back against the wall. A clanging wake-up and a meal of cold powdered eggs, the regimented shower, the indifference of the women guards.

She swore to herself that she would not let them take her so easily, but it was difficult finding a mechanism to deal with it, to keep the loss of herself under control. She felt her will eroding, and she knew that's what they wanted. To turn her into a victim again.

She'd really believed she was through with that for good. If Owen had done anything for her, it was that. She would not be a victim. That was something she could control.

She sat cross-legged on her mattress and closed her eyes. If she did not have a physical shrine, she would create one inside herself, even here. She had been this close to despair before. It was the day she had met Owen . . .

Alone in a darkened corner at Nissho, an exclusive Japanese restaurant near the Miyako Hotel in Japantown, a thick winter fog out the windows, she had sat contemplating her death. She would use seconal and alcohol, starting with a small bottle of *sake*. After lunch she would walk slowly back up to her apartment and sit by her window, watching the fog, and drink the bottle of Meursault. She would disrobe and take a hot bath. She would swallow the pills and draw the clean silk sheets up over her naked body. And she would go to sleep.

That was where life, after thirty-four years, had led her.

She could not have said precisely where she had failed, or which failure had marked her Rubicon. Should she have tried harder with her family? Tried to communicate more and break the icy bonds of reserve? There had been two sisters and a brother, living with her parents in a square and empty house under the flight path to Moffatt Field in Sunnyvale. Passive. "Remember, we are Japanese." Her father never able to get over his internment in Arizona during World War II, when he was a boy, snatched with his whole family from his home. The excuse for his whole life—"We will never belong." Harboring the hatred and disappointment in who he was, who they all were, doling it out to her mother, to his children, to May.

Starting college at Berkeley, glad to be rid of them, letting the family fall away. Running out of money in the first semester, taking a job selling shoes to *gaijin* with their huge feet; marrying Sam Hoshida, ten years older than she, because his landscape work got her out of the shoe store.

Another semester in college then, with Sam supporting her. Another year with a man who grew quiet and bitter as he came to know she was using him. Wearing better clothes, becoming conscious of her beauty, other men making her aware of it.

There was a teaching assistant, then, a half-Japanese, Phil Oshida, for whom she left Sam, for love. They married and she miscarried three times in two years; she could never have children. He hated her for that, felt pity and hate, trying to disguise them as love. She thought that was where the big fall had begun—when the only person she'd ever let herself care for gave up on her.

She got her meaningless degree in political science and her second divorce. She was a shell, empty and used up at twenty-four.

The first time it happened, she hadn't planned it. She had gone to Hawaii for a one-week vacation, her first vacation from her meaningless job at the Bank of America. Of course, as always, she was on a budget—the package was a round-trip ticket, hotel and one meal a day. She let a student on Christmas break from USC buy her an ice cream near the beach. He was big and built and blond and all-American and told her he liked her bathing suit. Could he buy her dinner? He had lots of money. His parents lived on Hilo. Next day he asked her if she'd like to go with him over to his parents' house. He was straightforward. He was going back to school in a week, he had a girlfriend, so no commitments, but they could have a good time.

No actual money changed hands, although he did pay for her rebooked return flight. But the experience gave her the idea of what could be done. She quit her job at the Bank of America, shortened her name to Shinn, and started to make a good living, alone, discreetly.

But there she was at Nissho's, still a shell, carrying her father's victim-load around with her. Men had been doing what they wanted with her for ten years. She couldn't be further debased or devalued. She was still in demand, but there was no May Shintaka anymore, not even, she thought, much of a May Shinn, and she didn't really care. Her usefulness, if she'd ever had any, was at an end.

Then Owen Nash had walked to her table. He sat down, uninvited. She raised her eyes to look at him. "Yes?"

"Are you as alone as you look?"

Of the many men she had known, she recognized something in Owen Nash that she thought she had given up on.

In her business—it was inevitable—you got to thinking all men were the same, or similar enough that the small differences didn't matter.

Here was a man, though, who on first meeting caught you in an aura, swept you up in it. He stood over her, looking down, giving off a sense of power, with a massive, muscular torso, a square face and eyes that vibrated with life and, half-hidden, suffering . . .

She stared at him, not wanting to acknowledge what she intuitively felt—that this man already knew her, knew what she was feeling. "Are you as lonely as you look?" An old pickup line. But this, she felt, wasn't just that. He was telling her that they were connected, somehow. Suddenly, with nothing else holding her to her meaningless life, she wanted to know how the connection worked and what it might mean.

He had reserved the private room in the back, but had been watching her from the kitchen, where he was helping prepare the side dishes to accompany his main course of fugu, a blowfish delicacy in Japan that killed you if you prepared it wrong.

After sharing the meal, they both waited for the slight numbness on the tongue. Owen had brought a bottle of aged Suntory whisky and sipped it neat out of the *sake* cups.

During the meal, he had gotten back some of what she would come to know as his usual garrulous persona. Now he ran with it, laughing, loud in the tiny room, emptying his *sake* cup.

"I think you're unhappy," she said. "If the fish had been wrong, it could have poisoned you."

He drank his whiskey. "There's risk in everything. You do what you need to—"

"And you need to risk death? Why? Someone like you?"

They were alone in the room, sitting on the floor. The table had been cleared—only the Suntory bottle and the two cups were left on the polished teak.

"It's a game," he said, not smiling. "It's something I do, that's all."

She shook her head. This wasn't any game for him. "I think that's why you came over and talked to me. You recognized me. I am like you."

She told him she wanted him to follow her—she would show him what wanting to die was really like. They walked twenty blocks in the deep fog to her apartment. He followed her up the stairs. In the foyer, she stepped out of her shoes and went into the bathroom, where she turned on the bath. She went to the refrigerator and got out the wine, opened it. It was as though he weren't there.

She went to her dresser and took off her earrings, her necklace. Unbuttoning the black silk blouse, she felt him moving up close behind her, but he didn't touch her, didn't speak. That was the understanding. She continued to disrobe—her brassiere, her slacks, the rest.

She finished the first glass of wine in a gulp and poured herself a second, which she brought to the bathroom. The bath was ready, the mirror steamed. He sat on the toilet seat, watching her lather, occasionally sipping from the Suntory bottle he'd carried with him.

She stood and rinsed under a hot shower, then stepped out and over to the medicine cabinet, where she took down the prescription bottle and poured the pills, at least twenty of them, into her hand. She lifted her glass of wine, threw back her head and emptied her hand into her mouth.

Which is when Owen moved, knocking the glass out of her hand, smashing it to the tiles, grabbing her, his fingers in her mouth, forcing the pills out into the sink, the toilet, onto the floor.

That had been the beginning.

The shrine was gone in the clang of the bars, the door opening. "Shinn. D.A.'s here to see you. Move it."

Remember who you are, she told herself. You are not what they think you are.

It wasn't quite eleven in the morning. Out the windows, through the bars, she saw the sun high in the sky.

The interview room was like a cell without toilet or bars. It was furnished with an old, pitted gray desk and three chairs. She sat down across from the man, casual in jeans and a rugby shirt. He introduced himself, Mr. Hardy, and some woman he called a D.A. investigator. He would be taping this interview. He asked how they were treating her.

"I need more phone calls," she said. "I shouldn't be in here."

She was not stupid. She was a citizen, and she wasn't going to fall into the trap that had ensnared her father. She had to believe that there was another reason she was arrested—it was not because she was Japanese. She told Hardy about her attempted call to Ken Farris.

"I could call Farris for you. He tried to call you several times last week, you know."

"I didn't kill Owen Nash," she said.

"I wouldn't say anything you didn't want to hear repeated."

"Then why are you here?"

"I thought you might want to tell me what happened. Maybe we could both get lucky."

"What happened when?"

The man shrugged. "Last night. The arrest. The last time you saw Owen Nash."

"Shouldn't I have a lawyer?"

"Absolutely. You have the right to one. You don't have to say one word to me."

But she found she wanted to explain, to talk. "I'm not sure I even understand why I'm here."

"I think trying to leave the country was a bad idea."

"But I knew—" She stopped herself. "Don't you see?"

"See what?"

She picked her words carefully, slowly. "When I saw my name in the paper, I knew I'd be suspected."

"Were you out on the boat with him?"

"No! I told the officer that, the one who arrested me."

"Then why would we suspect you?"

"I'm Japanese." No, she told herself. That was her father's answer. But it was too late to retract it now. "And it's true," she said. "You do suspect me, with no reason. Who I am, what I have done for a living." She knew she should be quiet, wait for an attorney, but she couldn't. "The gun, too."

"Your gun?"

She nodded. "I knew it was on the boat. That's where I left it. I didn't want it in my apartment. I couldn't even bring myself to load it. Owen thought I was silly."

"So you kept in on the *Eloise*?"

"In the desk, by the bed."

The man frowned, something bothering him. "You knew it was there when you went out on Saturday?"

"Yes, but—"

"So you did go out on Saturday."

"No! I didn't mean that, I meant when Owen went out. I knew it was there all the time. That's where I kept it."

"Did anyone else know it was there?"

"Well, Owen, of course." There was something else. She paused, not quite saying it. "Anyone could have."

"Anyone could have," he repeated.

"Yes!" She was starting to panic, to lose herself, and hoped it didn't show in her voice. She forced herself to breathe calmly. "It it were me, why would I leave the gun on the boat after I shot him? Why wouldn't I have thrown it overboard?"

"I don't know, May. Maybe you were in shock that you'd actually done it and reverted to habit, not thinking, putting the gun where it belonged. Why don't you tell me?"

"I loved Owen. I told that to the sergeant."

"You loved him." Flat, monotone. "Nobody else seems to think he was very lovable."

"Nobody else knew him."

"A lot of people knew him," he said.

The door to the room opened with a whoosh. "Just what the hell is going on in here?"

Hardy looked, then stood up. "Can I help you?"

The man wasn't six feet tall. He had curly brown hair and sallow loose skin. His shabby dark suit was badly tailored and poorly pressed. There were tiny bloodstains on his white collar from shaving cuts.

Nevertheless, what he lacked in style he made up for in substance. His brown eyes were clear and carried authority. The anger seemed to spark off him. "Yeah, you can help me. You can tell me what this is all about!"

Hardy didn't respond ideally to this onslaught. "Maybe you can tell me what it is to you!"

The two men glared at each other. The guard who had admitted the second man was still standing at the door; the woman investigator Hardy had brought along as a witness checked her fingernails. The guard asked, "You gentlemen have a problem with each other?"

The shorter man turned. "You know who I am?"

"I don't," Hardy said.

He was ignored. "I am representing this woman and she is being harassed by the district attorney—"

"There is no harassment going on here—"

"Save it for your appeal, which you're going to need. To say nothing of the lawsuit."

"Who the hell are you?"

"I'm David Freeman, Ms. Shintaka's attorney, and you don't belong here."

Like everyone else in the business of practicing law from either side of the courtroom, Hardy knew of David Freeman, and his presence stopped him momentarily. Freeman was a legend in the city, a world-class defense attorney in countless cases—and here was Dismas Hardy, novice prosecutor in a place he technically shouldn't be. He didn't know how there came to be a connection between May Shinn and David Freeman, but it was clear there was one now and it was hardly promising for Hardy's chances.

"How did you—"

Freeman cut him off. "Because, fortunately for justice's sake, some judges are available on weekends. Now you get the hell out of here, Counselor, or I swear to God I'll move to have you disbarred."

May spoke up. "But he wasn't—"

Freeman held up an imperious hand. "Don't say another word!"

Judge Andy Fowler watched his drive sail down the middle of the fairway, starting low and getting wings up into the clear blue, carrying in the warm, dry air. The ball finally dropped down, he estimated, at about two hundred ten yards, bouncing and rolling another forty, leaving himself a short seven-iron to the pin.

Fowler picked up his tee with a swipe and walked to his cart, grinning. "The man is on his game." Gary Smythe was Fowler's broker and, today, his match partner. They were playing best ball at $20 per hole and now, on the fourteenth, were up $80. Gary wasn't yet thirty-five, a second-generation member of the Olympic Club.

The other two guys, both members of course, were father and son, Ben and Joe Wyeth from the real estate company of the same name. Ben Wyeth was close to Fowler's age and looked ten years older. He teed up. "I think the judge here ought to rethink his twelve handicap." He swung and hit a decent drive out about two hundred yards with the roll, on the right side of the fairway. "That," he said, "is a proper drive for guys our age, Andy."

They got in their carts and headed down the fairway. "You are playing some golf today," Gary said.

Andy was sucking on his tee. He wore a white baseball hat with a marlin on the crest, maroon slacks, a Polo shirt. He followed the flight of a flock of swallows into one of the eucalyptus groves bordering the fairway. "I think golf must be God's game," he said. "You get a day like this."

"If this is God's game, he's a sadist." Gary stopped the cart and got out to pick up his ball. As had been the case most of the afternoon, Andy's ball was best.

Andy put his shot pin high, four feet to its left. Gary's shot landed on the front fringe, bounced and almost hit the flagstick, then rolled twelve feet past. "Your ball again," Gary said.

As they waited on the green for Ben and Joe, Gary told Andy he was happy to see him feeling better. "Some of us were worried the last few months," he said. "You didn't seem your old self."

"Ah, old man's worries, that's all." Andy lined up an imaginary putt. "You get lazy. You get a few problems, no worse than everybody else has, and you forget you can just take some action and make them go away. It's just like golf, you sit too long and stare at that ball, pretty soon it's making faces at you, and before you know it, hitting that ball clean becomes impossible. The thing to do is just take your shot. Let the chips fall. Pardon the mixed metaphor. At least then the game's not playing you. Which is what I let creep up on me."

"Maybe you could let it creep back just a little, give us young guys a chance."

Andy lined up another imaginary putt and put the ball in the hole. He looked up, grinning. "No quarter," he said. "To the victor goes the spoils."

19

Hardy had had better weekends.

Historical Martinez turned out to be a bit of a dud. Since Moses and Hardy had practically lived at the Little Shamrock bar on 9th and Lincoln in San Francisco's cool and breezy Sunset district for many years, an hour-and-a-half road trip to check out some small bars in another windy town was, at best, they decided, dumb.

They snagged a few not-so-elusive martinis—the gin first nagging at Hardy, then washing out the memory of the morning's disaster with May Shinn and lawyer David Freeman—then Frannie had driven them all home just in time to find out Rebecca had developed roseola and a fever of 106 degrees, which was worth a trip to the emergency room.

When they got back at midnight Hardy had been too exhausted to return the calls of Art Drysdale or Abe Glitsky.

But on Sunday he wasn't. He got an earful of rebuke from Art and was intrigued to learn from Glitsky, who'd worked yesterday, that Tom Waddell, the night guard at the Marina, had seen May leaving the place on Thursday night.

"Probably coming back, realizing she'd left the gun."

"Did she have a key?"

"That's just it. It appeared she couldn't get into the boat. Waddell was going to go help her when he finished whatever he was doing, but she had gone. Maybe that's when she decided to buy the ticket to Japan. The timing fits."

Hardy remembered that when he'd first gone to the *Eloise,* the boat had been left unlocked. May, knowing that, would have thought she could have just slipped aboard, taken the gun and disappeared with nothing left to link her to the murder.

"And there's another thing, maybe nothing, maybe a joke, but it could be the whole ballgame."

Hardy waited.

"I got a warrant for her suitcases and we found what looks like a handwritten will of Owen Nash's, leaving her two million dollars."

"Is it real?"

"We don't know, we're getting a sample of Nash's handwriting. We haven't even mentioned it to her yet, but let's assume Nash just disappears and his body doesn't show up on a beach. After he's declared dead, May appears with a valid will."

"Nice retirement."

"The same thought occurred to me." A good cop following up leads, building a case that Hardy hoped he hadn't already lost on a technicality.

Hardy spent most of the day inside worrying about Rebecca, giving her tepid baths every two or three hours. Frannie, as she did, hung tough, but he could tell it was a strain on her, to say nothing of his own feelings, memories of another life and another baby—one who hadn't made it—chilling the warmth out of the evening.

A dinner of leftovers—cold spaghetti, soggy salad, stale bread. They were all in bed for the night before nine o'clock.

Family life with sick child.

"Excuse me," Pullios said, "there is no issue here."

"Then I will take the folder and leave." It was nine-thirty on Monday morning and Hardy was, for the second time in a week, in District Attorney Christopher Locke's sanctum sanctorum. With him, in the second chair before the D.A.'s desk, was Elizabeth Pullios and, standing by the window, his back turned to the proceedings, Art Drysdale.

Pullios remained calm. "I am the homicide prosecutor here. What's the issue?"

"The issue is Art promised me this case." Hardy knew it sounded whiny, but it was the truth and had to be said.

"Art was out of line there, Hardy." Locke could smile very nicely for the cameras, but he was not smiling now. He leaned forward, hands clasped before him. "Now, you listen. I appreciate your enthusiasm for your work, but we work in a hierarchy and a bureaucracy"—he held up a hand, stopping Hardy's reply. "I know, we all hate the word. But it's a precise term and it applies to this office. Ms. Pullios here has a fine record trying murder cases, and on Saturday"—Locke pointed a finger—"*you* seriously jeopardized this investigation. The accused has an *absolute* right for an attorney to be present. You're aware of that?"

"I didn't force her to say a word."

"You shouldn't have been there at *all,* is the point. Thank God you taped what you did get."

Pullios swiveled on the leather seat of her chair. "Freeman could still make a case for procedural error."

"Shit." Hardy said.

"I beg your pardon." If anyone was going to swear in Locke's office, it was going to be him.

Hardy reflected on the better part of valor. "I don't think he can make a case there."

"Regardless"—Pullios was calm but firm—"this should not be up for debate. I am a Homicide D.A., is that right, sir?"

"Of course."

"Art?"

"Come on, Elizabeth."

"So I went up to Homicide and picked up a folder from Abe Glitsky, as I have done many times in the past. It happened, randomly, to be this Nash murder. There is a suspect in custody at this very moment, who was arrested while attempting to flee the jurisdiction. This is the kind of case I do." She wasn't yelling. She didn't even seem particularly excited. She had the cards.

Hardy gave it a last shot. "Elizabeth, look. I have put in some time on this thing. I found the hand. I've talked to the daughter, the victim's lawyer and best friend. Now I'm not on the case. What's that going to do to their confidence in this office?"

"That's irrelevant," Pullios said.

"More than that," Locke, to whom public perception of the district attorney's office was always the primary issue, spoke up, "it's not for you two to haggle about. Hardy, you've made a small but real point there. I can see you think you've got a legitimate right to this case, but so does Elizabeth. So here's what we do—you, Hardy, take second chair. Under Elizabeth's direction you keep contact with people you've already interviewed and you keep her informed at every step. Every single step. When we bring this thing to trial, Elizabeth puts on the show and you get to watch a master perform close up." The D.A. crossed his hands on his desk and favored the room with his patented smile. "Now let's cooperate and get this thing done. We're on the same team here, as we all sometimes forget. Art, Hardy, thanks for bringing this to my attention. I've always got an open door. Thanks very much. Elizabeth, could you stay behind a minute?"

* * *

"Talk about seeing a master perform close up."

Drysdale was juggling in his office. "My good friend Chris Locke tries to make sure everybody wins."

"Win, my ass."

The baseballs kept flying. "Pullios tries the case. You're on it. My authority in giving you the case is upheld. The office looks good. Everybody wins."

"Who was it said 'Another victory like this and we're ruined'?"

"Pyrrhus, I think."

"I'll remember that." Hardy shook his head. "I can't believe this. She doesn't know anything about this case."

Drysdale disagreed. "No, she knows, and I must say with some justification, that once a perp is arrested for whatever it might be, that perp is one guilty son of a bitch."

"How about innocent until proven guilty?" Hardy felt silly even saying it out loud. He wasn't sure he believed it anymore, after the tide of humanity that had washed across his desk in the past months, all of them—every one—guilty of *something,* even if it wasn't what they were accused of. The temptation to get whoever it was for whatever they could, regardless of whether it was something they did, was something all the D.A.'s faced. The best of them rose above it. Some didn't find the exercise worthwhile.

That still didn't make it a good argument for Drysdale. "Let's tick it off," he said. "She had a sexual relationship with the guy. Okay, already we're in most-likely-to-succeed territory. Two, what did she tell you this morning? She maybe benefits to the tune of a couple million dollars if the guy dies. This is a big number two. This is not insignificant."

"It may not even be true. And Elizabeth doesn't know about it in any event."

Drysdale kissed the air, a little clicking sound. "She will. Anyway, next, it's her gun and a witness puts her at the crime scene and she doesn't have an alibi for the day in question. Finally, she attempts to leave the country ten minutes after being warned to stay. It is not what I'd call farfetched to think she did it."

"I didn't say she didn't do it. I'm saying there's no real evidence that she did, not yet."

"Fortunately that's the jury's job."

"And Betsy's."

"And yours." Drysdale raised a finger. "And I wouldn't call her Betsy."

"Am I glad to be back working here?"

"Is that a question? You've got your murder case, quicker than most."

Hardy straightened up in the doorway. His name was being called over the hall loudspeaker. He had a telephone call. "Pyrrhus, right?" he said, before turning into the hall.

The snitch was named Devon Latrice Wortherington, and he certainly seemed to be enjoying the moments of relative freedom away from his cell. Devon had been picked up carrying an unlicensed firearm and a half pound of rock cocaine the previous Thursday night, outside a bar near Hunter's Point, and he had been in jail about twelve hours when suddenly he recalled his civic duty to assist the police if he knew anything that might help them in apprehending persons who had committed a crime. In this case a drive-by shooting that had left three people dead—including a small boy who reminded Glitsky of his son—and seven wounded.

He seemed to like Glitsky. Maybe he was just in a good mood. In any event, he couldn't seem to shut up. "What kind of name is Glitsky?" he asked while they were setting up the videotape for the interview. "I never knew no Glitsky."

"It's Jewish," Abe said.

"What you mean, Jewish?"

"I mean it's a Jewish name, Devon."

"Well, how you get a Jewish name?"

"How'd you get the name Wortherington?"

"From my father, man."

"Well . . ."

"You telling me you got Glitsky from your father? How'd *he* get Glitsky?"

Abe was used to room-temp IQs. Still, he thought Devon might be close to the range where he wouldn't be competent to stand trial. But he could be patient when it suited him, and now there wasn't much else to do. "My father," he said, "got Glitsky from being Jewish."

"No shit? You shittin' me?" Glitsky felt Devon eyeing him for some sign of duplicity. He kept a straight face.

"We're just about ready, Sergeant." The technician was a middle-aged woman of no looks and no humor. Maybe she dated the jail

warden who'd accompanied Devon down and who now stood inside
by the interview room's door.

"My father isn't black," Abe said.

He saw Devon take it in, chew it around, get it down. "Hey, I get it.
Your father *is* Jewish. I mean he is a righteous Hebe."

Abe wondered about how his father Nat would feel about being
called a righteous Hebe and decided he'd ask him the next time they
were together. He sat down across the table from Devon and asked
the first questions—name, age, place of birth.

"Okay, Devon, let's get to it. At about seven o'clock on the night of
Sunday, June twenty-first, you were standing at the corner of Dedman
Court"—Glitsky loved the name—"and Cashmere Lane in Hunter's
Point, is that correct?"

Devon nodded, and Glitsky continued, running down his mental list
of questions—establishing that Devon had been standing in a group of
neighborhood people when a green Camaro drove up with two men in
front and two in back. At the first sight of the car, someone at the
corner yelled and a few people dropped to the ground. Devon had
stayed up to see the barrels of guns poking out of the front and back
windows. Another man appeared to be sitting in the backseat window,
leveling a rifle or a shotgun over the roof of the car. "You have identified the shooter as Tremaine Wilson?"

"Yeah, it was Wilson."

Glitsky was wondering how Devon could have identified Wilson,
since two other witnesses had said that the shooters had worn ski
masks. "And he was firing from the passenger-side front window?"

"Right."

"Did anything obstruct your view of him?"

"No. He was only like twenty feet away. I seen him clear as I see
you."

"I hear he was wearing something over his face."

"What do you mean?"

"You know, a ski mask, a bandanna, something over his face?"

Devon stopped, his easy rhythm cut off. "It was Wilson," he said.

"I'm not saying it wasn't, Devon. I'm asking was there something
covering his face."

"What difference that make?"

Glitsky nodded to the technician, and she stopped the videotape.
Glitsky knew the tape recorder under the table was still going. "Okay,
we're off the machine, Devon. Was he wearing a mask or not?"

"Hey, look. I'm telling you it was Wilson. I *know* it was Wilson. So I give him up and you let me go, that's the deal."

Glitsky shook his head. "The deal is, you give us some evidence we can use in court. He was wearing a mask, wasn't he?"

Devon thought about it, figuring his chances, then shook his head no. "No way, man. No mask."

Glitsky sighed, then asked the technician to turn on the machine again. "Okay, Devon, for the record, was the shooter you've identified as Tremaine Wilson wearing anything over his face?"

"I just told you no."

"Tell me again. Was the shooter wearing anything over his face?"

"No."

It was, at this point, no surprise. Still, Devon seemed to be telling the truth about knowing the shooter was Wilson, but if he couldn't testify that he actually saw him pulling the trigger, it wasn't going to do anybody any good.

"Are you related to Wilson?"

Devon's face was a question mark.

"Cousin, half brother, like that?"

"No."

"Is he related to anyone you know?" Again Devon paused, but this time Glitsky didn't wait. He turned to the technician. "Shut that down," he said. "Okay, Devon, how do you know Wilson?"

It took about a minute, but it came out that Tremaine Wilson had recently moved in with the woman Devon had lived with for the past two years, the mother of Devon's child.

"So Devon figured he could cut himself a deal and put Wilson away at the same time, get his old lady back. Slick, right?"

"Très." Hardy had been sitting at Glitsky's desk, cooling off after the altercation with Locke and Pullios. "But it came up Wilson did it?"

"Yeah, sure. Devon thinks he was the target himself. That's why he bought the gun we found him with on Thursday. Wilson wanted to take him out, but as they always do, they miss who they're actually shooting at and kill a few folks standing around."

"So Devon's back upstairs."

"No evidence, no deal. Devon's sure Wilson was the shooter—he probably was. So big deal, we know one of the shooters. You want to try and sell Devon's ID to a jury?"

"Why don't you cut Devon a deal, let him back on the street, give him back his gun? He goes and shoots Wilson, then we pick him up again."

Glitsky smiled, his scar white through his lips. "It's a beautiful thought." He gave it a moment's appreciation. "Now how about you give me my chair?"

Hardy rose. He took the folder he'd been holding and dropped it in the center of Glitsky's desk. "While we're giving things back," Hardy said.

Glitsky spun the folder around, facing him. "How'd you get this?"

"I got a better one—how did Pullios get it?"

"I gave it to her."

"You gave it to her."

"Sure. Happens all the time. She comes in, says 'Hi, Abe, what you got?' and I give her a homicide."

"Did it occur to you this might be my case?"

"I told her you'd been working on it, and she said she knew that and she'd take care of it."

"Well, she did that. She's got the case."

"You got the folder, though, I notice."

"Yeah, I get to be her gofer. I follow up."

Glitsky leaned back, his feet on his desk. He dug a LifeSaver from his coat pocket and put it in his mouth. "So what's the problem?"

Hardy could continue bitching about internal strife in the D.A.'s office, but it would be wasted breath and he knew it. The best thing would be to do his job and wait for another chance. He settled against the corner of Abe's desk. "There's no problem," he said, "but I was going over the file and you say you found the gun in the rolltop desk."

"Right."

"Top right drawer? Maps and stuff like that?"

"That's it, so?"

"So I looked in that drawer on Wednesday, and there wasn't any gun there."

Glitsky took a breath, chewed up his LifeSaver, then brought his feet down off his desk. "What?"

Hardy told him about his own search of the *Eloise*.

"But Waddell, the guard, he was with you, right? Hurrying you up?"

"A little, yeah, but I checked that drawer."

"How close?"

"I opened it, I looked in. What do you want?"

"The gun was back a ways, Diz. How far in did you look?"

Hardy remembered back, remembered feeling pressure from Tom, the guard, to stop going through things. He'd pulled that drawer out, had seen the maps. He was sure—almost certain—he would have seen a gun. But to be honest—he hadn't looked or felt around anywhere near the back of the drawer.

"So you missed it," Glitsky said. "I wouldn't worry about it. It happens. That's why we have a team go and look."

The phone rang on the desk. Hardy got up, grabbed his file and walked to the back window, which overlooked the hole for the new jail and the freeway, on about the same level four stories up as Homicide. Traffic was stopped southbound. The sun was still out in a pure sky—day four of the hot spell.

Glitsky came up beside him. "That was Ken Farris," he said. "This morning when I got in I faxed him a copy of the will, the alleged will—two million dollars, remember? I figured he'd be the quickest way to verify the handwriting."

"And?"

"And he says it looks like Nash's writing, all right, but it can't be real. Nash wouldn't have done that."

"Why not?"

"He just says he wouldn't have. He let Farris handle all his legal stuff."

"But it's his writing?"

"Looks like. Could be forged, of course. No telling at this point. It's also, if it is his, a legal form for a will. Blank paper, dated, nothing else on it. But legal or not, I'll tell you something."

"What's that?"

"I'm glad I brought the Shinn woman in. She almost pulled it off."

Hardy kept looking at the stalled traffic on the freeway, the glare of the reflected sun. He felt a stabbing pain behind his left eye and brought his hand up to rub it away. "Almost," he said, "almost."

20

Hardy marveled at how busy Abe must have been. No wonder he'd been working through the weekend; smaller wonder still that he'd been so reluctant to arrest May without a warrant or indictment. On a no-warrant arrest, as May's had been, the arresting officer has forty-eight hours to bring all the paperwork on a case to the district attorney's office. Forty-eight hours was by Sunday night—last night. By then he had to have a complaint, any relevant incident reports, witness interviews, forensics, ballistics if available—enough evidence so the D.A. wouldn't throw it out.

This morning a typist had worked like a dog to type up the complaint and transcripts, then two copies of the folder were prepared—the original stayed with the D.A., one copy went to the clerk for putting it on a docket and one copy was saved for the defense attorney.

Pullios not only had gotten to the folder first, she had evidently convinced the clerk to get it on a docket for that day, in the early afternoon.

Rebecca's fever had broken at noon; spots were showing all over her skin. Otherwise, everything at home was fine. Frannie was planning on taking a nap, catching up if she could on the sleep she'd missed the night before.

Hardy was back from lunch—ribs at Lou's. Club soda. He threw three games of Twenty Down at his dart board and by the third game was nailing two numbers a round, sometimes all three. For the tenth time he considered registering for the City Championship Tournament. Someday he really would.

He got a black three-ring binder and started filling in some tab labels. Police Report. Inspector's Chronological. Inspector's Notes. Coroner. Autopsy. Witnesses. The drill, except for Coroner and Au-

145

topsy, wasn't all that different from his prelims—proof was proof. A trial was a trial.

There was one definitely new tab here, though, in Hardy's own folder—Newspaper. He had gone back and cut out all of Jeff Elliot's stories to date. Most crimes in the big city didn't get any ink. This one was already on the front page. Hardy figured he'd see the name Pullios in the paper within a day or so and he wanted to have a record of it.

He hadn't gotten far that morning on Glitsky's reports, when the gun issue—that he hadn't seen it on Wednesday—had stopped him cold. He'd been looking for an excuse to blow some steam anyway, get out of the office. Well, now he'd done that. He'd checked in on his baby, had a good lunch. It was time to go to work. He opened the folder again, turned to the first witness interview, the transcript unedited off the tape:

Three, two, one. This is Inspector Abraham Glitsky, Star number 1144. I am currently at the office of the Golden Gate Marina, 3567 Fort Point Drive. With me is a gentleman identifying himself as Thomas Waddell, Caucasian, male, 4/19/68. This interview is pursuant to an investigation of case number 921065882. Today's date is June 27, 1992, Saturday, at 1415 hours in the PM.

Hardy skimmed quickly through the preliminaries, down to where Abe had started talking about putting May at the crime scene.

Q: You remember locking up the *Eloise* with Mr. Hardy?
A: That's right. It wasn't locked before then.
Q: It was just left open?
A: It happens all the time. We notice it, we lock 'em, but we don't do a regular check, like that.
Q: But you locked it, when, Wednesday night?
A: I'm not sure. When the D.A. guy came by, after that.
Q: That was Wednesday.
A: Okay.
Q: And did you see anybody else board the boat, the *Eloise*?
A: No, not exactly. You guys, you know, the police, were still here Friday when I came on. You mean besides that?
Q: Right. What do you mean not exactly?

A: Well, you know I remembered 'cause of locking it up special, but Mr. Nash's lady friend came by.

Q: His lady friend?

A: You know, the Japanese lady? She was out here a few times. I recognized her all right.

Q: This is a snapshot of a woman named May Shintaka. Do you recognize her?

A: Yeah, that's her. She was by, like, Thursday night, out on the float.

Q: What time was that?

A: Still light. Maybe seven, seven-thirty.

Q: What was she doing there? Did you talk to her?

A: No. I don't know. She walked by the office when I was with some other people, went out onto Dock Two by the *Eloise,* stayed a minute, then when I got done and looked up, she was gone.

Q: Did she go aboard the boat?

A: It was locked up.

Q: I know it was. Maybe she had a key?

A: I don't know, I guess she might've. I don't know. I didn't see her again, and later I went to check the boat, and it was still locked up. She wasn't in it.

Q: How do you know that?

A: Well, the lock is outside. You can't go in and lock the door from inside. So if she was still inside, it couldn't have been locked.

Q: But you didn't actually see her leave?

A: No, sir, but I wasn't looking. People are going by all the time. I only put it together about Mr. Nash after she was already out there.

Hardy couldn't put his finger on it, but he wasn't happy gathering these nails for May's coffin. She wasn't his anymore, maybe that was it. She was Elizabeth Pullios's. And the more he looked at it, the more nails he seemed to find.

Glitsky's theory—that May had gone back to the *Eloise* to pick up her gun because it was the only physical evidence tying her to the crime—was starting to look pretty good. And certainly her idea that she and Owen Nash were going to be married was ridiculous.

He went around his desk and absently grabbed his darts again. His door was closed and he threw, not aiming, not paying any attention. He used his darts like Greeks used worry beads.

Thursday, the twenty-fifth, had been the day of Elliot's story linking Owen Nash, the *Eloise* and May. On that same day, she'd bought her ticket (without a return) to Japan and gone down, presumably, to get her gun back. And failed.

Why did he so badly want her not to have done it?

He thought it might be that so many of the people he'd been seeing on his other cases had been the kind you'd expect to be doing bad things. May Shinn, when he'd gone up to see her in jail, wasn't that type at all. She'd talked to him openly, until Freeman had shown up, unconcerned about her rights, the way innocent people might be expected to start out until they found out how the system worked.

Hardy was willing to believe she was a liar, but if she was, she was very good at it. Hardy knew such people existed. He just hadn't run across too many of them among the lowlifes—liars, sure, good liars not often.

There was a knock on his door, it opened and Pullios was in, watching him poised, dart in hand, ready to toss. She grinned her sexy, charming, I'm-your-best-friend grin and leaned against the doorjamb. "Reviewing the Shinn case?" she asked.

Hardy wanted to put a dart in her forehead, but thought he'd have a hard time pleading accident. It was one of the drawbacks of having talent.

"As a matter of fact, I am," he said. He threw the dart and sat down.

"You're mad at me." She actually pouted.

"I'm not much at games, Elizabeth. How do you want to play this?"

She sat herself down, the kitten disappearing as soon as it saw it wasn't going to get petted. "Come on, Dismas, we're on the same team."

"That's what Locke said, so it must be true."

"Look, I know how you feel."

"Good," he said. "That's a load off my mind. The thing is, I don't know how you feel, so we're not even. I don't, for example, know why you let me jerk myself off on this case for most of a week before you showed any interest in it, other than encouraging me to push for my rights, beat the bureaucracy."

"I meant it."

Hardy studied her face. Elizabeth Pullios, he was coming to understand, had a gift for sincerity. It probably played well in front of juries. "But then it was a skull case, and now it's hot ink."

"No, what it is, is a homicide and I do homicides. I've worked my way up to there."

Hardy looked longingly at his darts stuck in the board across the room. In lieu of them, he picked up his paperweight and leaned back in his chair, passing it from hand to hand. It might be unfair, and it might be manure, but it was a done deal, and he didn't want to discuss it anymore. "Farris says the will was Nash's handwriting," he said.

Pullios was right with him. "Definite?"

"Until we get an expert, but it looks like it."

"That's great, that's what we need."

"What do we need?"

"It's a hell of a motive, don't you think? Two million dollars?"

Hardy couldn't help himself. Things were just falling too easily. If Pullios wanted this job, she ought to do a little work for it. "It seems to me," he said, "that if May were going to collect money on Nash's death, she wouldn't have dumped him in the ocean."

"Didn't she?"

"I mean it was pure luck he washed ashore. How could she have known that?"

"So?"

"So if you were going to kill somebody for two million dollars, wouldn't you want to make sure they found the body? You don't get the money until he's dead, right? And he's not dead till there's a body, unless you want to wait seven years or so."

"But there is a body."

"But she couldn't have known that."

He enjoyed watching her stew over that, but it didn't last long. "I'll be prepared for that argument," she said. "It's good you brought it up. The great thing is the money angle."

"The great thing?"

"Murder for profit. Makes it a capital case."

"A capital case?"

"Absolutely," Pullios declared. "We're going to ask the State of California to put May Shinn to death."

21

Hardy sat next to Pullios in the courtroom, randomly chosen by computer for Department 11 in Municipal Court, which was where the arraignment in a no-warrant arrest, even on a capital case, was scheduled.

Glitsky was there, sitting next to Jeff Elliot in the mostly empty gallery seats. David Freeman, looking more disheveled than he had on Saturday, came through the low gate and shook hands cordially with both Pullios and Hardy, which was some surprise. Hardy found himself liking the guy and warned himself to watch it. If he was good at trial, he was by definition—like Pullios—a good actor. You could admire the technique, but beware of the man.

The judge was Michael Barsotti, an old, gray, bland fixture in his robes behind the desk. Barsotti had been in Muni Court forever and he wasn't known for moving things along.

The court reporter sat at a right angle to Hardy, midway between the defendant's podium and the judge. Assorted functionaries milled about—two or three bailiffs, translators, public defenders waiting to get clients assigned.

Hardy leaned over the table, organizing his binder, not knowing what his role, if any, would be. He wasn't prepared for his first sight of May Shinn.

She looked so much smaller, diminished. The yellow jumpsuit hung on her. He supposed she'd been in her jail garb on Saturday, but his focus had been talking to her, eye to eye, concentrating on her face.

She walked up with the bailiff, hands cuffed, and stood at the podium next to Pullios, giving no indication she'd ever seen Hardy before, or anyone else.

The gravity of a murder case was underscored by the judge's first words. Even Barsotti gained a measure of authority, casting off his boredom, caught up in the drama of the formal indictment being pronounced, the courtroom getting still.

"May Shintaka," Judge Barsotti intoned, "you are charged by a complaint filed herein with a felony, to wit, a violation of section 187 of the Penal Code in that you did, in the City and County of San Francisco, State of California, on or about the twentieth day of June, 1992, willfully, unlawfully and with malice aforethought murder Owen Simpson Nash, a human being."

"How do you plead," Barsotti asked.

"Not guilty, Your Honor." Freeman spoke for May. After Freeman's booming oratorio in the interview room on Saturday, Hardy was struck by the modulation of his voice. He was matter-of-fact, conversational. But there was a fist under the glove. Suddenly, he put on his trial voice. "Your Honor, before we continue with this charade I'd like to move to have all charges against my client dismissed due to procedural error."

"On a murder charge, Mr. Freeman? And already?"

"Mr. Hardy of the district attorney's office interrogated my client on Saturday morning without informing her—"

"I object, Your Honor." Elizabeth Pullios was up from the D.A.'s desk, where she'd appeared during the recess. "Mr. Hardy informed Ms. Shintaka that she had the right to have an attorney present and Ms. Shintaka waived that right. The prosecution has a tape recording of that meeting."

"I think we can establish coercion . . ."

Barsotti tapped his gavel. He sighed. "Mr. Freeman," he said, "save it for the hearing. In the meantime, we'll move on to bail."

He adjusted his glasses and double-checked the computer sheet in front of him. The handwritten notation next to the computer line read "No bail."

"The prosecution asks that no bail be granted?" he asked Pullios.

"This is a capital murder case, Your Honor."

Freeman turned and looked directly at Pullios. "You're not serious."

Barsotti tapped his gavel again. "Mr. Freeman, please direct your remarks to the bench."

"Excuse me, Your Honor, I am shocked and dismayed by this mention of capital murder. I can see that this is alleged as a special-circumstances case, but I can't believe that the state is asking for death."

Pullios stood up. "Murder for profit, Your Honor."

"I assume you have some evidence to substantiate this claim, Ms. Pullios."

"We do, Your Honor."

"Your Honor, Ms. Shintaka poses no threat to society."

"No threat? She killed somebody last week!"

The sound of the gavel exploded in the room. "Ms. Pullios, that's enough of that. Both of you hold your press conferences outside this courtroom.

Hardy was impressed. Barsotti might be a bland functionary, but he was in control here.

Freeman had recovered his cool. "Your Honor, my client has never before been accused of a crime, much less convicted."

Pullios wasn't slowed down by the rebuke. "Your Honor, the defendant was attempting to leave the jurisdiction when she was arrested."

"Mr. Freeman, was your client attempting to flee?"

"She was going to Japan on business, Your Honor. It's our contention the arresting officer overreacted. She was intending to come back. There had been no warrant issued. She was going about her normal life, which included a previously planned trip to Japan."

"She'd only bought the ticket the day before, Your Honor, and she didn't buy a return. She'd also packed many personal effects."

"And she'd left many more. She wasn't fleeing the jurisdiction. She was going on a trip. She will gladly surrender her passport to the court. There is no risk of flight here."

Pullios started to say something more, but Barsotti held up a hand. "I'm going to set bail at five hundred thousand dollars."

Pullios leaned over and whispered to Hardy. "Close enough."

"A half million dollars is a lot of money, Your Honor."

"I believe that's the point, Mr. Freeman. We'll set the preliminary hearing for—"

"Your Honor." Freeman again.

Even Hardy the novice knew what was next. Although the defendant had an absolute right to a preliminary hearing within ten court days or sixty calendar days of arraignment, no defense lawyer in his right mind would agree to go to prelim that soon, at least until he'd gotten a chance to see what kind of evidence the prosecution had gathered. "The defense would request three weeks for discovery and to set."

"Will the defendant waive time?" Which meant that in exchange for this three-week delay, May would give up her right to a preliminary hearing within ten days.

"Yes, Your Honor."

Barsotti scratched his chin. "Three weeks, hmm." He looked down at his desk, moved some papers around. "Will counsel approach the bench?"

Pullios, Hardy and Freeman moved around their respective tables and up before the judge. Barsotti's eyes were milk-watery. The drama hadn't lasted long. "We're getting ourselves into the beginning of vacation season here. Would there be any objection to, say, the day after Labor Day?"

"None here, Your Honor," Freeman said.

"Your Honor, Labor Day is over two months away. The defendant has a right to a speedy trial, but the people have no less a right to speedy justice."

"I don't need a lecture, Counselor."

"Of course not, Your Honor. But the prosecution is ready to proceed in ten days. Two months is a rather lengthy delay."

This was not close to true, and everyone knew it. Barsotti looked at Pullios over his glasses. "Not for this time of year, it isn't. We got a full docket, and you know as well as I do it can go six months, a year, before we get to a hearing." Barsotti clearly didn't expect to get any argument, and it put his back up. He shuffled some papers, looked down at something on his desk. "We'll schedule the prelim for Wednesday, September sixth, nine-thirty A.M., in this department.

"Thank you, Your Honor," Freeman said.

Pullios had her jaw set. "That'd be fine, Your Honor."

"That's all now." He brushed all counsel away and looked over to the bailiff. "Call the next line," he said.

Prelim courtrooms were on the first and second floors. The hallway outside the courtrooms on both floors was about twenty feet wide, the ceilings fifteen feet high, the floors linoleum. But except for the sound of falling pins, it had all the ambience, volume and charm of a low-rent bowling alley.

During the hours court was in session there were seldom less than two hundred people moving to and fro—witnesses, lawyers, clerks, spectators, families and friends. People chatted on the floors against the walls. Mothers breast-fed their babies. Folks ate lunch, kissed, cried, cut deals. On Monday and Thursday mornings, after the janitors had cleaned up, the hallway smelled like the first day of school. By now, seven hours into the workday, it just smelled.

Hardy, Glitsky and Jeff Elliot stood in a knot outside Department 11. All of them were watching Pullios's rear end as it disappeared around the corner down near the elevators. "Good thing justice is blind," Glitsky said, "or Freeman wouldn't have a chance."

"I don't know," Elliot said. "He's got May."

"Yeah, her dress though, that baggy yellow thing doesn't show it off like old Betsy." Hardy liked calling her Betsy. He knew he was going to get used to it and slip someday. He kind of looked forward to it. He pointed at Elliot. "That was off the record."

Jeff was happy to be included again. "Of course."

"Just making sure."

"So what do you think," Glitsky asked. "Christmas for the trial? Next Easter?"

Hardy said he didn't know how long Freeman could delay if he wasn't going to make bail. He wouldn't want to leave May in jail for a year, awaiting trial.

"I don't know. Maybe she'll make bail," Glitsky said.

"How's she gonna make bail?" Elliot asked. "Half a million dollars?"

"How much does David Freeman charge? Half a million dollars? If it goes a year, it could easily come to that."

"How'd she get Freeman anyway?" Hardy asked.

Glitsky shrugged. "If we only knew an investigative reporter or something . . ."

"She's got to have some money. What's her house look like?" Hardy asked.

"Apartment," Glitsky answered. "Small. Nice, but small."

"Maybe Freeman is one of her clients." Elliot clearly liked the idea, was warming to it. "That's it! Freeman is one of her clients. Nash was another."

Glitsky held down his enthusiasm. "And the will is collateral on the come after he gets her off."

"What will?"

Glitsky stopped short. He took a beat, then smiled down at the reporter. "Did I say 'will'? I don't think I said 'will.' "

Hardy shook his head. "No, I'm sure I would've heard it. I was right here and I didn't hear anything like 'will.' "

"Are we on the record here or what?" Elliot leaned into his crutches. "Come on, guys."

Hardy glanced at Abe. "What do you think?"

"It's gonna come out anyway," Abe said, "but it would be sort of nice to find out how Freeman got connected to May. Pullios is really going for capital?"

Hardy nodded. "You heard her."

Glitsky laid it out for Jeff—the $2 million will, the profit motive, Farris tentatively authenticating the handwriting.

"Well, there's the money if he gets her off," Elliot said.

Glitsky looked at Hardy. "This guy must not know any defense attorneys," he said. Then, explaining, "Jeff, listen, if there's one thing all defense attorneys do, they get their money up front."

"Think about it," Hardy said. "You're found guilty, you don't pay your attorney 'cause he didn't do the job. You're not guilty, you don't pay him 'cause you don't need him anymore. Either way, your attorney is stiffed. Maybe you're grateful, but not a half million dollars' grateful."

"Maybe he just gets the rights up front for the book deal. Maybe that's his fee."

"Pico was telling me that we—him and me—ought to go for a book deal. We found the hand, after all."

"Hey!" Rare for him, Glitsky got into it. "I arrested May. I ought to get the book deal."

Elliot said, "Somebody is paying Freeman. You still don't think maybe he's one of her clients?"

Glitsky put a look on Jeff. "A *half million dollars'* worth of ass?"

"Not including bail," Hardy put in.

Glitsky said, "If she makes bail."

"I don't know," Hardy said. "I've got a feeling here. Freeman's going for delay. He doesn't want delay if she's cooling her heels upstairs. Which means she makes bail."

22

"I think you're innocent. That's why." This was not close to true. David Freeman's words were tools to produce the effect he desired. That's all they were.

May Shinn was drinking Chardonnay in a booth at Tadich's Grill. David Freeman, her rumpled genius, sat across from her. Before the arraignment, he'd gone down to her bank with power of attorney and withdrawn $50,000, just about cleaning out her life savings. He'd known exactly the amount they'd set bail for. He'd gotten the clothes they'd taken from her and got them pressed before they gave them back to her. He'd bought her new makeup.

He'd followed the story in the newspaper. When he read of her arrest on Saturday morning, he knew he had to help her, that she would need an attorney, that a Japanese mistress of a well-known and powerful man was going to have a very difficult time making a defense against the arrayed powers. Now, having talked to her, he also had the advantage of believing she was innocent.

"But I am unable to pay."

He lifted his shoulders, sipped lugubriously at his own wine. The curtain was pulled across the booth. They had been through this before. He had started by trying to convince her that he was taking her case *pro bono*. Once in a while, he had told her, you just had to do something because it was the right thing to do. Which had caused her to smile.

"If I can't lie to you, you should not lie to me."

"May, why would I lie?"

She put her glass down, twirled it around, kept her eyes on him. Finally he cracked, laughing at himself. "Okay," he said, "okay, but it's not a terrifically flattering motive."

"It's not been a very flattering few days," she said.

"No, I guess not." Freeman drank some wine, then took a breath and began. "Until about ten years ago, attorneys weren't allowed to advertise, did you know that?"

She nodded.

"And even now, when it's technically legal, it's still not particularly good for business unless you're doing divorce or DUI or ambulance chasing. I mean, it kind of puts you in the low-rent market. Good attorneys don't advertise because they don't need to, and if they do need to, they're not good." He had a good smile, a strong face. Sincere, brown eyes, a full head of dark hair. "It's a vicious circle."

"And I am advertising?"

"I've got seven associates left. I had to let three go in the last twelve months. Business is terrible. This is a high-profile case. Owen Nash was a well-known man."

It didn't surprise her. She was to the point where she thought nothing could surprise her. At least she knew.

But at the mention of Owen's name, a shadow fell within her. She didn't want to be sitting here, drinking wine, enjoying food. "I didn't kill him, David."

He patted her hand across the table. "Of course you didn't."

He didn't believe her. He'd told her Saturday, before they'd even talked, before he'd reviewed any of the prosecution's evidence, that it was irrelevant whether or not she'd killed Nash—he was going to get her off.

"But I didn't!"

He shushed her gently, index finger to his lips. "I must say, there is very little evidence that you did."

"What about the will?"

He brushed that away. "The will. Does the will put you on the boat? Did it give you the opportunity to kill Owen? Did it give you the means? You were home, weren't you?"

She nodded.

"All right, then. We will prove you were home. The will, like the rest of the so-called evidence, is completely irrelevant. What do they have? The will? The ticket to Japan?"

"I thought the police would . . ."

"Of course. Naturally." He emptied the bottle into their glasses and continued with the litany. "There is nothing physically tying you to the gun, no proof you pulled the trigger"—he held up a finger, stopping her. "Uh, uh. No more denials. They don't matter, you see? There is nothing that could prove you did it. I don't even see a case that will get to trial. At the preliminary hearing, we point out the racial discrimination, mixed in with your profession . . . It's really not going anywhere. There is simply no hard evidence."

May Shinn was back in her apartment. David Freeman had driven her home, then walked up and made sure she was safe inside her door.

She ran a bath and sank into the hot water, letting the memories wash over her. She thought it might have been the closeness to death that brought her and Owen back to life.

The first couple of weeks they were inseparable—she canceled her appointments with all her clients. She didn't know who Owen was then, didn't know that he had money. All she knew was he made her feel things, that there was some connection between her mind and her body that she'd lost touch with long before, and now while it was back, for however short a time, she was going to keep it.

There was strange behavior—they tied each other up, blindfolded each other, tried every position and every orifice. They went outside at two in the morning and did it on the sidewalk. They shaved each other bare. He ate her with honey and chocolate and, once, garlic, which burned hotter and longer than Spanish fly. Owen had his appetites.

The man was also in fantastic shape. Big, barrel-chested, hard everywhere. He drank scotch and wine and brandy and took pills to get to sleep. Gradually she became aware that he was doing business from her house—phone calls in the middle of whatever they were doing, mention of the Wheel, taking care of his daughter's problems. He had a real life somewhere out there, but it wasn't coming between them.

She didn't understand it exactly. She just knew that in some unspoken way they were in this together, finding something out, something essential for them both to go on. It wasn't the sex, or at least it wasn't only the sex.

She'd made her living from sex for fifteen years, and none of it had seriously touched her. Her life, even her professional life, had evolved into something remote. She made love with her clients, but not every time she saw them. When they needed it, predictably missionary after the first few times, then she was there. Often they couldn't make it. More often they wanted to hug, lie there afterward and talk.

She made them dinners, too. Scampi in brandy, raw oysters, rare filet and cabernet. She'd turned into a great cook. She sang for them, played piano while they sat with their bourbon or gin, gave them the companionship or escape or a kind of romance they didn't find in their homes.

Owen, though. Owen wasn't like anyone else. And not just his hungers. He didn't live a life of quiet desperation. He wasn't looking for respite, or peace, or a sheen of culture laid on top of the vulgarity of the world. He'd seen it for what it was, or more, he'd seen himself for what he was.

No games. And she was with him. The oblivion—the sex—the sex was the only way they both knew anymore to get to it, to get underneath the crust. Something was cooking inside each of them, threatening to blow if it didn't get some release, get through the crust.

It was morning, early, before dawn. The sky was gray in the east and still dark over the ocean.

May Shinn had been out of bed for an hour, walking naked in the dark. She moved away from her turret windows and went back through the kitchen to the bedroom, stopping to pick up her razor-sharp boning knife. Owen slept on the bed, breathing regularly, on his back.

She put the edge of the knife up under his throat, sitting, watching him breathe. The bedroom was darker than the rest of the apartment. Finally she laid the blade down across his collarbone and kissed him.

"Owen."

He woke up like no one else. He simply opened his eyes and was all the way there. "What?"

She moved the edge of the blade back up so it touched the skin above his Adam's apple. "Do you feel this?"

"Would this be a bad time to nod?"

"Do you want me to kill you?"

He closed his eyes again, took a couple of breaths. "That's where we're going, isn't it?" He didn't move.

"Owen. What are we doing?"

He took a moment. Perhaps he didn't know either. Maybe they both knew and it scared them too much. "What are we doing?" she asked again.

"We're showing each other each other." He swallowed. She could feel the blade move over his skin.

"I don't know what I feel."

"You love me." And as soon as he said it, she knew it was true. She felt her eyes tearing and tightened her hand on the knife. "And I love you," he said, "but I don't want you to put your hopes in me. I'm not saving your life, May."

"I'm what you want, though."

"That's right. You're what I want. But I play fair. I'm telling you straight, the best way I know how.

"I'm a whore, Owen. I'm nothing, but I play fair, too. You know me. I don't know how long I've loathed what I am. I don't want to care about you, but you're my last great chance . . ."

Owen had closed his eyes again. She pulled the knife away from his throat. "I've warned you," she said.

"And I've warned you." He pulled her down and kissed her, held her against his chest.

23

The next morning, Pullios was sitting in Hardy's office when he walked in at 8:25. She held the morning *Chronicle* folded in her lap. "Nice story," she said. She opened the paper to the front-page article, in its now familiar spot lower right: "State To Seek Death Penalty In Nash Murder." And under it: "D.A. Claims Special Circumstances—Murder For Profit—In Tycoon's Death."

He came around the desk, opened his briefcase, started removing the work he'd taken home and ignored—some stuff he'd let slide while concentrating on May Shinn. Moses had come over, worried about Rebecca (and about Frannie and probably Hardy, too) and had stayed to eat with them and hang out.

"I read it," he said.

"I'm surprised Elliot didn't get the news about the bail."

Hardy stopped fiddling. "She made bail? I had a feeling she'd make bail. Freeman put it up?"

Pullios closed the paper, placed it back down on her lap. "I don't know. We can subpeona her financial records if we can convince a judge that we think she got it illegally."

"Not Barsotti."

"No, I gathered that. We'll look around."

"How about prostitution? Last time I checked, that was illegal."

"Maybe. It's a thought, we should check it out." She recrossed her legs. "Look," she said, "I came by to apologize again. I was out of line. It should have been your case. I'm sorry."

Hardy shrugged. "There'll be other cases."

"Thank you." She didn't try her smile or her pout. "'Cause we're going to be busy."

"I don't know," Hardy said. "We've got two months now and I've let all this stuff back up." He motioned around his office.

161

Now she was smiling, but he didn't get the feeling it was for any effect. "You believe we're going out on a prelim in two months?"

"I got that general impression."

Pullios shook her head. "We're not letting that happen. There's no way Freeman and Barsotti are putting this thing off until next year. I talked to Locke after the arraignment, and he okayed it—we're taking this sucker to the grand jury on Thursday. Get an indictment there, take it into Superior Court and blindside the shit out of the slow brothers."

"Can we do that?"

"We can do anything we want," she said. "We're the good guys, remember."

"I don't want to rain on this parade, but isn't there some risk here? What if the grand jury doesn't indict?"

Pullios rolled her eyes. "After you're here awhile, you'll understand that if the D.A. wants, the grand jury will indict a ham sandwich. Besides, the grand jury always indicts for me. We've got everything Glitsky had, which ought to be enough. But if it isn't, ballistics says the gun is the murder weapon. But one thing . . ."

"Okay, but just one."

She smiled again. They seemed to be getting along. "No leaks on this. This is an ambush."

David Freeman knew his major character flaw—he could not delegate. He couldn't even have his secretary *type* for him. He'd let Janice answer the telephones, okay, put stamps on letters if they were in the United States and less than three pages—more than that, he had to weigh them himself and make sure there was enough postage. He did his own filing, his own typing. He ran his own errands.

He was, after Melvin Belli, probably the best-known lawyer in the city. He had seven associates but no partners. None of the associates worked for him—recession or no—for more than four years. He burned 'em out. They'd come to him for "trial experience." But if you were a client and came to David Freeman to keep you from going to jail, he wasn't about to leave that up to Phyllis or Jon or Brian or Keiko —he was going to be there inside the rail himself, his big schlumpy presence personally making the judge and jury believe that you didn't do it.

His deepest conviction was that *nobody,* anywhere, was as good as he was at trial, and if you hired the firm of David Freeman & Associates, what you got was David Freeman. And you got your trial prepared —somewhat—by associates at $135 an hour. When David got to the plate—and he personally reviewed every brief, every motion, every deposition—the price went up to $500, and trial time was $1500. Per hour.

It was his pride, and he knew he carried it to extremes. This was why private investigators existed—to do legwork. But no one did legwork as well as he did. One time, when he'd just started out, he'd hired a private investigator to talk to all possible witnesses in a neighborhood where a woman had supposedly killed her husband. The woman, Bettina Allred, had contended she'd had a fight with her husband Kevin, all right—she'd even fired a shot into the wall. Terrified of herself and her own anger, she'd run from the apartment to go out to cool off. While she was gone, she said, someone had come in and shot her husband with his own gun. So the private investigator David hired had talked to everybody in the apartment and they'd all heard the fighting and she'd obviously done it. Except the P.I. hadn't talked to Wayne, the thirteen-year old son who hadn't even been home during the relevant time. When Freeman doubled-checked as he always did, he decided to be thorough—as he always was—and found that Wayne had been hiding terrified in the closet and when mommy had run out, he'd taken the gun and shot his daddy. He'd had enough of daddy beating up on him and mommy.

Since then, Freeman had done his own legwork. Though it was his precious time, he only charged his clients the $65 an hour he would have paid a private eye. It was, he thought, one of the best bargains in the business.

No one in May's building had seen or heard her on Saturday. Now he was going up the other side of the street, ringing doorbells, talking to people.

"You see the turreted apartment on the corner, up on the top over there? Anything at all? Shades going up, blinds being pulled? How about a shadow? Yes, well, it's confidential, but it has to do with a murder investigation, Jesus, don't tell my boss. I shouldn't have said anything."

The French deli across the street. The cleaners on the opposite corner. *Nada, nada, nada.* If May had been home, as she claimed, she had been invisible. Of course, he didn't believe she'd been home, but as he'd told her, what he believed was irrelevant.

He was on the fourth and last floor of the building directly across the street from May's. His feet hurt. He was considering raising his billing rate for this work up to $75 an hour. He rang the bell and listened to it gong for a moment. No one answered. There was one other door down the hall, and it opened.

"Mr. Strauss isn't in. Can I help you?"

Mrs. Streletski was a well-dressed elderly woman and he gave her his spiel. She invited him in and forced him to drink a cup of horrible coffee. She was sorry she couldn't really help him. She'd been out of her apartment for the last ten days—in fact, she'd just gotten back from visiting over in Rossmore. She was considering moving into Rossmore with Hal. They did so much there. It was an active place, even if you were a little elderly, no one treated you like you were old. There were lots of classes, movies, lectures. It was a fun place, a young place.

Mrs. Streletski showed Freeman that you couldn't see anything of May's building from her window. He thanked her for the coffee and left his card so that Mr. Strauss, who lived alone next door, could call him when he got in if he had the time.

"He's not home very often, I'm afraid," she said. "He travels a lot. He's always working. He got divorced last year and I think he's very lonely. We've played Scrabble a few times and I tried to get him to go out with Hal and me, but I think he misses his wife and his boys."

"Well, if you could have him call me, he might have been home, remember something."

She said she would. He thanked her and started walking down the steps, thinking that even when you didn't get anything, this was probably worth more than $75, call it $100 an hour.

"Two months before you even set a date for a preliminary hearing?"

Hardy was biting his tongue, held to the stricture not to leak anything about Elizabeth's upcoming appointment with the grand jury. Ken Farris, in the interview room down by the evidence lockers, wasn't happy, and Hardy wondered how far he could go to make him feel better.

"We're working on something." Lame, he knew.

"Let's hope so. And meanwhile she's out walking around."

"That's how it works."

Farris shook his head.

Hardy thought he'd get away from it. "So how are things down in South City? Getting any better?"

Farris didn't look better. There were bags under his eyes. His shoulders slumped. He sat kitty-corner to Hardy at a gray-topped metal table, his arms half-cupped—protectively—around the original of Owen's will. May's gun was also bagged on the table. The snake ring.

Farris shrugged. "The stocks went down, then back up. We've got contracts. People have work and life goes on." He looked back down at the piece of paper in front of him. "This, though, this is unbelievable. What was he *doing?*"

"Who's that?"

"Owen. Two million dollars. Christ. Celine told me she talked to you."

The man was jumping around, trying to find a foothold. Hardy still wasn't comfortable talking about Celine. He'd been able to put her out of his mind, but if something came up that put her back in, she tended to stay. He didn't really understand it. "When did you see her?"

"Sunday. The cremation."

The cremation. Farris—and Celine—they were both coming off that, too. They'd had a rocky week. "How's she holding up?"

Farris seemed to be studying the will some more. "What? Oh, she's pretty fragile right now. A little fixated on May. I talked her out of going to court for the arraignment."

"Good idea. What's she say about May?"

"She wonders why we waste all the time with arraignments and hearings and trials. And then there'll be appeals. Somebody ought to go and just kill her. Celine says she'd do it herself."

"Try to talk her out of that, too, would you? It would be frowned on . . . You're sure she did it, huh?"

That woke Farris up. "You're *not?*"

"Whoa, I didn't say that. We just can't put her on the *Eloise.* It's kind of a major detail."

"Well, I've got her on the *Eloise.* Celine told me Owen was meeting her on the *Eloise.*"

Hardy nodded. "She told me that, too."

"Well?"

"Well, what? It's hearsay. Inadmissible."

"Bullshit. She was on the boat."

"I didn't say she wasn't. We're trying her for murder."

"Okay. Sorry." Farris looked down again, tapped the paper. "This is definitely Owen. Why didn't he tell me about it?"

"Maybe he thought it would never come up."

"How wouldn't it come up?"

"If he didn't die, how's that? Maybe it was a goof, maybe he wrote the thing drunk. She might have dared him or something. The point is, it's here, and it's a damn good reason to kill somebody."

"Another one," Farris said.

"What do you mean, another one?"

Farris frowned, as though surprised he'd be caught saying anything out loud. He rose from the chair, pushing the physical evidence back toward Hardy. "Nothing," he said. "Figure of speech."

24

Jeff Elliot went blind in Maury Carter's office.

It had started, he guessed, on the night after he'd gone to the morgue. The tension of those moments, coupled with his first front-page article and the background stuff, had produced too much stress, and there had always been—and his doctors agreed—a correlation between stress and the onset of his attacks.

But MS was a sneaky thing. It wasn't like it came up and wopped you upside the head. With his legs, it had begun with pins and needles one morning. His left leg just felt a little bit like it was asleep, like a low-voltage current was passing through it. Then, over the course of a couple of weeks, the feeling not only didn't go away, it got worse and his leg became a weight he dragged around. Which was when he'd gone to the doctor and the bomb dropped.

The right leg had gone two years later. But since then he'd had five good years, three on Prednisone and then, because he hated the steroid, trying to get along without it. And, he had come to think, successfully.

So successfully that he hadn't really related it to the MS when he woke up with slightly blurred vision. He ignored it. If he wasn't looking directly at something, it was nothing.

This morning, though, he'd noticed it a lot. The right eye didn't seem to focus at all, and there was a brown smudge over half of what he could see through his left eye. He should go to the doctor, but this was the chance he'd worked so hard for. He was the man of the hour. Once he got a few more things tied up here he'd go see about his vision.

Maury Carter did business out of a building about two blocks from the Hall. There was a black-and-white four-foot-square sign above the doorway outside, bolted up against the old brick, that read "Bail Bondsman." Inside, a desk for Maury's secretary took up the big front

window. Behind that desk were file cabinets and acoustic baffling that
served to separate Maury's private office from the street.

It was Tuesday afternoon. Jeff had spent most of the morning following up on what he'd missed the day before—May's bail. It wasn't a
stop-the-presses story anyway—people, even murder suspects, made
bail all the time—but it bothered him that he'd found it out on television. He had to keep concentrating on his story, not worry about his
eyes.

And the real story now, if it existed and he could get it, was the
Shinn/Freeman connection. Along with the fact that May had made
bail, he'd discovered Freeman's billing rates, so Hardy and Glitsky
must have been right—there was a source of money somewhere.

But Dorothy, Maury's secretary, said she wasn't supposed to talk
about their clients, "but we can talk about anything else. Maury's over
at the Hall. Do you want to wait? I can get you some coffee."

Jeff thought she was about the nicest girl he'd met in San Francisco. She wore a print dress and her skin was fair with a few freckles.
It occurred to Jeff that she might even think he was okay, in spite of
his crutches.

She, too, was from the Midwest—Ohio—and had been out here for
four months, living with a girlfriend in the Haight, which wasn't anything like she'd expected it to be. She was going back to school to get
her nursing degree; she'd already majored in bio, so it shouldn't be too
hard, but she was going to be doing it at night and until then this job
paid the bills.

Jeff could have listened all day, was even starting to feel comfortable telling her a little about himself. He found himself looking
around the growing brown smudge, willing it away in the vision of her,
but then Maury came in, who'd actually put up the bond. And the
reason Jeff was here came back.

Maury wasn't going to tell him, though. It was confidential information. They were back in Maury's part of the office now, behind the
partition. "But we know how much the bail was."

Maury had a shiny, deep forehead with white steel-wool for eyebrows. On the map of his face, his nose was a small continent. His
ears stuck out and his jowls hung. He leaned back in his chair, feet on
his desk, and brought his cigar to his purplish lips. He seemed to be
enjoying himself. Blowing out a line of blue smoke, he chewed reflectively on his tongue. "Then what can I tell you?"

"May Shinn put up fifty thousand dollars?"

"As you say, you know how much bail is."

Jeff was fighting a kind of ringing panic attack. He looked down at his notepad and found he couldn't make out what he'd written there.

"Bail was half a million," he persisted. It was the stress, this circular discussion. He should end it and get out of here. The room was closing in—the cigar smoke, the funny light. "Let's be hypothetical," he said. "Your normal fee—suppose I'm a client now—is ten percent, right?"

Maury threw him a bone and nodded, blowing more smoke.

"So if I've got bail of half a million, I give you fifty thousand."

Maury nodded. "That would be the fee, yes."

Was the smoke getting thicker, the light worse? Maybe he was just getting dizzy. He squirmed in his chair, got the blood flowing a little. "Then you pay that to the court?" It still wasn't clear. Jeff knew, or thought he knew, this stuff, but suddenly it wasn't making any sense.

"No, I pay the court the half million. All of it. Not the fifty thousand, the full half mil." Maury pulled his feet down and pulled himself up to the desk. "Look, I keep the fifty no matter what. That's my fee for incurring the risk. Let's face it, these guys—my clients—call a spade a spade, they got lousy credit. Hey, are you okay?"

Jeff heard Maury's chair move back. It was funny—it felt as though he just closed his eyes a minute, then he'd opened them again. But if his eyes were open, how come he couldn't see anything? He guessed he was moving his head, trying to scan the room and find a flicker of light.

The panic was taking over. He had to get out of here. He went to reach for where his crutches were, but missed, and knocked them to the ground, now grabbing wildly at nothing, pushing himself from the chair, falling, falling.

Over the ringing that filled his head, he heard Maury yelling, "Dorothy! Dorothy, get in here!"

After Farris left, Hardy had put in what he thought was a pretty good afternoon's work. He pleaded out three assaults—a purse snatching and two robberies. A couple of dope cases were going to prelim. A teenage gang member had "tagged"—graffitied—six police cars, doing $9,000 worth of damage. Hardy was moving toward the opinion that possession of a can of spray paint ought to be punishable, like carrying a concealed weapon, by mandatory jail time. At four-thirty, he left the office and went down to the Youth Guidance Center, where he talked a pregnant sixteen-year-old girl into giving up the name of her thirty-year-old boyfriend who was letting her take the fall for a little friendly welfare fraud.

But, like to a hole in a tooth, Hardy kept coming back to Owen and May Shinn.

The drive back home from the YGC, top down on the Samurai, was over Twin Peaks, down Stanyan Street—and other sorrows—by the Shamrock, then the Aquarium, Golden Gate Park, out Arguello through the Avenues. It gave him enough time to worry it.

The motive thing was a real problem. If they couldn't sell it to a jury, they didn't have capital murder, and Hardy couldn't think of a rebuttal to his own argument: if May had killed Owen for the money, did it make sense for her to leave it to chance that his body would be found? He thought the answer had to be no. Resonantly, obviously, absolutely no.

So the strategic issue became whether they could keep Freeman from asking the question. He didn't see how.

But more immediately, and this was what occupied him as he ran the red light on 28th, once that initial chink in the motive worked its way around, would the jury start losing faith in May's guilt altogether?

He heard the siren and pulled over to the right. It was not yet six o'clock, a glorious night, the warm spell miraculously hanging on. He was surprised when the patrol car pulled in behind him and the cop got out.

"How you doin'?" Hardy asked.

The cop nodded. "May I see your license and registration please?"

Hardy reached into his pocket and pulled out his wallet. He opened it to where he had his D.A.'s badge pinned in across from his driver's license. He was reaching across into the glove box to get his registration when he felt the cop's hand on his arm.

"Sorry to bother you, sir, but you ran a red light back there."

Hardy half-turned. He must have. He didn't even remember seeing it. He apologized. Besides, he had no intention of failing the attitude test.

The cop handed him his wallet. "Eyes on the road, huh."

"Gotcha."

He waited until the cop was back in his car, then started up again, getting into the traffic with a nice signal, turning right off Geary at his first opportunity.

* * *

Hardy pulled up in front of his house still feeling foolish and a little guilty. It was the first time he'd experienced that particular professional courtesy—getting a break on a ticket—and he wasn't sure how he felt about it.

Rebecca was in her stroller next to Frannie, who was sitting on the front-porch steps, wearing sandals, Dolphin shorts and a tank top. The sun hit her hair just right, like a burning halo around her.

"You ought to get prettier," Hardy said, coming through the gate. "It's hell coming home to an ugly woman. And try to look a little younger while you're at it."

He was almost to her when she jumped with an animal growl. She hit him high, wrapping her legs around his waist, her arms around his neck, kissing him, then biting his ear, hard. He held her, marveling at her tininess, her smell, her fit to him. "Okay, okay, I guess you don't have to look younger."

She clung to him. "Wet willie," she said.

Hardy bore up under the torture. "See, you're making the baby cry." He took the last step to the porch and made a face at the baby. "It's all right, Beck, your mother's just a little bit insane. I'm sure it's not hereditary." Rebecca kept crying and Hardy kissed Frannie, then let her down and reached into the stroller. "I'll carry this neglected child," he said. "You push the stroller."

They walked east on Clement, past the Safeway and the little Russian piroshki houses and Oriental restaurants, the antique shops, Rebecca now happy in the baby seat, Frannie's arm through Hardy's, his coat hung over the stroller's handles.

They caught up on everything—Rebecca's spots mostly gone now; the decision about the second car they were considering buying as soon as the Shamrock profit payment came in, which ought to be when the fiscal year closed this week; Pico's weight, which led to Frannie's own weight gain (monitored daily); the Fourth of July picnic this weekend. The pregnancy was going smoothly. Boys' names. Girls' names. The ticket Hardy almost got for running a red light.

They walked as far as Park Presidio—over a mile—before they turned around and started back home. Hardy told Frannie about Pullios and her decision to get an indictment before the grand jury, move the proceedings to Superior Court.

"Why does she want to do that? What's the problem with a delay? I thought all trials took forever."

Hardy walked on a few steps, strolling really, relaxed, squinting into the sun. "This is a hot story. She's not going to let it cool off."

"Jeff Elliot," Frannie said.

"Exactly, but we've got a real problem." Hardy briefed her on it, moving on to what had concerned him when he'd gotten pulled over. "The thing is, once you start asking about the motive, you open another can of worms."

"If she did it for the money, why did she dump the body? But if she didn't do it for the money, why didn't she burn the will or something?"

"Right."

They walked along, pondering it. The sun had gotten behind the buildings. It was not cold, but there was a nip in the shade, and Hardy stopped and tucked his jacket around Rebecca. "Another thing, too," he said, "although I hate to mention it."

"What?"

"The ring. May's ring."

"What about it?"

"He was wearing it. Owen was wearing it."

"Does that mean something?"

"I don't know what it means, but it *could* mean that he put it on, that he left it on, that they had a relationship, that he wasn't leaving her. And if that's the case, *and* if she wasn't killing him for money, bye-bye motive."

"That's a lot of ifs."

"True, but they don't start with an if. He *was* wearing the ring."

"Couldn't they just have had a fight, got to arguing, the gun was there . . . ?"

"If that was it, it's not first-degree murder. It's definitely not capital murder."

Frannie hugged herself closer to Hardy. "I feel sorry for the woman. I'd hate to have you going after me."

"I did go after you."

"See?" She beamed at him. "That's what I mean."

25

There were things about the job Glitsky would never love. One of them was the reality of subpoenas and arrests.

The way you got people where you wanted them was to go out to their houses early in the A.M. and knock on their doors. Astoundingly, nobody expected to get arrested in the morning. So it was the best time to make an arrest.

But he'd been out last night on this drive-by again. They had received a tip—probably from a rival gang, but you took your leads where you could—that the shooter's car, with a cache of weapons in the trunk, was in a warehouse out in the Fillmore.

So Glitsky and a couple of stake-out officers had gone down there, letting the warm evening dissipate into a bitter, foggy cold as they sat drinking tea and eating pretzels in his unmarked car, and waited for someone to come and open the warehouse. Which had happened.

And they found the guns. Tonight's suspect, coked out of his mind and scared to death, had admitted that he'd driven the car, but they'd forced him, man, and he hadn't done any shooting. That was Tremaine Wilson. He was the shooter. Wilson. This witness, unlike Devon Latrice Wortherington, could actually put Wilson in the car with a gun in his hand, and if he didn't go sideways, which he probably would when he straightened out, Glitsky might be able to make a case against Wilson.

So now, four hours of sleep later, the dark not yet completely gone and the fog just as cold as when he'd left it, Glitsky found himself once again in the projects. The path to the door was a cracked cement strip that bisected a littered and well-packed rectangle of earth that might as well have been concrete except for the stalk of a tree that had made it to about one foot before someone whacked it off. Now the bare twig struggling out of the ground, maybe an inch thick, struck

Glitsky as an example of what happened to anything that dared to try to grow up here.

As always, they were going to try to do it neat and quick. Sometimes it worked, sometimes not. Just in case, though, three uniformed officers had gone to cover the back door of the duplex. Glitsky had two other guys, guns out, behind him on the walkway and another team in the street, out of their car and using it for cover on the not impossible chance that the frameless picture window would suddenly explode in gunfire.

It seemed a miracle that one of the streetlights still worked. The half-life of a streetlight in any of the projects could be measured in minutes after nightfall before some sharpshooter put it out. In the light from this one it was easy to make out the closed drapes in the front window. The screen door hung open, framed by a riot of graffiti.

Glitsky looked at his watch. The back entrance should be covered by now. He turned around and gestured at the guys huddled behind the car out in the street. They gave him the thumbs up—the place was, in theory, secured.

Now there was no fog and no cold and no darkness. There was only his pounding heart and dry mouth—it happened every time—and the door to be knocked on. Three light taps. He had his gun out and heard shuffling inside. The rattle of chains and he was looking at a four-year-old boy, shirt off, feet in his pajama bottoms, rubbing his eyes with sleep.

"Who's 'at?"

A woman's voice behind him, and the boy backed away, leaving the door open. Glitsky didn't like the boy between him and his perp. He'd seen guys—strung out on drugs or not—take their own children hostage, their wives, mothers, anybody who happened to be around.

Glitsky didn't wait. He had a warrant and Tremaine Wilson was wanted for special-circumstances murder. Tremaine wasn't going to be getting himself any slick lawyer to bust him out on the technicality of illegal entry. The boy had opened the door—that was going to have to do.

He pushed the door the rest of the way open and stepped between the boy and his mother. "Police," he said so she'd be clear it wasn't just another gang hit. "Where's Tremaine?"

One of the guys behind him hit the lights and a bare overhead came on. The woman was probably twenty. She had a swollen lower lip, short cowlicked hair, giant frightened eyes. She'd been sleeping in a men's plaid shirt that didn't quite make it down to her hips. She made no effort to cover herself below, but stood blinking in the light, separated from her boy by this tall black man with a gun. She made up her mind quickly, pointing down a hallway and moving to clutch her son as soon as Glitsky stepped aside.

The door to the room was open. The light from the hallway didn't make it back this far. One of Glitsky's men had stayed behind with the woman and her child, so Glitsky and his remaining backup moved quickly down the hallway. The sergeant went through the open door, his partner crouched in the dark hall, gun pointed in.

There might have been a bed, but he couldn't see it. He flicked on the light—another bare overhead. There it was—the bed—against the other wall, the only furniture besides a Salvation Army dresser. The man stirred in the bed, pulled the thin blanket over him. "C'mon, shit," he said, "get that light."

Glitsky was at the bedside, pulling the sheet all the way down and off the bed, at the same time putting the barrel of his gun against the man's temple. Wilson, naked except for a pair of red bikini underpants, blinked in the harsh light.

"Don't blink any harder, Tremaine," Glitsky said, "this thing might go off. You're under arrest."

Glitsky's partner had his cuffs out, was flipping Wilson over, snapping them in place. Glitsky went to the doorway and turned the light on and off, the signal that everything was all right. He heard the cops from outside come to the door. He went out to the front room, where the woman sat on the floor in the corner, holding her son. He lowered himself onto the green vinyl couch, letting his adrenaline subside.

The domicile looked the same as all the others—no rug, no pictures on the walls, stains here and there, a lingering odor of grease, musk, marijuana. Holes in the drywall.

Tremaine Wilson, untied shoes and no socks, pants and shirt thrown on, was led out. At least it had been an easy arrest. Small favors.

Now, nine o'clock, Tremaine booked, Glitsky was at the Marina and he was cold. July 1, and cold again. The past few days of warmth were already a dim memory. He thought maybe he ought to start keeping a log of certain dates, maybe the first of every month. He could see it, year after year, a microcosm of San Francisco's cute little boutique microclimate: January 1—cold. February 1—cold. March, April, May

—cold and windy. June and July—foggy and guess what. August 1—chilly, possibility of fog. September and October—nice, not warm, but not cold. November, December—see January, etc.

José was out doing something with one of the lunatics who was taking a yacht out this morning onto the choppy Bay. Glitsky stood over a portable electric heater behind the counter, wondering what he was supposed to be doing here.

When he'd gotten back to his desk from booking, there had been a message to call Pullios. He found out she was taking the Nash murder to the grand jury, top secret, and he should clear his calendar because he—Glitsky—was going to appear tomorrow as a witness before the grand jury and explain that he arrested May Shinn because he was sure she was trying to flee the jurisdiction to avoid her inevitable trial for murder. And by the way, did he think he could take another shot at a few witnesses before tomorrow and see if he could dig up any more evidence?

Sure, he'd told her, no problem. Always here to help. Except, what witnesses? The case was pretty much characterized by lack of witnesses. The only true interrogation he'd written up was the night guard at the Marina, Tom Waddell, and that, he thought, hadn't provided squat in the way of convictable testimony.

But you kept at this long enough, you got a feeling about these things. Some cases were light on eyewitness testimony. Didn't mean they weren't any good. Prosecutors were always wanting a little more, a look under one more rock for that fabled smoking gun. Pullios had asked him how he really felt about the case against Shinn, and he told her he thought it was tight as a frog's ass—watertight, but not airtight.

"Airtight would be better," she said.

So here he was. And here was José, the morning guard, back from the pontoons, going straight to the coffee machine. Normally tea was Glitsky's drink, but on less than four hours' sleep he thought a little Java wouldn't hurt him.

This was going to be another formal interview, another report, and he got José comfortable, sitting at his desk while he loaded a fresh tape into his recorder.

"Three, two, one," he said. He stopped, smiled, sipped at his coffee, and listened to it play back. "Okay . . ."

This is Inspector Abraham Glitsky, star number 1144. I am currently at the office of the Golden Gate Marina, 3567 Fort Point

Drive. With me is a gentleman identifying himself as José Ochorio, Hispanic male, 2/24/67. This interview is pursuant to an investigation of case number 921065882. Today's date is July 1, 1992, Wednesday, at 9:20 A.M.

Q: You have said that when you arrived at work a week ago Saturday, June 20, the *Eloise* had already gone out.

A: *Sí.*

Q: Had it been out the day before?

A: No. When I leave the day before, it's at its place at the end of Two out there. Where it is now.

Q: And what time did you leave the day before?

A: I don't know. Sometime normal. Two, three o'clock, but the boat was there.

Q: And it was back on Sunday morning when you came in?

A: *Sí.*

Q: Do you get any days off here?

A: Sure. It's a good place. I get Monday and Tuesday, but we can switch around. Long as it's covered.

Q: But no one switched on the morning in question?

A: No.

Q: All right, José.

[Pause.]

During which Glitsky drank some coffee and tried to find another line of questioning.

Q: Let's talk about Owen Nash and May Shinn. I have here a snapshot of Ms. Shinn. Do you recognize this woman?

A: Oh sure, man. She come here a lot.

Q: A lot? What's a lot, José?

A: Last three, four months, maybe twice a month, three times.

Q: So you've seen her here at the Marina, a total of, say, ten times, twelve times?

A: About that, maybe more, maybe less.

Q: Did you ever see her at the helm of the *Eloise?*

A: Well, sure. She always with Mr. Nash.

Q: I mean alone, guiding the boat in herself, like that.

[Pause.]

A: I don't know. I try to remember.

Q: Take your time.

[Pause.]

A: Yeah, she take it out under motor one time, at least to the jetty. But that's only like, you see, maybe two hundred feet.

Q: But Mr. Nash wasn't at the wheel?

A: No. I remember. He's standing out on the bowsprit, laughing real loud. That's when I look up. I remember.

Q: And she's alone. May is alone, under power?

A: *Sí.*

Q: And have you seen her since?

A: Steering the boat?

Q: No. Anytime.

A: *Sí.*

Q: When was that?

A: I don't know. Last week sometime. I remember, 'cause, you know, you guys . . .

Q: Sure, but do you remember when? What was she doing?

A: I don't know. She was out there, on the street. Walking back to her car, maybe, I don't know. I see her going away.

Q: And you're sure it was May?

A: *Sí.* It was her.

Q: Are you certain what day it was? It could be very important. [Pause.]

A: I think it was Thursday. Oh sure. It must have been. I remember, I got the note from Tom he'd locked the boat, which was Wednesday, right? So I go check it. It's still locked. Thursday, I'm sure, *sí*, Thursday.

26

"I need to see you."

Hardy felt his palms get hot. He leaned back in his chair at his desk. Without thought, he reached for his paperweight, cradled the phone in his neck, started passing the jade from hand to hand. There was no mistaking Celine's husky voice. "Ken says you don't think May did it."

"I'm sorry I gave him that impression. I do think May did it. I just don't think it's going to be easy to prove."

"What do you need?"

"What do you mean, what do I need?"

"I mean, what could make it more obvious?"

"It's can be obvious enough to me, Celine, but our job is to sell that to a jury—"

"Your job," she said flatly. "It's not our job. It's your job."

"Yes, right."

She was breathing heavily, even over the phone. She might as well have been in the room with him. It could be she was still worked up, just off the phone from Farris. There was no avoiding it, the principals —the victim's circle—tended to talk among themselves.

"What more do you need?" she repeated.

Hardy temporized. "We've got more since I talked to Ken. We've got ballistics now. May's gun did kill your father."

"Well, of course it did. We've known that all along."

He didn't know how to tell her they hadn't *known* it, they'd just assumed it. That the assumption turned out right was fine for them but it hadn't made the theory any more or less true before the ballistics report came in. "And her prints are on it. And no one else's." Silence. "Celine?"

"I need to see you. I need your help. I'm worried. I'm afraid. She's out on bail. What if she comes after me?"

"Why would she do that, Celine?"

179

"Why did she kill my father? To keep me from testifying? I don't know, but she might."

"So far as I know, Celine, we're not having you testify, at least not about that."

"But I know she was on the boat."

"How do you know that?"

"My father told me he was going out with her."

"That's not evidence."

He heard her breathing again, almost labored. "It is evidence, he *told* me."

"You father might have intended to go out on Saturday with May, but that doesn't mean he was actually out with her."

"But he *was*."

How do you argue with this? he thought. The woman is struggling with her grief, frightened, frustrated by the system's slow routine—he couldn't really expect a Descartes here.

"Celine, listen." He filled a couple of minutes with Glitsky's saga of Tremaine Wilson, how the first witness had known he was in the car, holding a gun, using the gun. But he hadn't actually seen his face. He knew it was Tremaine, he'd recognized him, ski mask and all, but there was no way to even bring that evidence to a jury because it wasn't evidence. It was assumption. It wasn't until the next witness showed up and could connect the car, the murder weapon and—undoubtedly—Tremaine, that they'd been able to make an arrest. "It's a little the same thing here, Celine."

She was unimpressed with the analogy. She didn't want an analogy. "I need to see you," she said for the third time.

She was fixating on him. He didn't need this. He didn't need any of it, common though it might be. His reaction to her was too unprofessional. Maybe on some level she knew that, was reacting to it, using it in her own desperation. "I'm here all day. My door's always open—"

"Not in your office."

"My office is where I work, Celine."

"That bar, the last time, that wasn't your office."

Hardy was starting to know how people got to be tightasses. It really was true that you gave people an inch and they took a mile—they expected a mile. You didn't give 'em the full mile and they felt betrayed.

Her voice softened, suddenly without the hint of a demand. "Dismas, please. Would you please see me?"

He sighed. He might know how people evolved into tightasses, but that didn't mean he wanted to become one himself. "Where's a good place? Where are you now?"

It was three-thirty now and she was just going to change and then work out. She would be at Hardbodies! near Broadway and Van Ness until around six. If he pushed it a little, he could tell himself it was right on his way home.

Jeff didn't have a private room, but he had the window, and the other bed was empty, so it was just as good. He was at the Kaiser Hospital near Masonic, and his window looked north, the red spires of the Golden Gate poking through the cloud barrier beyond the green swath of the Presidio. Closer in, the fog had lifted and the sun was bathing the little boxes along the avenues.

Jeff Elliot wouldn't have cared if there had been a monsoon blowing out there over a slag heap—at least he could see it.

His vision, coaxed by the Prednisone, had begun to slide back, furtive as a thief, sometime early in the morning, a dim, lighter shadow amid all the darkness.

He was afraid to believe it. This disease didn't give back. It took away, and kept what it took. First his legs. Now his sight? And besides, there really wasn't anything to see. Some shapes, but dark.

He could press his hands into his eyes and hold the pressure for a minute, and there would be little explosions of light—purple, green, white—that seemed to take place inside his brain. He didn't know if real blind people experienced that. The stimulus, though, didn't come from outside light. He was sure of that. Could it be his optic nerve was still working?

By morning there was no doubt. At least he wouldn't, thank God, be stone-blind. And all during the day, between naps, it had gotten better, until now he could see. Not perfectly, still fuzzy, but enough.

Dorothy Burgess—from Maury's office—had been in before she'd gone to work that morning just to see if he was all right, bringing flowers. Now she was coming through the door again—visitors' hours —smiling, concerned, the most lovely sight he had ever seen.

She sat down. "How are you feeling?"

He pushed himself up, half sitting now. "Much better. I can see you."

He hadn't called his parents back in Wisconsin. He didn't want to worry them. He thought he'd call them when the attack was over, when they could assess the latest damage. After he'd been admitted last night, he'd made a call to the *Chronicle,* but nobody from there had been in to visit.

He didn't know what to say to Dorothy. Before the MS, he hadn't done much dating to speak of, and since losing the use of his legs, his confidence in that area had dipped to zero. He'd concentrated on his career. But he was doing all right—he wasn't asking for anything more.

If you were crippled, you couldn't expect women to be crawling all over you, except the pity-groupies, and he didn't want any part of them. He knew he was probably the last mid-twenties virgin in San Francisco, if not the known world, and it was okay. He could live with it. At least he was alive. You had to keep your priorities straight.

Dorothy moved her chair against the bed and rested her arm down by his legs. Her hair was the color of wheat just before it was harvested. The white blouse had a scoop neck, a scalloped row of blue cornflowers that perfectly matched her eyes. Freckles on a tan bosom. He found he couldn't stop taking her in, like the air he breathed. "I'm staring."

She laughed, more sunlight. "I'd stare too if I'd been blind yesterday."

"I'm sorry," he said. He always felt apologetic about this damn disease. "I didn't mean to get anybody involved in all this. Don't feel like you have to come visit. I'm okay."

"It *is* a terrible inconvenience." Was she teasing him? "I was just saying to Maury today, 'I guess I've got to go visit that awful Jeff Elliot again. He is really making my life difficult, going blind in our office like that.' "

"I was just saying—"

"I know what you were saying. And it's silly." She patted his leg. "Are they feeding you all right here?"

He tried to remember. "I guess so. I must have had something. It doesn't matter. I'll be out tomorrow anyway. They just wanted to observe me for a day."

"Kaiser," she said. "Keep those beds empty. You never know when someone might need one."

"It's okay," he repeated. "All I need is steroids. I don't need to be in the hospital."

"You need food."

"I guess so. I never really thought about it."

"You never think about food? I think about food all the time."

His eyes traveled down over her slim body. "Where do you put it?"

"Don't worry," she said, "I put it. Now who's picking you up when you leave here? How are you getting home?"

He hadn't thought about that, either. He supposed he'd take a cab. He hoped his car was still parked in one of the handicapped stalls behind the Hall of Justice.

"Okay, it's settled then. I'm coming by tomorrow, taking you home, and cooking you a meal. After that, you've just got to stop bothering me." She stood up, leaned over and kissed him. "Don't get fresh," she said, then was gone.

Hardy reflected, not for the first time, that he was too much in touch with himself. Wouldn't it be nice to sometimes be able to truly fool yourself? Not know every motive you had down to about six levels.

He wanted to see Celine, and not in his office. That was the problem.

He had simply decided—last week, as soon as it had come up—that he was not going to do anything about it. It was too risky—for him, for Frannie, for the new life that was making him more content than he'd ever thought possible. It seemed to him that sometimes you met people who were immediately recognizable as having an almost chemical power to insinuate themselves into your life. Those people—men or women—could power your engines if you weren't yet settled down. But if you had a career and a family and a rhythm to your life, a blast like that could only destroy things. If you wanted to keep your orbit you avoided that extra juice. Simple as that.

Hardy could control himself—that wasn't it—but Celine was fire. And the best way to avoid getting burned, even if you were careful, was to avoid the fire.

"Dumb," he said, pausing a moment before pushing open the semiopaque glass doors of Hardbodies! He was greeted by twenty reflections of himself. Mirrors, mirrors, on the wall.

"Can I help you?"

The name tag said "Chris," and Chris, Hardy thought, was the Bionic Man. Muscles on his muscles, green Hardbodies! headband, yellow Hardbodies! t-shirt, black Spandex shorts. Wristbands on both wrists. Perfect shiny black Beatle-length hair. Behind the long counter he could see three girls and four guys, all from the same mold as Chris.

"I'm meeting somebody," he said.

"Sure, no problem," Chris said. "We got a pager at the desk here."

He heard her name called while he waited on a padded stool. There weren't any chairs, only stools. And little mushroom tables with magazines on them: City Sports, Triathloner, Maximum Steel, The Competitive Edge. There was music playing, heavy-beat stuff. He heard what sounded like a lot of basketballs getting dribbled on a wooden floor.

The place already seemed packed, and people were filing by him as though they were giving away money in the back room.

Suddenly, though he jogged four or five days a week, he felt old and flabby. Everybody in here was under thirty, except for the ones who were fifty and looked better than Hardy figured he had at twenty.

And Celine, who wasn't anywhere near fifty and looked better than any of the twenties, even with a good sweat up. Especially, perhaps, with a good sweat up. A blue sweatband held her hair back, a towel was draped around her neck. She wore a fluorescent blue Spandex halter top soaked dark between her breasts. The bare skin of her stomach gleamed wet and hard. The leotard bottoms rose over her hips at the sides and dipped well below her navel in the front. A Spandex bikini bottom matched her top. White Reeboks.

He was standing almost before he was aware of it. They were shaking hands, hers wet and powdery. She brushed his cheek with her lips, then wiped the slight moisture from the side of his mouth. "Sorry. Thank you for coming down."

Hardy stood, wanting to rub the spot on his cheek. Fire burns.

"I feel a little funny here," he said. "I'm afraid this isn't my natural environment, especially dressed like this."

She took him in. "You look fine."

"Is there someplace to talk?"

Celine told him there was a juice bar on the second floor. Would that be all right? Hardy followed her up a wide banistered granite staircase to the upstairs lobby, the entire space bordered by hi-tech metallic instruments of torture—exercycles, Climb-Masters, rowing machines, treadmills. Each was in use. You couldn't avoid the panting, the noise of thirty sets of whirring gears, occasionally a moan or a grunt. Beyond the machines, the glass wall to the outside showed off another of the city's famous views—Alcatraz, Angel Island, Marin County. You could see where the fog abruptly ended a mile or so inside the Golden Gate.

The juice bar was about as intimate as a railroad station, but at least the noise level was lower. The aerobic music wasn't pumped in here, although it did leak from the lobby. Celine ordered some type of a shake that the perfect specimen behind the bar poured a bunch of powders into. Hardy thought he'd stick with some bottled water; he paid $4.75 for the two drinks.

They sat at a low table in the corner of the room where the glass wall met brick. "Do you come here a lot?" Hardy asked.

"Sometimes it's like I live here. Then since Daddy . . ." She sipped her shake. "It works it off. I don't know what else to do to fill up the time."

"What did you do before?"

"What do you mean?"

"Before your father died. Sometimes the best thing you can do is go back to your routines, what you were used to."

A tanker that appeared through the fog bank on the Bay seemed to take her attention for a minute. "But I didn't really do anything routinely," she said. "I mean, I don't work or anything. I just lived. Now . . ." She let it trail off, went back to staring.

"Did you see your father every day?"

"Well, not every. When he wanted to see me, I had to be there. I mean, I know that sounds weird, but he'd get hurt."

"He'd get hurt if you didn't drop everything to see him?"

"Well, not everything. I had my own life too."

"That's what I was talking about. Getting back to your own life."

She was shaking her head. "But it's like there's no point to it now. Don't you see? It's like the center's fallen out."

"Yeah," he said, "that's how it feels, but it hasn't really. You've got your own center. You do. You just have to find it again."

But he seemed to keep losing her. Again, her eyes were out toward the evening sky. "Celine?" He brought his hand up and laid it over hers, exerting a little pressure. She came back to him. "You mind if I ask you how old you are?"

"No, I don't mind. You can ask anything you want." She met his eyes, solemn, then suddenly broke into a smile. "Thirty-nine," she said. "Almost got you, didn't I?"

Hardy nodded, smiling himself. "Almost."

"So what about thirty-nine?"

"I'm just thinking that's not too young to stop being dependent on your father."

He felt the shift in her tension just before she pulled her hand out from under his. "I wasn't dependent on my father. I loved my father."

"Of course, I'm not saying anything else. But, well, isn't thirty-nine a little old to be at his beck and call?"

"I wasn't at his beck and call."

"But he made you feel guilty if you weren't there when he wanted to see you. That's pretty classic parental control."

"It just hurt his feelings. I didn't want to hurt his feelings, that's all."

Hardy knew he was digging a hole, but thought he might get all the way through to China and see some light. "Remember when we were talking the other day, what you said about being so mad at him? Maybe that's why."

"I'm not mad at him! Ken's the same way."

Hardy leaned back, slowing down, wanting to make the point and not get in a fight over it. "Your father controlled people, Celine. Ken too. Maybe that's why he was so successful."

"My father did not control me."

She clearly didn't want to hear it. Time to back off. "Okay, okay."

"And who are you to talk? What makes you such an expert?"

Hardy held up a hand, trying to slow her down. "Whoa, I didn't say—"

"I know what you were saying. That my daddy was this control freak who was ruining my life because he loved his daughter and wanted to see her. Well, that's all it was. We loved each other. We had the best times. You didn't know him. We loved each other!"

She was starting to cry now, punctuating her speech by punching her glass into the table. Other people were looking over at the commotion.

"Celine . . ."

"Just go away. I don't need your help. Go away. Leave me alone."

Hardy leaned forward in the chair, put his hand again on the table. "Celine."

She slammed her glass down onto the table, the drink spilling out over her hands, over the glass. "Get out of here! Now! Get out of here!"

"I think she's nuts."

"She's bereaved, Diz. The girl's father dies, you don't pick that moment to point out to her he was a prick."

"I didn't say he was a prick. I was trying to give her something to help her break away, give her a little insight—"

"Insight comes in its own sweet time."

"That's beautiful, Mose. I'll remember that. Give me another hit, would you?"

Hardy was drinking Bushmills at the Shamrock. It was Wednesday, date night, and he was meeting Frannie at seven, in another half hour. There weren't more than twenty patrons in the place and only two others sat at the bar, nursing beers.

The Little Shamrock had been in existence since 1893. Moses McGuire had bought it in 1977 and pretty much left it the way it had been. The place was only fifteen feet wide, wall to wall, and about forty-five feet deep. The bar itself—mahogany—extended halfway to the back along the left side. Twelve tables, with four chairs each, filled the area in front of the bar on the linoleum floor. Over that area hung an assortment of bric-a-brac—bicycles, antique fishing rods, an upside-down sailfish and the pièce de résistance, a clock that had stopped ticking during the Great Earthquake of 1906.

The back of the place had an old wall-to-wall maroon Berber carpet and several couches, armchairs, coffee tables, a fireplace. It wasn't designed to seat the maximum amount of bodies, but to make it comfortable for what bodies there were. The bathrooms had stained glass in the doors. There were two dart boards against the side wall in the back by an old-fashioned jukebox.

The entire front of the bar was comprised of two picture windows and a set of swinging doors. Out the windows was Lincoln Boulevard. Across the street was Golden Gate Park, evergreen and eucalyptus. Three years ago, after working as a bartender there for nearly a decade, Hardy had acquired a quarter-interest in the place. It was almost as much his home as his house was.

McGuire walked down to the taps and came back with a pint of stout. "And what I am supposed to do with this? I see you come through the door, I start a Guinness. It's automatic. So now I got a Guinness poured and tonight you're drinking Irish."

"It's that element of surprise that makes me such a fascinating guy to know. Tonight I needed a real drink."

"My father told me that the secret to controlling alcohol is never to take a drink when you feel like you need one."

"Those are noble words," Hardy said. "Aphorism night has come to the Shamrock. Hit me again, though, would you?"

Moses sighed, turned and grabbed the Bushmills from the back bar and poured. "We're never heeded in our own countries, you know. It's the tragedy of genius."

"Leave the Guinness," Hardy said. "I'll drink it, too."

Moses pulled over his stool. Hardy had often said that Moses' face probably resembled the way God's would look after He got old. His brother-in-law was only a few years older than Hardy, but they had been heavy-weather years. He had long, brown hair with some gray, ponytailed in the back, an oft-broken nose. There were character lines everywhere—laugh lines, worry lines, crow's-feet. He was clean-shaven this month, although that varied. "So why'd she want to see you in the first place—Celine?"

Hardy shrugged. "Hold her hand, I don't know. She seemed to be hurting. I thought I might be able to help her out. Now I'm thinking we ought to get some protection for May Shinn."

"You don't really think she'd do anything to her, do you?"

"I don't know what she'll do. I don't think she knows what she'll do."

Moses took a sip of his own Scotch, a fixture in the bar's gutter. "She's upset, can't exactly blame her. She probably won't do anything," he said.

"It's the 'probably' that worries me." He took his dart case out of his jacket pocket and started fitting his hand-tooled flights into the shafts. "I think I'll go shoot a few bull's-eyes," he said. "Do something I'm good at."

David Freeman picked up his telephone. It was after work hours, but he was still at his desk, back after dinner to the place he loved best. He didn't have any particular work to do, so he was doing some light reading—catching up on recent California appellate court decisions for fun.

"Mr. Freeman, this is Nick Strauss. I got your card from a neighbor of mine, Mrs. Streletski. How can I help you?"

"Mr. Strauss, it's good of you to call. As Mrs. Streletski may have mentioned, I'm working for a client who needs to establish what she was doing during the daytime on Saturday, June twentieth. The woman in question happens to live directly across the street from you on the same level—that other turreted apartment?"

"Sure, I know it, but I can't say I'd know any particular person who lives there."

"She's an Oriental woman. Quite attractive."

"I'd like to meet her. I could use a little attractive in my life." A little manly chuckle, then Strauss was quiet a moment. "Sorry. June twentieth, you say?"

"That's the date. I know it's a while ago now."

"No, it's not that. Normally I probably wouldn't remember. It's just that's the day I picked up my kids. They'd been traveling in Europe with their mother—we're divorced—and I picked them up at the crack of dawn at the airport."

"And they didn't mention anything, seeing anything?"

"I don't know how they could. They'd slept on the plane and were ready to go, so we just stopped in to have a bite and drop their luggage. Then we took off, exploring the city. It was a great day really, they're good kids."

"I'm sure. But you saw nothing?"

"No, sorry. What did she do, this attractive Oriental woman?"

"She's being charged with killing someone, although the case is weak. If anyone saw her at home during that day, we can make a case that there is no case."

"I'll talk to the boys, double-check, but I really doubt it. Who'd she kill, by the way?"

Freeman kept himself in check. This was the natural question. "She didn't kill anyone, Mr. Strauss."

"Oh yeah, that's right. Sorry."

"It's all right. Thanks for the call."

"Sure."

Freeman sat back with his hands crossed behind his head. So the alibi wouldn't hold up. It was no great surprise.

27

The grand jury convened at ten A.M., Thursday, July 2, 1992. It was Hardy's first appearance there. He wore a brand-new dark suit with nearly-invisible maroon pinstripes, a maroon silk tie, black shoes. When Pullios saw him outside the grand-jury room door, she whistled, looked him up and down. "You'll do."

Hardy thought she didn't look so bad herself in a tailored red suit of conservative cut. Instead of a briefcase, she carried a black sling purse.

"No notes?"

She tapped her temple. "Right here."

At her knock, the door was opened by a uniformed policeman. This was light years from the bustling informality of one of the Municipal or Superior Court courtrooms.

The grand jury was a deck so heavily stacked in favor of the prosecution that Hardy thought a case could be made against its constitutionality. The fact that no one had brought such an appeal was probably a reflection of the reality that nobody representing the accused was allowed in the room. He thought the prosecution winning on an indictment before the grand jury was kind of like a Buick winning the Buick Economy Run.

Hardy sat next to Pullios at the prosecution desk and studied the faces of the twenty jurors arranged in three ascending rows behind long tables.

He couldn't remember ever having seen such a balanced jury of twelve. These twenty were comprised of ten men and ten women. Three of them—two women and a man—were probably over sixty. Four more—two and two—were, he guessed, under twenty-five. There were six blacks, two Orientals, he thought two Hispanics. Most were decently dressed—sports coats and a few ties for the men, dresses or skirts for the women. But one of the white guys looked like a biker—

190

short sleeves, tattoos on his forearms, long unkempt hair. One woman was knitting. Three people were reading paperbacks and one of the young women appeared to be reading a comic book.

The room wasn't large. It smelled like coffee. At what would have been the defense table—if there had been one—was a large box full of donuts and sweet rolls that about half the jurors had dipped into.

The grand jury wasn't chosen like a regular jury—if a trial jury was a time commitment and minor inconvenience for the average taxpayer, selection to the grand jury was more like a vocation. You sat one day a week for six months, essentially cloistered, and the only kinds of crimes you discussed were felonies. And if you mentioned *anything* about the proceedings outside of this room, you were committing a felony yourself. There were stories—impossible to verify—that D.A.'s had come in and said, "Off the record, I don't believe our eyewitness either. We've got no credible evidence at this time. But I've been doing homicides now for twenty years and I tell you unequivocally that John Doe, on the afternoon of whatever it is, did kill four Jane Does. Now we've got to get this guy off the street before he kills someone else. And he will, ladies and gentlemen, he will. You can count on it. I will stake my reputation and career upon a conviction, but we've got to get this man indicted and behind bars and we've got to do it now." Of course they were only stories. Whatever, the grand jury was a cornerstone of the criminal system, and it behooved prosecutors to take it seriously, which Elizabeth did, in spite of her "ham sandwich" rhetoric. She stood up, greeted the judge and the jurors pleasantly and began her attack.

"Ladies and gentleman of the jury, this morning the people of the State of California present the most serious charge in the matter of the capital murder of Owen Nash. You may have read in the newspapers something about this case, and specifically you may be aware that the defendant, May Shintaka, has already been scheduled for a preliminary hearing in Municipal Court in this jurisdiction. However, the delay proposed by the Municipal Court is, in the opinion of the district attorney, terribly excessive. No doubt many of you are aware of the legal axiom that justice delayed is justice denied. It is the contention of the people in this instance that the proposed delay would in fact constitute a denial of justice for this most heinous crime—the crime of cold-blooded, premeditated murder for financial gain, a crime that calls for the death penalty in the State of California."

Pullios paused and walked stone-faced back toward Hardy, to where he sat at the table. She picked up a glass of water, took a small sip. Her eyes were bright—she was flying. Immediately she was back to business. Hardy couldn't help but admire the show.

"So in a sense," she said, "the indictment the people seek today is simply an administrative strategem to move the trial for this crime to Superior Court, where it can be heard in a timely fashion. But in a greater sense, an indictment before this body will reinforce the state's contention that, based on real and true evidence, there is indeed just cause for issuance of a warrant for the arrest May Shintaka and a compelling need for a fair and speedy trial in pursuance of the interests of the people of this state."

Hardy thought it was getting a little thick, but he also realized that Elizabeth Pullios, looking like she did and fired up as she was, could probably read the telephone book to these people and keep their attention. She went on to describe the witnesses she would call: Glitsky, Strout, the cab driver, the ballistics expert, the two guards from the Marina, a handwriting analyst. Then she got to Celine Nash. Hardy remembered the other giant lapse in evidentiary rules before the grand jury—hearsay was technically inadmissible, but there was no judge or defense lawyer there to keep it out.

How could Celine not have mentioned to him yesterday that she was testifying today? Well, they hadn't had much time to get to it before she went off on him. It could have been that the initial reason she called him was nerves over this appearance today, testifying against Shinn. She'd even said something about it.

Hardy found himself unhappy in a hurry, wishing he'd reviewed the witness list before they'd come down here—he still did have a lot to learn. Pullios had been doing her homework while Hardy pursued his own agenda. They were going to nail May Shinn six ways from Sunday.

Then, at lunch, Pullios told him she wanted him to take Celine Nash.

"No way, Elizabeth. She's mad at me." He explained and she thought it over for a moment, then overruled him. "No, you're better. Just get her confidence back."

"You've already got her confidence."

"No, I don't. I've never met her personally, but Sergeant Glitsky tells me she's stunning."

"I guess."

Pullios shook her head. "Then it's not a good match. The jurors will see something between us. It might even be there."

"What's to see? What are they looking for?"

"This will maybe sound arrogant, but it's true that people don't identify with two attractive women on the same side. Right now I've got the jury on my side—our side. If Celine comes in, human nature is going to tell the jurors that we—she and I—are natural enemies. Somebody's credibility is going to suffer. Whoever's, it's bad for our side. If you question her there's no conflict. It's only natural she'd want to cooperate, especially looking all spiffy like you do today."

Hardy shrugged.

Pullios put her straw in her mouth and sucked up some iced tea. "You'd better believe those jurors are a fairly good representation of the average man, or average woman. I couldn't care less if I sound enlightened or liberated or anything else. I'm playing to win, and I'm telling you that if I depose Celine Nash it's a weak move. We can probably afford a weak move, okay, but it's a bad tactic. You don't give anything away. Even to grand juries. You still take your best chance every time. And you're our best chance with Celine."

She whispered she was sorry—more mouthed it—as soon as she sat down. She was elegant in cool blue. She'd put on extra eyeshadow, and Hardy wondered if she'd slept last night. Or cried.

It wasn't supposed to be lengthy. All he was supposed to do was nail down what Owen had said to her about going out with May on the day he was killed.

It had been the Tuesday before—the sixteenth, in the morning. She had called him at his office. Celine had intended to go away the upcoming weekend and wanted to make sure her father hadn't made plans that included her.

"Don't you think thirty-nine's a little old to be at his beck and call?"

"I wasn't at his beck and call. My father didn't control me!"

He put that out of his mind. That was last night. This was today. He had a limited role and he'd better keep to it. "And Ms. Nash, tell us what your father said regarding the day in question, June twentieth."

She kept trying to catch his eye, give him a look that promised forgiveness, but he kept himself focused on the judge, on individual jurors. He would look at her as she answered questions.

"He said he was planning on going over to the Farralons on Saturday with his girlfriend, with May."

"Had he told you of such plans in the past?"

"Yes, all the time."

"And in your experience, did your father tend to follow through on these types of things?"

This was shooting fish in a barrel. He kept expecting to hear somebody object to the nature and thrust of his questions, but since there was neither a defense attorney nor a judge in the room he could ask what he liked.

"Always. If Daddy said he was going to do something he *did* it."

"All right, but just for the sake of argument, what if, for example, Ms. Shinn had gotten sick Saturday morning?"

"Daddy would have done something else. He wouldn't have wasted a day. He wouldn't have done that."

"He wouldn't have gone out alone, perhaps, since he'd already made those plans?"

Celine gave it a moment, chewing on her thumbnail. "No, I don't think so. He wasn't a solitary man. Besides, we know he didn't go out alone, don't we?"

"You're right, Ms. Nash, we do. Indeed we do."

It took until three-thirty, but they got the indictment.

There was no immediate flurry of activity. The bail was still in effect. There would be no immediate arrest of May Shinn, but the fur would really begin to fly when David Freeman got the news, which would be very soon.

Meanwhile, Hardy packed his briefcase, hoping that Celine Nash had decided not to wait around until the jury adjourned.

Celine fell in beside him just outside the door.

"I am sorry," she said. She linked an arm through his and he felt the heat of her body where they came together.

"It's okay, people get upset. It happens."

"I don't know what happened. I didn't mean for anything like that to happen."

"It's all right, forget it. We'll just move ahead on the trial. It ought to go pretty quickly now."

He had stopped walking, waiting by the elevators. She was standing too close and his heart was beating enough that he felt it. "What do you want me to do, Celine?"

"I just don't want you to be mad at me."

"I'm not mad at you. I was out of line, it wasn't exactly professional."

"I don't care about professional."

"That's our relationship," he said, clearly as he could say it. Then, "It doesn't matter."

"It does, it does matter. Do you know what it is to be completely alone?"

Not a professional question.

The elevators opened, jammed as usual. Hardy got in, Celine cramming next to him, thigh to thigh, arm in his. He smelled the powder she used, the same powder she'd left on him as she'd greeted him with a kiss at Hardbodies! last night—that he'd scrubbed off in the Shamrock before Frannie had come in for date night. He didn't press the button for his floor and they rode it all the way down to the street level in silence, everyone else chattering away.

They went outside the front doors, turned east on Bryant, away from the bright sun. A cool wind was up off the Bay. They went two blocks before Hardy said he did know what it was to be alone.

Celine took that with no response. Then: "You must think I'm crazy."

He grinned tightly. "People do crazy things. It doesn't necessarily mean they're crazy."

"It doesn't?"

Hardy walked a couple more steps. "I don't know, maybe it does."

It was a little Cuban coffee shop, unnamed, dark as a cave. The table was of finished plywood—there were seven such tables, four with people at them. A Spanish television station whispered from the back corner. The good smell had stopped their walk and brought them inside. They were drinking café con leche made with heated Carnation evaporated milk, sweet.

If you walked in and saw them sitting across from one another, aside from knowing they didn't belong here in their Anglo clothes and complexions, you would assume many true things about them. Though they didn't know each other very well, there was a powerful attraction between them. They had to control it by putting the table between them. They weren't lovers; if they were they'd have moved together. Well, maybe they were in the middle of a fight, but they weren't acting angry. No, the first call was right. They were getting to something.

The man was leaning forward, hands clenched around the wide, deep coffee cup. He was more than leaning, in fact, more like hunched over, rapt, mesmerized?

She seemed more controlled, but there were giveaways, invitations. She sat sideways to him, very well put together. Her dark suit was muted but a lot of her excellent legs showed, tightly crossed and curled back under her chair. She held her cup lightly in one hand— her other extended out, subtle enough, toward him, there if he wanted it, if he dared take it.

She was doing most of the talking. You would think this might be the day they would do it. From here they'd go to one of their places, or maybe a motel. You could feel it, even halfway across the room.

28

After Dorothy had gone, Jeff Elliot called Parker Whitelaw at the *Chronicle* and told him his sight had returned—he'd be back at work the next day.

This wasn't completely true, but Parker wouldn't have to know it. Most people were ignorant about how MS worked. They could see the results—the weakened limbs, weight loss, lack of coordination—but they had no clue about the way the disease progressed. Jeff thought this was just as well. It was actually to his advantage if Parker thought that whatever had laid him up for a day had now completely passed and he could go back to being the ace reporter he'd been before.

In reality, his sight was still very poor. Yesterday, which had begun in total blackness, had heartened him as some sight, then quite a bit, had returned. But, testing it, he found the left eye still all but worthless, the brown smudge blotting all but its extreme periphery. The right eye was a little better—the range of vision was wider, though all of it was fuzzy. But he thought that he could get by. He didn't particularly think it would be wise to try and drive, but he could fake the rest.

The doctor had told him that since there had been some almost immediate remission in the total blindness, there was a small chance he could expect gradual improvement with continual steroid treatment. He might even regain normal sight. Maybe.

This morning he called Maury Carter's office and told Dorothy he really had to go in to work, but he would like to see her tonight as they'd planned.

"Well, how are you getting to work?"

"I'll just take a cab."

She wouldn't hear of him taking a cab. She told him she could take some time off—"Maury feels terrible about this, too. He's a nice man underneath"—and be down there by lunchtime. Would he please wait for her?

"You don't have to do this."

"Of course, I don't. Who said I did?"

They let him take a shower and shave. He still had his clothes from two days before, but they were okay, better by far than the gown. Dorothy was there by twelve-thirty and pushed him in a wheelchair out to her car. The morning fog out in the Avenues hadn't burned off, and the daylight glared. She put his crutches in the trunk and he got himself settled on the passenger side in the front seat. His legs weren't completely dead yet.

They had sandwiches at Tommy's Joynt and he got to the office close to four. She left him at the *Chronicle*'s front door and said she'd be back at six, he'd better be there. She'd kissed him again.

He had a message from an Elizabeth Pullios at the district attorney's office and the memo line said it was regarding Owen Nash. It brought everything back—the bail question, Hardy and Glitsky, Freeman's strategy. He hoped he hadn't missed much in his day away. He returned the call to Pullios and scanned the last two days' newspapers, turning up his desk light, squinting at the blurry print. After the little blurb on page nine that May had made bail, the story disappeared.

Of course they'd dropped it. Nothing had happened. The court's decision to schedule the prelim at the end of the summer had taken the wind out of those sails. It was frustrating. Unless he found something about the Freeman/Shinn connection he was going to have to get himself another story, another scoop.

He loved being on a hot story. It changed his whole view of the job, the world. People cared about him, asked his opinion, included him in their jokes. He wasn't just that crippled guy anymore.

The phone rang and it was Pullios—she didn't know if he'd heard from Hardy or anyone else, but the grand jury had just indicted May Shinn. The case was going to Superior Court. She just thought he'd like to know.

The grand-jury story was written and submitted. Parker had come by, impressed by the line on the grand jury. Parker said it was good to see a reporter hustling, working his connections. It might be old-fashioned reporting, but it got the best results. By the way, how were the eyes?

Fine. The eyes were fine.

Dorothy was at the curb at six sharp, the door opened and waiting for him. He saw flowers in the backseat, a brown grocery bag with a loaf of french bread sticking out the top.

He lived in a first-floor studio apartment on Gough Street, where it leveled off at the top of one of San Francisco's famous hills.

"My, isn't this cheery," she said. The room featured sconced lighting, hardwood floors and a mattress on the floor in one corner. In the other corner there was a stack of old San Francisco *Chronicles* about three feet high. The white walls were bare except for one black-and-white poster of Albert Einstein, daily reminding Jeff that great spirits have always encountered violent opposition from mediocre minds. The rest of the furniture consisted of a stool pushed under the overhang of the bar that separated the cooking area from the rest of the room.

Dorothy picked up the mail that was lying on the floor and put it on the bar along with her bag of groceries. She held up the flowers. "Any old vase will do," she said. "Don't break out the Steuben."

He loved the way she talked. Not mean, but squeezing out the drop of humor in situations. Like his apartment. He hadn't wanted to come here, but she'd teased him into it. "Didn't get time to call your girlfriend, huh? Afraid she'll be mad?"

"There's no girlfriend, Dorothy."

"We'll see about that."

Now here they were. She cut the top off a milk carton and poured out the four ounces of sour milk that was left in it—"It's so neat you make your own yogurt"—and arranged the flowers, a mixed bouquet of daisies, California poppies and daffodils, sitting them at the end of the bar.

She made him chicken breasts with onions and peppers and mushrooms and some kind of wine sauce that they poured over rice. They ate on the floor, their places laid on a blanket from the bed, folded over. When they'd finished, Dorothy pulled herself up and leaned against the wall. She patted her lap.

"Why don't you put your head here?"

His eyes hurt and he couldn't see her clearly. The only light they'd eaten by was cast by the tiny bulb over the stove. He put his head down on her thigh and felt her fingers smoothing his hair.

"Can I ask you something?" he asked.

"I'm sorry. I'm afraid not." Then her finger ran along his cheek.

She flicked his chin lightly. "You're a bit of a bozo. Anybody ever tell you that?"

"No. People don't kid with me."

"People are missing out," she said. "What did you want to ask me?"

There was no avoiding it. He had to know. "Why are you doing this? Being nice to me?"

"Oh, I get four units for it. It's a class project." Now she took his cheek and gave him a hard squeeze. "Haven't you ever had any girl like you?"

"Sure. Well, not since . . ."

"What? Your legs?"

He shrugged. "You know. The whole thing."

"I don't know. What whole thing? Your personality get deformed or something?"

"It's just a lot to ask somebody to deal with."

"It seems like it might just be a good crutch, no pun intended. I mean, nobody's perfect. You get involved with somebody, you're going to have to deal with their imperfections."

"Yeah, but romance doesn't exactly bloom when you see them right out front."

"Sometimes it does," she said. "Less gets hidden. It might even be better. It's definitely better than being fooled and finding out later."

"I don't see too many of yours. Imperfections, I mean."

"Well, that's just a fluke. It so happens I am the one person who doesn't have imperfections." Her fingers were back in his hair, pulling it. "Except, I warn you now, I am pretty Type-A. I like a clean house. If you squeeze the toothpaste in the middle I go insane, I need to fill up ice trays immediately. Nothing makes me madder than a half-empty ice tray. Also I'm impatient and outspoken although I have to say I'm not really bitchy. But I'm very organized, too organized."

"Those are not exactly major imperfections."

"I'm also pushy. And pretty selfish. I think of myself first a lot, what I want."

"I haven't seen any sign of that. Not with me, at least."

"Yes you have." She dipped her finger into her wineglass and traced his lips with it. "If you think about it. For example, I am in a highly selfish mode right now."

Hardy was back where it started, at the shark tank at the Steinhart Aquarium.

He sat on the gurney, listening to the vague bubblings and vibrations emanating from the walls around him. Although he knew the water in it wasn't even remotely warm, a thin veil of steam rose from the circular pool in the center of the room. The walls were shiny with distillation, the light dim and somehow green-tinged. He'd let himself in with his own key.

After dinner Frannie had been tired, and he'd felt flabby and soft, so he changed into some sweats and told her he was going for a run. Why didn't she turn in early?

Now it was close to nine-thirty. He hadn't done much running, more a forced walk to no destination. In any event, it had taken him here. He'd worked up a light sweat and he sat, his elbows on his knees, his hands intertwined in front of him.

"Do you know what it is to be completely alone?"

He certainly did. He was there now.

His family was at home. Some of his friends, undoubtedly, were a quarter mile away at the Shamrock. He could call Glitsky, or Pico, go out and drink a few brewskis, shoot some darts. But he knew somehow that none of that would make a difference. He was completely alone, knocked out of his orbit, trying to feel the pull of the other bodies, the old familiar gravity. He couldn't get it, couldn't get to it.

The thing to do, he thought, was to go into Drysdale's office tomorrow morning and resign. Just stop. Shut down the rockets. Go back and ask Moses for your old shift at the Shamrock and go back to that earlier life.

He didn't need the money. He could walk out on the law right now and the world would keep right on turning, May Shinn would still go to trial, Pullios would get another notch in whatever it was she notched.

Stiffly, he pushed himself up off the gurney and walked up to the side of the pool, a concrete ring four feet deep. He had his hands in the front pockets of his sweatshirt, felt his keys on the right side.

There was only one other person in his orbit right now. And she, he believed, was completely alone, too. Yesterday, he'd thought maybe she was crazy. Today he saw it differently. Celine was barely holding herself together. Her father had been her life. Whether or not you liked or admired Owen Nash, whether their relationship was good or bad—control or no control, she was left with a gaping hole. If she'd broken down around Hardy, it had been because she was strung too tightly, holding it all back. That's why the long workouts—to loosen the coil.

But it wasn't working. Not yet, anyway. She was trying, and she'd get there. She knew what she needed—she needed some surcease from the emptiness, the loneliness, the pain of the fresh wound. She *was* trying, she just needed time.

And one other thing, face it, she needed him. For whatever reason, he was the lifeline. Like she'd said, she didn't care about their professional relationship. He was connected to her . . .

Which was exactly why he should quit. This wasn't his job. It wasn't his concern. It couldn't be in his life.

But she was. He tried to tell himself it was the level he had to control. He could not allow himself to do anything to threaten Frannie; she too depended on him. And so did Rebecca and the unborn child. If he had any view of himself at all, it was, he hoped, as a man of some honor, and he'd given Frannie his absolute vow. And he loved Frannie. His life satisfied him. His own endless emptiness seemed to have vanished over the last year, thanks to her. She was his rock and he knew he had to get back to her orbit. His own salvation, he knew, lay there, with her.

But he also knew he wasn't going to quit—either the law or the case—and he knew why. He hoped—normally he didn't pray but he prayed—he wasn't going to do anything about the attraction, the connection. He told himself again that he could keep the level under control.

But if Celine had to see him again, he would see her. He would have to see her.

29

"Beware of what you wish for—you just might get it." Judge Leo Chomorro had heard it a thousand times from his father. It had always struck him as misguided advice. The way you got things was to wish for them, focus on them. It had gotten him everything he had today—a judgeship by forty, a beautiful wife, three intelligent children, a home in St. Francis Wood.

But lately he was beginning to think that his father's advice might have had something to it after all. He had wished and wished that someday he could get out from under the burden of being a good administrator, which was itself something to be proud of. Leo had always been an organizer, a team player, intelligent enough to be a leader, but a subscriber to the theory that a good leader must first know how to be a good follower.

And his talents had gotten him out of Modesto and his father's auto shop. He always thought it was his study habits more than his brains that had pulled him through San Jose State and then gotten him into Hastings Law School in San Francisco.

At Hastings he hadn't made Law Review, hadn't been in the top ten percent, hadn't been rushed by the big firms. But he'd gotten through, passed the bar on the second try, got a job as a clerk for the State Attorney General.

He worked hard. No one could say he wasn't a loyal and diligent staffer, and when the Attorney General finally made it to the State House, Leo was a top aide on budgetary issues. He was the organization man, efficient and objective. Guys weren't doing their jobs, fire them. They got families, tough—they should have worked harder, seen the ax coming.

The numbers of the budget game appealed to him. It was pretty simple. You had so much money to spend, first you looked around at who had been good to you, then you factored in services you needed and you cut where you had to—or wanted to—make a point, where the system wasn't working efficiently. And then you made the numbers balance. For an organized guy like Leo, it was a cakewalk.

For example, during some budget committee meetings Leo had made a big stink about liberal judges, especially in San Francisco, getting paid a lot to do nothing—letting off people caught in stings, like that. Clip, clip. Cut back on salary adjustments, do away with judicial raises.

Of course, to survive, yourself, you didn't make too many friends. You really couldn't afford to. You had allies instead—the Attorney General-turned-Governor, for example, was a damn good one. Leo's wife also, Gina. Brilliant, much smarter than he was—and attractive. A Santa Barbara Republican, she'd been a staffer, too, but after they'd had Leo Jr., all thought of politics left her head. Now she was an ally. She was loyal and did her jobs. That was life, right?

And then, according to plan, Leo got what he'd wished for. On his way out of office, his mentor the Governor had rewarded him for his sixteen years of loyal service by appointing him to a judgeship in San Francisco. Except that now that he was here, he found the job had all the glamor of a stockyard, except the cattle were human.

Before Leo Chomorro had arrived eighteen months before, Calendar judges in the City and County of San Francisco were rotated every six months. The work was so dull that no one could be expected to keep at it longer than that. But Leo's budgetary philosophy when he'd been with the governor, combined with his lack of belief in personal friendships, had created for himself a cloud of political resentment, and San Francisco's judges wasted no time putting him in his place— which was Calendar, where he had remained and remained.

It was ironic. Leo was a judge who believed there was justice in the world. Or should be. He had believed that if you worked hard and did a good job, people came to value you. You got promoted. You moved up.

Ha.

Today, Tuesday, July 7, Leo Chomorro sat sweating under his robes in Department 22, overseeing work he wouldn't have assigned to his clerk. The Calendar was a necessary evil in all larger jurisdictions— there had to be some mechanism to decide which suspects went to what courtroom, whether or not cases were ready for trial, all of the administrative work that went along with keeping eight courtrooms and their staffs reasonably efficient so the criminal justice system could keep grinding along.

It was the kind of work for which Leo was suited by experience and temperament. He thought he'd never get out of it, and it was driving him mad.

"Okay, Trial Calendar line six, what have we got here?"

This morning was never going to end. The bailiff brought in Line Six—all the cases were given line numbers off the huge computer printout that had to be processed every Monday. Except Monday had been a holiday. So the list was longer.

He forced himself to look up. Line Six was a guy about Leo's age and, like Leo, an Hispanic, although Leo couldn't have cared less about his race. Line Six shuffled behind the bailiff to the podium in front of the bench. Mr. Zapata was represented by the public defender, Ms. Rogan. Chomorro looked down at the list for the next available judge. Fowler, Department 27. He intoned the name and department.

"Excuse me, Your Honor." Leo looked up. Any interruption, any change in the deadly routine was welcome. It was the summer clerk who'd been quietly monitoring proceedings at the D.A.'s table all morning. "May I approach the bench?"

The boy reminded Leo of himself when he'd been a student. Dark, serious, intent, fighting down his nerves, he whispered. "Mr. Drysdale would like to ask you to reconsider your assignment of Mr. Zapata to a different department."

Leo Chomorro cast his eyes around the courtroom. He and Art Drysdale went over the Calendar on disposition of cases every Friday night, and he'd mentioned nothing about Zapata at that time. Well, maybe something new had come up, but Art wasn't in the courtroom.

"Where is Mr. Drysdale?"

"He's in his office, Your Honor. He asked if you'd grant a recess."

"When did he do that if he's not here?"

"That's all he's asked me to say, Your Honor, if you could grant a recess and call him."

Leo frowned. He wanted to keep things moving but felt empathy for the kid, and Drysdale made up the Calendar with him every week. In a world full of no friends, Art was as close to one as he had. He looked up at the defendant.

"Mr. Zapata, sit down. We'll take a ten-minute recess."

* * *

"It's pretty unusual, Art. It's circumvention."

"I know it is." Drysdale wasn't going to sugarcoat anything. This was Locke's call, and he was delivering a message, that was all. He was sitting back, comfortable in the leather chair in front of Chomorro's desk. "We don't want Zapata going to Fowler's department. He threw out the last one."

"I know. I read about that. Zapata's another sting case?"

Art nodded. "I just plain missed him on Friday or I would have mentioned it then."

Chomorro was moving things on his desk. "I've already assigned it, Art. Rogan might make a stink." He'd called out Department 27—Fowler's courtroom. If the defense attorney he'd appointed was on top of things, she'd know Fowler's position on these kinds of cases. From Rogan's perspective, Fowler was a winner for her client—he'd throw out the case. Any other judge probably would not.

Art leaned forward. "We're ready to lose one like that. What we don't want is Fowler getting any more of these—start another landslide and screw up this program."

Chomorro shuffled more paper. His life was shuffling paper. He didn't believe he could do what Art was suggesting. It was at the very least close to unethical. The D.A. or the defendant could challenge one judge, on any case. A judge could be recused from a case because of conflicts of interest, because he or she knew the defendant, for no reason at all, but such a public challenge always involved a political fight that both sides lost. Usually such problems were settled privately in the chambers of the Master Calendar department—certain cases just never happened to be assigned to certain judges. But here, Mr. Zapata's case had been publicly assigned for trial. "I don't think I can do it, Art."

Drysdale wasn't surprised. He nodded, then leaned forward, forearms on knees, and settled in. "Leo, Your Honor, how long have you been on Calendar here?"

It took Chomorro a minute, a subtle shift in posture, like Art's own. His mouth creased up. "Year and a half, maybe."

"Any talk of you getting off?"

Chomorro shrugged. "Somebody's got to retire soon, die. I'm the low man."

Art leaned back. "The job used to rotate, Leo. You know that?"

Again, a tight smile. "I'd heard that rumor."

"But if somebody carries a grudge around, maybe a little superior attitude, doesn't make any friends, do any favors . . ." Art held up a hand. "I'm not talking illegal, I'm talking little things, amenities. Things could change, that's all I'm saying. Chris Locke is pals with some of your colleagues, so is Rigby. They both like this program, the one that got Zapata. And no one—not even Fowler—is denying these guys are stealing. They've still got to be found guilty by a jury. They get a fair trial. We're not circumventing justice here, maybe just fine-tuning the bureaucracy."

Chomorro did not for a moment buy Drysdale's argument that they weren't circumventing justice. Of course they were. But Chomorro was not a newcomer to politics, deals. He knew a deal when he heard one, and—assuming you were going to play—it wasn't smart to leave things up in the air. "Labor Day," he said. "I'm off Calendar by Labor Day."

Art Drysdale stood up, reached his hand over the desk. "Done," he said.

"Line Six." Mr. Zapata was back up at the podium. "I'm sorry, there was a scheduling conflict, my mistake. The trial will be in Department," he looked down again, making sure, "Twenty-four, Judge Thomasino."

Leo watched Line Six being led out in his yellow jumpsuit. Time was standing still. It wasn't yet noon and he'd just had a recess. His blood was rushing. Well, it was done. It was possible that Ms. Rogan would never understand the significance of the change of department. Art would make sure he would be forewarned on any other Zapatas, and the whole thing would never have to come up again. Still . . .

He shook himself, chilled in the hot room.

"On the arraignment calendar, line one thirty-seven," the clerk intoned. "Penal code section 187, murder."

Suddenly the chill was gone. Something about murder cases got your attention, even when you were already familiar with them. This was the one he and Elizabeth Pullios had discussed after the indictment on Thursday—Owen Nash. They were dragging their feet over in Muni and the D.A. wasn't going to stand for it. On Friday, Art Drysdale told Chomorro it would hit this morning, and they were going to move ahead if not with haste then with dispatch. Send a little message to the junior circuit.

Line 137, May Shintaka, had surrendered on the grand-jury indictment and bailed again. She was in the gallery. Chomorro had noticed her earlier this morning, the one flower in a field of weeds. This was Line 137? He raised his eyebrows, then looked back down. Now she stood, unbowed, at the podium. Next to her was David Freeman, about the best defense attorney in the city. The defendant and her rumpled attorney were a study in contrasts. Leo theorized that Freeman's sloppy dress was a conscious ploy to appeal to juries as a common man, one of them, regular folks.

But regular folks didn't make half a million or so a year.

"Mr. Freeman," he said, "how are you doing today?"

Freeman nodded. "Fine, thank you, Your Honor."

During his recess with Art, Elizabeth Pullios had come into the courtroom and sat at the prosecution table with her second chair, one of the new men. He nodded to them.

"Is the prosecution ready to proceed?"

"I object, Your Honor." Freeman, wasting no time.

"We are, Your Honor." Simultaneously, from Pullios.

"Grounds?"

Freeman's voice rose. "As Your Honor knows, Municipal Court continued proceedings on this matter until after Labor Day."

"Well, you're in Superior Court now, Mr. Freeman. What's the point?"

"There is no evidence to support—" Freeman stopped, started again. "The preliminary hearing would have revealed insufficient evidence to proceed to trial, Your Honor."

"Evidently the grand jury doesn't agree with you. They issued an indictment."

"Your Honor." Pullios was standing. "The people—"

Chomorro brought down his gavel. "Excuse me, Ms. Pullios. I understand the people's position here. Mr. Freeman, we're not going to debate the evidence at this time. That's for a jury to decide. Perhaps a request for a shorter continuance in Municipal Court could have avoided this problem."

"Your Honor, my client should not be subjected to the expense of a trial on this charge. I'm going to move for remand back to Municipal Court."

Chomorro smiled. Freeman was pulling out the stops early. "I'm afraid that option is foreclosed, Mr. Freeman."

Defense counsel didn't seem to take a breath. "This hurry-up show trial is clearly motivated by state's counsel enjoying the publicity of this high profile—"

"Your Honor, I object!"

Chomorro nodded to Pullios. "I think I would, too."

Freeman kept right on. "—to say nothing of the blatant racial and class discrimination evidenced by—"

"Mr. Freeman! Enough. I remind you that this court operates under the grand-jury system. I will not tolerate these outbursts. The prosecution says it is ready for trial. If their evidence is weak it seems to me that should be to your advantage. All right, then."

Chomorro didn't even have to look down to see where the next trial was going. "It sounds like there will be extensive motion work in this case. I'm sending the whole matter—arraignment, motions, pretrial and trial—to Department Twenty-seven, Judge Fowler. Forthwith. You can fight it out down there." He brought his gavel down again, allowed himself a small smile. "Goodbye, Counsel. Now."

It wasn't a long walk down the hallway, so there wasn't much time for Hardy to tell Pullios about his relationship with Fowler.

"It doesn't matter," she said. "Have you discussed the case with him outside the office?"

"No, no place, in fact."

"Then I wouldn't worry about it." It was another opportunity to remind him of their respective positions, so she took it. "Besides, you're not the attorney of record here. I am. You're assisting me."

"I think if Freeman even gets a whiff of it, though, he'll move to dismiss."

"Freeman moves to dismiss if the bailiff has a runny nose. So what?"

"So I'm a little worried about it."

She stopped and faced him. "Dismas, look. He's not your father-in-law anymore, is he?"

"No."

"So essentially it boils down to the fact that you've met the judge socially. Well, I've met the judge socially and we get along like pickles and milk. I wouldn't be surprised if Freeman's met him socially. Hell, they're both in the rich men's club, they probably play poker together. Maybe they trade stock tips. It's irrelevant. Judge Fowler and you are *not* related, legally or otherwise. It's not an issue."

Pullios, Hardy thought, was good on things that weren't issues. She was good on everything. It got to you.

Pullios got to the doors of Department 27 and held one of them open for Hardy. "Age before beauty," she said.

The orbits had aligned themselves.

Friday had been a busy day, a couple of prelims, some plea bargaining, a lunch with four of the office gang, nobody even thinking about homicides.

Frannie and Hardy had made love twice over the long Fourth of July weekend. The first time, Friday night, intense and silent, then the closeness, body to body, lying there, talking until after midnight.

Saturday was the picnic with Moses, his current girlfriend Susan, all the Glitskys, and Pico with Angela and their kids. And Rebecca was healthy again, finally—her jolly gurgling wonderful little self. Baseball, beer and barbecue. America's birthday party on another miracle of a warm day.

Then Sunday morning they went out for brunch and shared the best paella in the city. Afterward, back home, Frannie telling Hardy it was okay, Rebecca might remember that her parents had laughed and wrestled a lot when she'd been a baby, but it probably wouldn't damage her psyche.

On Monday, the sixth, back on his own center again, Hardy and Frannie had spent the morning stenciling some pastel horses and dolphins onto the wall in Rebecca's room. In the afternoon he did a little work in his office, asking if Abe could get hold of May Shinn's phone records for the day Owen Nash had been killed. He realized that if she had made a call on that day, their case was in trouble, and as far as he knew, no one had checked those records. He asked Abe if they could pinpoint flurries of gas or water use, electricity, anything that might indicate somebody had been home, and Abe had told him no, those utilities weren't monitored that way.

Celine wasn't clouding things. Hardy knew that Pullios in a hurry was not the imperial wizard of detail, and after his oversights on Thursday with the grand jury, he was simply double-checking himself.

30

Jeff Elliot hissed at him from the gallery side of the rail in Department 27. He must have also been in 22 for Calendar, though Hardy, his mind on other things, hadn't seen him. In fact, come to think of it, Hardy hadn't seen Jeff for a few days, and now he didn't look so good —his face was puffy and he was wearing dark glasses, even here inside the courtroom. Still, he was smiling, his usual high-energy self. And why not? His story was back in the fast lane.

Jeff was motioning him back toward the rail. He nudged Pullios. "That's Elliot back there," he said. "The reporter. You wanted to meet him."

"Oh," she said. "Good." She was putting down some papers, starting to turn, Hardy waiting, when the bailiff called out, "Hear ye, hear ye! Department 27 of the Superior Court of the City and County of San Francisco is now in session, Judge Andrew Fowler presiding. All please rise."

The judge appeared in his robes from chambers. Elliot would have to wait.

Seeing Andy, Hardy felt a twinge of guilt—he hadn't followed up worth a damn on seeing how the judge was doing, whatever it was that had been bothering him. He should have called and set up a squash date. Something.

He hadn't heard from his ex-wife, Jane, either. Maybe the crisis—if there had been one—had passed. Certainly, up on the bench, Andy looked as he always did, magisterial and commanding. He gave Hardy a friendly nod. His eyes rested on the defense table for a moment— May Shinn was looking directly at him, meeting his gaze. She was one tough lady, although antagonizing a judge wasn't recommended defense strategy. Freeman was busy emptying his briefcase. He seemed to miss the exchange of glances.

Fowler broke first, his eyes drifting back to Pullios, then Hardy again. He arranged some work in front of him while the bailiff read the indictment again—Section 187, murder.

The gallery had filled up already. It was so unlikely as to be impossible that the trial would begin today. Normally the earliest trial date would be sixty calendar days from the arraignment. But setting that date would be up to Fowler. It was his courtroom.

Nevertheless a murder trial, especially this one, was news. After the indictment on Thursday, Hardy had heard that Locke had gotten calls from Newsweek, Time, all the big ones—they couldn't escape it.

Fowler welcomed counsel to his courtroom. He barely got a word in before Freeman predictably requested his continuance. The district attorney was using this as a publicity vehicle, there was racial discrimination. Hardy heard it with half an ear.

Fowler listened to most of it, nodded sympathetically, then touched his gavel to its block. "We'll set a date now, Mr. Freeman, and before that, if there is good cause for continuance, you can make a motion." He smiled. That was the end of that story. The trial would begin about when the Municipal Court would have held the preliminary hearing. This was a good sign.

The judge adjusted his robes and addressed the courtroom. "Mr. Freeman," he said, "did you have the opportunity to exercise a challenge in Department Twenty-two?" Defense counsel had a one-time right to challenge the judge to which the trial had been assigned, on no grounds whatever. If Freeman didn't like Andy Fowler for any reason on earth, he just had to say so and they would go back to Calendar for another department.

But Freeman barely rose to answer the question. "No challenges, Your Honor."

Fowler paused a minute, his face darkening. "Mr. Freeman?"

Freeman was still fiddling with his binders, laying out papers, whispering to May. "I said no challenge, Your Honor."

The judge seemed to be moving things around behind the rim of his desk. He leaned back in the high chair, arms straight out before him. His frown was pronounced. The instant passed. "Would defense counsel approach the bench, please?"

Hardy became aware of a growing stillness in the courtroom as Freeman pushed his chair back, patted May on the shoulder and stepped up before the judge. Fowler leaned over and there was the briefest of whispered exchanges, after which he straightened up, hit his gavel and announced a recess. He would see Mr. Freeman in his chambers.

"What the hell is going on?" Pullios asked Hardy.

"I don't have a clue. Maybe they're trading stock tips again."

Jim Blanchard from the *Tribune* came up and touched Elliot on the shoulder. "You got a call upstairs. Some girl."

Jeff had been trying to get Hardy's attention since the recess was called. He knew there was an element of cheating in it but he had to get caught up, since he hadn't given five minutes of thought to anything but Dorothy Burgess since Thursday night. He thought he would use Hardy to catch up, grab back the inside track he seemed to have lost to both the local and national media over the long weekend.

And now it looked as though something between Freeman and Fowler was happening right here at the outset. He wanted to be here when the judge returned to court, see if an explanation would present itself.

But Dorothy—it had to be Dorothy—was the priority. There would be other stories. He would not have traded the last four days for anything—not for his job, not even for the use of his legs.

Hardy and Pullios appeared to be in some kind of argument. He wasn't going to get anything out of them, so he grabbed his crutches and awkwardly crabwalked out of his row in the gallery, then out the doors.

In the reporters' room he picked up the telephone. "This is Jeff Elliot," he said.

"Mr. Elliot," she said. "This is Ivana Trump. You've got to stop pestering me." Jeff lowered himself into the school desk. Dorothy's voice got lower. "Jeff, you've got to get over here. You're not going to believe what I found."

"What?"

"I'm not sure what it means, but Maury's been out all morning and I finally got to typing up the paperwork on that story you were working on, the May Shintaka bail?"

"Yeah?"

"You've got to come see this, the collateral on the bail loan. You said you needed a paper trail, someplace to start. This looks like the trailhead. But you realize you're going to have to pay for this information."

"Of course."

"It won't be cheap."

He smiled, remembering the bartering system they'd developed over the weekend to pry secrets from each other—secrets they couldn't wait to tell. "I'll be ready," he said.

Andy Fowler sat back down, banged his gavel, and continued the trial until September 14, at nine-thirty.

"Your Honor!" Pullios was up.

"Counsel?"

"Permission to approach the bench?"

The judge nodded and motioned her forward. She walked firmly, with none of her usual sway. "What is it, Elizabeth?"

"Your Honor, with respect, the state would be interested in the substance of your conference with defense counsel."

Fowler, *gravitas* intact, glared down from his elevated position. There was no love lost between these two. "With *respect,* Counsel, what I do in my chambers is none of your business. But—" He leaned forward with his hands folded in front of him—"but you're right, we must avoid even the appearance of impropriety. You think defense counsel and I are colluding?"

"No, of course not, Your Honor, I—"

"But you think it may look like that to others. I appreciate your concern. Do you read the newspapers, Elizabeth? Watch television?"

Pullios stared at him. "Yes, Your Honor, occasionally."

"You might have noticed that this Owen Nash murder has attracted more than a modicum of publicity."

"Yes, Your Honor."

"Well, in keeping up with this story over the past week or so, it occurred to me that a fair trial might be hard to obtain in San Francisco. I was quite certain defense counsel would move for change of venue. And, as you've no doubt noticed, Mr. Freeman made no such motion. I wanted to make it clear to him that this strategic decision— if it backfires—could not be used later on as grounds for a mistrial. How's that?"

"That's very fine, Your Honor, thank you. No disrespect intended."

Fowler allowed himself a chilly smile. "Of course not, Counsel. An honest question."

After Fowler left the bench Pullios stomped out of the courtroom, leaving Hardy to gather their papers and eventually follow along. Free-

man came over to the prosecution table and told Hardy he hoped
there were no hard feelings about their initial meeting in the visitors'
room at the jail.

"None at all."

"You know, if you wouldn't mind a little free advice, I wouldn't
recommend using my client's little slip about being on the *Eloise*. She
really wasn't there."

Hardy smiled. "That's seems debatable, doesn't it?"

Freeman had his hands in his pockets, his leg thrown casually over
the corner of Hardy's table. "I've listened to the tape several times.
The way you phrased it, it will come out as a trick question. It will only
cast the prosecution in a poor light, make the playing field uneven."

"Well, we wouldn't want that." Hardy finished picking up the papers, closed the briefcase. "Thanks for the tip," he said. "I'll pass it
along."

Hardy was beginning to get used to it. These trial attorneys played a
no-limit game and didn't go about it according to Hoyle. How could
Freeman get the balls to offer such advice? Did he think he was so
green he'd be taken in by so transparent a bluff?

But the more Hardy thought about that, the more it made no sense
at all. So maybe it wasn't a bluff, it was a double reverse. Which made
it a very effective bluff, if it was one.

Slick, he thought, walking along the hall back to his office. You had
to admire it.

What did Freeman really want? He wanted to win. In a circumstantial case like this, if he could cause the prosecution to have doubts
about bringing up any evidence whatever, it could only help the defense. On the other hand, on the surface his advice was sound—
Hardy hadn't planned to bring up May's slip of the tongue, which had
seemed to imply she'd been on board the *Eloise*—because not only
was it in itself unconvincing, Hardy didn't want to introduce into the
record his impropriety in visiting May in jail without her attorney
present.

But now Freeman had told Hardy it wouldn't be a good idea to bring
it up. Certainly Freeman wasn't actually trying to be a nice guy, help
out the new kid. But his advice was something Hardy had intended to
do anyway.

Which meant—what?

*   *   *

"So why are we continuing until tomorrow? What's the point of that?"

It had been less than five minutes since Pullios left the courtroom and now she sat in her office, door closed. Hardy, entering, had been shocked to see tears in her eyes. He started to tell her it was all right, he didn't mean . . .

She stopped him and pointed to her eyes with both index fingers. "This is anger, Hardy. Don't confuse this with having my feelings hurt. That bastard."

Hardy had thought he'd discuss Freeman and strategy, but that clearly wasn't going to be on the agenda. "He's probably continuing it so he can read the file. He just found out he had the case this morning," Hardy said.

"There's no excuse for that tone."

Hardy put her briefcase on the desk and sat down across from her. "Maybe he resented having his own motives questioned?"

She didn't buy that. "You wouldn't have asked him?"

"I don't know. I was curious, sure."

"When you're curious, ask. It's one of the rules."

"I didn't think there were any rules."

She looked straight at him. Her eyes still glittered. "There aren't," she said.

31

It had turned into this.

Owen Nash stood on a balcony twenty-three floors above Las Vegas, his skin still damp from his shower. A towel was tucked under his protruding stomach, a fresh cigar remained unlit in his mouth. He liked the desert, especially now at twilight. It was still hot and dry after the scorching day, but the water evaporating from his skin kept him cool.

He fixed his eyes beyond the city. The mountains on the horizon had turned a faint purple. From far below, street noises carried up to him softly. More immediately, he heard May turn the shower off in the bathroom. He leaned heavily, with both hands, on the railing.

Sucking reflectively on the cigar, he felt rather than heard the soft tread of her bare feet crossing the rug behind him. After a moment, he felt her behind him, her hands massaging his bare back. He sighed again, started to say something, but May hushed him. She opened her kimono and pressed herself against him, then she led him silently back into the room and pushed him onto the bed.

"Lie down," she ordered. "You're getting a back rub."

She started kneading his shoulders. The muscles were knotted tightly, but May was in no hurry. She knew what she was doing. Gradually, the stiffness began to work itself out. He began breathing deeply, regularly. For a moment she thought he might have fallen asleep, but then he groaned quietly as she moved to a new knot.

Outside, the twilight had deepened. May stretched out on top of him, ran her hand up along his side. "Pretty tense, you know that?"

He nodded.

"You want to talk about it?"

He didn't answer immediately, just lay with his eyes closed, breathing heavily. "We've got dinner," he said. It was to be their first public appearance together. He thought it was important to her.

217

May didn't push. She lay quietly in the growing dark.

"I'll decide in a minute," he said.

Even in the dimness, May could make out the lines in his face. His high and broad forehead showed a lifetime of living. His thin lips were tight. "I don't know," he said, his voice strangely flat, "I don't know."

"What?"

"I think things may be getting a little out of hand."

May stiffened—she'd been trying to let herself believe that she'd never hear this kind of thing from him. "With us?"

He laughed, pulling her tight against him. "Shinn, please. Well, maybe it is us, but not the way you mean."

"You tell me."

"You know the bitch about life is you can't do everything. You take one road and it means you can't take another. And either way, you're going to miss something."

"Are you afraid of missing something?"

He laughed dryly. "I'm afraid of missing anything. I never felt I had to. I never made any commitment that way. It just wasn't in my life. Now I'm thinking about it. It scares the shit out of me. I keep thinking you're going to find out."

"Find out what?"

"What I am. What I've been."

She pressed herself long against him. "Haven't we been through that. What do you think I've been?"

"I don't care what you've been, Shinn."

"I don't care what *you've* been, Nash. Are you worried about those other roads, what you're going to miss?"

"Not so much. It's making the change."

"Nobody's forcing you."

"You're wrong, Shinn. You're forcing me. But it's okay, it's what I want. It's the only thing I want anymore."

She tried to believe him.

Freeman chewed on a pencil, looking out the sliding glass doors to the little courtyard, enclosed on the other three sides by the bricks of the surrounding buildings. A pigeon pecked on the cobbles.

May was sitting next to him at the marble table in the conference room. There was a fresh spray of flowers in the center of the table. The room smelled faintly like a walk-in humidor. "Did you ever go out?" he asked.

"What do you mean?"

"I mean that night. You said it was supposed to be your first public appearance. I just wondered how it went."

She seemed to gather inside herself, as she'd done before. Freeman wasn't sure he'd call it a visible withdrawal, but it was somehow palpable. He would have to try and define it better, get her trained not to do it, whatever it was, in front of a jury. "No," she said finally. "No, we never met any of his friends."

She raised her eyes, seeing how he took that. Perhaps emboldened, she added, "He . . . we never needed to, we were enough for each other."

Hardy reached a hand out over his desk. "Those the phone things?"

Glitsky held what looked like a small booklet of yellow paper. He passed it across the desk. "I think some clerk got carried away. I just asked for June twentieth. I think they gave us the whole year."

"Well, how's the twentieth look?"

"Good. For us. Not so good for Shintaka."

Hardy intended to merely glance at the printout—he had his binder open, ready to put it in. Given it was half a year, there weren't all that many calls, maybe fifteen pages, each of them five inches long. He began flipping through quickly. "Look at this," he said.

Glitsky nodded. "I noticed. No calls to Japan."

Hardy looked up. Glitsky, he knew, rarely missed a trick. "You're no fun, you know that."

If May did business in Japan, it made sense she would at least occasionally need to call there, especially if she were planning a trip. Even if she did most of her work by fax, Hardy thought he could reasonably expect one or two calls. "Well, it can't hurt. You check any of these?" Hardy was scanning the pages, turning them backward, now on March.

"No. I checked the twentieth. I just happened to notice Japan. You want, I can assign a guy."

"No, I'll . . ." Suddenly Hardy's eyes narrowed. He stopped flipping.

"What?" Glitsky asked.

"Nothing." He closed the pages and put them on his desk. "I just remembered I've got to pick up some stuff for the Beck."

"You're a good daddy."

"I know. I amaze myself." He tapped the pages, back to business. "I'll go through this stuff. Thanks."

Glitsky stood up. "Thank you. That is not my idea of a good time."

Hardy kept it loose. "God, they say, is in the details."

"Wise men still seek Him. Want me to get the door?"

"Please."

He hoped he was wrong, but he didn't think so.

Hardy wasn't great at math, but he had a natural affinity for numbers, especially telephone numbers. He hadn't called the number on the March listing recently, but as soon as he saw it, he knew that at one time he'd known it.

He grabbed the pages and looked back to the beginning. The number appeared in February, too, more frequently. Twice a week in January. Eighteen total calls.

Maybe the number had changed, but Hardy didn't think so. He picked up the telephone on his desk and dialed the number. There were three rings.

"This is 885-6024. Please leave your name and number and I'll get back to you."

Hardy's mouth had gone dry. His left hand gripped the paperweight so tightly his knuckles were white. The paperweight!

He thought of Owen Nash's jade ring, the distinctive filigree, the animal motif. Frannie's early theory. For a second he couldn't think of what to say. The tape hissed blankly in his ear. He forced himself to speak into the home answering-machine of Superior Court Judge Andrew B. Fowler.

"Andy," Hardy said, "this is Dismas. We've got to talk. I'm going by your office now, but if I haven't reached you by the time you get this, please call me immediately. It's urgent, it's extremely urgent."

PART III

32

Casually as he could muster, Hardy put the paperweight into his pocket and walked out past the other suites in the D.A.'s office. Thinking "not now," he saw Jeff Elliot coming out of the elevator and turned to duck into the criminal investigations room just outside the D.A.'s doors. He wasn't quick enough, though. He heard his name called and stopped, caught, hands in his pockets.

For a reporter Jeff had a knack of seeming to be sensitive, even reasonable. Maybe, Hardy thought, it was the crutches, that and the grin. To say nothing of today's puffiness, the indoor sunglasses. You wanted to help the guy.

"Bad time?"

Hardy nodded. "A little."

"You go ahead then. I'll talk to Ms. Pullios."

There was a perverse satisfaction in Elizabeth now being the attorney of record. Naturally she would be a valuable source. But Hardy felt that, at the very least, he ought to have some control over the flow of information to the *Chronicle*. This wasn't in the office hierarchy and he didn't want to give her a freebie on what she most craved—ink. "I've got a minute, Jeff, what can I do for you?"

"Can we talk somewhere? I need to go off the record."

They walked back into the D.A.'s hallway and Hardy unlocked one of the waiting rooms, provided for the families of victims, witnesses, the odd conference. There was a yellow couch—the city favored green and yellow—and matching armchair. A picture of the Golden Gate Bridge in a special limited edition of three and a half million livened up the wall space.

Jeff lowered himself into the chair.

"Where have you been lately? You don't look too well."

"Just some new medication. Makes me puff up and get light sensitive. Prednisone."

"Steroids?"

Jeff smiled. "That's what they use. It's okay, I wasn't going for the Olympics anyway."

Hardy liked him, no getting around it. "Okay, so what's off the record?" He pointed a finger. "And it *is* off the record."

Did Hardy remember last week, after the Municipal Court arraignment, standing in the hallway with Elliot and Glitsky, talking about the bail, the money connection?

"Sure, of course, what about it? You find something?"

The reporter shook his head. "No, not yet, maybe. But you guys said, didn't you, there were ways to subpoena the bail bondsman for his records."

Hardy shook his head. "Not in this case. Only if we think the money for the bail came from criminal activity."

"Well, how would May Shinn get half a million dollars?"

"What half a million? She only needed fifty thousand for a fee."

Jeff Elliot shook his head. "I thought that at first, too. She still needs collateral on the loan."

Hardy nodded. "Yeah, we've gone over that." He chewed it around again. "I don't know, investments? Maybe she inherited it? We don't have any sign of anything. Drugs. Like that."

"How about prostitution? That's illegal, isn't it?"

It was something to wonder about, but that, too, had already been discussed. "Maybe. Technically. But there's no judge going to give us a warrant to seize records on that." He shrugged. "Maybe the bondsman accepted Owen Nash's will."

"Even if she killed him? Could she collect on that?"

"That," Hardy said, "is another legal battle. Fortunately it's not mine. Whichever way it goes, even if she gets the whole two million, lawyers will wind up with most of it. What do you have that's so off the record?"

Elliot leaned forward and took off his sunglasses. There was something clearly unfocussed there, dark rings in sockets deepened by swelling. Hardy couldn't conceal his reaction and interrupted Jeff's response. "Are you sure you're okay?"

Jeff smiled and the bags seemed to lift a bit. "It looks worse than it is. Actually I'm feeling much better." He put on the glasses again. "The chipmunk cheeks go away after a while."

"You getting any sleep?"

Now the grin was wide. "Not enough." Then, slyly proud. "I'm seeing somebody. First time." He lifted his shoulders with exagger-ated nonchalance. "Sleep's not a big issue."

"You dog!"

"Yes, well . . ." Suddenly Jeff didn't want to be talking about it, reducing it, bragging as though it were some casual victory. This wasn't a conquest, it was Dorothy. "Anyway, about the bail, I don't have any names yet, nothing I can print, but before I even move ahead at all, I want to protect my source."

"So how do you do that?"

"I provide a plausible explanation of how I came to look at some records. Maybe I shouldn't tell you this?"

Hardy passed over that. "Have you seen some records?"

"No." Jeff leaned forward. Hardy thought if he took off his glasses he was lying. But he didn't. "Really, no."

"Okay. And I'm the leak?"

"Unnamed, of course. Off the record."

Hardy found himself reminded of Freeman's advice to him in the courtroom, of Pullios's insistence that there were no rules. This was high-stakes poker, and if Jeff could provide Hardy—oops, the prosecu-tion—with the source of May's bail, it would only help his, their, case.

"If anything comes out of this and I can't explain how I got my information, my source loses her job, so I thought I'd cover that up front."

"But we're not subpoenaing the records."

"I know, but that doesn't matter. I just need an answer if the ques-tion comes up."

"I'm not giving you an answer to anything, Jeff. I'm just telling you a procedure, you got that? The way the D.A. would do it if certain criteria were met, which they have not been."

"I got it."

"Clearly?"

"Clearly."

Hardy picked up a tall pile of blue chips and dropped them into the pot. "Okay then."

Hardy thought he might be getting paranoid, but he took the file home with him anyway. In it was everything they had to date, including the phone records on May Shinn. He stopped out by Arguello and Geary and spent forty-five minutes copying it. He couldn't have said exactly why it seemed like such a good idea—Pullios might be taking it away from him, maybe he wanted to be able to check up on her in the privacy of his office.

Maybe he was trying to protect Andy Fowler.

No. There was a fine line between the backstabbing, gamesmanship and duplicity that seemed to be the norm and downright unethical conduct. He was going to find out about Andy Fowler's relationship with May Shinn. Then he would deal with it. He thought.

But first, and in the meanwhile, what he didn't want was some D.A.'s investigator, spurred on by Pullios's zeal, to discover this apparent connection and ruin Andy's life. And in fact, there might be no connection, or an innocent one. Although Hardy couldn't imagine what it might be.

Nevertheless, the Boy Scout in him deemed it best to be prepared. He copied the file.

David Freeman thought it had been a long day, but not without its rewards.

The trial falling to Andy Fowler had been a godsend, one that he, Freeman, had never given up hope on but one which he couldn't possibly have counted on.

He had finished a decent meal and a couple of solid drinks at the Buena Vista Bar—not the birthplace but the American foster home of Irish Coffee—and was taking the cable car up toward Nob Hill, named for the Nobs who had originally claimed it as their own: Leland Stanford, Mark Hopkins, Charles Crocker and Collis P. Huntington. Freeman lived there himself in a penthouse apartment a block from the Fairmont Hotel, just above the Rue Lepic, one of his favorite restaurants.

But tonight he didn't want to go straight home. It was full dark, surprisingly warm again. He sat on the cable car's hard bench, cantered against the steep grade, rocking with the motion, surrounded by the tourists. It was all right.

He was a man of the people and yet, somehow, above the people. He looked on them tolerantly, with few illusions. They were capable of anything—thirty-five years practicing criminal law had shown him that—but there was something he sometimes felt in a bustling rush of humanity that brought him back to himself, to who he was.

He remembered why he had chosen defense work—and there hadn't been much glamor, and even less money, in the beginning. The field had attracted him because he knew that everyone made mistakes, everyone was guilty of something. What the world needed, what people needed, was forgiveness and understanding, at least to have their side heard. He described himself, to himself, as a cynical romantic. And he had to admit he was seldom bored.

He dismounted the cable car at the Fairmont and decided to prolong the night and the mood, take a walk, reflect. May Shinn was constantly referring to Owen Nash and always managed to mention his cigars. Freeman found it had given him the taste for one, and he stopped in at the smoke shop and picked up a Macanudo. Outside, while he was lighting up by the valet station, a well-dressed man tried to sell him a genuine Rolex Presidential watch for three hundred dollars. Freeman declined.

He strolled west, over the crest of the hill, craving another sight of the Bay at night. The cigar was full-flavored, delicious.

After the conference he'd had today with Andy Fowler, he was sure he was going to win.

Fowler shouldn't have gotten the trial. Certainly, when he'd hired Freeman, that couldn't have been contemplated. May was in Municipal Court and there was no possible way it could wind up in Andy's courtroom.

Even after the grand-jury indictment had moved it into Superior Court, the odds were still six to one against Fowler getting it. But, even at those odds, Fowler should have gone to Leo Chomorro, spoken to him privately, and taken himself out of the line.

Except that feelings between Andy Fowler and Leo Chomorro were strained, to say the least. Forgetting their philosophical differences, and they were substantial, on a personal level Fowler had been one of the few judges singled out by name in Chomorro's report to the governor on the "candy-ass" nature of the San Francisco bench. Fowler, in turn, had been an outspoken critic of Chomorro's appointment to the court. More, Freeman knew through legal community scuttlebutt that Fowler was the man most responsible for Chomorro's extended sojourn on Calendar. So, for any and all of these reasons, Fowler hadn't gone to Chomorro, and that's when he'd cut himself off at the pass.

Because he'd gone on the assumption that he had a fallback, failsafe position even if the trial came up in his department. Freeman smiled, thinking of it—not unkindly, it was consistent with his view of the folly of man, even judges. Fowler had thought that of course, without a doubt, there was no question that if the Shinn trial came to his courtroom, David Freeman, defense counsel, would exercise his option to challenge the presiding judge, not having to give a reason, and that would be the end of that—the trial would go to another judge.

But Freeman hadn't challenged, which, of course, was what had prompted the conference.

Fowler, arms crossed, stood just inside the door to his chambers. "David, what the hell are you doing?"

"I'm defending my client. That's what you hired me to do."

"I certainly didn't think she would get to this courtroom."

"No, neither did I."

"Well, you have to challenge. I can't hear this case."

Freeman hadn't answered. His hands were in his pockets. He knew he looked rumpled, mournful, sympathetic. Two weeks before he'd been Andy Fowler's savior, now he was his enemy.

He loved the drama of it.

Fowler had turned, walking to the window. "What am I supposed to do, David?"

"You could recuse yourself, cite conflict."

"I can't do that now."

Freeman knew he couldn't.

"I can't have my relationship with her come out."

Chomorro, even Fowler's allies, would eat him alive for that. It was bad form for judges to go with prostitutes. But sometimes the best argument was silence. Freeman walked up to the judge's desk and straightened some pencils.

"David, you've got to challenge."

Freeman shook his head. "You hired me to do the best job defending my client. A trial in your courtroom is clearly to her advantage. I'm sorry if it is inconvenient to you."

"Inconvenient? This is a disaster. It's totally unethical. I can't let this happen."

"That, Judge, is your decision." He was matter-of-fact. "If it's any consolation, I have no intention of betraying your confidence."

Fowler's eyes seemed glazed. "Does May know?"

"I'd bet against it. I told her it was free advertising for me. It seemed to go down."

"Jesus." He ran a hand through his hair. Suddenly he looked haggard and old. "Jesus Christ." He walked around in little circles, then stopped. "Do you think I could give her a fair trial, David?"

There it was, the rationality kicking in. That's what people did, Freeman knew. They made their own actions, however wrong, somehow justified.

Fowler continued, "If it ever comes out, I'm truly ruined. Would she say anything?"

"Why would she, especially since I'm going to get her off? It wouldn't be to her advantage. Now or ever."

"You're going to get her off?"

"Of course. There's no evidence, Andy."

The judge lowered his voice. "But she did it, David."

"No one can prove my client killed anybody. If the prosecution can be kept from sexual innuendo and racial slurs, she will be acquitted. It will be essential to control the tone in the courtroom."

The cigar had gone out and he chewed happily on the butt. It had been a satisfying performance, its outcome so sweet he almost wanted to dance a little jig when he left chambers.

Of course, on the downside, Andy Fowler, with whom he'd always gotten along, had his neck on the block. Andy couldn't recuse himself without admitting his relationship with May, and he wasn't going to do that. He was right, it would end his career, and the revelation at this late date in the proceedings would be particularly damning.

But he'd gotten himself in this position. You made your own luck. Good or bad. Andy was a big boy. He should have known better.

The walk had taken Freeman across the top of Nob Hill and back down its north side. He became subliminally aware that his steps were leading him somewhere, and he let them. Slowly, no hurry. He still chewed the cigar.

By night, the corner that May lived on was quiet. The cable cars had stopped running. The surrounding hills were steep, and people heading for North Beach or back out to the Avenues would take one of the larger thoroughfares, Broadway or Van Ness, Gough or Geary. He crossed the street and stood leaning against the window of the French deli, looking up. There was a light on in what he knew to be May's kitchen. The front of the apartment, the turreted window, was dark.

Across the street in Mrs. Streletski's building shadows danced across the turret, and suddenly Freeman remembered a fourteen-year-old boy named Wayne Allred who'd been hiding in a closet when his mother ran from his apartment, who'd come out to shoot his father dead.

He threw his cigar butt into the gutter. He wasn't quite disgusted with himself for being less than completely thorough earlier. It had been the end of another long day and he hadn't been holding out any hope that May was innocent. In fact, he still didn't.

But his feet, his subconscious—something—had taken him here, and now he knew why. He crossed the street and rang the bell to number 17, Strauss. The speaker squawked by his ear.

"Who is it?"

Freeman apologized and explained briefly.

"It's ten o'clock at night. Can't this wait until morning?"

He apologized again, and for a moment it appeared that he was going to strike out. But then the buzzer sounded and he was quietly climbing the carpeted steps. The door stood ajar and Nick Strauss leaned against the jamb, wearing white socks and a terrycloth robe. He was a big man, far bigger than Freeman, his black hair still wet from the shower.

"I'm sorry," Freeman repeated. "But a person's life is at stake here."

"Could I see some ID?"

The lawyer smiled. "Of course." It was the standard first line of protection, as foolish, Freeman thought, as most human endeavor. As if—were he a burglar or a murderer—possession of a driver's license would make him any safer, as if all IDs weren't routinely, expertly, forged or altered.

But he took out his wallet and offered it. He had a business card in his jacket breast pocket and he gave Strauss one of those too.

The man opened the door further. Freeman saw two boys—teenagers or a little younger—sitting together on the couch, trying to get a look at him. He gave them a little friendly wave, and Strauss said to come on in. "But I've already told you we didn't see anything."

"Well, Mr. Strauss, actually you told me *you* didn't see anything. You said you'd ask the boys and get back to me."

"If they saw anything—"

"What, Dad?"

"Just a second, Nick. I'm talking to this man. This is Mr. Freeman, guys. These are my boys—Alex, the big guy, and Nick, the big little guy. Aren't you, Nick?"

The younger boy, Nick, seemed an echo not only of his father's name but of the attitude—cautious, watchful. Freeman kept his hands in his pockets, the supplicant. "I don't mean to push. People forget these things all the time. It's just so terribly important."

Strauss made some motion that Freeman took for acquiescence; he looked to the boys, then back to Strauss. "Would you guys like to show me your room, if it's okay with your dad?"

The older boy, Alex, said "sure" and jumped up. This was an adventure.

"How about you, Nick?"

"Naw. I'll just wait here."

Freeman said fine, but Alex was all over him. "Come on, you wimp, chicken-liver, baby."

"Alex!"

But that did it. Nick got up. "It's all right, Dad. Alex is such a nerd." Then, to his brother, "you jerkoff," remembering the last time he had seen the Chinese women through the telescope . . .

Nick Strauss loved his dad's apartment at the corner of Hyde and Union, especially after the month of traveling with his mom and Alex, staying in those tiny stuffy rooms in Europe. First of all, Dad's place was humongous, twice the size of his mom's in Van Nuys, rickety-rackety pink stucco with peeling paint and cars parked all over the place where there should have been grass. Then, at Dad's, nobody was above them—no Mrs. Cutler and her two sons and the bass and drums coming down through the ceiling all day and night like in the Valley. No adjoining hotel rooms with people staying up all the time.

Plus the cable cars; it was a snap to get on and off without paying. And hills for skateboarding like you couldn't believe, and no damn palm trees. In fact, no trees.

And finally this glassed-in turret in the front upstairs corner of the apartment, which was part of his and Alex's bedroom when they came to visit on Saturday. And this time, since they'd been with Mom so steadily with school and then Europe and all, they were staying three weeks.

So after the lights went out you could take out the telescope and spy on anybody in the neighborhood, nobody noticing a thing. Or in the daytime, just drawing the drapes and making it all dark in there, looking all around, checking it all out.

And since they'd gotten here, checking her out.

Alex saw her first—across the street, upstairs just like them, proba-

bly figuring nobody could see her. It was supremely worth the fifty
cents Nick had to pay for the first look—he wondered what Chinese
custom it was to walk around your house naked, but he wasn't com-
plaining. Except for Mom (and she didn't count anyway), he'd never
seen a live naked woman. Even Playboy was hard to get when you
were eleven.

And he thought this woman looked as good—at least—as anybody
in Playboy, except for the smaller boobs. And being Chinese was a
little funny at first. He kind of wished she was a regular American—he
wondered if it really counted as seeing a naked woman if she was
Chinese, but he asked Alex and Alex said it sure counted for him, and
he was thirteen so he ought to know.

She hadn't been there for a few days; the last time had been a
couple nights ago. It had been almost eleven o'clock. He couldn't get
his weenie to go down and he couldn't get to sleep. He also didn't
want to waste a minute when her lights were on. He put his eye to the
telescope. It looked like she was doing some kind of exercise, taking
things down off shelves, reaching up, then bending over. She turned
toward him, her face so full in the telescope he almost jumped back. It
looked like she was crying, and that made him feel guilty, spying on
her and all.

"See anything?" Alex had whispered.

Darn. Nick thought Alex had been asleep. He quick stuffed a blanket down over his hard little weenie. He took a last look, thinking
about the way boobs changed shapes when women moved around,
leaned over, stretched up. His brother had called him a "boob man"
last week. Well, he guessed he was, if that's what interested him, and
he wore that knowledge like a badge of honor. A man, not a boy.

He pulled the drapes closed in front of the telescope. He'd keep the
crying a secret between just him and her. "Naw," he had told Alex, "I
think she went to sleep."

David Freeman, Nick, Alex and their father walked through the living
room, Mr. Strauss saying he was sorry about his sons' language, referring to Nick calling Alex a jerkoff. Their mother wasn't very strict with
them and the language thing was impossible to correct in the six
weeks or so he had them every year. You had to pick your fights.

Freeman saw the telescope as soon as he entered the room, and
walked over to it. "This is pretty cool," he said. "This looks like a real
telescope."

"It is a real telescope," Alex said.

Freeman put his eye to the glass. "What can you see through it?" What he was looking at, what it had been set on, was the turret across the street, the room beyond. He saw May at her kitchen table, drinking something, so close he could see the steam rising off her cup.

There was a knack to putting a little twinkle in your eye, to sounding conspiratorial and friendly. "You ever spy on people?"

Alex answered quickly, too quickly. "No way."

"How about you, Nick?"

Nick pulled himself further behind his father's robe. Big Nick broke in. "What are you getting at here?"

"Take a look."

Freeman moved aside and Big Nick came over and lowered his eye to the eyepiece. He stayed that way a minute.

"That's her," Freeman said. "My client."

Big Nick was angry, turning on his boys. "You guys have got to—"

"Mr. Strauss, please. Just a minute." The stentorian voice stopped everything. The boys stood transfixed. Freeman muted it, sat on the bed, and gave them Gentle and Soothing. "You guys are not in trouble, no matter what. I *guarantee* it."

He explained the situation then, slowly, calmly, no judgments. He told them what their father had said about the Saturday they'd first come here, that they'd only changed and had lunch and then gone out for the day. He just wanted to know if that was *all* they'd done, and were they sure? He didn't want to lead them.

The two boys looked at each other. "I think so," Nick said.

"Alex?"

His eyes went back to his brother, to his father. "It's all right, Alex, just tell the truth."

"Well, you know, the telescope was up, so I started looking around a little, just looking at things."

"And did you see anything? Anything interesting or unusual, maybe across the street there?"

Alex looked at Nick, shrugged, and gave it up. "She was naked. She was walking around naked."

"When was that, Alex?"

"Just before we had to go, when Dad called us, just before lunchtime."

"And you're sure it was that day, the very first day you were here, the Saturday?"

The boys checked each other again. Both of them nodded and said yeah, it was.

33

Hardy picked up the phone on the kitchen wall on the third ring. He'd gotten out of his warm bed from deep sleep.

"Dismas, this is Andy Fowler. Did I wake you up?"

The kitchen clock said 10:45. "That's okay, Andy."

"I just got your message. What's so urgent?"

Hardy was coming out of his fog but he wasn't yet awake enough to beat around the bush. "May Shinn."

A pause. "Since you're on the case, Diz, I don't think we should discuss it."

As bluffs went, Hardy thought, except for the pause it wasn't too bad. "I think we have to, Andy. I think you know what I'm talking about."

In the silence Hardy thought he could hear Fowler's breathing get heavier. Then he said, "Where can I meet you?"

They met at a fern bar on Fillmore, half a mile from Andy Fowler's house on Clay near Embassy Row. When it was not happy hour it was the local watering hole for doctors and nurses at the local medical center. It wasn't Hardy's type of bar but he wasn't here for the ambience.

He was wearing his prelawyer clothes—an old corduroy sports jacket over a misshapen white fisherman's sweater, jeans, hiking boots —and felt better for it. At a place like this, at this time of night, those clothes put out the message that he wasn't a yuppie looking to get laid with the accepted props of elegant threads and the attitude that went with them.

The music was some New Age stuff that was supposed to make you believe real people played it—bass pops, synthesized everything, music that eliminated the strain of having to listen to words or follow a melody. It was just There, like the ubiquitous television blaring in the corner, like the *National Enquirer* at checkout stands, like McDonald's.

Surprised that the judge hadn't arrived yet, he pulled up a stool at the corner of the bar in the back. He ordered a Guinness, which they didn't have on tap, so he went with Anchor porter, an excellent second choice.

Maybe it was being awakened from a good sleep, but he realized he was in a foul humor.

Andy Fowler's appearance didn't pick him up any. The judge hadn't changed out of his tuxedo. He had his trim body, his thick hair, his guileless smile so different from Hardy's weathered one.

These good-looking older guys—who were they trying to kid? Suddenly he saw a different man than the Andy Fowler he'd known—vainer and shallower, the august presence and appearance not so much a reflection of an enviable and confident character as a costume that concealed the insecure man within.

Coming back through the bar, the judge checked himself in the mirror. A man who checked his hair in a burning building had his priorities all wrong.

Hardy gave a small wave, and Andy brought up the stool next to him, ordering an Anejo rum in a heated snifter. There was a moment of cheerful greeting, ritual for them both, but it subsided quickly. Hardy reached into his pocket, took out the paperweight and laid it on the bar between them. He gave it a little spin.

There it was—Andy's Fowler's whole world in an orb of jade. There was no more avoiding it. "May Shinn gave this to you, didn't she?"

Fowler had his hands cupped around the amber liquid. There was no point in denial anymore. "How'd you find out?"

"Phone records." He told him how he'd made discovery, put the jade jewelry—his paperweight, Nash's ring—together. "Anyway, there were a dozen calls to your number, maybe more."

"That many?" Did he seem *pleased*?

"What's happening here, Andy? You can't be on this case."

"It's going to come out now, isn't it?"

"I don't see how it can't."

"Who else knows but you?"

Hardy sipped his porter. It wasn't the direction he'd expected. "What do you mean?"

"I mean who's put it together, Diz?" He brought his hand down on the bar, a gavel of flesh. "Goddamm it, what do you *think* I mean? Who else knows about this?"

Hardy stared into the space between them. They were the first harsh words the judge had ever directed at him. Immediately Fowler put his hand over Hardy's. "I'm sorry, Diz. I didn't mean that."

But it was done. All right, he was stressed out. Hardy could let it go, forget it, almost.

Fowler raised his snifter, took a sip, put it down. His voice was under control again. "I guess what I'm asking is, what happens now?"

"I'd say that depends on what's happened before."

Fowler nodded. "So nobody else knows."

"I didn't say that."

"Yes, you did."

Everybody was a poker player. It was all check, bet, raise. "Okay. Why don't you tell me about it? We'll go from there."

The bartender was coming down the bar toward them. "Double it up here, would you?" Fowler said. "And give my friend another pint."

They were at a large corner booth, nobody else within twenty feet, at right angles from each other, almost knee to knee, the older, good-looking man in a tuxedo, and the other one, maybe a construction worker, probably the man's son. Definitely they weren't lovers—in San Francisco two men alone were always suspect. But the body language was all wrong for that. They were close, involved in something, and it was putting a strain between them.

"It was at one of the galleries down by Union Square. I'd had lunch at the Clift and the sun was out so I thought I'd walk a little of it off, maybe drop in at Magnin's and visit Jane. I so rarely get to see downtown in the daylight.

"The place was empty except for the saleswoman—she turned out to be the owner—and May. I don't know what made me stop. They were showing some erotica—I guess that's what got me to look, but then I saw this Japanese woman standing there, her face in profile, and I walked in. We got to talking, probably talked for half an hour, analyzing all this stuff. It was erotic, I admit, discussing all these positions and anatomies, alone with a beautiful woman you had just met."

"So you picked her up."

"If only it had been that simple. I hadn't done anything like that in thirty years, Diz. When you're a judge . . ."

Hardy drank his porter, waited. "So what happened?"

"She left, said it was nice meeting me but she had to go. I stayed around a little longer and thought that was that." He paused. "But it wasn't. I found I couldn't get her out of my mind, kept picturing her in some of the positions. Sorry, I know it's not my image."

Hardy shrugged. "Everybody needs love, Andy."

"That sounds good enough when you say it. Try denying it, though, try burying it under your work and your image and your public life until you really believe you don't need it anymore."

"I did it after Michael, and Jane."

"So you know. You tell yourself your life is just as good, just as full. It's not like you don't do things, but you're so alone. Nothing resonates." Andy got quiet and stared outside at the empty street. "So a couple of days later," the judge went on, "I came back to the gallery and asked the owner if she remembered the woman I'd spoken with. She said she was a regular client."

"So she does deal in art?"

"Who, May? No, she collects some, but I wouldn't say she deals in it. Anyway, the owner knew her, but she wouldn't tell me her name, even after I told her who I was. Not that I blame her. As we know, there are a lot of nuts out there, even among my colleagues. So I gave her my card, asked her to have this lady call me. She said she would."

"So you got together."

"No. Not yet. She didn't call." He swirled his rum, put it back on the table untouched. "But I wanted her, I didn't know her at all and I didn't care. I had to see her again. I don't know what it was."

The vision of Celine Nash danced up before Hardy's eyes and he drowned it in porter. "Okay, what?"

"I gave it a week, then I went back in and bought one of the woodcuts, forty-five hundred dollars, and told the owner to send it to May."

"That'll eliminate the riffraff element."

"The money wasn't important. I've got money. In any event it got her to call and thank me, and I told her I wanted to see her and she still said no, she couldn't do that.

"I asked her why, was she married, engaged, not interested in men? No? At least tell me why. So she agreed to meet me for dinner. And she told me."

"Her profession?"

"What she did, yes. She was scared, me being a judge, that I'd bust her." He laughed, clipped and short. "I had to promise her immunity up front. I did want her, Diz. What she had done made no difference to me. I told her I wasn't interested in that kind of relationship, paying her—I liked her, I wanted to see her, take her out legitimately. She laughed. She didn't do that. So I asked if I could see her at all, under any conditions."

"Jesus, Andy . . ."

"No, it wasn't like that. I wasn't groveling. It was more good-natured negotiating."

"So what'd the negotiating get to?"

The judge focused across the room. "Three thousand dollars."

Hardy swallowed, took a long drink, swallowed again. "Three thousand dollars? For one time?"

"No, per month."

"You paid May Shinn three thousand dollars a month?"

"Yes."

"Lord, Lord, Lord."

"After the first couple of months I would have paid anything. Don't laugh. I fell in love with her, Diz. I still love her."

"Andy, you don't pay somebody you love."

"The money was never discussed after that first night. I thought she was coming around."

"To what? What could she be coming around to?"

"To loving me."

It was so simple, so basic, so incredibly misguided, Hardy didn't know what to say. "What about her other clients?"

"She dropped them all, almost immediately. That was one of the things that gave me some hope . . ."

"That she would love you?"

"I suppose."

"And then what? You marry her and have a happy little family?"

Fowler shook his head. "No, I never thought we'd get married. She made me happy, that was all. She was there for me. She filled up that space. I thought I was doing the same for her."

"But you weren't."

"For a while I'm sure I was. She started cooking me meals, making special dishes, giving me presents—the paperweight, for example—things like that. Then four or five months ago it just ended. She called and said we couldn't go on."

"Owen Nash?"

"I assume so. I didn't know it then. She said to just make believe she had died. But she was happy, I shouldn't worry. I shouldn't worry . . ."

Hardy sat back into the leather of the booth. All this tracked with Andy's malaise over the past months, his explanation to Jane about a friend dying. Frannie and Jane had both, independently, been right. A woman had broken a man's heart, the oldest story in the world.

But now, that story told, the judge had to move on. He took a gulp of his rum. "So that's it, Diz, now you know."

"I don't want to know."

"That's what Eve said after she ate the apple. It was too late then, too."

Hardy leaned forward again, arms on the table. "You can't be on the case, Andy. I just don't understand how it could have gotten this far."

The answer—the same one that Fowler had given Freeman earlier in the day—was that it had come a step at a time: the Muni-Court arraignment with no chance of getting to Fowler's courtroom anyway, then the grand-jury indictment leaving only one chance in six it would come to him, then his decision not to go and beg off privately to Leo Chomorro because that Hispanic Nazi would use the Fowler/Shinn relationship as political ammunition against Fowler. Andy didn't mention the ace-in-the-hole that hadn't worked—Freeman challenging out of his courtroom. He didn't have any intention of opening that can of worms. So far, no one else knew he had hired Freeman, and he intended to keep things that way.

"So then I figured if, after all that, it dropped in my lap, well then, it was fate. You know there's going to be prejudice against her being Japanese, her profession. At least I could give her an even playing field. I could have helped her. She might have come back to me. There was no reason it had to come out. There isn't now. I wouldn't obstruct justice, Diz. I just wouldn't do it."

Hardy wanted to tell him he already had. Instead he said, "The rationalization maybe moves it out of disbarment range, Andy, but you and I both know it's still unethical. You know the defendant—hell, you've been intimate with the defendant. If that's not a conflict . . ." What could he say? Andy knew this as well as he did. "You've got to take yourself off the case."

"If I did, I'd have to give a reason and I can't do that."

Hardy's drink was gone. He picked up the glass, tried it, put it down. "You could retire."

"Right now, without notice?"

"The trial isn't tomorrow, Andy. There's plenty of time. It'll get reassigned. The phone records in the file aren't strictly relevant to the murder. The police only asked for June twentieth. The rest doesn't have to be there."

This was not ethical either, and Hardy wasn't sure he could do it. The file was the public record. Tampering with it, suppressing potential evidence—even if its relevance hadn't been demonstrated—was a felony. Still, he wasn't telling Andy he'd take the earlier phone records out, not in so many words. And if he didn't say it explicitly, he didn't say it at all. That was this game, and Andy Fowler played it, too.

Hardy, with the problem of where to draw the line between personal loyalty and the public trust, knew he had to get Fowler off the case and he didn't want to blow the whistle on him. If a white lie could accomplish both results he thought it might be worth telling. He also thought it might not be. How many venial sins make a mortal sin? How many angels can dance on the head of a pin?

"Dismas, I'm only sixty-two, I'm not ready to retire—"

"You know, Andy, you've got to cut your losses, and you're going to have 'em. At least you'll still have your reputation. Maybe you'll get a call to the federal bench."

They both got a wry smile at that. They were making last call, the lights coming up, the music going down.

Hardy had to push it. "I've got to know by the morning, Andy. I'm real sorry."

Fowler patted his shoulder. "I'm sorry I put you through this, Dismas, although I'm glad it was you who found out. Anybody else . . ."

"Andy, we've been friends a long time, but in this case I am anybody else. I'm just giving you one day to correct an oversight. But it's got to get corrected, one way or the other. I want to be clear on that."

The judge was relaxed again, the situation worked out. "It's clear, Diz, it's clear. Don't you worry."

34

David Freeman had a tradition he'd carried over from his days in law school. Whenever he scored what he considered a clear-cut victory he would celebrate it immediately. His theory was that you never knew when or if you'd get another one, and you'd better savor every drop of satisfaction from the one in hand before it was swept away into the river of your past.

So Tuesday night, after he'd arranged to have the boys and their father meet him at one-thirty the next day for a press conference in his office, he'd called a cab and taken it back to the Fairmont.

After booking a room there he took the outside elevator to the Crown Room and ordered a bottle of Paradis cognac, which went by the snifter at $12.50. The bottle set him back $350 but he could save it and take it home, a trophy for the job well done. He arrived at the Crown Room just after ten and stayed until it closed at two, putting about a six-inch dent in the bottle, sitting at one of the north-facing windows, watching his city sparkle beneath him, a Nob in his own castle.

Which explained why he wasn't up anywhere near nine-thirty. If he had been, if he'd somehow gotten to Chris Locke and let him know that the May Shinn case couldn't go to trial, that her alibi was rock solid, then he might have saved Superior Court Judge Andrew Bryan Fowler the trouble of announcing his early retirement, effective September 1.

In a computerized age, Jeff Elliot considered this manual search for title to a piece of property the most unnecessarily tedious job he'd ever done. Yesterday, after only two hours at it, his blurred vision had forced him to give it up.

Now, three hours into it again, not yet noon, he was having second thoughts, wondering if it could really matter. He'd thought of all sorts of plausible reasons to talk himself out of the search, not the least of which was that May Shinn herself might easily have accumulated enough for a down payment on $500,000 worth of real estate.

He remembered stories in Playboy and Penthouse when he'd been in college about coeds who'd turned to hooking and pulled in $10,000 a month. Even allowing for the hyperbole of the publications, he knew it was possible for a high-class call girl to make $200 a night, plus all of her normal living expenses. So a smart one could save $4,000 a month, $50,000 a year. A little administrative acumen could provide a shelter for tax purposes—interior design, import/export, licensed sexual therapist.

He'd seen May Shinn in court in her tailored suit. It required no leap of faith to think she had the collateral for her own bail—she'd had the cash to pay Maury, after all. Why not the rest of it?

But—what if she didn't?

And, as always, it was that possibility that pulled him along. The chance that under the obvious and the plausible, there might lurk the secret, the hidden, the dangerous—the story.

The title clerks could have been more helpful. But they were busy with their own work, with realtors they saw more often. He was a nosy crippled guy who didn't even know what to ask for. So, like good bureaucrats everywhere, the clerks volunteered nothing.

But the learning curve was kicking in. Even if you knew the city— and Jeff wasn't yet up to speed even there—the search took some getting used to. There were huge grid books that divided the land into areas that seemed to bear little relation to current neighborhoods. At first glance, street names were useless in determining which grid book —out of more than a hundred—held your property. But he felt he was closing in.

The collateral was a six-unit apartment building three blocks up Powell from Washington Square. After his frustrating search of records the day before, Jeff had come up with the idea that he could just stop by the place and ask one of the tenants who owned the building, and he and Dorothy had tried that.

The one person who'd been home—a mime artist who was preparing to go out and work the streets, whiteface and all—told them she sent her rent checks to a management company.

Jeff thought it unlikely that he'd befriend another secretary who would divulge private records to him, and decided that if he wanted the story he'd have to work for it, like always.

He estimated the books weighed fifteen pounds each. Up close, they smelled like wet newspaper. He had to wait in line, return his previous request, using only one crutch, holding the title book in his other hand. He'd gone through twenty-six books so far, but the closest plot in the last book ended a couple of blocks north of his site.

Why couldn't you just type an address into a computer and push a button? He'd never figure it out.

Jane was furious. "You didn't have to tell anybody! Daddy's whole life is the bench. How could you do that to him?"

It was close to one o'clock. Jane had had her own early lunch with her father and he'd told her all about it. Hardy wasn't too thrilled to learn that the judge had told his daughter, since he himself had elected to treat the entire sensitive subject on a need-to-know basis, hoping no one would.

Frannie hadn't liked it either. "You can't tell me? What do you mean, you can't tell me? I'm your wife. We tell each other things, remember?"

"I can tell you it has nothing to do with us."

"You go out in the middle of the night and stay out until God knows when and I don't even get a hint of an explanation?"

"Frannie, no. It doesn't have to do with us. It's confidential, attorney-client—"

"Well, la di *da*. And whose attorney are you? I thought you worked for the city." She had him there, but he had made his decision. He had all sorts of conflicting loyalties. "This job is changing you," she said.

Maybe. Life changed people, big deal, live with it. But he wasn't stupid enough to say that. Instead he'd gone off to work with the stomachache he got every time they fought.

And now Andy Fowler had told his daughter, or she'd wheedled it out of him. But either way, here was another person—and not the soul of discretion—who knew.

"I didn't do anything to him, Jane. If anything, he did it to himself."

"You didn't have to tell anybody!"

"I didn't tell anybody. I haven't told anybody, at least not yet. I hope I won't have to."

"Have to? My, aren't we getting sanctimonious here."

Hardy's door was open. He told Jane to hang on and he got up to close it. Pullios was coming down the hallway, deep in conference with Chris Locke. His stomach tightened further and he shut the door before they saw him.

Back at the phone, he asked Jane if Big Chuck—he'd taken to thinking of her new boyfriend as Big Chuck—if Big Chuck had been there, too, when Andy had told her.

"What's that supposed to mean?"

"I think it means I don't have to take any abuse from you, so leave me alone."

He hung up.

There were lots of ways to do it, and Freeman naturally chose the most flamboyant. Well, perhaps not altogether naturally. The inclination to do things with flair, while meshing well with his personality, had been drummed out of him in law school, but over the years of private practice he had put it back in.

In the first years of his practice he would have taken evidence he had dug up (such as the Strauss boys' corroboration of May's alibi) and brought it into the D.A.'s office, where it would be discussed and some decision would be made about whether it eliminated the need for a trial.

But over the long run he had found that this cooperative attitude did little for him. Prosecutors often disbelieved what he brought them, doubted its truth or relevance, impugning his motives while they were at it. He had found that if he did it only sparingly, when his findings were unambiguous and, as in this case, critical, a public airing of evidence had a way of getting more action out of the D.A. than any attempt at amity, goodwill and cooperation. District attorneys, he had found, were acutely sensitive to public perception—more so, often, than to justice.

A news conference made hairs stand up in the Hall, made young lawyers (and even a few old ones) fear you—a force who dared go outside the system if he had to. They'd call him a loose cannon, and watch out, guys. Loose cannons go boom.

He stood now in the lobby of his office, surrounded by a totally unnecessary phalanx of some of his associates he'd sent home earlier to put on their best threads. He himself was as rumpled as usual in an old brown tweed and scuffed wing tips.

In front of him was a makeshift podium with several microphones.

Opposite the podium, facing him, stood a knot of some fifteen reporters, which was a pretty fair showing, considering the short lead time he'd given them. There were three sound trucks double-parked in the street outside, which meant he'd be on television. KGO radio was represented—so he'd get some sound bites on the most popular talk station.

May was a good sport about it. He told her it was time to collect on his advertising fee. He'd come to admire her quite a bit, especially after finding out she had probably been telling him the truth the whole time. Now she was standing next to him, not yet daring to smile, flawlessly turned out as usual.

His fingers did a little tap dance over the microphones and he smiled. Gosh, he wasn't used to all of this, regular old working stiff that he was. Were these things on? He spoke extemporaneously. "Ladies and gentlemen, I'd like to thank you all for coming here today and I won't take much of your very valuable time. As you know, a couple of weeks ago Owen Nash, one of the giants of American business, was felled by a gunshot. No one would deny that Mr. Nash was a powerful and fascinating man."

He glanced at May Shinn and got another bonus. At the mention of Nash's name, a tear had sprung from her eyes and was rolling down her cheek. Don't wipe it, he thought to himself. A couple of bulbs flashed.

Freeman took her hand, gave it a squeeze. "In cases like this, there seems to be a natural inclination to fasten guilt on somebody, to lay the blame somewhere. Who can say why? It could be it satisfies society's need for order. Maybe our outrage is so great we crave any action that seems to redress the great wrong that murder represents.

"How many of us, in our heart of hearts, blame Jack Ruby for killing Lee Harvey Oswald? No, when the king falls, the king's killer must, in turn, be killed. Of course, I'm not comparing Owen Nash to our martyred president. Like Dan Quayle, Owen Nash was no Jack Kennedy."

He waited for the laughter, stole a glance at May and squeezed her hand again. "But Owen Nash was, in his own way, a titan. And there was that same rush to judgment.

"Unfortunately, in this case, that rush centered upon the person who now stands here on my right, May Shinn, a natural American citizen, a woman with *no* criminal record of any kind, a woman whose sole fault, if it is one, was to become involved with, to fall in love with, Owen Nash.

"In a perfect world the district attorney would never have even condoned the kind of public vigilantism that has been the earmark of this case from the beginning. It is, however, a sad fact that this is not a perfect world and that our own district attorney's office was from the beginning in the forefront of the racist witchhunt that brought this young woman to the dock without a shred of physical evidence that could implicate her in this horrible deed."

He stopped, enjoying a minute of eye contact with the journalists and reporters. He had them.

"From the beginning, Ms. Shinn has contended that on the day Owen Nash was brutally murdered she stayed home, waiting for his return. She did not use the telephone. She did not go out to buy a newspaper. She did not play the piano or hammer nails in her wall or sing in the shower. I submit to you all that this is not criminal behavior.

"And yet, ladies and gentlemen, and let me make this very clear, this was the sum total of the people's case against May Shinn. That she did nothing to make anyone notice she was home! Imagine that! Time was when that would have been the mark of a good citizen, an ideal neighbor. But because she is of Japanese descent, because she dared have a relationship with a powerful man"—he lowered his voice —"because she was, in fact, a woman powerless to defend herself against the might of the state, she was the perfect scapegoat. She spent a quiet day at home and she is suspected, indeed, accused, of murder.

"I'd like now to introduce you to two young men—Nick and Alex Strauss—who happen to live directly across the street from Ms. Shinn's apartment."

He nodded to one of his associates, who went into the adjoining room and brought out the two boys and their father.

"If the district attorney had been interested in the truth, he too could have found the Strauss boys. They got back from a trip to Europe on June twentieth, the day Owen Nash was killed. You'll never guess what they saw."

35

He was getting a Diet Coke in the lounge, when one of the guys two doors down, Constantino, stuck his head in.

"Hardy, you better get to Drysdale's," he said.

It was five minutes to three. Drysdale had gotten a tip from one of his connections at KRON, and now Pullios, Chris Locke himself and a third of the rest of the staff were gathered in front of the television set. Hardy squeezed himself into the doorway, reminded of other gatherings like this—the day Dan White had killed Harvey Milk and Mayor Moscone at City Hall, the Reagan assassination attempt. He wondered who'd been shot.

Somebody called out. "Okay, okay, it's on, turn it up." The room went quiet, except for the anchor's voice, talking about an exceptional development in the Owen Nash murder case, and in a minute there was David Freeman on the screen in front of a bunch of microphones, May Shinn beside him.

"He's paying those kids, or the father. It's a setup." Pullios didn't believe it, or she was pretending she didn't believe it.

"Two kids?" Drysdale shook his head. "What about the naked part? He wouldn't have made that up."

Locke was silent, standing by the window, looking out.

"It is for sure going to play," Hardy said.

Everyone else had gone. Ironically, the room seemed smaller with only four of them in it.

"How could they be sure it was the same day?" Pullios.

Drysdale picked up his baseballs and began to juggle.

"Would you please not do that!" The exasperation of Elizabeth Pullios. Hardy didn't mind seeing it, thought she'd earned it. It was, after all, her case.

"Sorry," Drysdale said. He caught the balls and palmed them all in

248

one hand. "I think they covered that pretty well. It was the day they came back from Europe, they'd just gotten off the plane. It's pretty solid documentation."

"Maybe they're just plain lying. He's paying them—"

"Pretty risky. Cross-exam would kill them and Freeman knows it."

"I want to interview them."

"I would think so," said Drysdale.

She stood flat-footed in front of his desk. She kept looking over at Locke's back, but he wasn't turning around. Freeman's hammering of Christopher Locke wasn't lost on any of them. Locke was the district attorney, they weren't. So far as the public was concerned, Christopher Locke—personally—had screwed this one up. He, a black man, was a racist. He had picked on a woman. An ethnic. It was a disaster.

"Goddamn it!" Pullios said.

Drysdale nodded. "Yes, ma'am," he said.

When Jeff Elliot discovered at the title office that the owner of the collateralized apartment was Superior Court Judge Andrew Fowler, he was pretty sure he had hit the jackpot.

Then, finding out he'd missed Freeman's press conference—"Why didn't somebody call me?"—he saw it all slip away.

Finally, hearing the news about Fowler's retirement, he knew he had himself the story of his career. There was only one person who held in his hand all the elements to this thing, and he was it.

To Glitsky it meant something else entirely—he'd arrested the wrong person, and they still had a live homicide. He was in the office of his lieutenant, Frank Batiste, after five, chewing on the ice that was left in his styrofoam cup.

Though one outranked the other, the two men had come up together and knew that politics outside of either of their control had dictated Batiste's promotion—they still viewed themselves more as partners than anything else.

"You're lucky the grand jury indicted," Batiste said. "It takes the heat off."

"I'll probably still get sued." Glitsky found a spot for his cup on Batiste's cluttered desk. "Let's see, false arrest, sex discrimination, race discrimination . . . I might as well give you my badge now." It wasn't funny, but they both were smiling. Cop humor. "Maybe Locke won't drop it."

Batiste looked hard at him. "Maybe it'll snow tomorrow."

"The kids *could* be mistaken."

"There could be peace in our time."

"You know, Frank, you are solace to a troubled soul."

"I try to be." Batiste had his feet up on his desk, a legal pad on his lap. He started doodling. "So what do you think we've got here, the perfect crime? I hope not, because I've got a feeling this one isn't going to go away. Anybody else could have done it?"

"Maybe. Nobody looks near as good as Shinn did." Glitsky told his lieutenant that he'd take another look at the business side, Mr. Silicon Valley, somebody else who might benefit, but the evidence was slim and none if it wasn't Shinn. He flicked ice into his mouth and chewed. "You know, this one time I thought I might have a case with, you know, witnesses who weren't already in jail, maybe a motive aside from lack of imagination."

"Maybe next year," Batiste said. "And in the meantime we still have a very important dead person."

Hardy called Celine after he returned from Drysdale's office—he told himself that she at least deserved to be among the first to know that her father's killer was still on the streets.

He reached her at Hardbodies!, where she'd been working out again. After he told her, he listened to the background noise in the phone—the throbbing music, the torture machines. Finally she asked him what he meant.

"I mean May's alibi checks out. She wasn't out on the *Eloise* with your father."

"But what does that *mean?*"

"It means she didn't kill him, Celine." He waited, not pushing, for another minute. "Celine?"

Okay, he thought, you've done your duty. Now tell her you'll keep her informed of developments and hang up. Just hang up, go home and have a date night with Frannie.

"So what do we do now?" Celine asked him quietly, shock in her voice. "Can I see you?"

No, I'm busy. How about coming by the office tomorrow? "All right," he said.

He met her at Perry's on Union, a meat market in the classic sense— fine food, big drinks, good vibes.

Though her hair was still damp, pulled back by a turquoise band, she'd found time to make herself up. But somehow Hardy found her physical presence not quite so overpowering as before. It was the first time he'd seen her since their original meeting that the contours of her body—under the baggy purple sweater, the black and blousy pants—weren't immediately evident. He was grateful for that.

It was early dusk but the place was already jammed. She was standing near the entrance, which was on the side down an alley, an orange juice in her hand, talking to another man who was about Hardy's age, though taller, broader and better dressed. When Hardy came in, her face lit up and she moved to him, kissing him briefly on the lips. She took his hand and turned; the man had already started for the bar.

"I told him my boyfriend was on his way," she said, "but you know this place. A woman alone is fair game." She didn't let go of his hand. "Come, let's see if we can get a table."

"I can't eat, Celine. I'm just on my way home."

She stopped pulling him along, still didn't let go of his hand. "You mean you're going to leave me here alone? I won't last five minutes."

"Oh, you will if you decide to."

Another side of her, a little more humanity, a trace of humor. She did have a real life he knew nothing about.

A couple vacated their table two feet from them and Hardy let go of Celine's hand and guided her to it. A waitress appeared and he ordered a club soda. He could feel the heat of her thigh where it pressed against his.

"Are you always alone?" Hardy asked her. "Every time I see you, you're alone."

"Wrong. Every time you see me, I'm with you." She leaned away from him. "Why do you want to know? You're married."

"Yes, I am," he said. "I just wonder."

She accepted that. "Not right now. Does this have to do with my father?"

He tried and failed to find some connection. "No, I don't suppose so."

She reached for her orange juice, took a sip and cradled the glass in both hands in her lap. "I was married one time. I was twenty-one, going through one of my rebellious phases. He was a musician, a good player. He finally made a couple of albums. Heavy metal, which now I truly hate. I think I despised it then, and I know Daddy did."

"Did your father and he get along?"

She started to laugh, then stopped herself. "No. Daddy hated everything about him."

"Is that why you broke up?"

"No, not really. He was a jerk, which I suppose I knew all along, but Daddy had him followed when he was on the road and he didn't act like he was married. So," she continued, shrugging, "we had it annulled. It's ancient history now, but it kind of soured me on men for a long while. Plus, there's being rich. You know, it's hard to find people you believe. Guys try to pick you up, first it's your looks, then if they find out you've got money . . ."

Hardy's club soda arrived. He held it, staring out the window. It seemed to not be getting any darker outside.

"What are you thinking?" she asked.

"I don't know exactly. That there's more than the pickup scene. I mean, didn't you meet anybody in your regular life?"

She shook her head. "Sometimes, once in a while. But my regular life always had Daddy in it."

"I think this is where our problem started last time."

She reached over and took his hand again. "We're not going to do that again. I can't explain to people about me and Daddy. It was all right, we did everything together."

"But *he* seemed to have a personal life, I mean women friends, and you apparently weren't allowed to. How can that have been fair? How was it living with that?"

"I don't know how to say it or explain it, but it was okay. You did things with Daddy, you felt a certain way. Ask Ken."

"But it couldn't be the same with him. He's married, he's got a life."

She tightened her hold on his hand. "I've got a life, Dismas, don't worry about me."

"I guess I do," he said. "I don't know why, but I do."

"I know." She let him go and moved her palm up and down over his thigh. "You are a very good man, Mr. Hardy. I wish . . ."

She didn't finish what she was saying. She didn't have to.

They never got around to mentioning the name of May Shinn.

Hardy got home just at seven. Rebecca was in bed asleep, one of their regular baby-sitters was in the living room talking to Frannie, and Frannie was dressed up, ready to go out.

He was in the house for less than five minutes. He wanted to peek in on the Beck, to feed the fish. Pit stop.

They walked out to the car, parked two blocks away on Clement, holding hands. "Are we still fighting?" he asked.

"I wasn't fighting with you."

"Neither were you singing my praises."

"I didn't agree with you. I don't agree with you. I think your job is taking too much of your time and is threatening you and me and our family and I don't like you not telling me what you're doing and where you're going."

"You've got to learn to speak out, Frannie. Express yourself a little more clearly."

"Not funny."

They walked on another half block without talking. "So if you can't make a joke out of it you're not going to say anything?" she asked.

"I'm going to say something."

The last of the chivalrous men, Hardy held the door for her, then went around to his side. The sun had at last gone down. He put the sides up on the Samurai, it was warm with the breeze off the ocean.

"When?"

"When what?"

"When are you going to say something?"

Hardy turned in his seat. Confidentiality obviously meant little to Andy Fowler. Since Jane knew, then certainly by now Chuck Chuck Bo-Buck was in on it. And Hardy had never promised Andy he would keep it private—he'd only promised himself.

He'd *only* promised himself. He liked that.

This was how it started, he thought. This was the kind of rationalizing that people everywhere seemed to be so good at. And once it was okay to break a promise to yourself, then it wasn't all that big a step to break one to anyone else. Just so you could end a fight.

Or maybe tell a little white lie to keep from getting into a fight in the first place.

All he had to do was give in, tell Frannie about Andy and they would have a pleasant and well-deserved date. And Hardy's supposed private integrity would only be slightly diminished—he could make it up on the weekend, do some good works.

"Did you hear about the May Shinn thing today?" he asked her. She hadn't yet, and he filled her in on it.

She listened, and when he'd finished, she told him that it was interesting but that it wasn't what their fight had been about. Did he want to tell her where he'd been last night or not?

"I went out to meet a guy who's got a legal problem, which I can't discuss. Period. If you want to be mad at me about that, it's up to you."

She was biting her lip, not so much angry, he thought, as worried. "What about the other stuff?" she said. "These hours at work, getting home when it's dark, leaving in the middle of the night. What's that doing to us?"

The two front seats in the Samurai were separated by a well, and he reached for her and put his arms around her. She leaned into him. "We're not being threatened," he said. "The job is not threatening us. I love you, Frannie, okay?"

She nodded against him, her arms around his neck. Her reserve broke. She started to cry.

When they got home there were calls from Ken Farris, Jane apologizing, and Abe Glitsky wondering about the direction the D.A. was going with this thing.

Hardy went into his office while Frannie drove the baby-sitter home and began rereading the file on the now-dead case. At least it was dead so far as May Shinn was concerned.

He didn't know what the D.A. was going to do, but he thought he personally was going to go back to doing his prelims, earn his stripes, win a lot of cases and eventually move up the ladder to where he might get a couple of righteous homicides.

There was nothing else he could do. He wasn't an investigator. He knew Glitsky, after the false arrest, would be super-cautious. He wasn't inclined to stir things up with Pullios anymore. Frannie had been right . . . he was putting in too many hours, not having enough fun. He was becoming a *lawyer,* and if he wanted to do that he could get some corporate work and bill sixty hours a week for five or six years and make some money while he did it.

He'd left Celine at Perry's, thinking what a good man am I. He thought she might be a little in love with him. Although he knew he was infatuated with her on some level, he wasn't going to pursue it. He'd made his choice, and not only was he going to live with it, he was going to be happy with it.

That settled, he decided to close up the binder and file it away in the cabinets next to his desk. He arranged the yellow sheets from his own private notes at the beginning of the investigation—his initial talks with Ken Farris, impressions from Strout and so on—and laid them on top of the copies he'd made of the official file.

His office was quiet. From the bedroom the bubbling of the fish tank registered subliminally. Not really looking for anything, waiting for Frannie's arrival back home, he reread the early notes. All of this seemed so long ago, so distant in time and experience.

He flipped pages, the police reports, Glitsky's interviews, killing time. Elliot's articles.

And then the bubbling fish tank was gone. There was nothing in his world but a nagging, half-recognized contradiction. He flipped back to one of Jeff Elliot's first articles.

Ken Farris had told him that he'd last seen Owen Nash on Friday around lunchtime, after lunch. The article, quoting Farris as the source, said Nash had last been seen by his household staff on Thursday night.

He looked back at his notes—Friday around lunchtime, after lunch. Elliot's article—Thursday night. Thursday night was not Friday near lunchtime.

He shook his head, rubbing his eyes. What was he thinking of? Farris wasn't any kind of suspect in this. He had been Owen Nash's best friend. All right, so he effectively inherited the business when Owen died, that wasn't—

Or was it?

But all he had done was tell Hardy one day and Jeff Elliot another. The stress of those first days after Nash's death had undoubtedly played some havoc with his short-term memory.

But Farris was a detail man.

Ridiculous.

He shook his head again . . .

Frannie was in the doorway to the office. He hadn't heard her come in or close the front door or walk down the long hallway. She had turned on the light in the bedroom and it hadn't registered.

"You look like you've just seen a ghost."

He came out of his trance, shook himself. "More of this madness," he said.

"I thought you were done with it."

It was as tantalizing as that last cognac, where you knew if you had it you were going to hurt tomorrow. He would, perhaps, mention it to Glitsky. It wasn't his job.

"I am," he said, closing the file. "I was just waiting for you to get home."

36

JUDGE GUARANTEES BOND IN NASH MURDER CASE
But Defense Attorney Verifies May
Shinn's Alibi; D.A. to Drop Charges
by Jeffrey Elliot
Chronicle Staff Writer

In a startling series of developments surrounding the murder trial of financier Owen Nash yesterday, Superior Court Judge Andrew B. Fowler resigned just hours before it was discovered that an apartment he owns had collateralized the half-million-dollar bail for defendant May Shinn.

According to sources in the district attorney's office, investigators may subpoena a defendant's financial records if there is probable cause that the money used for bail, or for paying a defense attorney, is the result of criminal activity, such as drug dealing or, in this case, prostitution. Ms. Shinn has admitted that she has been a highly paid call girl.

In a related story, however, Ms. Shinn's attorney, David Freeman, produced two young boys as witnesses who have testified that, using a telescope, they saw Ms. Shinn in her home during the time the district attorney had contended she was aboard Owen Nash's sailboat, the *Eloise.*

District Attorney Christopher Locke last night personally interviewed the two boys and announced that all charges against Ms. Shinn related to the murder would be dropped.

"Two eyewitnesses confirm her alibi," Locke said, "so there is no case. But remember, her gun *was* the murder weapon, we believed we had a solid motive. But we are dealing with a very clearly defined window of time in this case, and if Ms. Shinn was in her apartment on Saturday afternoon, she could not have killed Owen Nash.

257

"This office is, of course, distressed by implications of racism used against Ms. Shinn, and we intend to investigate those charges and take disciplinary action if appropriate."

The relationship between Judge Fowler and Ms. Shinn remains unclear. The judge has reportedly left the city, but California Supreme Court Justice Marshall Brinkman, who serves on the state's Committee on Judicial Ethics, stated that he is "deeply concerned" over reports of Judge Fowler's purported involvement with the defendant. "Where there is any relationship, however tangential, between a judge and a defendant, the judge must immediately recuse himself from the case," Brinkman said. "Any failure in this area is gross judicial misconduct. At the very least it's a disbarment issue."

David Freeman refused to comment on Judge Fowler, although he certainly knew the details of the bail arrangement. Citing the attorney-client privilege, he also defended Ms. Shinn's right to her privacy. "My client has been through enough," he said. "She did not commit this murder. She is an innocent woman, falsely accused, wrongly charged."

"Wow!" Frannie said.

"Yeah." Hardy was on his third cup of coffee. He had read the article twice. He was astounded that Andy had essentially put up bail for May Shinn and hadn't felt compelled to mention that fact to him during his soul-baring two nights ago.

The sun was coming through the skylight over the stove, shining off the pots and pans hanging from the opposite wall. Rebecca was breast-feeding.

"I'm sure this has nothing to do with a friend of yours who is in legal trouble that you can't say anything about."

The shifting sands of the moral high ground. Hardy smiled at it, had some more coffee.

"Where do you think he is?" she asked.

"I think he's probably home, holed up, not answering the phone."

"How much more do you know about this?"

"A little. Not much."

"I don't know how you can keep this in. How long have you known about it?"

He pulled the paper back in front of him. "This stuff, about fifteen minutes. The relationship a little longer."

"So what was the relationship?"

"What do you think, Frannie?"

Frannie was still in her bathrobe. She had a diaper over her shoulder, the baby against it, patting her gently. Rebecca let out a long, satisfied burp. "That's a girl," she said.

"Let me hold her."

Hardy took Frannie's daughter—his daughter—into his arms and made a face that was rewarded with a delighted gurgle. "Are you my big girl? Am I not spending enough time with you?" He put his face down by hers, breathing in her scent, rubbing his cheek against hers. Frannie came around the table and pressed herself against him, looking over his shoulder. "We're the lucky ones," she said.

"I know."

But the newspaper kept drawing them both back. Frannie reached down and turned it back to the front page.

"What's going to happen to him now, Diz?"

"I don't know. Since May Shinn didn't kill Nash, the whole thing might just blow over. Couple of days of bad press. You were right, by the way. Remember his paperweight?"

"She gave it to him."

Hardy nodded. "Reminded him of his broken heart, so he gave it to me. She dumped him for Owen Nash."

"So they weren't together anymore, Andy Fowler and Shinn?"

"No, I mean that was kind of the point."

"So then why would he put up her bail? Why would he be the judge on her trial?"

"I don't know. If he helped her out, maybe he could get her back eventually."

"That never happens," Frannie said.

"What doesn't?"

"You don't dump somebody for someone else, then go back to the first one. If you're the one dumped, okay, you might. But if your heart goes cold on somebody . . ." She shrugged. "It just doesn't happen."

"I don't know if it was May's heart that went cold, Frannie. The woman is a hooker. Maybe she really fell for Nash, but it was probably just a better financial deal with him. So Andy helping her out with the bail . . . it might have just been him putting out the word that he had money, too, and he'd spend it on her. Hell, half a million, that's serious good-faith money."

"And he'd be satisfied with that?"

"I don't know. I guess so. Anyway, that's what he had before."

She was rubbing his back, rocking back and forth against him. "Nope," she said. "He loved her, and however she felt about him, he had to *believe* she loved him too. The paperweight, remember? That's a special gift. That's a message."

"So?"

"So what was it? *After* she left him I don't believe he really thought he was buying her back. By then he had to realize she didn't love him, even if he'd made himself believe it before. So there must have been another reason."

Hardy shook his head and leaned back into Frannie's body. "Well, until *you* get it figured out, at least you'll know why this thing has kept me up nights." He stood and shifted the Beck over his shoulder. "But it's not going to anymore."

"I just feel sorry for Andy. I mean, if the Shinn woman really is innocent, then he just gave up everything for nothing."

"That's right," Hardy said. "People do that all the time."

He stopped by Glitsky's before going to his own office, but the sergeant wasn't in. He wrote him a short note about the discrepancy in Ken Farris's recollection of when Nash had last been seen, and figured that was the end of his active involvement with Owen Nash.

Then, taped to the center of his desk, he read the summons from Drysdale to see him as soon as he got in and to bring all of his binders on the Nash matter.

It was getting to be a habit, the walk down to Locke's office, although this time with the bulging, special "lawyer's briefcase." Hardy sat in the anteroom, listening to muffled sounds through the closed door. The secretary seemed unusually preoccupied, typing away, filing. The intercom buzzed and she punched it and said yes, he was out here.

Another few minutes and Hardy sat back, relaxed, crossed his legs and picked up the sports page from the low end table next to his chair.

In the day's latest, Bob Lurie was trying to move the Giants to either Sacramento, San Jose, or Portland, although he mentioned Honolulu —the great baseball tradition in Hawaii. Talk about a homeless problem, he thought. This is the team nobody wants to take home. He turned to the standings. Halfway through the year—nine games out, third place. Not terrible, not great. How could they have traded Kevin Mitchell?

The door opened and Elizabeth Pullios came out. She didn't appear to be in any particular hurry, yet she walked by Hardy, ignoring his greeting as if she'd never seen him before. "Have a nice day," he said to her back.

Drysdale was at the door, gesturing with his forefinger.

"Why do I get the feeling this isn't a hundred-percent social?" Hardy asked.

Locke got down to it immediately. "Did you tell this reporter Elliot that our office subpoenaed Andy Fowler's financial records?"

"No. Somebody tell you I did?"

"We've had a discussion about leaks and so on before, right?"

"Yes, sir. Somebody tell you I was the leak? Did we subpoena his records?"

"I want you to tell me everything you know about Andy Fowler."

"Was it Pullios? If it was, she's a liar."

Drysdale, who'd been standing halfway behind Hardy, hands in his pockets, stepped forward. "We've got a problem, Diz. A real problem. You've got a problem."

"Fowler." Locke didn't want to leave the issue.

"How is Fowler my problem?"

"You were seen entering the witness waiting room the other day with Jeff Elliot."

"Can I ask who saw me? Or rather, who thought it was important to tell you?"

"It's irrelevant," Locke said. "What's relevant is that you knew something critical to a murder case and withheld it from us."

Hardy found himself getting pretty hot. "Like hell it's irrelevant! You accuse me of something and you don't let me face my accuser. I thought perhaps in an office practicing law we'd give a nod to the niceties of getting to the truth."

"We already know the truth. Fowler was your father-in-law, wasn't he?"

"That came from Pullios. Deny it."

"I don't have to deny anything. Pullios, unlike you, is a damn good lawyer."

"Oh, that's right. She really did a great job with May Shinn, locked her up tight."

Drysdale tried to slow it down. "Guys . . ."

"If Elizabeth knew that Andy Fowler had gone the bail for May Shinn, she would have come to me with it, not the newspaper."

"Well, isn't she the nice little Gestapet."

Drysdale butted in. "When did you know about Fowler, Diz?"

Hardy stopped and took a breath. "You know, Art, it's funny, but I don't believe we've established that I *did* know about Fowler yet. We have some unnamed source finking me into a room with Jeff Elliot. Although I'm beginning to suspect that in Mr. Locke's little fiefdom here, if you're accused, you're guilty."

The district attorney was on his feet. "Don't get any smarter with me, Hardy."

"It's too late for that." He paused, then added, "Chris. From what I've seen, I'm already smarter than you."

"What you are, is out of a job."

"And what you are, Chris . . ." Hardy slowed down, pulling out of it. He looked him in the eye. "What you are, Chris, is a total flaming asshole."

He thought about it at Lou's over his third black-and-tan. They'd planned to fire him all along. They didn't want any new information out of him, anything incriminating. That had been a front.

Figure it out—before they'd asked him question one they'd told him to bring all the Nash files down to the office. They were planning on taking them from him. Which they'd done.

Ha, guys. Guess what?

The funny thing was he *had* withheld information from them. But he really hadn't leaked the news about Fowler and bail. He'd only found that out this morning when he'd read the newspaper. Jeff Elliot had discovered it and used the information Hardy had given him about subpoena policy to make it appear it had been a D.A. leak. He was a clever guy, Jeff Elliot, and he'd cost Hardy his job, though at the moment Hardy was thinking that fell more into the category of a favor.

So maybe Locke and Drysdale had had grounds to fire him after all —he had known about Andy Fowler's relationship with May Shinn and hadn't come forward with it immediately. That wasn't being a *team player*. But, he told himself, even if they had reasons they didn't have the *right* reasons.

It still wasn't noon. He thought he'd call Frannie, see if she was home, take her and the Beck out for a nice lunch.

37

Of the three men A.D.A. Elizabeth Pullios slept with on a fairly regular basis, two were married and two worked in the district attorney's office.

There was District Attorney Chris Locke, who called her Pullios. She had him for the rush and the control—intimacy with your superior might be a double-edged sword, but so far it had cut only one way. Actually, in this case, Locke was the one who had most to lose if it came out. She knew not only the law on workplace harassment but the implications, if played right, and she knew how to play them. If a strong man who happened to be your boss had a relationship with you, it was his problem. You were the employee, he was the boss. And he could—and often did—fire you if you weren't cooperative. The true vulnerability of many women in the workplace was something that played into the hands of someone like Pullios. Further, the odds of a backlash were long in her favor. For example, the way she had pushed and manipulated to get May Shinn indicted after lifting the file from another prosecutor . . . most any other assistant D.A. would have been stripped and flayed by Locke. Instead, since Locke knew Pullios was a damn good prosecutor, as well as "one helluva squeeze," diverting his gaze and rage to a junior scapegoat like Hardy had been so easy it was almost unfair. Except that nothing was unfair. If you won, fairness was a concept that didn't apply.

Her second lover was Brian Powell, to whom she was Elizabeth. Brian had been her "boyfriend" for three years. Forty-five, handsome, politically correct, he was a divorced, childless stockbroker who made six figures and did not hassle her. He understood when she was busy. She considered getting engaged to him (he hadn't asked yet but she could lead him to it if she wanted) when it was time to run for D.A. and a mate would be helpful; until then he was someone pleasant to be with and be seen with.

The other man in the office—and in some ways the only one personally dangerous to her, called her Molly. That was Peter Struler, married and the father of three. He gave her the impression that he could take her or leave her, though he'd been taking her with some regularity for the past four or five months. With a law degree from Duke and three years in the FBI, Struler was both brain-smart and street-smart. He was also irreverent and funny. As an investigator for the district attorney's office he worked under a separate jurisdiction from both the SFPD and the sheriff's department. It was the private police arm of the district attorney's office and was used to protect attorneys going out to see witnesses in bad areas, to deliver subpoenas and, occasionally, to carry on its own investigations.

The danger of Peter Struler was that Elizabeth Pullios liked him a lot. She had met him when he had escorted her, in his official capacity, on an interview with some lowlifes she needed to put away even lower life-forms. After she had been her very efficient self, talking to witnesses hiding behind their drawn curtains, she had come out into the sunlight to see Struler playing basketball, shirt off, with eight black high-school dudes on a glass-strewn court—a little boy having the time of his life. She had fallen for him, gotten uncharacteristically shy and made excuses for them to get together officially until he called her on it and she told him, driving out to another site, that she thought maybe she was in love with him. He didn't have to worry about it, though, she added quickly. She would get over it. And she didn't want to hurt his marriage.

"My marriage is solid," he had said, pulling the car over. "Nothing is going to threaten my marriage. But I think we ought to get something straight between us."

And they did, right there in the car.

Now they sat, again in his city car, eating Chinese takeout at a parking lot at the Presidio. There were whitecaps on the Bay and you could see halfway to Alaska.

Struler was quoting from the front of his chopsticks wrapper. " 'Welcome to Chinese Restaurant. Please try your Nice Chinese Food with Chopsticks, the traditional and typical of Chinese glorious history and culture.' "

She nodded. "It's a wonderful view, too."

"Now look at this," Struler said. "If this is true, why did they have to invent cranes."

"Cranes?"

"You know, derricks, cranes."

"If what's true?"

Struler read: " 'Learn how to use your chopsticks Tuck under thumb and hold firmly Add second chopstick hold it as you hold a pencil Hold first chopstick in original position move the second one up and down Now you can pick up anything!' "

He tried to lift the briefcase. "It's just not true. How can they get by with that. I can't even lift this thing. I bet there's no way you could even pick up a dog."

"A dog?"

He pointed at the paper. "It says 'anything.' 'Now you can pick up anything!' You're missing a bet here, Molly. You're the lawyer. I smell a major lawsuit. Class action, false advertising, big bucks."

She let him rave. It was one of the things she liked best about him, his capacity to run with essentially nothing. "Plus their punctuation is really weak. They don't use periods. Did you ever notice that?"

She reached over and grabbed the briefcase herself, placing it on her lap, snapping open the clasps.

"Why do I sense you don't share my fascination with this topic? The future is the Orient, mark my words."

She kissed him on the cheek. "Business before pleasure."

He put his hand between her legs. "Who made that up? Some lawyer, I bet."

"You're a lawyer, Mr. Struler."

"No, I just went to law school, I never took the class on business before pleasure. Come to think of it, that's probably why I flunked the bar." He moved his hand a little. "Actually, I never took the bar, did I?"

"Peter."

He made a face. "Molly." But he put his hands in his own lap. "Okay, what?"

"This is a two-week-old murder . . ."

"My favorite."

"My point is, the police have already embarrassed themselves over it—the Owen Nash thing. Abe Glitsky has been handling the case and he made the original bust."

"Lucky guy."

"Right. He's not going to do it again. There's very little evidence. Plus the guy who got fired today—Hardy—they're at least pretty good friends. Anyway, the police cooperation is going to slow down for a while."

"And you turn to me. I am touched."

"I'd just like you to take a fresh look at it, that's all. This is an important case and I don't want it to go away. I made a big pitch for this one to Locke. Whoever killed this guy, they've made me look pretty bad."

Struler thought a moment, then took some papers out of the brief-case and glanced at them. "Is this all of it?"

She nodded. "That's all the paper. There's some other evidence logged, the murder weapon, like that, but it's been pretty well gone over."

"So what do you want me to do?"

"Start over. We need a new theory and it's in here somewhere. *Somebody* killed Owen Nash."

"If you tell me you don't have any ideas who, that would be a fib, wouldn't it, and then I'd have to spank you."

She leaned toward him and licked his ear. "I don't have any ideas."

In spite of Elizabeth Pullios's belief that the police were going to let it lie, Glitsky jumped on Hardy's discrepancy. There was nothing better than a suspect who told a lie. It opened up all the doors and windows, let some new air in. Of course, he didn't know for a fact that Farris had lied—he could have simply made a mistake, remembered incorrectly. But he was on the record—Glitsky had been in on the conversation, he remembered it—as having said white was white one time and then white was black the next. It deserved reflection.

Glitsky's own reports revealed that Farris had been at Taos during the weekend of the murder. What was at Taos? Hadn't he said it a place with no phones, no electricity? Had anyone else seen him there? Were there records of his plane flight? A hotel? Rental car?

He took some notes, placed a call to the Albuquerque police, then reached Farris at his office at Owen Industries in South San Francisco.

"Sergeant, what can I do for you?" A busy man, sounding like it.

"You know we've got an open case again, sir. It looks like May Shinn wasn't on the *Eloise*. And if that's true she didn't kill Mr. Nash."

"Of course, I read that. I'm not sure I think it's true."

"Well, yes, sir, but the D.A. seems to think it is. And while that's the case, we have to go on with the investigation." There was one of those infernal beeps again. Glitsky had forgotten about them.

"Just a minute, would you?"

He sat on hold for twenty seconds, keeping time with a pencil on his blotter.

"Sergeant? Sorry about that. It's still crazy here. I know, I tried to call the D.A. this morning but they told me some nonsense that your man Hardy wasn't working there anymore and nobody's gotten back to me."

"They said Hardy didn't work there anymore?"

"That's what they said."

Glitsky shook his head. "Well, that's ridiculous. I'll give him your message, but I'm calling to clear up a little inconsistency. We're kind of starting over here, so I apologize."

"It's all right, but what's this story on this judge knowing May? That's really a shock."

"We're looking into that, too. But what I'm wondering is when you last saw Mr. Nash alive." He did not explain about the apparent conflict in Farris's testimony.

"I remember distinctly. We had lunch down at the Angus."

"Yes, sir. And you told us it was on Friday."

Beep.

"I did? I don't remember which day it was. If I said Friday, I must have been mistaken."

"This was the weekend you went to Taos."

"I remember what weekend it was. I always fly out to Taos in the morning, which would have been Friday, so the lunch must have been Thursday. I could call the restaurant and double-check."

"That would be helpful."

"You want to hold, I can do it right now."

He came back in about a minute, saying that the restaurant still had the reservation records and it had been Thursday.

There was no way to make this next question sound innocuous, but if the answer was yes, it would save Glitsky a lot of footwork. "Mr. Farris, is there staff at the place where you stay in Taos?"

You didn't have to draw Farris a map. He didn't answer right away. Glitsky heard him take a breath on either side of the recording beep.

"Owen Nash was my best friend, Sergeant. I don't benefit in any conceivable way from his death. To the contrary. I'm personally devastated and professionally handicapped in ways you can't imagine by

Owen's death. I'm sure there's a substantial paper record of my comings and goings that weekend and if you decide it's your duty to look
into it, you go right ahead . . . If I were you, Sergeant, I'd first spend
some time on this judge. But that's up to you. And now if you'll excuse
me, I've got a full load here."

The connection went dead in Glitsky's hand. He tapped his pencil
on his blotter. Farris's reaction was not unusual—folks were generally
unappreciative when told they were under suspicion. But, Glitsky
couldn't help but notice, he didn't say that anybody had seen him in
Taos or anywhere else. Could be an oversight, like Thursday or Friday
or whatever day it had been when he'd last laid eyes on his best
friend. Could be.

It was the kind of thing, though, that Glitsky thought he'd remember.

The nap helped a little, but not much.

After the three black-and-tans in the morning, Hardy and Frannie
and Rebecca had shared some outstanding *gambas* at Sol y Luna.
Also, because Frannie wasn't drinking at all, he'd had a bottle of a
light white Rioja. Hell, he was celebrating.

He'd broken the news about his job and she took it in very much the
same vein as he had himself. They had most of a quarter million
dollars in the bank, the profit check on Hardy's percentage of the
Shamrock was coming in this week—money wasn't the biggest problem in the world, and she didn't like what practicing law had been
doing to him.

Which called for a little Fundador after lunch.

Frannie drove home and Hardy got his shirt off before he crashed to
sleep, waking up to Rebecca's wails and a thundering head. He
walked into the back room and picked up the baby, patting her gently,
holding her against him. She tried to fasten herself onto his nipple
and cried all the more at the lack of result. Frannie was coming
through the kitchen.

"We're really having another one of these baby things?" he said.

"She didn't have the lunch you did."

"She doesn't have the head I've got either." He held Rebecca in
front of his face. "Look," he said, "I know for a fact I feel worse than
you, and I'm not crying."

The logic didn't have any effect. He handed her off to her mother
and in seconds she was suckling.

"That's an excellent trick," Hardy said. He was changing into his running clothes, his green jogging suit next up in the drawer. "You mind if I run a little of this off?"

He took the four-mile circular route out to the beach, along the hard sand south to Lincoln. The air was clear, the temperature was in the low seventies and got a little nippier with the wind off the breakers.

Here he was, unemployed during a major depression, and he smiled as he ran, the headache gone in the first twenty minutes. Down the beach, back along the park, up the Avenues to his home.

He was sitting on his porch, cooling down, the sun still up but hidden now behind the buildings across the street. On the back-half of his run he had decided that, with his calendar suddenly free, the Hardy family should book a flight to Hawaii and disappear for a couple of weeks. He was daydreaming about some serious beach time, rum drinks, Jimmy Buffett riffs on a balmy breeze.

From Hardy's porch the six-story apartment buildings on either side blocked his vision both up and down the street, so there was no warning when Celine Nash appeared on the other side of his picket fence —stonewashed jeans, sandals, magenta silk blouse.

He might have expected something like this to happen—perhaps he should have called her, Farris, even Glitsky with the news of his termination. Was she coming to offer her condolences, ask what happened, get news about who would now be handling the case? How did she get his address?

He stood up, deciding he was going to change his phone number and have it unlisted. Get his address out of the new book. He should have done it—he now realized—when he had been re-hired at the district attorney's office last February, but with the new marriage, new job, new baby, other things had filled his mind.

He took a couple of steps off the porch. Celine saw him and stopped in her tracks.

He came down toward her and he realized her face was frozen. Had something else happened? She stood stock-still, as though in shock.

"Celine, are you all right?"

He took a few more steps toward her, stopping just before the gate. There was a long moment. She stared at him with a look that seemed to combine horror and loss.

Hardy heard the front door open, heard Frannie say, "Diz?"

Celine's eyes went behind him, to Frannie, fastened back, first it seemed hopefully, then almost in panic, on him. "I'm sorry," she said, starting to back away, "I'm sorry. This is a mistake."

"Celine. What's the matter?"

She shook her head, looking him up and down. Everything between him and Celine had always been too personal. Now, seeing his house and his wife, she couldn't ignore the reality. Not only was he a good man, he had a life that didn't include her on any level. She backed further away, then stopped and seemed to regain some control.

"I'm sorry, Dismas. I don't know what I was thinking."

"It's all right. What is it?"

She shook her head. "Nothing. It's a mistake." She was backing away again, turning. She lifted a hand, a diffident wave, and walked away.

"Who was that?" Frannie was up next to him, arm in his.

"Celine Nash. Owen Nash's daughter."

"God, she's beautiful, isn't she?"

Hardy tightened his arm around her. "You're beautiful."

She bumped her hip against him. "What did she want?"

He shrugged. "I don't know. Maybe she heard I got dumped."

She was getting in her car, parked halfway down the street. They both watched her.

"So why didn't she stay?"

"She's been sort of unstable since the loss of her father." They were going back to the porch. He told Frannie about Celine's explosion at him the other day, her mood swings. He neglected to mention the after-hours meeting at Hardbodies!

"I know after Eddie I was a bat case."

Hardy tightened his hand around her waist. "You were a *mensch,*" Hardy said. "She's not holding up so well."

"You shouldn't be too hard on her."

Hardy kissed his wife. "I'm not going to be anything on her. I'm fired, remember? All that's over.

PART IV

38

Hardy did take Frannie and Rebecca to Hawaii, where they stayed for two weeks.

In San Francisco the Owen Nash case fell out of the headlines. During August and September there was no outward sign of activity, although Peter Struler (not Abe Glitsky) kept himself very busy on the case that Elizabeth Pullios didn't want to close; the police department, and Abe, had moved along to other, more pressing crimes.

Now it had been over three months since Hardy had been fired, and Struler and Pullios had put together their case. When they did finally move, they moved very quickly.

The sealed indictment was passed down by the grand jury on the morning of Tuesday, October 13. Superior Court Judge Marian Braun read the indictment and decreed that there would be no bail on the bench warrant. In an unusual move, the warrant itself was hand-delivered by the district attorney himself, Christopher Locke, accompanied by assistant D.A. Elizabeth Pullios and Police Chief Dan Rigby, to Lieutenant Frank Batiste of the Homicide Division at 11:45 A.M. Reading it, Batiste sucked in a breath.

Had this case gone to the grand jury in the normal way, after an investigation by an assigned police officer, service of the warrant would have been assigned to that officer, in this case Inspector Sergeant Abraham Glitsky. But Glitsky, along with the rest of Homicide, was unaware of Peter Struler's work on behalf of the D.A.'s office. So the service was assigned to Marcel Lanier, who was lounging around the office waiting for something to happen.

Judge Fowler had weathered a cyclone of vitriol and criticism, gossip and embarrassment, but, like all storms, this one had passed. The reprimand he received from the Ethics Committee, due to his long and distinguished career stopped far short of having teeth, and the

Bar Association told him that had the May Shinn trial gone on, it would have seriously considered suspension or even disbarment. But in the end, three months later, he was back in the business of the law with a spacious corner office at Embarcadero One—a partner in the firm of Strand, Worke & Luzinski.

When Wanda buzzed him and told him Officer Marcel Lanier was waiting to see him he said of course, he knew Marcel, send him on in. Fowler hadn't been completely ostracized at the Hall—a lot of the attorneys and staff saw his side of things, the human side. His colleagues on the bench were less understanding but he'd expected that. There was nothing he could do about it.

To the cops, the Shinn fiasco had been the district attorney's screwup, not Fowler's; it hadn't gone down as a loss for the police department, except for the false arrest, but the grand-jury indictment had *de facto* corroborated Glitsky's judgment anyway, so even that wasn't an issue.

Fowler came around his desk and extended his hand to Lanier. "How are you doing, Marcel? Social call? How can I help you?"

Lanier remained standing. "No . . . not a social call, Judge."

"Andy, please."

"Judge." He took the warrant out of his coat pocket, "I don't know how to say this, but I've got a warrant here for your arrest."

"For my arrest?"

"That's right, sir."

Andy tried to smile. Marcel Lanier wasn't smiling. "Is this some kind of joke?"

"No, sir. The grand jury issued an indictment against you this morning on the murder of Owen Nash."

Fowler found he needed to put his weight back against the corner of his desk. "The grand jury," he repeated. He had gone pale, poleaxed. "Owen Nash?"

Lanier stood mute.

Wanda was buzzing again, and Fowler punched the intercom button. "It's your daughter, Judge. Lunch."

"Just hold her a second—"

But Jane had already opened the door. "Hi, Dad. Oops, sorry. Wanda didn't say you had a meeting." Seeing him so pale, she stopped. "Dad? What's going on?"

"Jane, hon, why don't you wait outside a minute."

"Are you all right? What's happening?"

"I'm fine. Scoot, now. Go."

The door closed behind her reluctant retreat. "This is ridiculous, Marcel. It's Locke, isn't it? Payback time."

"All I know, sir, is I've got to bring you in."

"Sure, I know, I understand, of course. It's not you. What in the world do they think they have?"

"Sir, I have to tell you that you have the right to remain silent, and anything you do say . . ."

"Marcel, please," Fowler said, holding up a hand. "You have my word I won't plead Miranda."

"It's got to be pure harassment. Locke swore a thousand times he'd crucify me. Now he thinks he's got the chance."

The crumbs of a hero sandwich littered David Freeman's desk. The last few bites had been interrupted by Andy Fowler's telephone call from the Hall of Justice. Fowler hadn't spoken to him since he'd refused to challenge his department that day last July in the May Shinn matter, but now, in trouble himself, he had called again.

What Fowler was saying made little sense to Freeman. Christopher Locke might in fact hate Fowler's guts, but he wasn't going to take another hit being wrong on a high-profile murder like Owen Nash. They must have found some real evidence. And Freeman knew Fowler had more motive to kill Owen Nash than had ever been even imputed to May Shinn.

"Listen, Andy, I'm not sure I can take this one."

"What do you mean you're not sure? What would be the problem?"

"Well, two come to mind. I'm not saying no just yet, Andy, but I'm going to have to consider it. Number one, I'm still representing May Shinn in some civil work. I'd want to avoid the appearance of any conflict there."

"I can't see how that would apply, David. May and I are totally separate."

"Yes. Well, the other one is our collusion . . ."

"Collusion?"

"That's what it was, Andy, so damn close to conspiracy I still get nightmares. And I believe you know it."

"There was absolutely nothing illegal about that relationship and *you* know it."

"Well, be that as it may, I'm having a little trouble envisioning the two of us together at a defense table and getting anything like reasonable treatment from the bench."

"So we'll file for change of venue."

Freeman leaned back in his chair and took another bite of his sandwich. Again, he didn't agree with Andy. Change of venue was called for when you didn't think you could get a fair trial in a certain locality because of pretrial media coverage or other excessive public awareness of the purported facts in a case. But it presumed that the prejudice you'd encounter would be on the jury.

What Fowler was ignoring, and what Freeman knew to be true, was that there wasn't a judge in the state, perhaps in the country, who didn't know what he'd done, and wouldn't be prejudiced against him for it. He was this year's legal Benedict Arnold.

Any judge of Freeman's acquaintance, and he knew most of them, would be far tougher on one of their own—on an Andy Fowler—than they would on other miscreants, all other things being equal. Andy Fowler had, in their *official* view, befouled their collective cave, and David Freeman understood that. It would be this side of a miracle if Fowler could get a fair trial *anywhere,* and with Freeman, his colluder, beside him, the chances became more remote.

"Venue is an issue all right, Andy. But I'll really have to give this some consideration."

"Meanwhile, David, what do you recommend?" Freeman was surprised to hear the note of anger in the judge's voice. There was nothing personal here, and Fowler must know that.

"I could recommend an interim counsel, Andy. Several, in fact. What did they set bail at?"

Fowler clipped it. "There's no bail on the bench warrant. They want to be sure I'm here for the arraignment. Look, David, my two minutes are about up and I need some representation here."

"I'll see what I can do."

Freeman put down the receiver and popped the last bite of his sandwich. There must be something in the San Francisco air, he thought. Dry salami, mortadella, sourdough bread. Any food that sat and fermented picked up something from it, some essence, that enhanced its flavor.

He put his feet up, chewing. He figured Fowler's bail would be at least a million, if he got it at all. He could guarantee offhand that three judges out of the six on Superior Court would let the judge rot in jail just to express their displeasure. And it would all be impartial, impersonal, within the bounds of their prerogatives.

Institutionalized pettiness. Perfectly legal. The law was a many-splendored thing.

39

Jane Fowler walked into the Little Shamrock and back to the dart boards, where Dismas Hardy was playing for money. She let him finish his round, let him turn and see her. They hadn't spoken in three months, since she'd yelled at him about forcing her father to retire. He hadn't returned her phone calls—four of them altogether, one about every three weeks.

After seeing her father led from his office wearing handcuffs—that was the drill—she didn't care what he thought about it, she was going to see him, so she'd driven out to his house. Frannie, obviously pregnant again, had about six other infants and a few other women in their house. Had they opened a daycare center or what? No, this was their playgroup—other new mothers supporting each other. There was a pang. This hadn't been a feature in Jane's life during the months she and Hardy had been new parents.

Frannie had been, as always, polite, and had told her where she could find Dismas, who always left the house on Tuesday afternoons. She explained that Dismas was good around one infant or perhaps even two. But when the number got to four plus their mothers, he reached his critical mass and tended to want to disappear. He was undoubtedly playing darts at the Little Shamrock. She should try there.

Seeing Jane, Hardy lit up briefly, then frowned. "What's the matter?" he asked. She told him in about twenty seconds. Hardy's dart opponent had finished his turn. "Hardy," he said.

He told Jane to give him a minute, went to the chalk line and threw three darts—a twenty, a seventeen and a double six. The other man swore and took out his wallet. Hardy was already pulling the flights from his darts, putting the shafts back in his leather case.

"Double or nothing?" the other man asked.

Hardy shook his head. "Can't do it." He pocketed the man's bill and led Jane up to the bar.

"What do you want me to do, Jane?"

"I want you to see him, I want you to *help* him."

"How?"

She didn't know. Hardy had been unemployed for three months. He had put on thirteen pounds. Under the guise of improving his dart game and preparing to play in some big tournaments, he was drinking about six Guinnesses every day between one, when the Shamrock opened, and about five, when he went home. The latest Guinness arrived.

"Daddy needs you," Jane said. "It's ridiculous. He wouldn't kill anybody, Dismas, you *know* that."

Hardy said nothing. He didn't know that, nobody knew that.

"Come on," she said.

"What am I supposed to do?"

"You'll think of something. You're the lawyer."

"So's he, so are all his friends." Hardy shook his head. He'd think of something; he liked that. "I'm sure he's already got a lawyer."

"But he needs somebody he can count on, not just somebody he's paying."

"I'm not a lawyer anymore, and even if I were, I'm not a defense lawyer. I've never defended anybody in my life."

"Look, I'm only asking you to see him. He's done you favors, more than one. You owe him."

In a way, maybe so. He still felt bad—justified but bad nonetheless —about Andy's early retirement, guilty that he'd forced it so quickly when the whole thing had proved unnecessary. Since their meeting at the fern bar, Hardy and Andy hadn't spoken. "I didn't leak it, Jane."

Jane narrowed her eyes. "But you were the only one who knew about him and May. It had to be you."

Hardy shook his head. "From the phone records. I didn't know anything about the bail. The *Chronicle* guy, the reporter, he's the one that found the bail story."

"Daddy thought it was you."

"Well, it wasn't. And if he did, why would he want to see me now?"

"He didn't exactly say he did. I'm saying it. I think it would be good for him, for both of you."

Hardy sighed. Jane wasn't going to go away. Besides, he wasn't doing anything else. How could it hurt?

*   *   *

Hardy followed Jane in his own car.

It was a warm October day, Indian summer in San Francisco. The top was down and there was plenty of time to ponder. He found it nearly impossible to imagine that they had arrested Andy Fowler for the murder of Owen Nash. He knew that Locke personally disliked the man and that Pullios was capable of carrying a grudge of impressive proportions, but all that aside, you needed evidence to indict a man, a former *judge,* for murder, even more to convict. Hardy hadn't heard about any new evidence turning up, and he was sure he would have.

He still saw Glitsky once a week or so, talked to him every few days. By the time he and Frannie had gotten back from Hawaii, the Nash case had faded from the newspapers, but Glitsky had come by the house, filling Hardy in.

Apparently Ken Farris had made an honest mistake about the last time he had seen Nash. In fact, it had been on Thursday. People made mistakes. He had flown to Taos on Friday, ate out in restaurants in Taos on both Friday and Saturday nights, flown back Monday morning.

Austin Brucker, Mr. Silicon Valley, had vacated the presidency of the company Owen Nash had set him up in and started a new venture of his own—something to do with ceramic fibers—down in San Jose. With a staff of five engineers he'd been in his shop all day every day for the months of April, May and June, and according to all sources, would remain there until next Groundhog Day at the earliest.

Glitsky, being thorough, had even looked into Celine. Her fingerprints had been all over the *Eloise,* which was to be expected—she said that she had often gone sailing with her father. The friends she had visited in Santa Cruz were an unlikely trio of two gay bodybuilders and one of their mothers, all of whom verified that Celine had spent the weekend with them, helping with the remodeling of their old Victorian house.

The one surprise was that Celine's fingerprints had shown up in the arrest database. If you had never been arrested, your fingerprints might be on file with the Department of Motor Vehicles, but by far the most accessible record to the police, and thus the first place they looked, was the database of people who had been arrested.

"Celine was arrested?"

"Twice. Shoplifting when she was twenty, reduced to reckless trespass, dismissed. And prostitution."

"Prostitution?"

"I know, like she needed the money, right. Anyway, it was fifteen years ago. I questioned her on it. It's not what you would call one of her favorite memories. She says it was a misunderstanding. She also says it was just after her first marriage ended, and she was having a bad time."

"Which was it, a bad time or a misunderstanding?"

"I know, that was a little iffy. Either way, it never got charged. When your father's Owen Nash . . ."

"Money keeps talking, doesn't it," Hardy had said, and Glitsky said he believed it did.

So with Farris, Brucker and Celine accounted for, only one righteous suspect was left, and that was Andy Fowler. But—and what had plagued this case from every angle since it began—Glitsky could find no evidence linking him to Owen Nash, or to the *Eloise*.

Andy had been out of town, hiking in the Sierras, though apparently he had seen no one. But he hadn't known Owen Nash—there was no record of their having met. While Hardy was in Hawaii, it had come out that Andy Fowler had had a long-term relationship with May Shinn but that it had ended about the time she met Nash.

"I don't think that was a coincidence, Abe."

"No. I don't either. So what? Fowler swears he never heard of Nash until he read about him in the papers."

"Do you believe that?"

"There's nothing to contradict it. Nothing to put him on the boat. What's the motive? Eliminate a rival, get her back. Oldest one in the world. You've got to understand, Diz. People do think Fowler might have done it. Locke wants his ass in a big way. But if he did do it, he did it right. There's no way Locke or Rigby or anybody else is going to make a move until we've got more than we had with Shinn, which we sure as hell do not."

"So is he—Fowler—seeing Shinn again?"

"No sign of it, and believe me, people are looking. She seems to be laying low, trying to collect her money, suing me and the City and County. Freeman's bill must be approaching the national debt."

Those had been Glitsky's facts.

*   *   *

To satisfy his own curiosity, Hardy had done some checking himself. He had the telephone records. Andy Fowler might have convinced himself that before Owen Nash came along he had May Shinn all to himself, but her telephone records included three other numbers, called with about the same regularity as those to Andy Fowler.

Hardy tried all three numbers. One was to a switchboard of the main office of the Timberline Group, a timber-lobby consulting firm with an address on Bay Street. Hardy thought it unlikely that May Shinn was doing a lot of lumber work.

When a woman answered at the second number, Hardy, feeling a little foolish, pretended to be taking a demographic survey for the Neilson ratings. The woman said that she and her husband, who worked out of the house (he was in software), were both in their mid-fifties. She didn't want to be too specific, but their income was in the low six figures. He let it go.

The third number was to the private office of an affable millionaire in the garment district.

So . . .

It seemed May had three other clients before Owen Nash came along. Four including Andy Fowler. And, from the phone record, she'd dropped them all around the beginning of February. Did Nash pay her more, or had she, as she contended, truly fallen in love with Nash?

Of course, he knew nothing that tied any of these men to Owen Nash. Not yet. Hardy spent a day wondering if he should mention them to Glitsky, then decided against it. He had promised Andy he wouldn't bring up the phone records if he didn't have to. The originals were there in the file downtown if anybody wanted to look at them.

It wasn't Hardy's job anymore, but it didn't take immense reserves of gray matter to realize this discovery would open things up again. If the motive they had all ascribed to Fowler, killing a rival, applied, then it applied as well to May's other three clients/lovers. But then, the D.A.'s office wasn't arrayed in a vendetta against any of these guys, as it was against Fowler.

Still, Andy must have made a mistake. Some evidence must have turned up, but where did they get it? Hardy was sure Glitsky would have called him with anything at all, so it hadn't been him. And if Glitsky didn't have it, who did? He was the investigating officer. It didn't make sense.

Hardy hadn't set foot in the Hall of Justice since the day after he was fired, when he went in to pick up his personal effects, his dart board, the paperweight.

Now, coming up the front steps with Jane, he found it hard to believe that he'd been talked into returning. The false accusations, the unnamed informer, the politics of the lifers—the gut reaction still kicked in.

He and Jane rode in the crowded elevator up to Booking. He didn't have much of an idea what he was going to do. It was late in the afternoon, and he thought at least he'd get the lay of the land. At the desk, the sergeant looked up and nodded.

"Hey, Hardy, taking the day off?"

It took him a minute—Hardy was in casual clothes. The sergeant thought he was still working there.

"Where you been, on vacation or something?"

"Or something. Listen, you got Andy Fowler processed yet?"

"Yeah, I think so, I'll check. Can you believe that? The judge?" He got up from his chair and disappeared for two minutes, during which Hardy devoutly hoped no one would recognize him. When he came out again he pointed to his right and told Hardy he could go on in, they'd be bringing the judge down.

He and Jane were admitted, then ushered into Interview Room A, the same room where he had first seen May Shinn.

Jane sat uncomfortably. "How'd we get in here?"

"I think under false pretenses. Now listen, when your father gets in here, be cool in front of the guard. Don't jump up and yell or anything. Since they think I'm working here, let's let them think you're my assistant, okay?"

But it wasn't so easy. Her father just didn't look the same in a yellow jumpsuit. Four hours before, in his pinstripes, Andy's handcuffs had been the ultimate indignity. Now Jane realized she hadn't known the half of it.

The judge played the game, entered cooperatively, nodded at both of them and sat down across the table. Hardy thanked the guard and told him to wait outside. As soon as the door closed, her father said, "Good. How did this happen?"

Dismas inclined his head a fraction, his hand to his mouth. "I cheated. How are you doing, Andy?"

"Badly. How about you?"

"All right."

The two men tried not to look at each other. Jane wasn't going to let this go bad. Or worse. "Dismas didn't leak your story, Daddy. About you and . . . May."

Her father didn't look beaten. In fact, he looked ready to fight. "You didn't?" Directly at Dismas.

"I said I wouldn't, I didn't." He shrugged. "I figured you had other things on your mind. So did I. I got fired over it, for example."

"I heard about that." More waiting. Jane realized she was squeezing her fingernails into her palms. She didn't understand this silence— the two men who'd been closest to her jockeying for something.

"I guess I just got a little tired explaining how I didn't do whatever it was somebody thought I did. It gets old."

"I'd imagine it would." Her father was inside himself, settling something. "Sorry, Diz, I just assumed . . ."

Jane's ex-husband had his hands folded on the table. He opened them. "I lived through it. What are you doing here?"

"Somebody thinks I killed Owen Nash."

"I know that. But who's representing you? You ought to be out of here already."

A tight smile. "You'd think so, wouldn't you? One of Locke's little object lessons. No bail until the arraignment." He paused. "At least."

"That Locke, he's a swell guy."

Fowler kept on. "I called David Freeman. He thought it might not be wise for him to represent me because of May. He intimated he'd put out the word. Meanwhile, it appears that I'm to stay locked up." Another tight smile. "Lousy pun."

"Daddy, they can't do that."

"They can, honey. How many times have I had a defense lawyer tell me his client *had* to get out of jail, wouldn't survive one night there, it was life and death. And I told them it would have to wait until the morning. Judicial process . . ."

"We can't let this happen, you can't stay here. Dismas can do something."

Hardy nodded. "I could try, Andy."

"Why would you want to do that? What would you try?"

"I don't know, I got me and Jane in here to see you, didn't I? I could try walking you downstairs and out the door."

Her father pulled at the jumpsuit. "Don't you think the outfit's a little conspicuous?"

"Goddamn it," Jane said. "Will you two cut it *out*."

"You're right, I'll have to think of something else."

The judge got serious. "You'd really do something? Why?"

Hardy shrugged. "At least until one of Freeman's wonders shows up. At least you'd be represented. I could pass it off after you decided who you wanted." Hardy straightened in his chair. "Not to mention, I wouldn't mind getting in the face of a few of these people here—they seem to have pissed me off."

"Can you get him out *tonight,* Dismas? On bail or something?" Jane looked at her father. "You cannot stay here overnight."

Fowler reached out and patted her hand. "It's all right, honey. I spent a night in jail once before—voluntarily, I admit—and it wasn't so bad. I wanted to see what we were putting people through. I'll survive, I promise you. Besides, I might as well get used to it. It could be longer than that if bail is denied."

"They couldn't do that!"

Her father and Hardy shared a glance. The guard outside the door gave a knock.

"I'll call Freeman, keep him on it," Hardy said. "And I'll be there tomorrow . . . You sure you want me representing you, even temporarily?"

Andy appeared, for really the first time, to consider it. "Maybe more than that."

"Why, Andy?"

The judge looked around the tiny room, then at his daughter, as though looking for verification of something. He knew he'd written Hardy off too easily before, when he thought he had betrayed his trust. There had been a mistake. He knew Hardy and he hadn't blown any whistle on Andy Fowler. Hardy didn't betray trusts and he didn't give up. "The devil you know?" he said, smiling.

40

He left Jane at the fourth floor. Getting out of the elevator, he walked down the hallway and turned into Homicide. If Glitsky was in maybe they could stop in at Lou's for old time's sake. But he wasn't around. Hardy leaned over his desk and was writing him a note when he heard some heels on the tile and looked up.

Pullios stopped in the door.

"Hi, Bets," Hardy said. "Getting any . . . exciting cases?"

Her smile was glacial. "How are you, Dismas?"

"Great," he said. "I'm writing my memoirs."

She didn't react. Her eyes searched the back of the open room. "Anybody seen Lanier?" she asked. One of the guys said he thought he was downstairs having some coffee with a witness. She came back to Hardy. "Well, take care of yourself."

She started to turn and Hardy spoke. "I hear Judge Fowler's been arrested."

She stopped. "My, news travels fast."

"Tribal drums. We're kind of family."

"Oh, yes, that's right."

"You really think he killed Owen Nash?"

"The grand jury thought there was enough evidence to issue the indictment."

Hardy folded his arms, leaning back against Glitsky's desk. "I have it on good authority that if the D.A. wanted, the grand jury would indict a ham sandwich."

Pullios nodded. "Well, it's been nice talking to you."

Hardy caught up with her out in the hallway. He turned conversational. "I guess there's some new evidence, huh?"

Pullios stopped. "Are you representing Fowler?"

"I'm merely a curious citizen who wonders what you've got new since Shinn?"

"Quite a bit. I'm sure it'll be in the newspaper."

She started walking again.

Hardy found himself planted to the floor with roots of rage. It just came up over him. His stomach turned over and he heard his blood pulsing in his ears.

Don't do it, he told himself. Don't say any more. Don't chase her through the halls. Nothing to be gained.

He watched her elegant figure disappear around the corner of the elevator lobby. Where had the air gone? Feeling as though he'd stopped breathing, he sucked a strained lungful. He needed a drink.

Or four. Or five.

On top of the three Guinnesses he had had before Jane had arrived at the Shamrock. He had the first couple of Irish whiskeys at Lou's, but then the guys started showing up. Guys that knew him, that wanted to know what he was doing, how he was getting along.

Yeah, he was busy, working on stuff, was looking into opening a second bar maybe, even a restaurant. No, he didn't want to go into private practice, wind up defending a bunch of scum.

Leaving Lou's, he remembered that he had forgotten to call David Freeman. He'd call him from the next place. And Frannie too. He couldn't forget to call Frannie. She would worry. She'd been worried for a couple of months now—worried about him, about them, their future, her baby, the pregnancy. Everything. Their wavelengths had ceased to coincide somehow. It worried him too, made him doubt himself. Sometimes he thought it was making him sick. Drinking seemed to cure it.

Entertaining the possibility that he should cut down on his intake, and forgetting his own oft-uttered advice that beer on whiskey was mighty risky, he stopped at a place down Seventh Street and ordered a Rainier Ale. The bar didn't have a pay phone.

He brought the bottle of green death over to a small table next to the door and stared up at the television screen broadcasting the evening news. The financier, the judge and the prostitute again. He moved to the other side of the table, where he didn't have to look at the damned set. White noise.

They'd enjoyed the vacation. The two weeks had been good for them. They'd come back refreshed, reinvigorated, reconnected. They'd purposely put off discussing his career plans—there would be plenty of time for that. Instead, they talked about babies and childbirth, about whether Moses and Susan were an item, about food and their past lives—Eddie and Jane. And if they should move to a bigger house before or after the next child came along.

Hardy had run daily on the beach. A couple of days of rum drinks, then he'd surprised himself by going on the wagon for the rest of the trip. He was tan and lean and liked it.

Then, the first week home, catching up with Abe about Owen Nash and May Shinn and Andy Fowler. Cleaning out some tanks at the Steinhart with Pico. Pouring a few shifts at the Shamrock to keep his hand in.

At first it was a nagging unease, a touch of insomnia. He hadn't wanted to admit how much he'd invested, how great had been the risk, when he'd given up bartending right after Christmas to go back to the law. But now, in the long and formless days stretching before him, he was starting to come to the numbing realization that he'd failed in one of the fundamental decisions of his life.

He'd been fired. His services were not wanted. It wasn't that the people he worked for were so honorable or talented or better at their jobs than he was, at least he didn't think so, but the fact that he'd been judged by those people and found unacceptably wanting. Never mind their standards. He was out, they were in.

It got to him. He found himself internalizing the rejection. More, he couldn't seem to get it out of him. Who was he at forty, anyway? A castoff, a reject. He had told Frannie what the hell, he didn't want to be underfoot all day, he'd go out and interview a few places, get some work, try to get some feeling back that he was doing something worthwhile—that maybe he was worthwhile.

People were nice. Men and women—lawyers and office managers—in business suits like he was wearing. But they didn't hire him. They'd call him back, it was just a slow time. Maybe he could try the public defenders.

He thought he was a logical man, and logic was telling him that in terms of the marketplace, worthless.

Well, shit, he wasn't going to accept that. He'd lived a pretty good life, thank you, and it damn sure wasn't over yet. The hell with the rest of you.

Then he made his big mistake.

Frannie was a rock at home, telling him not to push it, time would take care of it. Something would come up. She loved him.

But once you started thinking people didn't want you, it was easy to start believing nobody wanted you for anything. You were just a burden, a drag, plain and simple, not able to carry your own weight.

He thought he could feel Frannie pulling away. She swore it wasn't true, she wasn't. She was with him. But he found he couldn't talk with her anymore. He could tell it was making her lose confidence in him, and *that* was too much to ask her to carry. She needed him to be strong, especially now, building a family. So he resolved to put on a happy face. Lots of laughs, long silences between.

He idly thought of finding someone he could talk to where he wasn't constantly reminded of his situation. Of course, he wasn't going to, but wouldn't it be nice to be around someone who thought you were okay, not aware of any of the baggage?

He'd taken to stopping by the Shamrock after his interviews and having a round or two. It was more time that he didn't have to face her. He stopped working out.

He'd been home a month now, six weeks. He told himself enough was enough, it was time to beat this thing, not let the bastards get him down. The first step, he told himself, was physical—get back in shape, stop drinking, tighten up.

He stood behind Celine Nash as she pumped up and down on the Stairmaster. Her hair was fixed back with a hot pink headband. A patch of darker pink showed where she was sweating between her shoulder blades. Her ass was a phenomenal pumping machine. Up and down, step step step. Sweat was pouring off her. He thought about turning around and walking out.

It was okay, he told himself. He was here to work out and he'd chosen Hardbodies! because he'd already been in the place and it had the machines he was looking for.

He hadn't seen her since she'd stopped in front of his house before the vacation, when she'd realized she couldn't be in his life. Well, he wasn't putting her back into his life now. Enough time had gone by since then. He wasn't starting anything by showing up here.

He climbed onto the machine next to hers. "Yo," he said.

They were sitting together in the steam room. He was on a towel, leaning back against the cedar wall, in gym shorts and a t-shirt. She'd gone to the locker room after her workout, gotten rid of her leggings and changed into a one-piece black bathing suit.

The talking wound down. She was doing all right, she said, keeping busy. He wished he was. Well, at least he was exercising. That was doing something. Yes.

The temperature was near a hundred and twenty. The room was tiny, cramped, perhaps five by seven feet, with a furnace near the floor, which was covered with rocks. Celine got up and poured more water from a pitcher over the rocks and a cloud of steam lifted and hovered. She went to sit down on the wood where she'd been, then jumped and said, "Ouch."

"Here." Hardy moved enough towel out from under him to give her room. He could feel his heart pounding through his t-shirt. Their legs were together.

She leaned back next to him and took his hand, putting it high on her thigh.

"Celine . . ."

"Shh . . ." Her shoulder came up against him. "I've been coming here for six months and have never seen another soul in this room."

She lifted the elastic on her nylon suit and guided his hand under it. "Feel me," she said. She was shaved bare, the skin smooth as though it had been oiled, already wet where she was moving him.

"Oh, God," she said. "Oh dear God."

One hand held him in place against her and the other lifted his shirt, found the band of his shorts and reached under them for him.

Silk and oil. Honey and salt.

That proved he had been right. He was no better than anyone else, and worse than most. He tried to tell himself, once, that he hadn't been technically unfaithful. There had been no penetration, therefore he hadn't really made love to her. Feeble. Beneath contempt. More honest if he had.

Now he had proved that the world's assessment of him was valid. He wouldn't hire himself to do anything. He could barely look at himself in the mirror.

He started practicing darts, putting away gallons of Guinness. Avoiding Frannie, avoiding himself. Putting on weight.

Thank God, Celine hadn't tried to follow up. That, at least, seemed to be over.

But he resided in a deep cave, in total darkness.

* * *

It was ten-thirty. There were four bottles of Rainier Ale on the table now, a rocks glass with mostly water in the bottom, a faint taste of Irish to it. He blinked, wondering where he had been, and tried to focus on the clock over the bar. No use. He stood uncertainly.

Jesus.

Outside, the night had turned cold and the street came up at him, forcing him against the outer stucco of the building for support. Seventh Street stretched empty for what seemed like miles, shining as though it were wet. Was his car parked up at the Hall of Justice? Even if it was, how could he get it home?

He tried moving along but everything suddenly seemed to hurt, to throb—his shoulder where he'd been wounded in Vietnam, the foot he'd hurt last year in Acapulco.

There were noises behind him, laughter, then a skipping, leather on concrete. It finally registered, coming toward him.

He straightened up, turned around, saw an arm, something, a blur that hit him in the forehead, knocked him to one side. He heard another dull thud—was that him?—and his head cracked back against the stucco and he went down.

There were images. The gagging jolt of smelling salts. A light behind his eyes. Something sticky under his hand. The cold concrete.

"Let's take him down."

"Wait a minute. Is this him?"

Hardy forced his eyes open. The flashlight hit him again and he winced. Shadows emerged, recognizable. Cops.

A lucky break. One of them had found his wallet, less cash, in the curb. Hardy had never given his badge back to Locke. If he wanted it he could come and ask for it.

"Are you Dismas Hardy?" one of them asked.

He supposed he nodded, grunted—something.

"He as drunk as he smells?"

Another whiff of the salts. Hardy brought his hand up to his face, felt a crust. He looked down. His white sweater was matted dark.

"I'm Hardy," he said.

They got him up. Pain, nausea. "Watch out, guys." He staggered a step or two away and vomited bile and beer. He leaned against the building. "Sorry."

They stood back a couple of yards. He caught his breath, spit a few times, tried to see what time it was but his watch was gone.

If they could do it, he told them, he'd rather go home than the hospital. He didn't think anything was broken. He might have a concussion; his head felt like an anvil attached to his neck by some two-pound test. And someone kept swinging the smith's hammer.

They put him in the rear seat.

He rested his head back. Lights passing overhead, the freeway overpass. He closed his eyes. Nothing to see.

It was almost midnight, and Moses had been there for a half hour. To her brother, Frannie looked particularly vulnerable. She was now five months pregnant and showing it. Her arms looked thin, he thought. Her face was too hollow. Maybe it was the contrast with the fullness of her belly and breasts. There were circles under her eyes. She sat forward on the low living-room couch, her elbows on her knees, her hands crossed under the bulge of her stomach.

Moses was telling her that the best thing to do was wait. He'd turn up. Moses had had his own lost weekends, or nights.

"This isn't a lost weekend, Mose." She hesitated. "He's with Jane. I know he's with Jane."

Moses shook his head. "There's no way, Frannie."

"She came here today asking for him."

"Jane did?" He mulled that. "What did she want?"

"She wanted Dismas. She always wants Dismas. He's gone back to her before."

"Frannie. Come on. He wasn't with you then. He wasn't with anybody. It probably had to do with her father being arrested. He and Diz were friends, right?"

"Are, I think."

"Well?"

Why hadn't she thought of that? These raging hormones were making her crazy.

"He probably went down to get him out, help get him out, whatever they do down there. Lost track of the time."

"Diz never loses track of the time. What if he got Jane's father out, and then they all went out somewhere to celebrate, and then her father left them together . . . ?"

"What if he was snatched by invading space creatures and dissected alive in the name of intergalactic research?"

"I don't want to kid about it."

"I don't want to play 'what if.' He's probably just hung up. It happens."

They sat for a long moment. "It's just he's been so unhappy lately, like he's lost."

Moses cricked his back, got up slowly and crossed over to the mantel. He rearranged the herd of elephants, something he did differently with every visit. "You know, Frannie, I just don't think anybody's ever prepared us, guys like me and Diz, for how tough real life is." He tried to make a semi-joke of it, but he was serious, and she knew it.

"Life with me isn't tough, Moses."

"I'm not saying with you. I'm saying, you know, life in general."

She got up and moved some elephants back the way they'd been. "You're just getting old, brother."

Moses grabbed her gently and pulled at her hair. He was a year older than Hardy. He had raised his sister from the time she was eight. Of the ten things he cared about most in the world, he liked to say that eight of them were Frannie. The other two were closely guarded secrets.

Facing the bay window, Moses saw the police car pull up in front. "Here he is, anyway," he said. "See? He must've been doing something with the cops."

41

There was fog everywhere—in his head, out the bedroom window.

"I don't deserve this." Frannie had been up awhile, had taken a shower and gotten dressed. She sat across the room, by the door to the nursery, in her rocking chair. "I am very sad that this happened, but it wouldn't have if you'd come home."

"Frannie . . ."

She stopped him, pressing on. She wasn't crying but her cheeks were wet. "I know this is a hard time for you, although I'm not sure why. And you don't have to try and tell me. But I don't deserve you treating me this way. Not calling, letting me sit and worry all night. I won't have it in my life."

Hardy had a walnut-sized lump over his hairline. His left ear was raw and there was a gash in the scalp above it. They must have kicked him when he was down—his ribs jabbed at him. His headache was mammoth, his tongue bitten in several places. He still tasted blood.

"I'm sorry—"

"Of course you're sorry. So am I. Who wouldn't be sorry? What do you want, Dismas? What do you want? If you don't want me, I'm out of here, babies and all. I mean it."

He didn't doubt her. Frannie wasn't a poker player and this wasn't a bluff.

"I do want you," he said. He saw her take a breath. A miracle, he thought, she still wanted him. She was as mad as he'd ever seen her, but at least it wasn't over between them. "I know I've been a shit. I can't tell you the things—"

She held up a hand. "No litany. I just don't want to live miserable. I don't want that for any of us. This family doesn't deserve it. Including you."

Hardy held his head in his hands. "So why do I feel like that's exactly what I do deserve?"

"I don't know. You've somehow let those idiots make you feel they're better than you are, which is ridiculous. What's so hot about them? What have they done? Why does it matter what they think of you?"

"Okay, but what if they're right? They might be right—"

"Damn it, Dismas. They're not right. You're not a loser. Why? Because I'm smart and I wouldn't have married a loser. Don't let them do this to you—to me. If you do they *will* have won."

Why couldn't she see it? He'd been going around proving it for a couple of months. "You have to admit, Frannie, I'm not exactly on a winning streak."

Her eyes flashed now. "Thanks a lot. What am I? What's this house and the Beck?" She gestured down to her stomach. "What's this new guy, anyway? Doesn't this count as winning something?"

"I don't mean that."

"Well, then," she slammed a tiny fist hard into her leg and raised her voice. "Goddamn it! Don't say it then." She stood up, turned into the nursery. The rocking chair creaked on the hardwood. After a while he heard her talking to Rebecca. "It's okay, it's not you, sweetie. Back to sleep, now."

Hardy, sore and nauseous, forced himself out of bed, hurting everywhere. He stood by the nursery door, stopped the creaking rocker with his foot.

She turned around. "Look," she said, "whatever it is, just put it behind you. You can't undo it. Let's just move on, okay? We've got a good life here. But you've got to respect me. And you've got to respect you. End of sermon."

She crossed the room to him, touched his arm lightly. "Go take another shower," she said. "A hot one. I'll make breakfast."

Hardy sat on the mega-hard bench in the gallery of Department 22, Marian Braun's courtroom. Elizabeth Pullios in her power red-and-blue never gave him a glance from the prosecution table. Hardy recognized several well-dressed lawyers hanging around, probably sent over by David Freeman for Fowler to choose among—he guessed one of them would wind up representing Andy.

Jane came and slid in beside him. "What happened to you?"

Hardy was wearing a three-piece suit, white shirt, one of his best conservative ties. He'd gotten his shoes shined downstairs. He looked proper except for the bandage across the top of his forehead, the swelling around his eye.

He told her it was a long story, Jane's favorite kind, but didn't get to go into it because the judge was coming in and they all rose.

Braun had had chambers next to Andy Fowler for something like a decade. That she had been the presiding judge for the Superior Court —and so the recipient of the grand jury's indictment—had been a matter of timing. Since Leo Chomorro had moved up to fill Andy Fowler's seat upon his retirement, the duties of presiding judge were again being rotated. What was ominous was that Braun, who had known Andy well and might be considered to be one of his few allies, had accepted D.A. Chris Locke's recommendation and decreed that there would be no bail.

In the normal course of events, for a typical defendant, bail would not be set before arraignment in a murder case because the court wanted to guarantee at least one appearance, at the arraignment, of the accused.

In this case, though, there would have been little fear that Andy Fowler would not show up—the withholding of bail was a clear signal that there would be no professional courtesies. Andy Fowler was out of the club.

At least they weren't making him wait all morning—he was the first line called after the judge sat down. The bailiff escorted him in wearing the yellow jumpsuit.

His protestations that jail wouldn't kill him might have been valid, but the stay overnight hadn't done him any visible good. His skin looked gray, his lion's mane of hair hung heavy and wet-looking. He stood at attention, alone at the podium in front of the bench.

Hardy glanced at the jury box. None of the men were rising to stand by their client as, once again, the formula was carried out, the indictment for murder read out in full.

"I presume, Mr. Fowler . . ." So the honorific wouldn't be used, either. Andy wasn't going to be called "judge." If Marian Braun was any barometer, Hardy decided, Andy was in for some very rough weather. Braun asked if he had an attorney present.

"I do, Your Honor." He half turned. "Dismas Hardy."

A murmur ran through the courtroom. Hardy barely heard it, standing and moving by Jane. But he hadn't reached the aisle before Elizabeth Pullios was on her feet. "Your Honor, I object. Mr. Hardy was a member of the prosecution on this case. Aside from that obvious conflict, he has had access to material that falls under the attorney-client privilege. He cannot represent the defendant here."

Hardy found himself talking. "If the court pleases . . ." He got ignored.

Braun pulled her glasses down to the end of her nose, then took them off completely. "Write me a motion on that, Counselor, and have it on my desk by tomorrow morning." She scribbled something in front of her and raised her eyes. "Mr. Hardy, would you care to join us on this side of the bar?"

Hardy came up the aisle and through the gate. "Your Honor, I'd like to request a short recess. I'd like a few words with the judge here."

"I am the only judge in this courtroom, Mr. Hardy. Clear?"

"Yes, Your Honor."

"We've barely begun and I've got an exceptionally full docket today, so let's forgo the recesses and try to keep things moving. Is that all right with everybody?" Clearly it was going to have to be all right. "Mr. Hardy," Braun was saying, "you might save Ms. Pullios a long night if you feel there's a conflict with you representing the defendant."

Hardy wasn't inclined to save Pullios a long night—it was a small bonus. "No, Your Honor, I don't have a conflict."

Pullios got up again. "Mr. Hardy assembled the files on this case."

"That wasn't this case, Your Honor. Ms. Pullios perhaps has them confused because it's the same victim. Mr. Fowler wasn't the defendant."

"I don't have anything confused, Your Honor. Mr. Hardy was all over that file."

"If it please the court," Hardy said, enjoying this, "as Ms. Pullios knows full well, she was the People's attorney of record the last time a defendant was before the court for killing Owen Nash. I was specifically denied an official role."

Braun's gavel came down. "All right, all right. I'll read your motion, Ms. Pullios. Tomorrow morning." She put her glasses back on, seemed to be deciding something.

"Good work," Fowler whispered. "What happened to your head?"

Braun continued. "Meanwhile, let's keep to the business at hand, shall we? You've got a plea, Mr. Fowler?"

Hardy would have preferred to leave Andy to his permanent representation at this time—one of the suits in the jury box—but after the run-in with Pullios, thought it would be better to go ahead.

"Your Honor, before entering a plea, the defense would like some time, say two weeks, to review the file in this case."

Pullios started to object again, but Braun tapped her gavel, shaking her head. "I don't think you'll need two weeks to decide what to plead. We'll continue this arraignment and take defendant's plea next week."

"Thank you, Your Honor. Now on the matter of bail . . ."

"Yes, bail. The state has requested no bail in this case."

Hardy asked permission to approach the bench. Braun waved both counsel forward.

"Your Honor," Hardy said, "isn't no bail a little unusual?"

"This is an unusual case, Mr. Hardy."

"Granted, Judge, but the last time the state brought a person to trial here for killing Owen Nash, we had a risk-of-flight defendant and even she was given bail. There's no risk of flight here. The judge isn't going anywhere."

Pullios started to argue, but Braun responded quietly. "Mr. Fowler has given us an ample indication of the contempt in which he holds the judicial process. I have no faith that he will appear once, or if, he is released."

"Judge, please, you know that's ridiculous—"

Braun sucked in a breath. "You'd better brush up on your etiquette, Mr. Hardy. If I hear again that my judgments are ridiculous you'll spend some ridiculous nights in jail for contempt."

Hardy studied the floor a moment. "I apologize, Your Honor. But I would respectfully ask you to reconsider."

Walking back to where Fowler stood, Hardy shook his head. "Then plead now," Fowler whispered. "Not guilty."

Hardy met Fowler's eyes, feeling embarrassed but having to say it. "I don't know you're not guilty, Andy—"

"*Enter the plea,*" Fowler snapped. "Does your conscience also require you waste the week?"

It was a good point, and Hardy made the plea. The judge canceled the continuance and took Hardy's plea of not guilty. The case was set for calendar the next Monday, October 18, at 9:30 A.M., in the same department.

He wasn't even going to go and request the evidence files from the D.A. What he planned to do was meet Andy upstairs right away and discuss his choice for another attorney. He stood in the hallway with Jane, head throbbing.

"Hardy! Dismas, excuse me." It was Jeff Elliot, smiling his smile. "Remember me?"

Jeff leaned on one crutch and Hardy introduced him to Jane. "The judge's daughter? I'd love a minute with you if you could."

"Watch this guy." It was Hardy's escape line.

"Where are you going?" Jeff asked.

He stopped, half-turned. "After a brief career," he said, "I'm retiring from defense work."

"Don't do that," Jeff said. "You were great in there."

"Thank you. Now if you'll all excuse me . . ."

Elizabeth Pullios emerged from the courtroom. She was accompanied by a young male assistant D.A. who Hardy didn't know. Pullios touched her assistant's arm, stopping him, and walked over to Hardy's group. "Locke won't release any files to you until Braun rules on my motion," she said to him. "There's no way you can do this."

Hardy smiled. "I like your red tie," he said, "it kind of matches your eyes."

She stared at him. "You know, I almost hope I'm overruled," she said.

"Why is that?" Hardy asked.

"If you're doing the defense, it makes the case a slam dunk."

42

Hardy didn't go directly upstairs to see Andy Fowler. Instead, he left Jane and Jeff Elliot, then carried his pounding head out to the parking lot under the freeway. It was cold, but the chill suited him.

Pullios thought his involvement would make it a slam dunk, did she? It was tempting to find out.

He forced himself to consider Andy Fowler in a new light. He could help him for a day—some mixture of appeasing Jane, doing a favor for a man who'd done him a few. But this was not to be confused with actually defending him for murder.

He kept telling himself he wasn't a defense lawyer. There was a different attitude, an orientation he didn't have. He'd been a cop. He didn't believe many people got arrested when they hadn't done something. May Shinn had been an exception.

But to think it could happen twice with the same victim stretched things pretty thin. Hardy hadn't seen the new evidence they'd gathered on Andy, but it must be pretty damning. Even if every judge, D.A. and police officer in the City and County hated Andy, Chris Locke would never allow Pullios to go for another indictment on Owen Nash if he wasn't convinced he was going to get a conviction . . .

Still, there was the decidedly unusual if not unprecedented nature of the investigation. Whatever had gone on since May Shinn's release seemed to have circumvented the police department.

Glitsky would have told Hardy if they had found anything implicating Andy, as a matter of personal interest if nothing else. And they didn't replace an experienced homicide investigator like Abe Glitsky with another guy from the homicide team without any notice.

Abe was still in charge of the police investigation and he hadn't found anything, yet somehow there had been enough new evidence for a grand jury. Well, where had it come from? What had they—whoever "they" were—found, or invented?

The traffic throbbed on the overpass above him. He put his seat back and groaned as his sore ribs tried to find a way to come to rest. He closed his eyes for a minute.

What the hell *else* was he doing, anyway?

The events of last night, if he was listening, ought to be telling him something.

Okay, he'd gotten fired. Sure, no one else wanted his services. Yes, he'd really screwed up on Frannie. He'd also taken some pretty shabby advantage of Celine, in the steam room.

Celine.

If his own curiosity and the lack of evidence were two strikes for taking up Andy's defense, then Celine—by herself—was two strikes against it. If he stayed involved, he would have to see her, see her a lot, and now from the wrong side of the case. He would be the man defending her father's killer. *Alleged* killer, Dismas, remember that.

Would the distinction matter to her? Probably not. He tried to imagine her behind him in the gallery as he tried to present his case for the defense. How effective could he be with that going on?

But then there was Pullios. And there was Locke and Drysdale. There was the setup that had gotten him fired, set in motion his own personal tailspin. The injustice of that, the score to be settled. If he got Andy off, it would show them, and wouldn't that be sweet?

Hardy thought he just might beat Pullios. He'd gotten under her skin somehow—there was no other explanation for her challenge today. He could hammer there, let more of her anger, or whatever it was, come out, let the *jury* see it. Make them see it. And if she lost her cool, what about her arguments?

He could beat her.

He was smiling to himself, and it hurt. But so what? What else was new? You pushed through the pain and you got healed. That's how it worked.

Fowler sat across the table from him in Visitor's Room A. "I've more or less reached the conclusion you're my best shot, Diz."

"When did you decide that?"

"I think when I saw that line of vultures sitting in the jury box. I've seen 'em all work, Diz, and none of them approach David Freeman."

"Neither do I. I couldn't even get you bail, remember."

Fowler tried to smile. "I don't think Abe Lincoln could have gotten me bail. But you handled Pullios just fine. Plus you got in here last night, and with Jane. That was impressive."

"That was luck."

"Better lucky than smart. Besides, people make their own luck."

Hardy touched his bandage gingerly. "Lucky people do tend to say that, don't they? I don't believe it."

"You think I'm lucky?"

"I'd say you've had a good run."

The face clouded. "I'm sixty-two, my reputation is shattered, the woman I love won't see me—"

"Let's talk about the woman you love."

"Does that mean you're with me?"

Hardy shook his head. "I don't know, Andy. I don't know what they've got. I don't know how Braun's going to rule on my involvement."

Fowler waved that off. "File a brief before you even see what Pullios has. Your oral argument was persuasive as it was. I am entitled to the counsel I want and regardless of what Locke may say, I don't see a conflict. I don't think Braun will either. You weren't state's counsel for May, right?"

Every time that came up, Hardy liked it better. "Absolutely not."

"Then forget that. Write your brief. Let's talk defense."

But before they did, Andy wanted to talk money, an issue Hardy, most unlawyerlike, had never once considered. After chiding him for that, Andy offered a $25,000 retainer against a $150-an-hour billing rate for preparation, and $1500 a day for trial, which, he explained, would represent a cut in the hourly rate, since ten hours on a trial day would be a rock-bottom minimum.

Hardy listened to the figures. He supposed he would get used to them, and when Andy had finished, said they sounded all right to him. So much for being unemployable, he thought, feeling better.

Andy hadn't seen any of the file they'd gathered on him and didn't know who'd put it together. He assumed they'd gone over his life with a fine-tooth comb, but he had little or no idea about what exactly they might have found to tie him to Owen Nash. He had never met the man, he said.

Hardy, in fact, wasn't sure of that. What he was sure of was that if

Andy Fowler felt about May the way his actions—never mind his words—indicated, he had a solid motive for killing Owen Nash. Still, there were facts to establish and he might as well start here.

"And I take it, then, you've never been on the *Eloise?*"

"That's the same thing as asking if I killed him, isn't it?"

Hardy said that maybe it was. He waited.

"What's the point of talking about that, Diz? We've pleaded not guilty. Every defendant in the world tells his lawyer he didn't do it, but let's not muddy the waters, okay? The issue is whether they've got evidence tying me to that boat. I say they can't have. There isn't any."

"How about my peace of mind, Andy? How about if it's important to me that my cause is just?" Hardy grinned, realizing he sounded pompous, but it was important to him.

"Your *cause,* Counselor, is getting me off."

"So humor me," Hardy said. "Tell me one time. Did you kill Owen Nash or not?"

Fowler shook his head. "Not," he said.

"Hardy on defense," Glitsky said. "How can you do that?"

"Pullios says I can't."

They were at Lou's, where the lunch special was hot-and-sour lamb riblets with couscous. Hardy was filling in Abe on the Pullios theory of his conflict of interest.

"She may be right, Diz, although she is not my favorite person this week."

Abe understood that whatever investigation had taken place, it had been behind his back. Simple courtesy would have dictated that he be kept informed of any developments. But Pullios had gone around him, and Glitsky was angry. He crunched the end of a rib bone and chewed pensively. "You think maybe he did it?"

Hardy sipped some water. He'd stopped eating because eating hurt. "I'd like to see what they've got."

"He didn't deny it?"

Hardy wagged a hand back and forth. "Oh, he denied it. Sort of."

"Sort of? Do me a favor," Abe said, "if you find out he did it, don't get him off."

Hardy moved his hot-and-sour around. It was also greasy and congealed. "You know why dogs lick their balls, Abe?"

"Why?"

"Because they can."

Abe shook his head. "You want to identify with the dogs, you go right ahead."

"I'm just saying it's the professional approach." Hardy tried to shrug, but again, it hurt. "For your own peace of mind, and mine, I won't stay with it if the file convicts him. Which is what worries me. They must have something. This isn't just an administrative vendetta —they're trying Andy Fowler for murder and he says he never met the man, never went near the boat, hadn't seen May in four or five months."

Glitsky sucked a lamb bone. "That's about what I found. But obviously, somebody found something else."

Hardy put his hands to his face, moved them to the sides, rubbed at his temples. He knew that if Andy Fowler had told him he'd killed Owen Nash, he couldn't have let himself take the case, even to beat Pullios and Locke, even if the investigation hadn't been strictly kosher.

But, as Glitsky said, they must have found something important that pointed to Andy's guilt.

Which didn't mean he was guilty. He said he wasn't. Which didn't mean he wasn't. Okay, Hardy, that's why there are trials, and juries.

He'd gone from Lou's back to his car, then decided that, headache or no, he had more business downtown. He got to the *Chronicle* Building at about one and stretched out on a cracked black leather couch beside Jeff Elliot's desk, where he was left alone for almost two hours. Elliot shook him awake.

"What happened to you?" he asked.

"You owe me," Hardy said. He described to Jeff how he had come to lose his job, the misunderstanding with Judge Fowler and Jane, every other real and imagined consequence he could invent relating to Jeff's story on May Shinn's bail, leading up to last night's drunk and the beating he took.

Basically, Hardy conveyed to Jeff that his article had ruined everything in his life for the last three or four months.

"Okay," Elliot said, "so I owe you. I'm sorry about your problems, but the article never mentioned your name."

That wasn't worth a rebuttal. Hardy turned straightforward. "I may need some investigative help down the line."

Jeff leaned over his desk, talking softly. "I work here. I can't do anything like that."

"If I can leak to you, why can't you leak to me? Plus, what you find for me, you've got the stories. There's something here. Maybe I can point you at something you might miss, help out both of us."

"I'd have to protect my sources," Jeff said.

"Naturally."

Jeff was mulling it over but Hardy could tell he had him. It was, he thought, a nice turnaround—usually the Deep Throat went to the reporter. Now he would—if he needed it—have himself a personal investigator with the ideal cover. He loved the idea of Pullios leaking to Jeff, who would in turn keep him on the inside track.

"So did you have a nice talk with Jane?" Hardy asked.

"Do you know she knew Owen Nash?"

Hardy was sitting on the couch beside Jeff's desk, drinking tepid coffee from a styrofoam cup. He tried to keep his voice calm. "What?"

"Jane, the judge's daughter." The reporter kept typing away. "Your ex-wife, right?"

"She knew Owen Nash?"

"Yeah. Just a sec." He finished whatever he was working on, then spun a quarter-turn in his chair. "Are you all right?"

Hardy was sitting back on the couch, his hand to his head. "How did she know Owen Nash?"

"In Hong Kong, last year. She was over there on some buying thing. Just social stuff, a cocktail party for Americans abroad. But small world, huh?"

He remembered Jane's trip to Hong Kong. It was before he and Frannie had gotten together, or, more precisely, it was during the time he and Frannie had connected.

When Jane had left for Hong Kong she and Hardy had been—more or less—together, trying it out again after the divorce and eight years of true separation where they had not so much as run into one another in the relatively small town that was San Francisco.

While she was over there, while Dismas and Frannie were falling in love, Jane had confessed to Hardy that she had had her own small infidelity. Hardy knew a lot about Jane and a few things about Owen Nash. Jane was right around May's age. Both she and Nash liked excitement. Both were given to spontaneous action.

But Hong Kong was a crowded place. There was no reason to think that because Jane had met up with Owen Nash that she'd slept with him. But there was also no reason to think she couldn't have.

And if she did . . .

Driving home, another truly perverse thought occurred to him. His friend Abe Glitsky was unhappy with Elizabeth Pullios for building a homicide case outside the framework of the police department. Abe had even mentioned considering bringing obstruction-of-justice charges against the district attorney's office, and wouldn't that be a wonder to behold. Of course, it would never happen, but it indicated Abe's state of mind.

Now, Hardy thought, wouldn't it be sweet if Abe discredited Pullios's investigation by pursuing one of his own—teach her and her boss the D.A. a lesson in interdepartmental protocol . . . which would mean that Abe, in effect, would be doing police work for the defense. Smiling still hurt.

He sat with his arm around Frannie on the top deck of the ferry to Jack London Square in Oakland. There were still another two weeks of daylight savings time and the sun hadn't yet set. The Bay was calm and as they approached Alameda it seemed to grow warmer. Though only twelve miles separated the cities, it wasn't unknown to find twenty degrees of difference between the temperatures in Oakland and San Francisco.

This was a Wednesday, and headache or not, date night was a sacred tradition. He pulled her in closer to him. "You can hang in there?" he said. "It might be a while."

"I can handle a while—even a long time. Just keep me included, will you? We're on the same side."

"Promise," he said.

"And while you're making promises, I need one more."

He nodded.

"This baby is getting itself born in four months, and trial or no trial, I want you there with me, just like with Rebecca."

"Hopefully not just like Rebecca." Rebecca had been thirty hours of grueling labor.

"You know what I mean." His wife was leaning into him. She looked up. God, she was beautiful. Hardy and Frannie had come together when she'd been about five months pregnant with Rebecca—

five months like now. Hardy thought it had to be the most attractive time in a woman's life.

After this morning, the agonies had been put aside for both of them. They were moving forward. They'd gotten through a bad time. That's what "for better or worse" meant, didn't it—that you had some worse?

He kissed her. "I know what you mean," he said.

"So you promise?"

"Promise."

43

They were back home by nine-thirty and Hardy began working on his conflict-of-interest brief in his office, typing it himself. Without a law library at hand, he had to make do in a couple of places, but he had several rows of lawbooks and periodicals on his shelves, and anyway, the gist of his argument was the one he had presented orally in court.

The closest thing to a precedent against him had been in a case where an assistant district attorney had been in the midst of trying a case against a Hell's Angel when he'd been hired away from the district attorney's office by the firm representing the defendant. There, the judge had prohibited the representation.

And Hardy agreed that there, clearly, a conflict existed. He was sure that Pullios would try to draw a parallel to this case, but Hardy was certain that the differences here far outweighed the similarities: he had not been the counsel of record for May Shinn. Andy Fowler hadn't been the defendant. All they had was the same victim, and the evidence against May Shinn in that earlier case was part of the public record. Hardy believed he knew nothing—officially—that a concerned layman couldn't have discovered.

Of course, he knew about the phone records, but that wasn't official. Also, he didn't know whether anyone in the D.A.'s office knew about the phone records.

He finished at one A.M. and called an all-night messenger service. The brief would be at Judge Braun's office when she arrived at her office in the morning.

There was nothing to do but wait for Braun to read both briefs and make her decision.

He slept in until nine-thirty and went for his first run in weeks, the four-mile circle. His ribs were unhappy with that decision but he ran through the stitch in both sides. If he was going to do this, he would be in shape for it.

Frannie went to visit her mother-in-law down in the Sunset, and Hardy got out his black cast-iron pan and turned the heat up to high under it.

Now he cut up half an onion, threw in a couple of cloves of garlic, diced a small potato, opened the refrigerator and found two leftover porkchops and cut them up. He was humming some Dire Straits and stirring when the telephone rang.

It was Marian Braun's clerk saying the judge had ruled in his favor.

He would have to play it very close. He surely didn't want Abe to think that he'd been obstructing justice himself. Abe's fuse was getting justifiably short around that issue.

Hardy leaned across Glitsky's desk. "You've still got them," he said, "and by 'you' I mean the prosecution. They're still in the file."

"What do you know about them?" The phone records.

"Almost nothing." Not true. "I checked Fowler's calls to Shinn, but I just wonder if there might have been others, if she had other clients who might have had a motive."

Glitsky took a minute. "Diz, the state's got a defendant. It's not like I'm bored in my job. This city's got more murders than Cabot Cove, and I'm on five of them right now. The Nash homicide, from our perspective, is a closed case."

Hardy shuffled through some papers on Glitsky's desk. "Well, you do what you want, but I'm going to clear Fowler, and this case is going back to open status. And if Fowler's not guilty, then someone else is, right? If you found something, it might be interesting to let Pullios know where it came from. We're talking justice here, Abe."

"Also lots of 'ifs,' Diz. Plus lots of legwork."

"Isn't that what you do, Abe? Legwork?"

"It'd have to be on my spare time."

"Whatever," Hardy said. "I've just got a feeling I'm going to find a few stones unturned here. Locke wants to get Fowler. That message comes down, people might start thinking they see things that aren't there."

"There aren't any trails, Diz. I've looked."

"What if I find you some? What if these phone calls turn into something?"

"What if, what if."

"It's up to you," Hardy said.

It was one-thirty, and Hardy had read most of the file. He was in Visitor's Room B, the mirror image of A. Fowler entered, upbeat. As soon as the guard had gone back outside, he stuck out his hand. "Congratulations," he said. "Welcome, Counselor."

Hardy ignored the hand and cut to it. "Andy, I can't represent you if you lie to me."

"What are you talking about?"

"I'm talking about this file, which I'm about two-thirds of the way through."

The euphoria of his first win faded almost as soon as he'd picked up his copy of the file from reception in the D.A.'s office. He had taken it downstairs. Sitting on a bench in the hallway, he was immediately caught up in the grand-jury testimony of a prosecution witness named Emmet Turkel, whose name jumped out at him because he'd never heard it before.

This is Peter Struler, Badge Number 1134, Investigator for the District Attorney of San Francisco. The date is July 13, 1992 at 2:40 in the P.M. No case number is assigned. I am interviewing a gentleman who identifies himself as Emmet Turkel, a resident of the state of New York, with a business address at 340 W. 28th Street in Manhattan.

Q: Mr. Turkel, what is your occupation?

A: I am a private investigator.

Q: In your capacity as a private investigator, have you had occasion to work for a man named Andrew Bryan Fowler?

A: Yes. Mr. Fowler is a judge in San Francisco.

Q: And he retained you?

A: Correct.

Q: To do what?

A: Well, the judge was upset because a woman he knew, May Shinn, had stopped seeing him. He wanted to know why.

Q: Hadn't she told him why?

A: Well, yes, I suppose what I mean to say is that she'd told him why, that she was seeing someone else. The judge wanted to know who it was.

Q: The person she was seeing now?

A: Yes.

Q: She didn't tell him who it was?

A: No. She said she was seeing someone else and that they—she and Fowler—had to break up. That was his word, break up. I make that point because the relationship wasn't exactly typical.

Q: In what way?

A: I mean, you don't say you're breaking up with someone if you're being paid by them.

Q: And the judge was paying Ms. Shinn?

A: That's my understanding, yes.

Q: For sex?

A: Sex, companionship, whatever. She was his mistress.

Q: And what did you discover?

A: I discovered the man was Owen Nash.

Q: And what did you do with that discovery?

A: I reported it to my client, Judge Fowler.

Q: And when was this?

A: Oh, middle of March, thereabouts. I could give you the exact date.

Q: That's all right. Maybe later. I have one more question. Did you find it unusual that someone from California would come to you here in New York and offer you a job out there?

A: Not really. It happens when you want to keep things closed up. I knew the judge from work I'd done for other clients over the years. I'd testified in his courtroom a couple of times, like that. So he knew to look me up. And then he didn't want anybody in town—in San Francisco—even a P.I., to know about his relationship with Shinn. I guess he figured it would look bad. So he came to me."

Fowler crossed his hands in front of him on the table. His face was serious. "How did they find Turkel?"

"I don't know, Andy, but that's not the issue. If I'm representing you, you've got to tell me everything. How do you explain this?"

Behind Turkel's deposition testimony in the notebook were a couple of xeroxed pages from Fowler's desk calendar. On the page for March 2, the name Owen Nash was written, circled, underlined. On May 16, a note read: O.N.—tonight. The *Eloise*.

"I thought you didn't know Owen Nash." Hardy's tone was more a prosecutor's. So be it. If Fowler was guilty and lying on top of it, he wanted nothing to do with it.

"I said I'd never met him, Diz. I knew who he was."

Hardy stood up, walked to the window, looked out at the high clouds and shook his head. "Not true, Andy. You said you only found out it had been Owen seeing May after he turned up dead."

The judge didn't seem too shaken. "Did I? I don't remember."

Hardy sat back down across the table. "Andy, look. You've got to remember. Did you tell anyone else you didn't know Nash, hadn't met Nash, whatever it was?"

"I don't know. Probably while they were questioning me about the bond. I'd have to say yes."

"Jesus," Hardy said. He was flipping through the binder. There were tabbed sections with other names he hadn't looked at yet. He was starting to get the feeling most of them would be impugning the judge's character. They were going to sling mud, and Andy had given them the shovel.

"I never thought they'd dig up Turkel, Diz. And when you tell a lie, you'd better stick with it. It doesn't look good, I know, but it doesn't mean—"

Hardy waved him off. "So why'd you tell the lie in the first place?"

Fowler held up his palms. "For the same reason I went to New York for Turkel, Diz. It looked terrible. Embarrassing. I knew damn well how it would look if it came out."

"And that's so important, isn't it? How it looks?"

But Andy Fowler hadn't been a judge most of his life for nothing. His jaw hardened. "You don't give it all up at once, Diz. You conserve what you've still got."

"So what do you still have, Andy? You tell me."

"I've got nothing putting me on the boat. Why would I volunteer something that would tie me to Owen Nash?"

"How about because you had to lie to evade it? Innocent people don't lie—"

"Don't give me that, Diz. Of course they do. Innocent people lie all the time, and you know it."

Hardy knew he was right. "All right, Andy, but you'll agree it gives the appearance of guilt, and appearance is going to matter to the jury."

Fowler nodded. "It was one consistent lie. The fact that I told it several times is explainable. I wanted to hide an embarrassing truth, but, as I tried to say, it doesn't mean I killed anybody."

"Andy, we're not talking embarrassment here anymore."

"I *know,* I've accepted that." The judge stared out the window, looked back to the closed door. "They do like to bring down the mighty, don't they?"

"That's not the issue either, Andy."

Fowler pointed a finger. "Don't kid yourself, Diz. That's the issue."

"Let's get back to the facts, Andy. So where did these notes come from?"

Fowler pulled the binder over in front of him. "That's my calendar, my desk at the office here." He thought a moment. "The day I retired, when the story about May's bail came out. I stayed away from the office to let things blow over. Remember?"

Hardy remembered.

"They must have moved awfully fast. I went in and cleaned out my stuff the next week. Somebody must have had an idea back then I'd killed Nash."

"Pullios," Hardy said. "Sounds like her. Get a theory and find the evidence to back it up. Somebody ought to tell her she's doing it backward." Hardy pulled the binder back in front of him, getting an idea. "This means they went into your office without your permission, maybe without a warrant?"

Fowler shook his head. This was familiar ground for him. "Don't get your hopes up, Diz. It's probably admissible. In California employers own their offices. In my case, the City and County had a right to enter my room in the Hall of Justice at any time. That's why I had my own desk brought in. It's my personal property. If I lock it, they need a warrant to get inside. But anything on top of it is fair game." He brightened up. "It's not a disaster, Diz. We can make the point I didn't take anything with me, I had nothing to hide."

Hardy knew the prosecution could counter that the judge was so arrogant he thought no one would dare look in his office, though it was technically public property. But he didn't say that. "So, assuming it's admitted, what does it mean, Andy? 'O.N. tonight—the *Eloise*'?"

"A guy at the club," he began.

"What club?"

"The Olympic. One of the guys said he was invited to this fund-raiser on Nash's *Eloise,* this was back around March or April some-time, I think."

Hardy checked. *"May* sixteenth." Just about a month before the murder.

The proximity didn't faze Fowler. "Okay, May. Anyway, I thought I might go along, see the famous son of a bitch." He shook his head. "I decided against it."

"Why?"

"I'm not sure. A mix of things, I suppose. I thought May might be there and I didn't think I could handle seeing her with him."

Hardy went back to the window. Under the fluorescent glare at the table his head had started to throb again. He stood there a minute, then turned back. "Andy, this might offend you, but I want you to take a polygraph."

The judge pursed his lips. The request clearly annoyed him. "Polygraphs don't work, Diz. They're inadmissible."

"I know that."

The silence built. Hardy stood by the window. Fowler leaned back in his chair. "I told you I didn't kill him."

"I know you did."

"And you don't believe me?"

Hardy let his silence talk.

The judge pushed. "It's that one lie, isn't it, not knowing Nash? I told you about that. I didn't think you or anyone else needed to know. I didn't think it would come out."

"Well, it's out now, and it's not need-to-know anymore. I've got to know everything, and I'll decide what to hold back. You want me to defend you—I do that or I do nothing."

"And you need a polygraph for that?"

"To tear a page from the Pullios notebook, 'One lie speaks to the defendant's character, Your Honor.' "

"You think I'll agree to take a polygraph?"

Hardy drummed his fingers a moment, looked around at the walls, the barred window. "You know, Andy, I'm afraid this isn't a request."

"Diz, they're inadmissible!" Fowler repeated. He took a beat, slowing down. "You know *why* they're inadmissible? Because they don't work. They don't prove a damn thing."

Hardy nodded. "I know that." In a courtroom, at least, they were certainly suspect.

Fowler stared at him. "They why?"

Hardy found himself biting back the words—out loud they would sound priggish, self-righteous. Because the reason was that he wanted something that would let him, for his own conscience's sake, continue defending Andy, something that, if it didn't clear him, at least left open the probability that in spite of his untruths and peccadillos, he wasn't guilty.

For many legal professionals this would be irrelevant. The issue wasn't the fact, it was whether the fact could be proved. But Hardy used to be a cop, then a prosecutor. His mind-set was getting the bad guy and he wanted no part of defending a guilty man, even an old friend like Andy Fowler.

"I've got my reasons," he said at last, "and you either accept them or get yourself a new lawyer, Andy."

Fowler's gaze was firm, composed. "I didn't kill him, Diz."

Hardy spread his hands. "Then it ought to be no problem, right?"

Finally the judge nodded. "All right, Dismas. I don't like it, but all right."

44

Glitsky was wearing green khakis, hiking boots, a leather flight jacket. He stood about six-foot-two-and-a-half and weighed in at a little over 210 pounds. His black hair was short, almost Marine cut. When he was younger, partially to hide the top of his scar, he sported a Fu Manchu but he'd been clean shaven now for six years.

Elizabeth Pullios had worked with him on at least fourteen cases since she'd become a homicide prosecutor three years earlier. Their relationship had been mostly cordial and open. They were on the same side. It shouldn't, therefore, have filled her with any foreboding when Abe's substantial form appeared in her doorway. But it did.

He didn't say anything. She'd been reviewing testimony for a case she was taking to trial in two months, memorizing as she liked to do. And then he was there. She had no idea for how long.

"Hi, Abe," she said. She closed the binder and flashed him some teeth. "What's up?"

Glitsky was leaning against the door, hands in his jacket pocket. As though changing his mind about whatever it was, he shrugged himself off the jamb and inside. Jamie Jackson, her office mate, had gone home an hour ago. Glitsky closed the door behind him. He didn't sit down, and Pullios pushed her chair back slightly to get a better angle.

"How long you been a D.A.?" Abe asked.

Pullios still tried to smile, the charm that worked so well. "You're upset with me and I can't say I blame you."

Glitsky really wasn't much of a smiler. He'd seen too many cons and too much phoniness introduced by the glad hand and the ivory grin. Smiling set his teeth on edge. "About, what? Six, seven years?" He was a trained interrogator, and what you did was you zeroed in, you ignored the smoke until you got the answer to your question. "Since you got here?"

Pullios nodded. "About that, Abe. Just over seven."

"You know how long I been a cop?" It wasn't a question. "We've worked together a long time and I don't think you know anything about me at all."

She was still staring up at him. He was wearing the face he used on suspects. It was a look.

"I did four years at San Jose State on a football scholarship. Tight end. Actually, it was before they called it 'tight end.' It was just plain old 'end' back then. But I wasn't just a dumb jock, mostly because I was smart enough to realize I was a step too slow for the pros, so I kind of studied and pulled a three-point-four grade-point average. My counselor told me I could get into law school with that."

Now his mouth stretched, a caricature of a smile that stretched the wide scar that ran through his upper and lower lips. "Imagine that," he went on, "law school."

"Abe . . ."

He didn't acknowledge her. "But I was recruited into the Academy —yeah, they did that then—after I graduated, and I thought it looked like more fun, more action than the law, you know? I was twenty-three then. I'm forty-one now. Eighteen years, and the last seven I've been on homicides."

He stopped. Somewhere in another office a phone was ringing. Outside the window, an orange and pink dusk was settling.

Pullios had to struggle for breath, for control. "There were a lot of reasons, Abe," she said. He didn't reply, just loomed there like a malevolent statue, hands in his jacket pockets, feet planted flat. She swirled in her chair to get out from under his gaze. "The way the Shinn matter went down, the false arrest." She cathedraled her hands in front of her mouth, staring out to the Bay Bridge. "I know Hardy's your friend. I guess I just thought it wouldn't have your full attention."

"My work gets my full attention."

"Come on, Abe, you know what I mean. It would all be warmed over." She kept at it. "And nobody took you off it you know. If you'd found anything, we would have used it. Peter Struler just happened to find it."

"He just happened to go search Fowler's office? A lot of times, I'll do that—spice up a slow day and go and toss some judge's chambers."

"Well, I had a theory and mentioned it to him."

"Even a dumb jock like me could figure that out, Elizabeth. Traditionally, though, theories get told to the investigating officer, which happened in this case to be me."

"I know that, Abe." Contrite. She stood up. "It was a mistake, Abe. I'm sorry."

"Yeah, well, sorry is a big help. Look at the evidence Struler got, and then why don't you explain to my bosses how it was that I didn't find any of it. Like by the time I hit Fowler's office, after clearing it with my lieutenant because I thought it might be a touch sensitive, why there wasn't anything left to find."

"It wasn't only in his office."

Glitsky's voice went real low. Almost a whisper. "You know, Elizabeth, I don't care if it was in the Amazon rain forest. We've got a homicide team upstairs that works on homicides. We get you your evidence, without which you don't have a job anymore. You got a new protocol, fine, you go for it, but it's a two-way street."

"I understand that. Look, Abe, I've apologized. It won't happen again. I'm really sorry."

Glitsky nodded. Sometimes you let them have the last word, let them think it's all settled and forgotten.

"Just tell me you didn't sleep with him."

"That's none of your business."

"It's my business." Hardy lowered his voice into the telephone. "Especially if it was last September. And you know it." He was in his office. Halfway through the file, he remembered Jane.

He imagined her in her kitchen at her house—their old house—on Jackson Street, sitting on the stool, maybe a glass of white wine nearby. Nearing forty, twice divorced and suffering through the apparent decline in her market value that came as such a shock, Jane was still very attractive. Also intelligent, self-reliant, why was it men didn't see it? If they were her age they wanted a relationship and went —as Hardy had (and she had pointed it out to him)—for the younger women, the tighter, the firmer, the more *fun*. They could dream again with the young ones, pretend they were younger, too. Build a new life halfway through their old one. The older men knew you'd been around. You didn't have to play games. Everybody had sex. It was an itch to be scratched. Dinner, cognac, orgasm. Thanks a lot. You're a great kid. Or the young guys who dug the experience of an older woman, but never a thought of settling down with one . . .

Hardy had heard and read about all the stages. Jane had to be lonely as hell most of the time. Even with Chuck Chuck Bo-Buck, the latest.

But not, he hoped, please not with Owen Nash.

"Jane."

"It wasn't anything," she said. "It was one night."

Her voice sounded dead.

He had filled twenty pages of yellow legal pad. It was nearly midnight and he rubbed his eyes, the swelling around them having turned a faint purple now, the throbbing continuous but bearable. He had been letting his mind go, jumping from issue to issue and following the flow, tearing out sticking tabs and placing them on pages by subject: Venue. Bail. Evidence. Theory. Jury.

He thought he had to take another shot at getting Andy out on bail. Even if they set it for a million dollars, he couldn't let him stay in the clink. He knew he could ask the Court of Appeal to force Braun to set some reasonable bail and eventually they would do it. Drysdale would know that, too. Maybe he could talk to him and get some concessions without the procedural hassles.

After that, the first thing he would do would be to make a motion for judicial review of the evidence, which, now that he'd reviewed most of the file, still struck him as very light. Everything was circumstantial.

Perhaps bolstered by Andy's unsupported alibi, his lies (or one lie told many times) and the enormity of the risk he'd taken in defense of May, the evidence still didn't put him on the boat. Without that, Hardy didn't see how anyone could vote to convict.

Juries had been known to do almost anything, but he thought an impartial judge, if he could find one, would throw this thing out as a turkey.

Pullios and her personal grand jury notwithstanding, the system at least tacitly contemplated abuse of the indictment procedure, and so authorized a judicial review of the indictment to insure there was sufficient evidence to go to trial. It was not, after all, in the system's own self-interest to bring a case to trial where there was no evidence. Hardy thought maybe he could get Andy off there. It at least was worth a try.

If that didn't work, he thought he would try to get out of San Francisco. His own file, from the time of the original *Chronicle* blurb when he and Pico had found Owen Nash's hand, contained over sixty-five articles from both local and national publications on the case. Nash, Shinn, himself, Freeman, Fowler. And it was the kind of story people tended to read and remember, or stop what they were doing to listen to on the radio or watch on television.

At least he was coming to the theory he would use in defense. You needed a defense theory. He'd done enough prosecuting to know that those defense lawyers who just refuted his evidence, who debated his conclusions, got themselves beaten. What you needed was your own affirmative defense. Come out fighting, the voice of outrage at unfair accusation.

It had come to him today, and he thought it had some real legs. It also appealed to him because it gave things a personal edge—Pullios had done her job backward. The way it was supposed to work (he would argue) was that evidence is fairly gathered from all quarters by the police investigating the crime. When that evidence reaches some critical mass an indictment is sought and an arrest warrant is issued. None of that had happened in Fowler's case.

Hardy thought he could make a case to the jury that someone, Locke or Pullios or whoever, had fastened on Andy Fowler out of personal animus, out of anger at his professional lapses. It was a political vendetta based on his conduct on the bench but *not* because the evidence pointed at him.

Hardy had never before called Glitsky as a witness for the prosecution on any of his cases, but now he wrote his name under a new tab . . . the investigating officer of record as a witness for the *defense*. That ought to jolt old Betsy.

And he knew there was a further step he had to take, if he believed the judge was innocent. For that he was ready to use Jeff Elliot and Abe Glitsky and anyone else. *Someone* had killed Owen Nash. But juries were imperfect. They could make a mistake and convict Andy. Hardy's best hope of getting Andy off was to find out who *had* done it.

A tall order that, since evidently it hadn't been any of the suspects so far—Shinn, Farris, Mr. Silicon Valley. But there was an "X" out there. Jane? Impossible. A one-night stand, she'd said. She'd said . . . *No*. He knew Jane, she couldn't *kill* anybody. Besides, why would she have told Jeff Elliot she'd met Nash that once if she'd seen him since and it was an affair? Why open that door? Unless she figured it would come out anyway and she wanted to look like she had nothing to hide. No, ridiculous. Jane had no motive.

Farris? He was *numero uno* with Nash gone, or in a position to be the power behind the new man in charge, all his show of grief notwithstanding.

He sat back in his chair and stretched. Enough already, picking at straws. Abe hadn't even looked yet at May's other clients—the three men Hardy had discovered through the phone records. There was a whole universe of potential suspects. One of them, someone, had to have made a mistake but he wasn't likely to discover it practicing this sort of armchair reverie. He had to get someone moving on it.

He lifted the last dart from his desk and pegged it at his board where it stuck four inches below the bull's-eye.

Jane . . . had Andy known about Jane and Owen? Could that have been reason, another reason, for *Andy* to have killed Nash? . . . It might have been the last straw, Andy broken up over Nash—the "famous son of a bitch"—stealing his May, and then he's almost over that, maybe, when five months later he finds out the guy had also *fucked his daughter* and boom, over the edge . . . ?

You're playing devil's advocate, Hardy. Andy didn't do it, the polygraph he'd managed to schedule for the next morning, technically flawed as it might be, should eliminate any last doubts . . . not that he had many left—Andy resenting, sure, but also quickly agreeing to take the test was in his favor. Wasn't it?

He had read nearly everything in the file. He thought he was being fairly objective and still had no idea what *new* evidence Pullios had found to convince her to proceed. Certainly, on the evidence presented in the transcripts he'd been reviewing, she hadn't put it in before the Grand Jury. Pullios could have talked herself blue in the face, sweet and convincing as she could be, about what an immoral man Andy was, what a lousy judge, how he didn't have an alibi, the fact that he'd written Owen Nash's name in his calendar, he was involved with May Shinn, he'd thrown away his career and reputation, had been secretive and unethical—but, so what? What did all that prove about making him a murderer?

There had to be something else or the case wouldn't have gotten this far—but winning an indictment wasn't winning a jury trial. He was getting tired now but thought he'd take another pass at the stuff he thought he was already familiar with. The paper load had grown in one day to three binders and a couple of legal pads.

He scanned Glitsky's interviews with the two guards at the Marina —not much there. From his own notes he reviewed the previous May Shinn grand-jury testimony of Strout, Abe, Celine and the rest. So there wouldn't be any surprises, he reviewed the physical-evidence list the prosecution was planning to enter as exhibits. It was, with the additions from Fowler's calendars and the deletion of the two-million-dollar handwritten will, pretty much as he expected, and there still wasn't much—the autopsy photos of Owen Nash, the gun, the phone records establishing Andy's relationship with May, papers on the bail situation.

He closed the binders. Time to sleep on it.

45

There were stacks of papers on May's kitchen table.

Under David Freeman's guidance she had been, it seemed, suing most of the western world for what it had done to her—there were lawsuits against the officer who had arrested her, his superiors, the district attorney's office and the City and County of San Francisco. Freeman was citing a smorgasbord of offenses ranging from false arrest through various civil-rights violations, defamation of character, libel and slander.

Separately, they had been negotiating for the return of the many personal items—clothes, makeup and so forth—that she'd kept stowed aboard the *Eloise*. Four months after the murder, the boat was still sealed and winter was coming on. There were special things Owen had given her. She and David had made up a list, and David thought she ought to have all of it back—shoes, rain slickers, her beautiful down coat, a Siberian babushka, glass and jade pieces she'd kept in his rolltop, some exercise stuff. She had to laugh at the last one—she hadn't done a thing with her body since June.

By far, most of the legal work had involved the will. At first she hadn't cared about the money, or thought she hadn't. But gradually practicality and principle merged. Why should the estate, which didn't need it, get it. Or his daughter who had so much anyway? She —May—was the one who had loved him and he had *wanted* her to have it.

She stood holding her cup of tea, looking down at the stacks of papers, wearing a black-and-red silk kimono cinched at the waist. The mid-October day had come up clear and sunny.

The peace she'd found, or thought she'd found, with Owen, had been shattered by her time in jail, the craziness surrounding her arrest. David Freeman, a dear man, had seen the hopelessness start to rise in her again and wisely had proceeded to involve her with these distractions, the lawsuits.

And for a time it had kept away the nothingness. She had been busy, the way an ant was busy—going around piling up little things until they made a bigger thing. You don't stop because the busyness was the end in itself. Now there was something new, a written request, not a subpoena, that she appear as a state's witness against Andy Fowler.

She walked over to her turret and looked down on the street, the people going into the deli, that cute little cable car. She tried to conjure up some image of the way she'd felt, or remembered feeling, with Owen, the unity the two of them had discovered.

But it wasn't there anymore. She'd had a family that had never loved her, that had been too afraid of life to try living it. Two barren marriages, liaisons without meaning. Day after day, going through motions, hoping for someone she could admire, who could admire her. Then thinking she'd found it and having it all smashed.

And now all those papers. She supposed she owed it to David to keep at them. What did she owe Andy Fowler?

"Who was that?"

Dorothy woke up happy every morning. The mattress on the floor was lifted onto a sturdy platform with a modern pine headboard. There was floral wallpaper along one wall with some Degas and Monet prints dry-mounted and covered with glass. Einstein still counseled them about mediocre minds. New drapes, a large bright throw rug, a rattan loveseat, end table, coffee table, three modern lamps. It was a different place.

Jeff was even walking better, able to cross from the bar to his bed without his crutches. He didn't believe it would last forever but he'd take it while it was here. Maybe the Prednisone for his eyes had done something for his legs. There was no predicting these symptoms, so when a little good came along you didn't question it. He pushed himself back onto the bed.

"That was Hardy, the attorney I told you about. For the defense this time."

Gloriously immodest, she lifted her naked body against a reading pillow and pulled him back against her, pulling the blankets over them, rubbing her hands up and down his chest. "And what does Mr. Hardy want?"

"Fowler's taking a polygraph today. He wanted me to know."

"Why?"

He leaned his head against her. "If he passes it, it's news. It's not evidence, but it's news. And he figures it helps him."

"What if he doesn't pass it?"

"That's news, too. Either way it's good for me. But Hardy must think he's going to do okay or he wouldn't have told me."

"It seems a little risky . . ."

"Hardy's got to take some risk. They both win if Fowler is innocent."

"Do you think he is?"

"Innocent you mean?"

She nodded.

"Nope."

The gun.

Pullios and Struler, clever devils.

Hardy knew it would be unwise to file his 995 Penal Code motion for dismissal before he'd gone over every word of the file carefully. Most of it, as he'd noticed last night, was stuff he'd seen before, and the temptation was to skim it.

The discovery process tried to eliminate surprises in the courtroom; the Perry Mason, last-minute, rabbit-from-the-hat conclusions were really the stuff of fiction. Long before anybody went to trial, attorneys for the prosecution had to disclose everything they had in terms of evidence, proposed witnesses, expert testimony. In theory, the point was not to sandbag your opponent (although if you could, it was a nice bonus) but to lay out the evidence and its relevance before a jury.

If Glitsky or somebody else should chance upon some relevant evidence during the trial, then Hardy could introduce it at that time, but that would be a rare event. Most of the time, the parties knew the cards against them—the skill was in how they were played.

Which didn't mean that Pullios, having given Hardy everything she was supposed to, then had to sit him down and show him how to use it.

So Hardy was being thorough. There was no surprise in the gun being presented as an exhibit—it was, after all, the murder weapon.

What he did *not* expect was that Andy Fowler's fingerprints were on the clip.

So much for his motion for judicial review of the evidence. With this latest, Hardy realized there was at least enough evidence against Andy Fowler to warrant a trial.

"How could that happen? How could no one have seen that before. That puts him on the boat, and if he was on the boat, no jury in the world will believe he didn't kill him."

Hardy had caught Glitsky on the phone at his desk before he started driving downtown and now they were eating hamburgers far from the Hall of Justice. Glitsky understandably didn't want to be seen being buddy-buddy with a defense attorney. Friends or no friends, a new reality had kicked in.

Glitsky chewed ice, which he did every chance he got. It drove Hardy crazy. "Not necessarily."

"What do you mean, not necessarily? The gun was on the boat and Fowler's fingerprints were on the gun."

"They could have been on the gun before it got to the boat."

"Well, that's damn sure going to be my argument, but it doesn't exactly strengthen my case. How could he not tell me about that? How could he not know?"

Glitsky had a bite of burger. "He lied."

"Thanks."

Abe swallowed, took a drink of Coke, chewed ice. "You're welcome."

"How did we miss them last time, the prints?"

Abe rubbed his face. "Two ways, maybe. One, nobody looked at the clip. Shinn's prints were on the barrel, she was the suspect, end of search. Two"—Abe held up two fingers—"they got a print they couldn't match. Then, once they knew they were looking for Fowler, they ran it against his."

"That would have come up long ago."

"Nope. His prints weren't in the right databank. We run a print we find on the gun through known criminals and nothing comes up, what are we supposed to do, check every fingerprint file in the universe?" Glitsky shrugged. "It hurts me to say it, but these things sometimes slip through the cracks."

Hardy swore.

Glitsky nodded again. "Probably some combination of both."

"Abe, I forced myself to play devil's advocate, but the truth is, I can't believe he did it. *That,* he wouldn't lie about—"

After a moment's baleful stare, Glitsky rubbed a finger into his ear as though he'd heard something wrong. "Excuse me," he said, "I thought I heard you say a perp wouldn't lie to you?"

"This is not any old perp, Abe. This is my ex-father-in-law. I know him." Or at least he thought he did. "A Superior Court judge, for Christ's sake."

Abe reached over and grabbed the rest of Hardy's burger. "I can tell you're not going to eat this . . . You said you've got a polygraph for today, right. That'll tell you. Maybe. And maybe not." Abe smiled his awful smile.

The polygraph technician—Ron Reynolds, a tall, thin man in a gray suit, white shirt, blue-and-black tie—was waiting for him in the second-floor visitor's lounge of his office near the Civic Center.

After introductions they got right down to business.

"Are you going to stipulate for admissibility?" Reynolds asked.

"I'm not doing it for admissibility. I'm doing it for me."

This wasn't the first time Reynolds had heard an attorney say that. Occasionally, though not so very often, they wanted to believe their clients.

Hardy went on. "Also, though, I thought the fact my client was willing to take the test might have a positive effect on the jury."

"If you can get *that* admitted, which I doubt."

"Well, I can try." Hardy took out a pad of notes and they started to go over them. He had twenty-odd "yes" and "no" questions Fowler could answer that related to Owen Nash and May Shinn. Reynolds had ten-or-so more for what he called calibration.

"You'll go over all of these with him before the test? No surprises, right."

"Sure. Are you planning on being there?"

"Outside. Close by."

Reynolds thought that was the right answer. "It's better without interruptions," he said.

But before he had Andy Fowler take the test, Hardy needed some answers of his own.

They were again in Visitors Room A. The guard was still holding the judge by the arm when Hardy, who'd been pacing by the table, started. "You want to tell me how your fingerprints got on the *inside* of the murder weapon, on the clip?"

Fowler stopped dead. The guard didn't move, either. Hardy stared at his client for a moment, then recovered. He pointedly thanked the guard and waited until he withdrew and closed the door behind him.

Andy had recovered. "Are you kidding?"

"Don't give me that, Andy."

"My fingerprints?"

Hardy was angry. Every day brought him more into the case, more committed to getting Andy off, but that was mostly because he kept telling himself that the judge was innocent. He'd told himself that he would only stay with Andy's defense if he had a reasonable certainty that he wasn't guilty. Of course, no one but the murderer, Andy or not, would ever be one-hundred-percent sure of what had happened on the *Eloise,* but Hardy wasn't a hired gun. He wouldn't have gone on, he wouldn't go on, if he knew Andy had done it.

Fowler swore softly behind him, and Hardy turned around.

"I *loaded* the gun for her, Diz. This is unbelievable. It was months ago. It never even occurred to me, Diz, I swear to God."

"You loaded the gun for her?"

He nodded. "She was afraid to touch the thing. One of her earlier —someone had given it to her and she'd never even loaded it. It was in the headboard of her bed. I told her there was no point in keeping a gun for protection if it wasn't loaded so I loaded it."

"It wasn't on the headboard of her bed, Andy. It was on the *Eloise.*"

"She told me she didn't want it in the house. She hated it. *I* couldn't take it, I couldn't take a gun registered to another person."

"Because you were a judge and didn't want to break any laws?"

Fowler tried to smile. "Before my little problem with the Shinn trial, that's how I was, Diz."

Hardy slammed the table between them. "Goddamn it, Andy! That wasn't a 'little problem' at the Shinn trial. That's the whole reason we're here."

"I understand that, Diz." Said quietly.

"Well, then, how do you expect me to sell a jury on the idea that you were such a paragon of virtue that you wouldn't take May's gun to your house when six months later . . . ?" He checked himself; yelling at his client wasn't going to do either of them any good. He turned away.

"It's a good point, Dismas, but it happens to be the truth."

"So maybe when May started seeing Nash he didn't have your scruples and let her store the gun on his boat?" Hardy was back at the window. Andy Fowler had an answer for everything, all right, but it was easier to listen without having to see what he was doing with his face.

He felt for a moment like he was in *Gone With the Wind*. He'd think about it tomorrow. For today, at least he had an explanation for this latest revelation—tomorrow he'd decide if he could believe it.

They'd gone over the polygraph questions one at a time. Fowler advised Hardy to try and get Pullios to stipulate to the admissibility of the results of the test. He told him that if, before either of them knew how it came out, Hardy offered to permit her to use the results, no matter what they were, she might agree to let them be entered as evidence.

Of course, she might not. Andy's suggestion did have the effect of moving Hardy back toward thinking his client might be telling the truth, but of course Andy would know that. Circles within circles.

In any event, Hardy didn't hold out much hope Pullios would go for it. Sticking with polygraph inadmissibility was the smarter course from her perspective—she'd figure her case didn't need it, and a good showing on the polygraph by Fowler could only hurt her.

Unlike defense attorneys who only had a duty to their clients, the job of prosecutor included not just presenting state's evidence, but ensuring that the defendant got a fair trial. The defendant was a citizen of the state, one of the people the prosecutor was sworn to help protect.

Except Hardy knew Pullios, and this nicety was, he believed, lost on her.

Which led him to his bold, unorthodox strategy—

"How's jail treating you?"

Fowler shrugged. "It's like a good hotel, only bad. Why?"

"I don't want you mistreated. This bail situation is intolerable."

"I am a little surprised at Marian."

Fowler was a little surprised at *Marian*! At Judge Marian Braun. Hardy couldn't get over Andy's seemingly ingrained sangfroid. Like Marie Antoinette apologizing to her executioner for stepping on his toe. Fowler too was unfailingly polite, refined, even self-effacing. It wore well in the world, but here in jail, in his prison garb, it was somehow at once incongruous and pitiable.

It was going to be next to impossible to choose a jury resembling this man's peers.

"Well, *Marian* notwithstanding, Judge . . ."

"Better get out of that habit, Diz. Not judge, *Mister* Fowler. Remember, Marian made the point."

Hardy pressed on. "Marian notwithstanding, Andy. I think if you can live with your situation for a while we can use it to our advantage."

Hardy's theory involved doing away with many of the time-honored traditions of the Superior Court, but he didn't think he or Fowler could make any new enemies if they tried—all the available ones were taken.

His primary defense, of course, would be that the prosecution had failed to prove their case beyond a reasonable doubt. The evidence did not prove that Andy Fowler had killed Owen Nash. There was probably motive, or purported motive, but motive alone should not be enough to convict. So he had a defense, a passive defense. He wasn't sure it would be enough.

Pullios, he was certain, was going to use all of the physical evidence she had, but she would probably build her case around a "consciousness of guilt" theory by which a defendant's actions, such as flight, resisting arrest, lying to interrogators and so on, were admissible evidence showing the defendant to be "conscious of guilt"—even with little other evidence, those actions could as a matter of law be sufficient to establish guilt beyond a reasonable doubt.

There might not be a smoking gun here, Hardy knew, but Fowler's unethical behavior while on the bench rang, sang and went sissboom-bang with consciousness of guilt.

So he needed something else if he wanted to get Andy out of jail, and the court had steered him in the right direction. Beginning with Pullios as she proceeded backward from suspect to investigation, on through Marian Braun's decision to deny bail, this case, he could argue, had been riddled with demonstrable prejudice against Andy Fowler. Hardy, thinking it likely they couldn't get a fair trial on account of prosecutorial and judicial prejudice in San Francisco, had at first considered trying for a change in venue but then the other thought—the strategy—occurred to him.

In San Francisco it was likely they would get a judge hostile to Andy, possibly even to himself. They would, in fact, further antagonize both the judge and Pullios by demanding a trial immediately, as was their right. (In the Shinn matter, Pullios had wanted to proceed to trial quickly and had gotten hurt by it—now that she was slowly building what she thought was a strong case she'd be opposed to rushing it through.)

Hardy would argue that so long as his innocent client was being held without bail, it was unreasonable to ask him to suffer any delay. He was innocent until proven guilty and he was rotting in jail.

Hardy figured this approach could prevail in more ways than one. First, the presiding judge might reconsider bail. If that didn't happen, then scheduling an immediate trial would, he hoped, maybe disconcert Pullios—he'd seen how the swirling events with May Shinn had led even Pullios to slip on some details such as checking the phone records. She also could get testy, personal, which could hurt her credibility in front of a jury. He hoped. At least if he could keep her covering her fronts he figured he would cut down on her efficiency. Her effectiveness.

Finally, in the event they went to trial with Andy still in jail, with a hostile judge, and Pullios got the conviction, Hardy could make the argument on appeal that there had been a *de facto* conspiracy against Fowler to obstruct justice and due process, from investigation to incarceration to trial.

Fowler heard out Hardy's argument. "I'm not too thrilled with the idea of setting a mistrial in motion to win on appeal."

"It's a last resort, Andy, granted. But we'd be foolish not to think of it now. It would cut Pullios's prep time by two-thirds."

"And ours."

Hardy nodded. "True, but the evidence isn't going to do it, Andy. It's who slings it better, and I believe she'll feel rushed. I know her."

"How about you?"

Hardy let himself grin. "I thrive under pressure."

"It gives us less time to find out who really killed him."

Hardy had been sitting on the hard wooden chair. His ribs, black and blue and yellow under his shirt, stabbed at him as he shifted now. Grimacing, he stared across the table.

"Are you all right?" Fowler asked him.

"Yeah. You know what? That's the first thing I've heard you say that really sounds like you're not guilty."

46

EX-JUDGE ANDREW FOWLER'S POLYGRAPH RESULTS
"INCONCLUSIVE" IN OWEN NASH MURDER CASE
By Jeffrey Elliot
Chronicle Staff Writer

Former Superior Court Judge Andrew B. Fowler yesterday was not cleared in a polygraph test. The results of so-called lie detector tests are not admissible as evidence in California courts, but Fowler's failure to clear himself was characterized by the district attorney's office yesterday as a blow to the defense.

Fowler's attorney, former prosecutor Dismas Hardy, put the results in a more positive light. "The test did *not* say that Judge Fowler was not telling the truth. The judge *volunteered* to take the test. Would he have done that if he were guilty?"

Ron Reynolds, a University of San Francisco psychology professor trained in polygraphy, and the man who administered the test, agreed with Hardy. "The reason polygraphs are inadmissible in the first place is because they can have a wide degree of variability, of accuracy, according to the subject's mood, his familiarity with the testing procedure, his understanding of the questions. Judge Fowler seemed to be extremely uncomfortable with the entire process—we could not even get a good calibration on him in four passes."

Hardy added: "There was no indication whatsoever that Judge Fowler was not telling the truth."

Mr. Drysdale replied: "There was also no indication whatsoever that the judge was not lying."

In a related development, the *Chronicle* learned from a reliable courthouse source yesterday that Judge Fowler's fingerprints have been found on the loading chamber of the murder weapon, a .25-

332

caliber Beretta semi-automatic handgun registered to May Shinn, who had been the lover of both Owen Nash and former Judge Fowler.

The case will be scheduled for trial on Monday morning.

HARDY HAD TO LEARN TO HOLD HIS COMMENTS in front of the jailhouse guards, even though they might be known to the prosecution. He knew who the "reliable courthouse source" must have been about the fingerprints. His good statements to the press notwithstanding, the polygraph was a blow. It was all well and good to tell Jeff Elliot that there had been nothing that showed Andy was lying, but the test, from *Hardy's* perspective, had brought up his old doubts about Andy's innocence. On the other hand, he reminded himself, Andy's nervousness could have been real—after all, everything about his predicament in jail was strange and scary. And what about Andy's position that his best shot at proving he didn't kill Nash was to find out who *did*? But outside of Glitsky and maybe Jeff, who owed him, where did he go for finding that out? And even with them, a few tenuous leads, some serendipitous snooping by Jeff . . . none of these were too hopeful.

He stood in front of his desk and threw darts, round after round. There were household noises—Frannie was doing some vacuuming, Rebecca got hungry and cried, Garth Brooks serenaded a CD's worth from the living room. The sun got higher.

He was due in Master Calendar in two days. Based on the presumption that his client was innocent and being held without bail, he planned to push for an immediate trial. He would not waive time, and this would anger Pullios and whatever judge they got. They would not challenge the judge, whoever it might be. The newspapers were already leaning toward Fowler's guilt, and Hardy thought it would be easier to find a heterosexual on Castro Street than to find a prospective jury member in this city who didn't already have an opinion on Andy Fowler and Owen Nash.

Risks. Too many?

Leaving out the biggest—if Andy had in fact done it—Hardy's doubts came and went. He just didn't *know*. Not yet, anyway.

Personally Hardy's own blackness had lifted—it was gone, vanished like a virulent flu that had done its damage and moved on.

He could think of no better place to be than where he was now—

defending Andy Fowler. Since he had discovered Owen Nash's hand last June, this case had been central to his life—his marriage, his career, his view of himself. He would, by God, see it through—if he had to wring it from some collective necks, he would get to the truth.

47

Superior Court Judge Marian Braun gavelled the room to order.
Hardy had been sitting in the jury box to Braun's right. Twenty minutes before, Elizabeth Pullios had come in with her entourage—the
same assistant D.A. she'd had last time and what looked to be a law
student/clerk. She sat at the prosecution table, busily conferring, ignoring Hardy completely.

They had called six of the earlier "lines," and the various defendants had been paraded before the bench. Two of them had been
assigned to courtrooms, three were continued and defense attorneys
assigned, one was pled out then and there and ordered to pay a fine.

Hardy tried not to look at the gallery. Celine was there, dressed in
black, sitting next to Ken Farris in the second row. He hadn't seen her
since the day at the steam room in Hardbodies! He noticed Jeff Elliot
sitting among what Hardy assumed to be a group of other reporters.
Jane, of course, was in the front row, opposite Celine. Art Drysdale
came through the main doors and stood, arms folded, against the
back wall.

He and Andy had discussed it yesterday—Sunday—and decided what
he would wear in court. Andy didn't own a suit that cost less than
$700, so Hardy had asked Jane, the I. Magnin buyer, to hit a few
lower-price racks and find something in Andy's size with a little more
of a common feel. He wanted Andy to look good—if a jury thought you
looked like a criminal you were starting off on the wrong foot—but not
too good. Andy Fowler, ex-judge, was going to have a problem with the
jury empathizing with him in any event.

As the bailiff was reading the charge again, Hardy got up from the
jury box and met Andy at the podium, fifteen feet in front of where
Marian Braun sat. He heard activity behind him. Turning, he saw that
the door was open and a larger knot of reporters was pushing in.

Braun brought down her gavel. "Let's get seated out there. While I'm at it, I want to tell you all that I will not allow pictures to be taken in this courtroom. I want order. This isn't going to take long."

"Note that," Fowler whispered. "This is not going to take long."

Hardy nodded to Fowler, then addressed the court. "Your Honor?"

"Mr. Hardy."

"On the matter of bail . . ."

"Bail has been decided."

"Yes, your Honor, but I understood that you would reconsider your position."

Braun glared down at him. "What made you understand that? What could I have said that brought you to that conclusion?"

Hardy had expected hostility, but on a *pro forma* request such as this one, Braun's response still took him aback. "Your Honor, Mr. Fowler is a respected jurist—"

"Was, Mr. Hardy. Presently he is a defendant in a murder trial. It is not unusual to deny bail in such cases. I thought I'd made that perfectly clear. Ms. Pullios, was that clear to you?"

"Yes, Your Honor."

"Mr. Hardy somehow understood that I would reconsider."

No answer was called for. The courtroom was quiet. Marian Braun stared at her former colleague. She looked to the computer sheet in front of her.

"Bail will be set at one million dollars."

PART V

48

It was a cold and clear Monday morning, the fifty-first anniversary of Pearl Harbor. Out in the hallway in front of Department 27 Hardy turned from the group that had gathered around Ken Farris and Celine Nash. He pretended to lean down and tie his shoe, wanting to hear what she was saying. Her husky voice cut through the hubbub.

"I'm here, and I'm going to be here every day to remind the jury that Owen Nash was a real person, not just a statistic, not a quote super-rich financier unquote but my *father,* a living and breathing person whom I loved and whom I mourn every day."

Jane was next to him. "Chomorro," she said. "Isn't that the worst?"

Hardy hadn't spoken to his ex-wife since finding out she'd slept once—"only one night"—with Owen Nash. "Hi, Jane." He stood up. He hadn't seen any reason to burden her with his strategy of the antagonistic bench. In that light, he considered Chomorro was one of the best judges who could have come up.

"Are we going to challenge him?"

Hardy thought he'd move along down the hallway away from Celine and Farris. He saw Jeff Elliot having a few words with Pullios over to his right. They had about fifteen minutes before Chomorro would call the court to order.

"Chomorro? No."

"You're kidding."

Hardy thought he might as well practice for the newspapers. "Why would I want to challenge him, Jane? This is his first murder trial. Your dad wouldn't go to him to recuse himself on the May Shinn matter because Andy thought Chomorro couldn't keep it confidential. No, your dad and I have discussed it. Chomorro's ideal because he's got so much to prove—he's going to lean over backward to give a fair trial to someone who had perceived him as an enemy. It's a chance for him to make his good name—in that context he's probably the best judge we could have drawn."

Except for the last line, Hardy didn't believe a word of it, but he was pleased to discover that it flowed smoothly off his tongue.

They were inside Department 27, Fowler's old courtroom. Hardy turned around and checked the gallery—Jane, Farris, Jeff Elliot. Glitsky made it a point to come down. Hardy was glad to see him; he'd looked into one of the May Shinn phone calls with no results. Abe wasn't to be pushed, but for the time being he was the only investigator Hardy had, and even if he was technically working for the prosecution, Hardy was glad something about the manner in which this case had been brought to trial gnawed at him. At the least, it was good to have him involved. He went to Celine. He couldn't define exactly what he saw in her eyes, but they held his for a moment. He wondered what he could say to her when, inevitably, they spoke again. That he was sorry? That he'd been floundering and confused and hadn't meant to lead her on, if that's what he'd done?

In her expression he read nothing, and in that nothing saw anger, betrayal, disgust. He looked away as the bailiff announced that Department 27 of the Superior Court of the City and County of San Francisco was now in session, Judge Leo Chomorro presiding.

Chomorro looked young, fit and feisty. His wasn't the physique of lean good health seen in advertisements. He gave more an impression of heavy solidity—a lack of fat on a heavy frame, like an old-fashioned fullback. His face had a light olive cast. His eyes were dark with brows that nearly met. The razor-styled hair was short without a trace of gray.

When he had gotten settled at the bench, the clerk of the court raised her voice: "Calling criminal case number 921072979, section 187, felony murder. *The State of California versus Andrew Bryan Fowler.*"

Because of the passage of Proposition 115, after June of 1991 lawyers in California for both the prosecution and the defense were no longer permitted to conduct *voir dire* on prospective jurors. Now the judge did it. This didn't mean that lawyers had no say anymore in who eventually got on a jury—they still got their perremptory and other challenges—but the judge ran the show now. He or she asked the questions and gave instructions to prospective jurors, and people like

Hardy and Pullios had to make do as best they could on some combination of information, instinct and luck.

Hardy had asked Chomorro if he could at least ask pertinent questions during the process, and the judge had denied the request. Hardy then submitted a list of questions that he hoped Chomorro would ask, but he entertained little to no hope that the judge would go along.

The jury-selection process could take hours or it could take weeks. Under the new and improved rules it tended to go faster than it had in the past—indeed, that had been the intention of Proposition 115. Andy Fowler's jury would consist of twelve jurors and two alternates, and Chomorro had told both Hardy and Pullios that he would be very disappointed if they didn't have a panel sworn in by the end of the first day.

The predicted mob materialized in the gallery. In the past two months, besides preparing his defense, Hardy had given no fewer than a dozen interviews on the case—television, magazines, newspapers. Now, with the impending trial coming up on center stage, the first four rows of the gallery behind Pullios filled with the media. On the other side, he'd already seen Jane. He knew Celine would be in, and probably Farris.

Since there was no telling how long jury selection would take, Pullios had arranged to have a couple of her witnesses be on hand in the event it moved swiftly. Hardy thought he recognized the two guards from the Marina sitting together. John Strout could be summoned from the coroner's office in a matter of minutes. The waiting was nearly over.

Fowler, after his million-dollar bail had finally been granted, had resumed a semblance of a normal life. He went into his office every day, maybe had lunch with some senior partners, maybe even played a little golf and tennis. Hardy would meet him either at the Embarcadero Center or at the Olympic Club and they would hash out their strategy, the affirmative defense that they were beginning to have some confidence in.

It shouldn't have surprised Hardy, but somehow it did, that Fowler was turning into a real help in his own defense. He still acted removed from the process—as though it involved someone else entirely—but that was his personal style, and once he'd been released from jail, on his own refined turf, it wasn't so grating. Andy had a copy of all of Hardy's files—witnesses, interrogations, the evidence list, newspaper articles—and he took notes almost daily with ideas that might either weaken the prosecution's case or help to locate "X." In fact, his insistence that there was an "X" did a lot to keep Hardy's confidence up about Andy's innocence.

Nothing had panned out with Hardy's other "investigators." Glitsky still professed an interest in helping him out, but he had other active cases and so far every road he'd followed on Owen Nash had led to a dead end. All of May's other clients had had solid alibis and no particular motive, anyway. All had been cooperative, just so long as Abe wouldn't disclose the liaison with May Shinn to their wives/friends/business associates.

Jeff Elliot had kept in touch, but there hadn't been anything close to a scoop since Fowler's polygraph, and even that hadn't been much from Jeff's perspective. He was one of the people to whom Hardy had given his new telephone number, and last week he'd called with renewed interest now that the case was getting hot again, but he'd had nothing new to contribute.

So if it wasn't Andy Fowler—and Hardy had to believe it wasn't, except for the sweaty moments in the middle of the night when he still questioned—whoever *had* killed Owen Nash looked like they were going to get away with it.

Eighty people were called for the first jury pool.

There were as many theories of jury composition as there were attorneys. Hardy and Fowler had spent hours discussing the relative merits of various professions and "types" of people, ever aware that they might, when the crunch came, wind up empaneling an individual who went against type and killed them.

For example, every once in a while a secretary, who for some reason tended to be pro-prosecution, would show herself to have a soft heart and come up for the defense. On the other hand a long-haired musician (a typical pro-defense juror) could turn out to have a heavy-metal, neo-Nazi edge and lean to convict.

In spite of these possibilities the two men had come up with a general idea of who they wanted on the jury and who they didn't. Whether Chomorro would ask the questions to identify the traits or professions they were looking for remained a mystery.

As it transpired, Hardy's original idea to provoke some judicial prejudice had borne, and continued to bear, some sour fruit—witness Chomorro's denials about *voir dire*.

There was still, though, enough early prejudicial activity to use in an appeal if it came to that, but first, as Fowler had convinced him, there was a trial to be won. If you overconcentrated on your backup position you could find yourself needing it.

In fact, after all the preparation and discussion, it might after all come down, as it so often did, to old gut instinct.

There was, however, one rather unique wrinkle involved in choosing this particular jury. In the mind of the public, judges were generally held in high esteem, and Andy Fowler had been a judge. Would people who might be opposed to authority figures—defense jurors usually—find in Fowler a rebel they admired? Would the law-and-order types, normally pro-prosecution, view him as one of their own who'd just made a mistake, or would he be vulnerable to the wrath of the betrayed?

In the end they decided that their ideal juror would be a sensitive blue-collar white male with a good background and education. Either that, Fowler said, or Mr. Ed the talking horse.

They also thought they might have decent luck with an educated older black or Oriental woman. An Hispanic woman, they reasoned, might take too many cues from Chomorro, and most of those cues would favor Pullios. They agreed that an older Caucasian woman would be disastrous—how could Fowler throw away everything he had on *paid* sex with a Japanese prostitute? But a younger, liberated white woman, so long as she wasn't a secretary, might be all right—there was romance and drama in what Fowler had done for love. Gay men and women would probably be good for the defense—outsiders siding with an authority figure now on the outside and looked down on by the "respectables." But, of course, Pullios would no doubt challenge any she presumed were gay, without giving that as the reason.

If they got the chance they would try to keep any scientists or engineers—men or women—should they appear in the pool. Hardy was certain by now that the thrust of Pullios's offense would be consciousness of guilt, and therefore people who tended to believe in evidence as opposed to theory—scientists as opposed to philosophers—would better serve the defense needs. Of course, scientists as a rule tended to be conservative, and thus pro-prosecution, but what the hell, you couldn't have everything. Nobody, no group, was altogether desirable or predictable.

Both Hardy and his client found this stereotyping odious. Especially in San Francisco, it went against the social and personal grain. It was a cliché to say so, but two of Hardy's best friends were, in fact, the "mulatto" Abe Glitsky and Pico Morales, who was not of northern European ancestry. But they also felt they had to develop *some* criteria. They were looking, they hoped, at professions, affiliations, attitudes—if they ignored race and gender they weren't doing themselves any favors.

"I hate this," Fowler whispered. "I hated it before from behind the bench. I still do."

Each side had twenty perremptory challenges, where they could dismiss a prospective juror with no reason given. Hardy and Fowler had decided to use a diagram of the twelve jury seats in the pool, and to cross out those they wanted to challenge. With their legal pad in front of and between them this was a relatively subtle approach, chosen so they wouldn't have to confer and risk antagonizing the jurors who remained. People didn't like to feel they were being judged, even if they weren't challenged personally.

The jurors were sworn in, and Chomorro started talking to them, or rather reading to them. "Andrew Bryan Fowler has been charged with murder in the first degree in an indictment returned by the grand jury for the State of California."

Fowler, Hardy noticed, did not hang his head or show any outward signs of guilt or embarrassment while the indictment—again—was read in full.

Judges addressing juries, or prospective jurors, could be friendly and avuncular or tight and businesslike. Hardy thought Chomorro—relatively new to the process—struck a tone of studied affability. It was as though an effort to appear friendly to jurors had appeared on the job description. If he kept it up, it might be good for Andy, whose breezy geniality was, Hardy felt, genuine.

"I'm going to ask a series of questions to all of you." He addressed himself both to the panel of twelve on the courtroom side of the rail and to the sixty or so other prospective jurors waiting in the gallery. "If you answer yes to any of them I ask those of you up here"—he gestured to the jury box—"to raise your hand. Those of you in the gallery pool, please listen carefully, and if you are called up here and would have answered yes to any of these questions, inform us immediately."

Among the questions Hardy had submitted for Chomorro to ask, the most important was the most obvious: based on anything they had read or seen in the media, had any of the prospective jurors already formed an opinion about the innocence or guilt of the defendant?

Chomorro did ask that question, a fairly routine one he would have asked anyway. There was a lot of looking around, but no one put his hand up. Chomorro didn't let it go. "Let me rephrase that, or ask a related question. And you prospective jurors in the gallery, you may raise your hands directly here. How many of you have read about this case, or know about it from television or the radio?"

There was a scattered show of hands, eight in the jury box. Hardy swiveled to look back at the gallery. There were about ten more. In the two months he'd spent preparing for trial most of his "creative" ideas had gone out the window. If a change of venue would have a better chance of getting Andy a fair trial he would have gone for it. But he'd hired a consultant who had taken a poll and discovered that only between twenty-three and thirty percent of adults in San Francisco had ever heard of this case. At first it had shocked him. He knew people read less and less, were too busy for most current events, but still . . .

"Do any of you whose hands are up feel you know the issues in this case?" A few hands went down.

"You're going to be hearing evidence that may or may not corroborate what you think you already know. Would any of those remaining have any problem accepting those new arguments or evidence?" This was getting weaker than what Hardy had hoped for. Only four people, and none in the jury box, had their hands up. "All right, then, I think we can proceed."

Chomorro then began the general winnowing process. Did anyone in the panel know the defendant? Had anyone known the victim? The prosecutor or defense attorney? Chomorro read the list of proposed witnesses and asked if anyone knew any of them.

The tedious procedure continued. Were any of the panel themselves or any members of their families peace officers or lawyers? Ditto, victims of violent crime? What about nonviolent crime? Had anyone been arrested?

Five of the twenty jurors raised their hands during this period of questioning, a large percentage. Chomorro followed up individually with each one and ended by dismissing all five. Five new prospective jurors took their seats.

When the general questions had finished, Chomorro began taking the panel one at a time. This was where, before June of '91, Hardy could have narrowed things down considerably, but now he was at the mercy of Chomorro's questions.

Seat number one was a heavy-set woman of about forty. She gave her name as Monica Sellers. She had been married for seventeen years to the same man and had three children. For the past three years—after the children were old enough—she'd been employed as a part-time bookkeeper for a temp agency that worked out of the Mission district. Before that she'd been a housewife.

"Now, Mrs. Sellers—by the way, do you prefer Mrs. or Ms.?"

She laughed nervously. "Oh Mrs., definitely. I'm Mrs. Sellers."

"All right Mrs. Sellers, let me ask you this question, then. And would the rest of the panel please pay attention? I will be instructing you in certain matters of law, and one of the words you're going to hear a lot in the next few weeks is going to be 'evidence.' There are two basic kinds of evidence—direct evidence, for example, when an eyewitness sees something and swears to it. If you believe that witness, then his or her statement would be direct evidence. Circumstantial evidence might be, for example, a fingerprint—"

Hardy jumped up. "Objection, Your Honor."

Chomorro, interrupted in his monologue, frowned from the bench. "Objection to what, Mr. Hardy? I was about to say that a fingerprint on an object can be circumstantial evidence that the object had been touched by the person who had left fingerprints on it. Do you mean to object to that?"

"No, Your Honor. Sorry." He sat down, and Fowler whispered that he ought to reel it in a little if he didn't want the jury to start turning against him.

Chomorro turned back to the panel. "The classic analogy related to direct versus circumstantial evidence is something we call the cherry-pie analogy." Chomorro appeared a bit embarrassed by the homespun nature of his words. "If you walk into your kitchen and see your child eating cherry pie, then you have direct evidence that he was eating the pie. If, on the other hand, you come in and see a half-empty pie plate and your child's face and clothes covered with cherry pie filling, then you have circumstantial evidence that he's eaten the pie. I need hardly add that both types of evidence can be pretty convincing."

The jury nodded appreciatively, and Chomorro, more relaxed at the positive reaction, continued. "Let's take another example, since this evidence is central to what a trial is all about. How about lipstick on a cigarette, which can also be evidence? Mr. Smith sees Mrs. Jones smoking a certain type of cigarette and leaving a certain colored lipstick stain. Then let's say he walks to another room in her house and sees a similar cigarette butt lying in an ashtray in another room. That second cigarette butt is *circumstantial* evidence that Mrs. Jones has been in that room. She may have been in that room, but it is not a fact proved by direct evidence. I trust that's clear."

"This is good," Fowler whispered. Hardy nodded, agreeing, and glanced at Pullios. Her mouth was set tightly. She looked straight ahead.

"However," Chomorro went on, "that said, if I tell you as a matter of law that an abundance of circumstantial evidence, under certain conditions, can be sufficient to establish guilt beyond a reasonable doubt, would you have a problem with that?"

Mrs. Sellers looked thoughtful. "No, I don't think so."

Pullios looked to be suppressing a smile. Hardy put an "X" through seat number one (he didn't want to run through his challenges, but there was no option here) as Chomorro nodded to Mrs. Sellers. "Would any of you have a problem?"

First one, then two other prospective jurors, wanted some clarification. Chomorro took them one at a time, getting names, marital status, occupations—beginning to fill in the blanks. They were all men, two in their fifties, one, a black man of about thirty. Finally they all agreed they could accept Chomorro's instructions although there might have to be a lot of circumstantial evidence.

Which brought Chomorro to a pedantic discussion of quality versus quantity of evidence. A small amount of direct evidence might outweigh an abundance of circumstantial evidence, or vice versa.

Seat number two was Shane Pollett, cabinetmaker, a relic of the sixties with graying long hair and a tie-dyed t-shirt, a medium-length beard, an expression of amused tolerance. He was forty-four years old, in his second marriage, second family, three young kids. Two already grown up.

Hardy was beginning to understand Chomorro's technique. He would move quickly through the panel, asking a technical question or making a legal point or two to each member, opening it up to the rest. If his goal was to keep things moving along, it would work. For Hardy's purposes, it wasn't nearly enough.

"Mr. Pollett, let me ask you this."

"Sure," Pollett said.

Clearly, the informality, irreverence, rankled Chomorro, but he forced a smile. "If the state didn't have someone come in and say,

'This happened, I saw it,' would you accept that there'd be another way they could prove something happened? To use my example?"

"Sure, why not?"

Hardy leaned over and whispered to Fowler. "Why do I like this guy?"

Fowler shrugged. "Wrong answer for us but but the right tone. Gives one pause. Keep your eyes open."

Jane brought sandwiches into the room they'd been assigned on the second floor of the Hall. It was a little after one o'clock on the first day, and seven jurors were already empaneled—Chomorro wanted a jury in two days, max, and by God, they were going to have one.

"How are we doing?" she asked.

"Knocking 'em dead," her father answered brightly. He pulled a submarine and a soda from the bag Jane had brought in. "No chips?"

Jane smacked her forehead. "Sorry, I forgot the chips."

Hardy pulled the bag toward him. He realized the banter was in the "brave-front" department, but his patience was worn thin. "Let's chat some more about chips, chips are real important right now." He started unwrapping his own sandwich. "Okay, I've got it four to three, slightly toward us."

"Is there anybody you hate?" Jane asked, her face serious.

"Anybody I hate, I challenge, but there's damn little to go on."

"I know," Fowler said, "to call this a *voir dire* is a little misleading. I don't think Leo knows that much what he's doing."

"What's he leaving out?" Jane asked.

"It's not so much that," Fowler said.

Hardy spoke up. "He's not getting anybody to open up. Who are these people? What do they think about? What movies do they like? Hobbies? Anything. When he gets done we're not going to know anybody better than we do now. You look at what they're wearing, if they got a nice face, if they don't stare at us like they hate your father, that's about it. That and his so-called explanations of law."

"He does favor the leading question," Fowler admitted. "But he's a politician, what do you expect?"

"He's what I expect, all right, but I'm let down on so many other expectations, why couldn't we get lucky here? He's going awful light on the burden of proof, don't you think?"

"Well, we knew that going in."

Hardy chewed a moment. "There must be a rebuttal to consciousness of guilt."

"Not that I know of," Fowler said. "You can't prove a negative."

"If he'd only make a nod toward due process. I gave him twenty questions on the investigation, the indictment, the grand-jury process, all of that."

"What was that?" Jane asked.

"Jesus, everything," Hardy said. "Everything these people should know and probably won't—that an indictment is essentially a minimum showing of cause for trial, that no defense people can be present during the grand-jury proceedings, that basically it's the prosecutor's ballgame. These prospective jurors out there are intimidated enough. Then you tell them that another jury, a *grand* jury no less, thinks your father killed Owen Nash, what are they supposed to think?" Hardy turned to his client. "He's got to bring up some of that. Put it in context."

Fowler shook his head. "He won't, you can bet on it. He's telling us it's not relevant." Fowler smiled grimly. "What a judge thinks has a way of making it into the courtroom. Believe me, I know. Your due-process argument might make the appeal, but you're going to have to get clever and lucky to get it introduced here."

Jane tapped her bottle of soda on the table a few times. "Gosh, you guys are heartening to talk to," she said.

Chomorro finished his questioning and asked if either side would like to exercise a challenge. Hardy decidedly did not want to dismiss the first person interviewed—it would not enamor him to the jury—but since Mrs. Sellers had come down so strongly for believing in the accumulation of circumstantial evidence, he had no choice. He could tell it both surprised and hurt her as if she'd failed a test. He looked at the eleven faces to his left, most of them fixed solemnly on Mrs. Sellers as she walked back through the swinging door that separated the gallery from the courtroom. The clerk called a name to fill the vacancy.

By 4:25 they had empaneled a jury and two alternates. There were seven men and five women, four blacks—two men and two women—and, despite Hardy's initial misgivings, one Oriental—a fifty-five-year-old bespeckled Vietnamese shopkeeper named Nguyen Minh Ro. Fowler had crossed him off on their schematic almost as soon as he'd started talking, but then Ro, not perfectly understanding the laws of his new country, had asked the very question that Hardy had wanted to get in—just how was it that Mr. Fowler was to be considered innocent when the grand jury had already said he was guilty? Hardy could have kissed the man. He still might have dismissed him, but there was something in his body language toward Chomorro as the indictment process sunk in that looked promising for the defense. Surprisingly, Pullios didn't challenge, and he was in.

They could break it down demographically any number of ways—seven men, five women; seven whites, five non-whites. They did have a fortunate break with their hope for scientific/engineering types—three of the jury worked to some degree with computers. Additionally, one middle-aged black woman, Mercedes Taylor, was an architect.

There were no secretaries. They had kept Pollett, the cabinetmaker. Three computer jocks, an architect, two salesmen, one housewife, two small-business people (including Ro), a construction person and a high-school teacher.

Chomorro had put on reading glasses as the day progressed, his affability fading along, apparently, with his eyesight. By the time he began questioning the alternates at four o'clock, he was as clipped as a drill sergeant, asking them if they'd heard anything in the questioning and instructions to the other jurors that they felt ought to disqualify them. No? Okay, then. He finished them both in under twenty minutes.

49

"I don't blame her. Why should she want to help you?"

The "she" Peter Struler was referring to was May Shinn. He sat on his "Molly's" desk, facing her in her chair, his legs on either side of her. Pullios had pushed herself back nearly to the wall and looked up at him.

"I thought the letter made that very clear," she said. "She's got about a half dozen civil suits going. Freeman knows her civil jury will more likely pay off on an upstanding citizen who helped the authorities solve the murder of which she was wrongly accused. Besides, all the witnesses will be cops and D.A.'s. We could do her some good. She might be suing us but it's the City that pays off.

Struler shook his head. "I'd just bring her in."

"On what?"

Straight-faced, Struler replied. "How about a DWO, something like that?"

Pullios knew her law, and she'd never heard of a DWO. "Okay, I'll bite. What's a DWO?"

Struler grinned. "You know, Driving While Oriental. Gets 'em every time."

There was no training this guy. "Is it just me, or do I get the feeling your political correctness is slipping again?"

"Who gives," he said, enunciating clearly, "a big steaming pile of shit?" He put his feet up on the chair's arms. Outside the window behind Molly it was pitch black, though it wasn't far into the dinner hour. Her door was closed. "So hit her with a subpoena."

"I know, but the minute I do that, she goes on the official witness list."

"Yeah, well excuse me, but aren't those the rules?"

She graced him with a "get-serious" expression, and he asked if Hardy had interviewed her.

351

"She said he hadn't."

"So why'd she talk to you?"

Pullios smiled. "I asked Freeman to clear it for me to apologize personally for what I'd put her through."

Struler shook his head in admiration. "You are a cruel and terrible woman."

"Thank you, sir. It got her to talk to me about Fowler and the gun, but she said she wouldn't be a witness against him."

"Hey, she's not married to him. It's not like she has a choice."

"I want to keep her on my side as long as I can, though. The nice letter, all that."

"You need what she's got?"

Pullios nodded. "It's absolutely essential."

"Okay," Struler said, "here's what I suggest you do. Wait until the last possible moment so there's no notice to Hardy, then send somebody out—some D.A. investigator like my own self—and slap her with a submeister."

"What's that?"

Struler shook his head. "Come on, Molls," he said, "get hip. *Saturday Night Live*? Submeister, sub-a-rama, Mr. Sub, subster." At her continued blank stare, he finally relented. "You lawyers ought to get out more, I swear to God. A subpoena, Molly. Hit her with a subpoena."

Hardy plugged in the Christmas lights he'd strung up around his front porch over the weekend. Rebecca, walking now, clapped her hands, stopping to point and yelling what sounded like "why why why" at the top of her lungs. Hardy picked her up and held her closer to them.

"Light light light," he said.

The Beck shook her head, laughing.

"Is she the greatest kid in the world?" Frannie said.

"The universe," Hardy said.

"Why," Rebecca said. Some of the lights had started blinking. She pointed to them. "Why why."

"I think she's going to be a philosopher," Hardy said, "like her father."

"Like her uncle Moses, maybe, not exactly like her father."

Frannie, now in her eighth month of pregnancy, had her arm around Hardy's waist. The problems that had led up to Hardy's mugging in October were behind them. He was working a lot of hours but he was at least sharing it with her—plus they were laughing together, teasing each other, enjoying the Beck.

The car pulled up and double-parked in front of their house. "Who's that?" Frannie asked.

Hardy knew immediately. He kissed his wife on the cheek and handed the baby to her. "I'll be right back."

He'd been expecting this somehow. He walked down the few steps, then onto the path that bisected his lawn to the gate at the fence. Apprehensive, he met her there.

She was wearing a heavy coat against the chill, a cowllike head covering pulled down around her ears. Her hands were deep in her pockets. Vapor from her breath hung in the still air a moment before it dissipated.

"You shouldn't be here, Celine."

She seemed unsteady, as if she'd been drinking, but he was close enough to have smelled that and didn't. "I had to talk to you, you've changed your phone number."

"You were in court all day, Celine. I'll be there tomorrow."

"I didn't know what I wanted to say then."

He let out a breath. He had it coming. "Okay."

"I, I . . . ," she began, then stopped.

"It's all right." Hardy heard the door to his house close. Frannie and Rebecca had gone inside.

"I just wanted you to know that I understand. I don't want you to hate me, to think that I hate you."

Hardy nodded. "That's good to hear. I certainly don't hate you—"

"You were acting like it."

"No, I was trying to ignore you. That's different. It's something I have to do."

"Yes, of course, but I'll still be there every day. You have to know that."

"All right. But I don't think you ought to come by here. The last time—"

"I know. That was a mistake."

He recalled her panicked retreat the last time she'd come up to his gate. "My life is here," he said. "I forgot that for a moment. I'm sorry . . ."

"No, it wasn't that, it wasn't even you . . . you just suddenly reminded me so much of my father . . ." She gripped the gate, steadying herself. "I didn't mean to say it like that, but your wife, your baby . . . what I couldn't have."

Hardy had his hands in his pockets. The vapor from their breathing merged in the air between them. She seemed to gather herself then, regain control. "Your client, the judge. You obviously don't think he did it."

"No, I don't."

"Then who *did*?"

"I don't know. We're looking, but so far there isn't much—"

"Much?"

"To be very honest, nothing."

"Poor Daddy," she whispered.

There wasn't anything more to say. She glanced at his house behind him, nodded, turned and walked quickly to her car.

He had taken to following a routine every night. First, he was not drinking at all during the week, from Sunday through Thursday night. He would finish dinner and help Frannie with the dishes. They would talk about each other's day. He would bounce things off her.

Then he would take a cup of coffee and go into his office for a couple of hours of what he called creative leisure—toss some darts, read over some testimony he thought he already knew by heart, play devil's advocate with every position he could think of. Sometimes he'd call Abe just to keep the needle in. He tried not to work on the weekends, or on Wednesday nights, although he'd told Frannie that they'd have to suspend date night during the duration of the trial and, of course, for however many weekends the trial took, weekends as such would not exist.

His paper load now included six full binders, four filled legal pads and a dozen cassette tapes. It was amazing, he thought, that as many times as you went through it there was always something you'd missed. He remembered papers he'd done in college, proofing and proofing and rereading and then handing in what he thought was perfect work only to get it back with a typo or something screwed up in the first line.

But tonight the choreography was complete—the dance began in earnest tomorrow. He arranged his books, binders, pads and tapes neatly on his desk and turned out the light in his office and walked through his house.

He looked in at Rebecca, pulling up a blanket around her. The bedroom was bathed in blue light from the fish tank. In the kitchen, pots and pans hung neatly from overhead hooks; his black pan glistened on the top of the gas stove.

Moving forward through the dining room he caught a whiff of lemon oil from the polished table, then—unmistakable, seductive, mnemonic—the scent of Christmas tree and woodsmoke.

Frannie sat in the recliner next to the fire, feet up and hands folded over her belly. The only other light in the room came from the tree, blinking reds and greens and blues. Nat King Cole was singing quietly in German—"Oh Tannenbaum." Hardy took it all in for a moment.

"Are you ready?" she asked.

"As I'll ever be."

Frannie patted the side of the chair, and Hardy crossed the room and sat on the floor next to her. She idly ran her hand over his head, through his hair. "Have you thought about after this trial?"

"Not much. I thought we'd have this next baby, get back to real life."

"Are you going to be happy with real life?"

"I'm happy with *this* life, Frannie."

The fire crackled. He knew what she meant. He was in trial time—everything assumed an importance that was out of proportion to day-to-day prosaic reality. She was worried about a recurrence of the letdown he'd gone through over the summer.

"How far did it go with her?" she asked.

He looked up at her. Her hand still rested on his head. Her face was untroubled and unlined, beautiful in the firelight. "I don't want any details," she said, "and I appreciate you dealing with it yourself. I know what infatuation is and I don't think we need to get each other involved in them. But I need to know how far it went."

Hardy stared at the fire, suddenly aware that the music had stopped.

"It's funny, I thought it was Jane."

"No." He could embroider and skate around it but he knew what she'd asked. "It stopped in time. It didn't happen."

She let out a long breath. "I don't know everything you need, Dismas, but if you can try to tell me, I'll try to give it to you."

"You already do, Fran."

"I'm just telling you—whatever it takes—we stick it through together, okay? But you have to want me—"

"I *do* want you. Hey, that's why I'm here."

"All right," she said, "because that's why *I'm* here."

50

"Good morning."

Pullios looked nice—friendly, approachable, the girl next door. She wore low brown pumps and a tawny suit the cut of which minimized her curves. Shoulder-length brown hair framed a face nearly devoid of makeup. She smiled at one and all, pleasant, but on serious business.

"I want to begin by thanking you all for your patience yesterday. It was a long day for all of us, and I'm sure we'll have more in the days to come, but let me assure you that your presence on this jury is one of the most important duties that can be undertaken by citizens in our society, and your time and attention here is well appreciated."

Hardy gave some thought to an objection right away—Pullios had no business massaging the jury; that was, if anyone's, the judge's role. But he knew you had to walk a fine line with objections. The jury also had to feel good about *him,* and if he objected to Pullios saying they were appreciated, it would no doubt be misunderstood.

"Although, like a lot of important jobs," she continued, "the pay could be better."

A nice chuckle. Even Chomorro smiled. What a nice person this prosecutor was. She walked back to her desk, moved a yellow pad, then turned back to the jury.

"I'm going to tell you a lot about what we know about the defendant, Andrew Fowler, and the man he murdered, Owen Nash. I make the point that I'm going to tell you a lot because you are undoubtedly going to hear that . . ."

Fowler had poked him. Early or not, Hardy had to get on the boards sometime.

"Objection, Your Honor."

To his surprise, Chomorro nodded. "Sustained." He looked down at

357

Pullios. "Just make your case, Counselor. This is your opening statement. Don't editorialize."

"I'm sorry, excuse me, Your Honor." Gracious and unflustered, this one. She moved on. "Early in the morning of Saturday, June twentieth of last summer—a windy, blustery day—the victim in this case, Mr. Owen Nash, boarded his sailboat the *Eloise* and prepared to take what would be his last sail. The prosecution will prove to you, ladies and gentlemen, prove *beyond a reasonable doubt,* that with him on the *Eloise* that morning was the person who would murder him—the defendant Andrew Fowler.

"A former colleague of the defendant, a fellow member of the Olympic Club, will tell you that Mr. Fowler had talked of making an appointment to see Mr. Nash to solicit political contributions from him. This was the pretense for their getting together.

"The evidence will corroborate that Mr. Nash and his killer sailed under the Golden Gate Bridge and headed south down the coast. We have an expert in tides and currents who will tell you with a good deal of precision exactly where Owen Nash fell into the sea after being shot two times with a .25-caliber pistol. The coroner will explain that the first bullet struck Mr. Nash just above and to the right of his penis, the second bullet went through his heart. An expert in bloodstains will describe how this second bullet sent Mr. Nash over the rail of his boat and into the ocean, at first glance a very convenient circumstance for his killer.

"We will show you that Mr. Fowler is an an experienced boatsman in his own right, that he could easily have kept the *Eloise* at sea until the evening, when he could have guided it back into the Marina, even in high seas. A meteorologist will describe the weather on that evening—there were high winds, and small craft warnings were out. In this weather it is no surprise that there was no one at the Marina when Mr. Fowler returned.

"He tied up the boat, leaving it unlocked, and was not seen by another human being until he arrived at work, right here in this building, on the following Monday morning."

Here was another objection, but this time Hardy merely made a note of it. Counsel wasn't supposed to argue evidence in their opening statements.

Pullios didn't use notes but she returned again to her desk, playing down any appearance as a superwoman. After checking her props, she turned and continued.

"Rather than predict what the defense will contend relating to evidence in this case"—here a nod to Chomorro, a smile to the jury—"I will tell you right now that the prosecution has found no one who can point to Mr. Fowler and say, 'That was the man I saw on the *Eloise* on June twentieth with Owen Nash.' No one saw Mr. Fowler on the *Eloise* besides Owen Nash, and he's dead.

" 'Well,' you're asking, 'then why are we here?' We are here," she answered herself, "first, because Mr. Fowler's pattern of behavior over the course of several months cannot be explained other than by acknowledging his consciousness of his own guilt. Duplicity, deception, abandonment of the high ethical standards—"

"Objection, Your Honor."

Chomorro nodded. Two for two, Hardy thought, not too bad.

"Sustained. Let's stick to the evidence, Ms. Pullios."

She apologized again to the judge and jury. But it clearly didn't rattle her. "The prosecution will demonstrate that Mr. Fowler knew the precise location of the murder weapon on board the *Eloise* and that he had a compelling reason to kill Mr. Nash—the oldest and most lethal motive in the world—jealousy. Mr. Nash had superseded him in the affections of the woman he loved, for whom he subsequently risked—and this is a fact, not a conjecture—risked his entire career and reputation as a judge and a man of honor.

"We will show that the defendant first identified and then tracked down his rival with the help of a private investigator, that he concocted a plan for the two of them to meet, that he painstakingly arranged an alibi for the weekend of this meeting. All these *facts* speak to Mr. Fowler's consciousness of guilt.

"But all this is not to say there is *no* direct evidence. There is a murder weapon, for example. And on the murder weapon—not on the outside, but on the clip which holds the bullets for the gun—are the fingerprints of the defendant, Andrew Fowler."

A stir in the courtroom. Hardy had known this would be a bad point but there wasn't anything he could do about it. Andy's story was all he had to tell.

Pullios pushed on; they were captivated. "Now, this, of course, is not direct evidence that Mr. Fowler was on the *Eloise* with Mr. Nash. Nor, obviously, is the fact that he wasn't seen anywhere else. Nor, by itself, is the discussion with his colleague about meeting Mr. Nash for political reasons. Neither, finally, is his jealousy, his hiring of a private investigator, his attempts to hide or cover up all of his activities relat-

ing to his lover, May Shinn, or his rival, Owen Nash. But the people of
the State of California contend that, taken together, the evidence in
this case *can lead to no other conclusion—beyond a reasonable doubt,*
Andrew Fowler did with malice aforethought, sometime in the morning of June twentieth, 1992, shoot and kill Owen Nash."

Hardy thought she was finished and took a drink of water, preparing
to stand and begin his opening statement, but she turned back at her
desk.

"I would like to make two final but important points. One, circumstantial evidence can be sufficient to satisfy the burden of proof. Judge
Chomorro mentioned this to you yesterday, and it is a crucial point
here. Circumstantial evidence is still *evidence,* and the evidence in
this case inescapably convicts the defendant."

Hardy knew he could object but figured he'd run out his string with
the jury. Any further objections would look like he was trying to keep
something hidden from them. He let her go on uninterrupted.

"Secondly, why *is* there so little direct evidence? Does it make any
sense that a man could commit a murder and leave nothing behind by
which he can be identified? Well, let's consider that Mr. Fowler has
spent the better part of the last thirty years as a judge in this very
Superior Court of San Francisco. During that time, he has heard
hundreds if not thousands of criminal cases. Is it any wonder that a
man with this experience would leave little or no physical trace of his
presence?

"Ask yourselves this—if your job is evaluating evidence, if you are
intimately familiar with how the legal system works in all its detail, if
you know every test and every procedure someone will use to catch
you, don't you think you could avoid leaving anything incriminating
behind?

"I think I could. I think Andrew Fowler could. *And did.* The evidence will speak for itself."

"You'll have to bear with me," Hardy began. "I'm in a bit of a bind."
His legs were so weak with nerves he didn't trust himself to stand,
either at attention or at ease, in front of the jury, so he leaned back
against his table, hoping his legs would improve as he got going. "The
charge against my client is murder, the most serious of crimes, yet the
prosecution theory here is so bizarre that I hardly know how to discuss
it without losing my temper or insulting your intelligence, or both."

A sea of blank faces. Were these the same folks who had smiled,

frowned, chuckled and gasped on cue as Elizabeth Pullios stood before them? But there was nothing to do for it. Here he was, and he
had better get it together and press on.

"Stripped of all the rhetoric and polite verbiage, listen to the nonsense the prosecution presents. Here is their truly astounding theory
—because there is no evidence, the defendant must be guilty." Hardy
paused to let that sink in. "We've just heard that there's no evidence
in this case because Mr. Fowler was too smart to leave any. Well, I'm
going to tell you something. By that standard, everyone in this courtroom—all of you jury members, me, the judge, the gallery out there—
unless we're all ready to admit we weren't smart enough to think of a
way not to get caught, if Ms. Pullios's version of justice were the law of
the land, all of us could be found equally guilty of the murder of Owen
Nash."

The jury woke up. The gallery came to life and Pullios was on her
feet objecting. Good. Let them see both sides could interrupt. She was
sustained. Hardy had unfairly characterized her statement and was
arguing to the jurors. He told the judge he was very sorry. The
jury was instructed to disregard what he'd said, and he was sure they
would try and, he hoped, fail. His sea legs came in.

"All right," he said, "let me tell you, as the judge instructs me, what
the defense *has to* prove, and then what the defense *will* prove. The
first is simple—the defense doesn't have to prove anything. The burden of proof rests on the prosecution and during the course of this
trial, with all the direct and circumstantial evidence you will be asked
to evaluate, it will be up to the prosecution to prove that Andy Fowler
is guilty." Pullios objected again, Hardy was arguing the law, not stat-
ing the facts. She was sustained. Hardy didn't care. "When you've
heard and seen everything the prosecution has, the inescapable conclusion will be that the state has not met its burden of proof. It cannot
provide evidence to prove that Andy Fowler killed Owen Nash. And,
ladies and gentleman, fancy theories of guilty consciences notwithstanding, evidence is what a jury trial is all about. Until you twelve
people deliberate, knowing all the evidence, *and basing your judgment on it,* return with a guilty verdict, it is presumed that Andy
Fowler just plain didn't do it. That's the law and I'm sure you all
understand it."

Again—she was alienating jurors and didn't seem aware of it—Pullios objected. This time Chomorro overruled her with a pointed com-

ment about the latitude she had been allowed in her opening. Hardy kept his face impassive and went back to his work.

"But—my second point—the defense plans to go beyond that. A lot of you are probably sitting in the jury box here, wondering how an eminent jurist like—"

"Objection."

"Sustained. Mr. Hardy, Mr. Fowler is the defendant in a murder trial. He is not an eminent jurist."

"All right, Your Honor." Hardy walked to his table and took a drink of water. The jury was waiting for him when he turned back to them. "I'm sure all of you believe, to a greater or lesser extent, in our criminal justice system. It's why you're all here doing your civic duty. As Ms. Pullios said, you are doing an important job, giving up important other work, to be part of this process. We very much appreciate it."

Hardy had swiveled half away from the jury and nodded to Pullios. Back to the box.

"It is one thing to say you believe in the presumption of innocence. It is quite another to come here, as you are now, sit in a jury box and look at a man—a man who used to be a judge—sitting at the defense table accused of committing the most serious crime a man can commit, murder in the first degree, and not believe there isn't some powerful, compelling, overwhelming reason why that person is there. His very presence seems to be an argument for his guilt."

The judge rapped his gavel. "Mr. Hardy, we've gone over this in *voir dire*."

Hardy stopped, consciously slowing himself down. Not exactly given to theatrics, he suddenly found it completely natural to point at Andy Fowler. "That man," he said, lowering his voice, "has been a member of the legal community in this city for more than half his life—"

Pullios popped back in. "Objection, Your Honor."

"No, I'll overrule that, Counselor. That's a fact."

Hardy thanked the judge. "That man," Hardy repeated, still pointing, "will be the first to admit he made a grievous error of judgment. From that one mistake he was drawn to others, perhaps more serious, until at last he had sacrificed his good name, his standing in the community, the respect of his peers."

He found himself standing very close to the rail separating the jurors from the courtroom.

"Now who are Andy Fowler's peers? They are the professional prosecutors, the policemen, the other judges in this building. They are the very people who have brought this murder indictment against him."

"Your Honor!" Pullios was on her feet. "Mr. Hardy is impugning the entire grand-jury process."

Chomorro seemed to agree, but also seemed uncertain. "Is there relevance to some evidence here, Counselor?"

"Your Honor, the defense will present direct and incontrovertible evidence—eyewitness testimony from members of the district attorney's own staff and from the San Francisco police department—that there was nothing approaching an impartial investigation leading to the indictment of Mr. Fowler. The district attorney's office concocted a theory out of whole cloth and proceeded to fill in whatever blanks they needed to get an indictment."

There—Hardy had gotten it out, and Chomorro could overrule him if he wanted to.

Pullios took over. "Do we call this the paranoid defense, Your Honor? Someone was out to get Mr. Fowler, so we got together and accused him of murder?"

"Mr. Hardy?"

"It speaks to the interpretation of evidence."

"Interpretation of evidence is in the hands of the jury."

Hardy nodded. "My point exactly, Your Honor."

But Pullios wasn't ready to quit. "The evidence must speak for itself, Your Honor."

Chomorro banged his gavel. "All right, all right. Hold on a minute here."

The courtroom hung in silence. By its absence, Hardy for the first time noticed the ticking of the court reporter's keys. Finally Chomorro spoke up. "I'll overrule Ms. Pullios objection. You may proceed, Mr. Hardy."

Hardy took a deep breath and let in out slowly. He didn't want to betray that he was sighing in relief. He'd also blanked on where he was going. He walked to his table and checked his outline.

"You've already heard the term 'consciousness of guilt' in the people's opening statement. And I don't dispute that there are certain actions that would seem to admit guilt. These would include such behavior as flight to avoid prosecution, resisting arrest and so on. But we're on very slippery ground here when we're using consciousness of guilt—a very general legal area—as a catchall for a *specific* crime."

Hardy went on to describe an example of a situation where someone had resisted arrest and fled from arresting officers. If there had been a murder on that block, would that person's actions in any way *prove* he had been involved in the murder? Of course not. Perhaps the person had stolen a car. Maybe he had an outstanding arrest warrant for jaywalking. Maybe he was a member of a minority group in a neighborhood where minorities were routinely harrassed. "The point," Hardy said, "is that our person here can be guilty of *something,* and can act in what we would recognize as a guilty manner. But his actions don't automatically make him guilty of, or a suspect in, any specific crime."

He thought he'd nailed that point. "Now we have already admitted that Andy Fowler felt guilty. We'll go a step further—he *acted* in a guilty manner. The prosecution is telling you that they will prove beyond a reasonable doubt that Mr. Fowler's behavior *allows for no other explanation* for this behavior except that he committed murder. We don't believe they can do this. We don't believe that you will let them. Because it isn't true."

He took another three or four seconds to look up and down the jury box. Then he thanked them and sat down.

51

Fowler told his daughter that Chomorro had obviously talked to some of his lawyer friends at lunch. Which was why he had called the conference in his chambers before they began with the testimony of coroner John Strout in the afternoon.

"What's it about?" Jane asked her father.

She was beside him at the defense table, which was allowed when court wasn't in session. Behind them in the gallery the crowd was gathering again after the lunch recess.

"Chomorro's going over some rules," he said. "This is his first murder trial, remember. He doesn't want to foul it up and have it declared a mistrial."

"How could he do that?"

Fowler patted his daughter's hand. "See? All these years I guess I've made it look easy. You're not supposed to argue law during opening statements, for example. You can say what you're going to be showing, but you're not supposed to explain it, which—you may have noticed— Ms. Pullios did. Also, all this objecting and interrupting. It's already getting to be a little personal in what's supposed to be an impartial process."

"Didn't Dismas want that?"

Fowler nodded. "Yes, he did. And to that extent he's doing fine, but Chomorro—I'd bet anything—has got some ringers back there." He motioned to the gallery. "A couple of clerks taking notes. A trial's supposed to be about evidence, not personalities. If it gets too bitter it jeopardizes the trial."

"Do we want that?"

"No, Jane. I don't want a mistrial. I want a fair trial. Dismas wants one, too, although he also wants to fight, which is good up to a certain point. But if I'm going to have any life after this we've got to win fairly, so everybody knows I'm innocent. Even Diz."

"Daddy, he doesn't think you did it. He wouldn't be defending you."

Fowler wasn't so sure. Hardy's own uncertainties hadn't been lost on him. "I've known him a long time, Jane, longer than you have, remember. He's willing enough to pretend to believe—even to himself —that I'm innocent. But I wonder if it isn't more a case of his feeling the evidence doesn't prove I did it and—"

"Well, that's the same thing."

Fowler shook his head. "No, it isn't, Jane. It's not even close."

Hardy had read Dr. John Strout's grand-jury testimony twenty times. He'd memorized the autopsy report. He'd paid another doctor, a friend of Pico's named Walter Beckman, to spend a night talking about medical issues, and he'd come to the conclusion that Strout's testimony couldn't damage Andy Fowler. The coroner had to be called to establish the fact of the death, the means of death, but essentially his testimony would be neutral, a foundation for what followed.

Which, he soon discovered, was selling Pullios short, and he should have known better.

Strout, tall and lanky, pushed back the witness chair so he could fit his long legs into the space. He appeared to be the most relaxed person in the courtroom, which was to be expected. He had given testimony perhaps an average of once a week for the past twelve years. He sat straight, his elbows on the arms of the chair.

Pullios and Hardy had both been instructed not to come close to witnesses when they were interrogating them, so Pullios stood where she had delivered her opening statement, about in the center of a circle that encompassed Hardy, the jury, Strout and Chomorro.

After leading the doctor through his qualifications, which were not in dispute, she asked him to describe the wounds he had discovered on Owen Nash's body.

"Well," he drawled, "there were two wounds, both created by .25-ACP-caliber slugs. The lower wound, not in itself fatal, entered the body in the pubic area—"

"Excuse me, Dr. Strout," Pullios said. "Distasteful as this is, would you please be more precise as to the location of this first wound?"

The drawl became more pronounced. "Well, if we don't want to get into Latin, Counselor, the pubic area is relatively precise. It's the area covered by pubic hair above the genitals."

"In other words, within an inch or so of the penis?"

Hardy saw where she was going. If a man were eliminating his sexual rival . . .

"Objection. Leading the witness."

Pullios quickly said she'd rephrase. "Can you tell us the location of this first wound in relation to Mr. Nash's penis?"

"It entered just about at the base of the penis, slightly high and to the right."

Some of the men on the jury seemed to wince.

"Any more about this wound?"

Strout went into some detail about the bullet's passage through Nash's body, nicking the ilium, depositing some chips of bone in the greatest gluteal muscle before exiting through it. He went on, at Pullios's careful prodding, to make the point that this wound had in all probability been the first one.

"And why do you say that, doctor?"

Strout recrossed his legs. "Well, the second shot was fatal, almost immediately. It went right through the heart, struck a rib and ricocheted up into the left lung. Now, unless Mr. Nash stood a while on his feet after he was dead, we can assume he fell within about a second of being shot. And if he was on the ground, the bullet through his pubic area would have been lodged in the deck, not on the side under the railing, which was, I believe, where it was found."

Hardy objected, citing relevance, but he knew the testimony was relevant to what Pullios was doing, which was planting in every juror's mind a vivid picture of the actions of a jealous and jilted suitor. First he would shoot his victim in the crotch. Then he would aim for the heart, killing him after he'd maimed him as a man.

Chomorro overruled Hardy, but Pullios didn't pursue it. She graciously thanked Dr. Strout and told him she had no further questions.

So the dike was already leaking where he'd foreseen no damage. He had to try and put his finger in.

"Dr. Strout," he began. "These .25-caliber bullets that produced the wounds in Owen Nash. For the jury, can you describe their impact as opposed to different sized slugs?"

Strout, no less relaxed than he'd been with Pullios, sat back in the chair. He looked directly at the jury and answered in his pleasant twang. "Well, they're in the lower-end range according to size for handguns. The smallest is a .22 and it's slightly larger—the diameter is slightly larger than that."

"Thank you. Now was there anything you could determine from your autopsy about the load in the bullet itself? The amount of powder in the casing?"

Strout got thoughtful. This was the kind of question he liked. "Judging from the fact that the second bullet didn't make an exit wound, it could not have been a particularly heavy load."

"About average, you'd say?"

"Yes, about average."

"So, Dr. Strout, what we've got here is a small bullet with about an average powder load hitting a full-grown man. Would the impact of that bullet necessarily throw the man backward, even if it hit him squarely in the chest?"

"Objection, Your Honor. That's not Dr. Strout's area of expertise."

"What's the point, Mr. Hardy?"

"Ms. Pullios went to some length to bring out Dr. Strout's belief that the first shot was to Mr. Nash's pubic area."

Chomorro chewed on it a second, then overruled Pullios.

"Dr. Strout. Is it possible that a man, even if hit in the heart by a bullet of this size, with this sort of charge behind it, could remain standing for half a second, particularly if he were moving toward the gun when the bullet was fired?"

"Yes, I'd say so."

"And would that be enough time for his assailant to get off another shot with an automatic such as the murder weapon?"

"Half a second? I'd say it's possible."

"That's all. Thank you, Doctor."

"What bothers me is I didn't even see it coming."

"You did fine," Fowler said. "I doubt it's relevant anyway. Who cares where the first shot went?"

They were taking a ten-minute recess, still sitting at the defense table. Hardy explained what he thought was the connection and Fowler doodled on a pad for a moment. Then he said, "Look, Diz, it doesn't tie directly to me, therefore it's not relevant. It's speculation, conjecture, call it what you will, but keep me right in the center of this picture or we are in trouble."

"You were in the center of that, Andy."

Fowler, showing displeasure for one of the first times, shook his head. "No," he said, "the murderer was."

* * *

After Strout, they heard from a ballistics specialist who identified the murder weapon as a Beretta model 950, a single-action semiautomatic that held eight rounds of .25 ACP. The gun, registered to May Shinn, was introduced as Peoples Exhibit 1, and Hardy could tell the jury was surprised by the size of it—it was very small, with a barrel only two and one-half inches long.

The bullet that had passed through Nash's body had been found imbedded in the side paneling of the boat behind the wheel. There was a fifteen-minute slide show on the similarities of the striations on the recovered slugs with others fired from the same gun. When the lights came up, so did a few heads that had been nodding. Pullios was explaining the obvious—how this testimony conclusively proved that Exhibit 1, May Shinn's gun, was the murder weapon.

Big deal, Hardy thought, and chose not to cross-examine.

The fingerprint specialist was a young black woman named Anita Wells. She testified that there were two sets of identifiable fingerprints on the gun—those of May Shinn, the registered owner, and of the defendant, Andrew Fowler.

Hardy had badly wanted to get the May Shinn fiasco introduced into the record, and he knew Pullios had no choice but to let him if she wanted to get Fowler's prints in, which she had to do. It was, he was sure, why she had called Wells on day one.

When Pullios had finished a cursory interrogation, Hardy went to the center of the courtroom. "Ms. Wells," he asked, "have you had occasion to test People's Exhibit One for fingerprints more than once?"

Wells looked up at the judge, then at Pullios. She nodded, and the judge told her to speak up, answer with words. "Yes," she said.

"And when did you first see this gun?"

The witness thought a minute. "Around the beginning of July."

"And at that time, when you tested it for fingerprints, can you tell the jury what you found?"

Pullios stood up and objected. "Asked and answered, Your Honor."

Hardy shook his head. "I'll rephrase it. The first time you looked, did you identify the defendant's fingerprints?"

Wells swallowed. "No."

"Did you identify *any* fingerprints at that time?"

"Yes. May Shinn's."

"May Shinn. The registered owner of the gun. And where were Ms. Shinn's prints."

"There were several clear impressions, on the barrel and the grip."

"All right. Now after you identified Ms. Shinn's fingerprints, what did you do?"

"Well, first I verified the comparison—they were what I was looking for."

"So, in other words, you went looking for May Shinn's fingerprints? Isn't that true?"

"Yes."

"And after the case against Ms. Shinn got thrown out, you went looking for Andy Fowler's fingerprints, and you found them, isn't that true?"

Pullios objected, but Hardy didn't want to let this one go. "Your Honor, when the case against Mr. Fowler gets dropped, does the prosecution plan to go looking for other prints at that time? The defendant's fingerprints on this gun are critical to the case against him. The jury can't know too much about how they were identified."

Pullios wasn't quitting either. "Ms. Wells has already testified that they were on the gun."

"That's true, Mr. Hardy. We're talking about Mr. Fowler's fingerprints, not May Shinn's. You are arguing evidence that hasn't been presented *in this case*. Try not to confuse the jury by referring to what is not properly before it."

Hardy felt this was a big loss. He stood a moment, gathering his forces.

"You still with us, Mr. Hardy?" Chomorro asked.

Hardy had anticipated Chomorro's antagonism from the bench, but now, at its first appearance, he realized how powerful its influence could be. If Chomorro was allowed to patronize him, the jury would pick up on it and his credibility would suffer. Andy Fowler had been right—this wasn't an appealable issue. It had been bad strategy.

"Of course, Your Honor," Hardy said mildly. "I was waiting for your ruling."

Chomorro's face tightened slightly. "I thought I'd made that clear. The objection is sustained."

This time Hardy simply nodded. He spread his hands to the jury and smiled at them. "Sorry, my mistake." But the message was clear —he was a reasonable man, waiting to make sure he understood the judge's ruling. There was no antagonism between himself and Chomorro. He went back to Anita Wells. "Can you tell us how long a fingerprint can last?"

"I don't understand."

"I mean does it go away after a while by itself? Does it evaporate?"

"No, fingerprints are oil-based. They last until they're wiped away."

"So Mr. Fowler's fingerprints on the clip inside the gun might not have been placed there at any time near to when the gun was found or fired?"

"That's true."

"Did you find anything indicating it might not be true?"

"No."

"So Mr. Fowler's fingerprints might have been on the gun for as long as a year?"

Pullios stood up. "Asked and answered, Your Honor."

"I'll withdraw it," Hardy said. "No further questions."

"It's early, but I'd put us ahead on points." They had their coats off, their ties loosened. From Fowler's law office high up in Embarcadero One, the city glittered out the window, Christmas lights starting to appear below.

Hardy was not so sure. "I wanted to get Shinn in." He had wanted to call May as a defense witness from the beginning, but Fowler wouldn't hear of it. What could she possibly say that could make a difference, he had argued. Fowler hadn't seen her, after all, in the four months before the murder. To say nothing of the fact that she had turned down Hardy's several requests for interviews. She remembered him from Visitors Room A, thank you.

The prosecution, they both figured, wouldn't go near her. She would be understandably hostile to the San Francisco district attorney's office. So, strangely enough, the other central figure in this case would apparently play no active role in it. Hardy did not like that at all.

Andy had poured himself a neat Scotch from a tumbler on the sideboard and now took a drink of it. He stood and carried the glass over to the window.

Hardy watched his back a minute. "You haven't seen her, Andy?"

May Shinn was still the issue, the looming specter, an unmentionable apparition. The chronology could not have been simpler: a year ago Andy Fowler had been in love with May Shinn; in mid-February she had dumped him for Owen Nash; in July he had sacrificed his career for her; in October he had been arrested for murdering her lover; and in the two months that Hardy had been seeing Fowler every day, he had never, to Hardy's knowledge, made any effort to contact her.

Fowler's shoulders sagged. "No. What would be the point?"

"It just seems you might have."

Fowler gave it a moment, then nodded. "I suppose it does." He returned to the chair behind his desk and sat heavily into it. "What do you want me to say?"

"I don't know. Maybe she could help us. There's no doubt she can hurt us."

"How?"

Hardy shrugged. "Maybe she knows something. God knows we've tried everybody else, and we've got nothing resembling a lead for 'X'."

Fowler sipped and stared. "No, Diz, I don't think so."

Suddenly a frightening thought occurred—Andy was still carrying a torch. Hardy had kept the secret of Shinn's other clients to himself (excluding Glitsky), but he was coming around to thinking it might do Andy some good to know the truth, to *face* the truth. If nothing else, it might break him out of his reluctance to use what May might have.

"You know," he said, "there were other men . . ."

Fowler pushed his glass, a quarter turn at a time, in a circle on his desk. "What?"

Hardy spent five minutes explaining to Andy—checking the phone records, proving that May had lied to him. Fowler stared into space behind Hardy's head. "Why are you telling me all this now?"

"Because your life is at stake here, Andy, and I think maybe you're somehow planning on getting found not guilty, putting this trial behind you and doing nothing to jeopardize what you still think is your relationship with this woman. And if that's the case, you ought to know what that relationship really was."

He took a moment. "I know what it was. That's become clear to me. Before you told me this."

"Well?" Hardy asked.

"Well what?"

"Maybe you could talk to her, maybe she knows something." He paused, waiting for Andy. "About 'X', if nothing else."

The ex-judge, suddenly looking old and tired, leaned his head back against the chair and blew at the ceiling. "Don't you think she would have mentioned that in her own defense last summer?"

"She never got the chance."

"She got plenty of chance. She doesn't know."

"You think." He had to drive it home. "But you thought she had cut off her other clients for you, remember? She wasn't supposed to be sleeping with anyone else."

Fowler pushed his fingers into his eyes. "There must be some aphorism here about old fools and young women." He pulled his hands away from his face. "Okay, okay, do what you've got to do."

When Hardy got home at eleven the house was asleep. There was a Redi Delivery Service box on his front porch when he walked up and he opened it in his office—the dailies. Only death-penalty defendants, who got them free, and people as rich as Andy Fowler, who could afford them, got daily transcripts. One hundred eighty-eight typed pages of today's transcripts that he ought to review before tomorrow. Maybe someone had said something at the trial today he hadn't heard, or listened to carefully enough.

He saw Frannie's note by the telephone. Elizabeth Pullios had called with the message that the prosecution was adding May Shinn to their witness list "re Fowler knowledge gun on boat."

Shinn again. What did that woman really know?

Was this only the second day? He couldn't imagine ever getting to sleep. He'd already tried twice, once a little after midnight, then again around two. Now the clock by his bed read 3:15 and he'd just had a rush of adrenaline, remembering how he'd been so unsuspecting of Strout's testimony and then there had been a snake in it.

He recognized in a flash what had awakened him—Tom and José. He'd noted their presence both in the courtroom and on the witness list and, as he'd done with Strout, had reviewed and reviewed and finally reached the conclusion that neither of the Marina guards had anything damaging to say about Andy Fowler.

What had jolted him awake was the realization that he was wrong again—he *had* to be wrong. Pullios wouldn't call them to pass the time of day. There must be something there and he hadn't seen it.

Wearily, he threw back the covers and padded barefoot to his office.

52

"We talked to her last night," Pullios said. "I think she's tired of all this."

"It does get that way."

It was nine o'clock, and Hardy was leaning over the prosecution table, talking with his opposing counsel about May Shinn. "You want to tell me about her testimony?"

There had been an element of courtesy in Pullios's phoning him to let him know they were calling Shinn as a witness. It made him nervous.

"You know Peter Struler? He's been handling this. He's interviewing her today. Of course you can review the transcript."

Hardy said he planned to. "But you saw May last night? How'd you get her to agree to talk to you?"

"You know, she's very bitter about all this—all the litigation, the way she's been treated. I thought we might make some gesture. Well, Sergeant Struler did."

Hardy waited.

"You know we've been holding all of her clothes, personal items, knickknacks, things like that, from the *Eloise*. The sergeant thought we could cut through the red tape and at least get that stuff back to her. None of it is evidence here, strictly speaking."

"What is evidence here?" Hardy said.

"Well, her testimony will be." Pullios smiled sweetly. "Did your client tell you how he found out that the gun was on board, exactly where she kept it?"

Andy Fowler still appeared as exhausted as he had in the office the previous night. "Well, there's the missing link if she does it," he said.

Hardy kicked the wastebasket; it crashed against the wall, then fell on its side. "You knew she knew this! All along you knew it!"

Jane had come to the courthouse with her father and had accompanied them into their conference room. "Dismas, for God's sake . . ."

A guard opened the door and asked if everything was all right in there. Hardy told him it was and good-by.

Fowler, seemingly unmoved, shook his head. "She wasn't testifying, remember? Why do you think I didn't want to call her ourselves?"

"Well, *now* she is. How could you *not* tell me this?"

Fowler said nothing, then, "Maybe I can talk to her now."

"Last night you couldn't, though, right? Nice timing on the change of heart. She's talking today." Hardy looked around for something else to kick. "Goddamn it, I've at least got to have the facts, Andy. I can't defend you without them. Jesus, you know that."

"I honestly didn't think it would come up, Diz."

Hardy put both hands on the table and leaned over. "Well, it's come up. How about that? Is there anything else you want to tell me that you don't think is going to come up?"

Jane cut in. "Dismas, come *on.*"

He turned on her, trying to keep his voice under control. "You know what this is, Jane? Your dad's right—it's the missing link. There was no way they had first-degree murder unless he knew the gun was on board. Without that there's no way they could prove he'd premeditated it."

He'd only had two hours of sleep. His stomach was churning and his head buzzing with four cups of espresso. He had planned this argument as his ace in the hole, ready to unleash it during his closing argument. It was, in fact, a crucial point in his finally coming around to a belief in Andy's innocence.

He had even asked Andy directly, early on, "Did you know the gun was on the boat?" Just like that. Couldn't have been clearer. And he had looked right at him, figuring *it wouldn't come out,* and lied just like he had lied about not "knowing" Owen Nash. No wonder he hadn't wanted May on the stand.

"I'll tell you something, Andy," he said, "I'm tempted to withdraw."

"Dismas, you can't!"

"Yes, I can, Jane. You'd be surprised."

Fowler wagged his head back and forth. "Nothing's changed, Diz. I *still* didn't do it, if it helps you to hear it again. I never claimed my behavior with or about May was entirely rational, let alone sensible. But—"

"Jane," Hardy said, "could you leave us alone a minute?"

"It's okay, honey, go ahead," Fowler told her.

The door slammed after her but it barely registered.

"Listen up, here, Andy," Hardy said. "I'm not stupid. Yes, May has had you off-center and that may explain a lot. But you're also acting like nothing's changed, above it all, still the judge, even though you happen to be on trial for your life. You're still trying to save face, as though nothing you did or didn't do could matter because you're the *Judge* and a fine fellow and you want people to still see you that way. *Forget* it, Andy. That's all over. You're on trial for murder here. Trying to save some image so you won't look foolish or bad or whatever to me or anyone else is a total waste and dangerous. If there's anything else you want to tell me, tell me now. It doesn't matter a damn what I think of you, what anybody thinks of you. I know that goes cross-grain to the way you've lived your life, but it's true. The *only* thing that matters about you now is that you didn't kill Owen Nash."

Fowler's eyes were bloodshot. "I didn't," he whispered.

"I don't think you did," Hardy said. "That's the only reason I'm still here."

Hardy had been ready to stipulate that Owen Nash had been shot on the *Eloise* sometime during the afternoon of Saturday, June 20, as well as to several other timing and forensic issues. Pullios wanted to talk to everybody on the witness stand and would stipulate to nothing. Fowler thought it was because she had few enough facts to work with, and without a parade of prosecution witnesses her case would appear to have less factual support.

So they had to sit and listen to José relate how the *Eloise* had already been out when he'd come on around seven o'clock or so on Saturday morning, and had been back in at its slip the following morning. Hardy had a point or two on cross. He wanted to make sure that when José and Tom had boarded the boat on Wednesday, neither of them had tampered with it. José told him he hadn't boarded the *Eloise* or seen anyone else near it. Tom then testified that the Marina had been nearly empty all that day—the weather had been terrible, and he hadn't seen anything of Nash's boat. It hadn't yet gotten back in by the time he got off for the night.

When Pullios had finished with Tom, Hardy stood up. He didn't want the jury to become somehow lulled by unquestioned testimony, to his disadvantage, even if it appeared unimportant.

"Mr. Waddell," he said. "Did you check the *Eloise* on Sunday when it was at its slip?"

"What do you mean, check it?"

"Go aboard, see if it was secured, anything like that."

"No, I didn't."

"When was the first time you went aboard the *Eloise.*"

"That was with you on the following Wednesday night."

"I remember. And was the cabin to the boat locked when you went aboard?"

"No, sir."

"In other words, anyone could have gone aboard the *Eloise* between Sunday and Wednesday night—"

"Objection. Calls for a conclusion from the witness."

"Sustained."

Hardy took a beat. He didn't really need it. He thought he'd made his point and excused the witness.

He half-expected Pullios to do something on redirect, but she let Tom go. Hardy would take it—he had read over everything both Tom and José had told either him or Glitsky and had found nothing that looked like it could bite him. And there hadn't been. It gave him some hope.

Emmet Turkel combed back his forelock of sandy hair and smiled at Pullios. A character with a gap-toothed grin, the private investigator from New York had an old-fashioned Brooklyn accent. He had obviously spent many hours on the witness stand. Just as obviously, he admired the looks of the prosecuting attorney. The jury noticed and seemed to be enjoying it.

It was early afternoon, and Turkel and Pullios had chatted about the former's professional relationship with the defendant, covering the same ground as his tape.

Andy Fowler had hired him by telephone on February 20. Turkel had some other business to clear up, but he made it out to San Francisco by the next Wednesday, February 26, met with the judge at "some fancy pizzeria—hey, what you folks out here put on a pizza!"

It had taken him, Turkel said, only a few days to find out why May Shinn had ended her professional relationship with Andy Fowler. When Pullios asked him why that had been, he answered it was because she had gotten herself a new sugar daddy.

Hardy had objected and been sustained, but damage was done.

None of Turkel's testimony, covering Fowler's relationship with May, his efforts to hide his activities, and his character in general, put the defendant in anything like a positive light.

Still, Hardy had at least known what was going to be coming. Turkel didn't present anything in the first two hours that he hadn't prefigured in his taped interview with Peter Struler months earlier. No surprise, but definitely no help.

Pullios had introduced the March 2 page from Fowler's desk calendar showing Owen Nash's name and had it marked as Exhibit 7. Turkel said that had been the day he had informed Fowler of the results of his investigation. Pullios asked him if Mr. Fowler had given Mr. Turkel any indication of what he was going to do with the information.

"No, not then," Turkel said.

"Did he at any time?"

"Nah, not really, he was just kidding like, you know?"

"I don't know, Mr. Turkel. I'll repeat the question—did Mr. Fowler say anything about Mr. Nash at any time to you after you'd told him he was Ms. Shinn's current . . . paramour?"

"Yeah, well, we talked again sometime around April, May—I called him, just keeping up contact, you know, and I ask him does he still have his problem with this guy Nash, did he want I come out and clear it up for him?"

"Clear it up?"

"Yeah, you know."

"You asked Mr. Fowler if he wanted you to kill Mr. Nash?"

"Well, you might take it that way, but—"

"Can you tell us Mr. Fowler's exact words, please?"

"But I'm telling you, we was *kidding*. You know, people kid all the time."

"Nevertheless, Mr. Turkel, if you could tell the jury what was said."

Turkel glanced at Fowler and shrugged theatrically. Chomorro slammed his gavel and told him to refrain from the gestures and answer the question.

Turkel sighed. "I said 'Hey, I'm doin' nothin' the next couple weeks, I could use a vacation, fly out there, do this guy.' The judge said, 'No thanks, if I want the man disposed of, I'll do it myself.' "

"That's clear enough," said Moses McGuire. "No jury would buy that—"

"You never know what juries are going to think," Hardy told him.

"Yeah, but Turkel was right. People talk like that all the time, it never means anything."

"Except when it does."

It was Wednesday night. Not exactly date night, but Frannie had invited her brother over. When Hardy got home at seven-thirty she poured him a beer, told him she was giving him a special dispensation on his no-alcohol-during-the-week policy and guided him to his chair in the living room. He would be a better lawyer if he could recharge for a while. Moses would be around in a minute or two. They were having a fancy leg-of-lamb dinner and he was going to sit and eat it.

His plan had been to keep reading, reading, reading—the dailies would be in later tonight, probably also May Shinn's transcript. He wanted to go over every word Turkel had said—Chomorro had called it a day after Pullios finished with the private investigator and Hardy would start cross-examining him tomorrow.

Suddenly he realized enough was enough. Frannie was right, he was too beat to think. He finished his beer and lit the fire, turned on the Christmas-tree lights and listened to John Fahey play some seasonal guitar.

And now Moses was here. Frannie was humming, bustling around between the kitchen and dining room, setting a fancy table. He was having another beer. The claustrophobic feeling that had enveloped him for the past two days was letting up. So was the fatigue.

"The real problem," he said, "is that Turkel's in it, period. It's not so much his testimony, although that's bad enough, but the fact that Andy hired him at all."

"What's the matter with that? He wanted to find out what had happened, why May dumped him."

"So he hires a private eye? Would you hire a private eye?"

Moses shrugged. "He was a working judge. Maybe he didn't have the time personally. I don't know . . . what did he tell you?"

"That's what he told me. But what am I supposed to sell to the jury? I mean, we've all had relationships end, right? Do we go three thousand miles for a private eye to keep chasing it?"

Frannie was in the archway between the living and dining rooms. "I would chase you to the very ends of the earth," she said. "Meanwhile, dinner is served."

She'd gone all out. The soup was a rich consommé with tapioca and sour cream. The lamb, stuck with garlic and rubbed with rosemary and lemon juice, was served with potatoes and a spinach dish with nutmeg and balsamic vinegar. She even had a half glass of the outstanding Oregon Pinot Noir. They talked about Christmases past, Moses' memories of his and Frannie's parents, Hardy's memories of his. The trial wasn't there.

After Moses left, Hardy and Frannie cleaned the table and did the dishes together, catching up on each other, trying out names for the new baby, getting back to some teasing.

"Would you think I was a terrible human being if I didn't work tonight?" Hardy asked.

Frannie's eyes were bright. "I don't think I could forgive that." She put her arms around him.

"How about if I got up early?"

"How early?"

"Real early."

Frannie gave a good imitation of thinking about it. "So what would you do instead? Of working, I mean."

"Maybe go to bed, get a little sleep."

"Which one?"

53

Real early turned out to be four o'clock, but he woke up refreshed, the growing sense of panic he'd been feeling somehow dissipated. He got into some running clothes—long sweats and a thermal windbreaker—and chugged his four-mile course.

By quarter after five he had showered and dressed and was at his desk with yesterday's dailies and the transcript of May Shinn's tape with the D.A.'s office.

It was every bit as bad as he'd feared.

Q: You had stopped seeing Mr. Fowler by this time, isn't that right?

A: Yes, I think it was early in March. He just caught me at home. Normally I screen my calls but I was expecting Owen so I picked it up.

Q: And what did Fowler say?

A: He said he was worried about me.

Q: Why?

A: He said he'd heard I was seeing Owen. I guess he'd heard bad things about him or thought he had. He said he wanted to make sure I was all right.

Q: What did you tell him?

A: I mostly tried to say he was being silly. Look, I didn't want to hurt him. Then he said if Owen ever hurt me in any way I should come to him, I could always come to him. So, you know, I was trying to keep it light, I told him, if anything, Owen made me feel safer than he ever had. At least Owen had taken the gun.

Q: Which gun, Ms. Shinn?

A: *The* gun. I never liked to keep it around and I'd asked Andy to take it home with him—I hated it in the house. But he wouldn't do it, being a judge . . .

381

Q: Then what?

A: I told him we put the gun on board the *Eloise* in the desk right next to the bed in case there was an emergency and I needed it, but at least it wasn't at home anymore. It made me feel safer.

Q: And what did the judge—did Mr. Fowler—say to that?

A: Nothing, really. Then he asked me why I had stopped seeing him. It was really hard, but I told him . . . I was in love with Owen.

Q: How did he react to that?

A: He said he thought I'd been in love with him. I told him I *liked* him, that he had been very important to me. He asked what if Owen weren't in the picture anymore, did I think I could see him again?

Q: And what did you say?

A: I said I was sorry but I just didn't think so. Owen had changed me, or I had changed myself. I just wasn't the same anymore, I was a different person. He said if Owen wasn't there maybe I would be—the way I was, feel toward him the way I had. I thought Owen was always going to be there . . .

Q: It's all right, Ms. Shinn, it's okay, take your time.

A: I said I didn't know.

Q: Didn't know what, May?

A: What I'd do if Owen wasn't there. I couldn't think about that. I believed him, Owen I mean. He wasn't going to leave me. Then Andy . . . the judge . . . said what if something happened to Owen. What would I do then?

Q: And what did you say to that?

A: I think I said I didn't know, I didn't even want to think about something like that.

Hardy ran into Glitsky under the list of fallen policemen in the lobby of the Hall of Justice. It was 9:20. Court went into session in ten minutes and Andy Fowler had not yet arrived. Jane was calling his home, as she already had done twice since nine o'clock; there had been no answer either time.

Hardy told Abe a little about May Shinn's damaging testimony.

"Maybe Fowler just decided to cut and run."

"He wouldn't do that. He put up a million dollars' bail, Abe. He surrendered his passport."

Glitsky, more knowledgeable in such matters, smiled. "You want a new passport? Give me ten minutes. Cost you fifty bucks."

"He wouldn't do it."

"A million dollars doesn't stand up against a life in the slammer. And for a man like Fowler . . . you know how long a judge's life is going to be once he gets there? That's the good news—he won't suffer very long. The bad news is he'll suffer real hard."

"He's not going there, Abe."

"Right. I forgot."

Jane came up, shaking her head no.

"You know," Hardy said, "your dad is making me old before my time."

"He'll get here."

"So will Christmas, Jane."

Glitsky looked at his watch. "Contempt time starts in about three minutes."

"Yes, Mr. Hardy?"

"Your Honor, Mr. Fowler called from a gas station about twenty minutes ago. He has car trouble. He was taking a cab from where he was—it shouldn't be more than a half hour."

Chomorro spent a minute rearranging things on the bench. He tried not to betray how angry he was and was not entirely successful. "Ms. Pullios?" he asked.

"What's our choice, Your Honor?"

The judge tried to smile at the jury. Hardy knew this was another prosecution bonanza. Guilty and late. Thought he was still a big shot . . .

"Well, ladies and gentlemen, why don't you all go out and have yourselves another cup of coffee." The smile vanished. "Mr. Hardy, if Mr. Fowler is not here at ten-o-one, I'm going to cancel his bail and put him back in custody—is that understood?"

"Yes, Your Honor."

To say nothing, Hardy thought, of his own contempt if it turned out that Andy had left the country or taken off—it wasn't recommended procedure for attorneys to lie to the court, as he had just done. But what was his option?

He got up from the defense table and went back through the swinging door to the gallery, where Jane was sitting next to Glitsky, who had stayed around to view the proceedings.

"What if he doesn't show?" Abe said.

"Thanks, Abe, the thought never occurred to me." He looked at his ex-wife. "Any ideas?"

"About what?" Pullios had left the prosecution table and was standing at the end of the aisle, from where she just happened to overhear.

Hardy turned quickly around. "Lunch," he said. "We're trying to decide between Chinese and Italian."

How much had she heard? Whatever, she gave no sign. "It's going to be a long day," she said. "Chinese, you eat it and a half hour later you're hungry again. I'd do Italian." Her eyes left Hardy and went to Glitsky. "Hello, Abe. I almost didn't recognize you at the defense side."

The sergeant nodded tightly. "The other side was filled up," he said.

Pullios decided against whatever she was going to say, then moved crisply back through the gallery.

"Bitch," Jane said.

Hardy said nothing. He crossed one leg over the other, looked at his watch and waited.

"Your car broke down—the clutch went out. You called me from out on Lombard and took a cab."

It was 9:58. Andy Fowler strolled up the center aisle as though he had the world by the tail. He shook Hardy's hand and kissed his daughter on the cheek. Hardy thought he'd give him the short version and fill it in later.

"My car is out in the parking lot. How about if I had a flat and they fixed it?"

Hardy sometimes wondered if the reason he hated to lie was because once you started it got so hard to remember exactly what you'd said. Had he told Chomorro it was the clutch? Or was it just car trouble? He knew to keep it simple. He probably kept it simple. "All right, it was a flat. Jesus Christ, Andy, where the hell were you?"

Fowler had an embarrassed look. "May's," he said quietly. "I finally went to see May."

Before Hardy could react, the clerk was calling the court to order. The jury, by and large, hadn't left the box. It was precisely ten o'clock.

Hardy didn't hope to get much out of Turkel. The private investigator was wearing a turtleneck and a lime-green sports jacket. After he was sworn in he again made himself comfortable in the witness chair, making eye contact with the jury.

Hardy let him perform awhile, wasting time pretending to read his notes at his desk, then went to the center of the courtroom. "Mr. Turkel," he began, "when Mr. Fowler first called you, back in February, how did he sound?"

"Objection. Conclusion."

"Sustained."

Hardy tried again. "Can you recall any of the conversation you had, exactly?"

Turkel still had eyes for Pullios, but she seemed to have antagonized him somewhat by pushing yesterday—the private investigator hated rinky-dink testimony—especially being forced to give it by the rules of the court. He was now giving Hardy his full attention.

"Well, the judge said, 'Hi, Em,' asked if I was busy and I said 'Yeah, a little,' like I always do." He smiled at the jury. "Trade secret."

Pullios spoke up. "Your Honor . . ."

Chomorro leaned over. "Just answer the questions."

"Sure, Your Honor, just like I did yesterday."

Chomorro, not getting it, nodded. "That's right."

Hardy thought he did get it . . . a prosecution witness deciding he might be able to do something for the defense. Cover your ass two ways to Sunday. "Go on," he said.

"All right, then the judge said—"

Chomorro interrupted. "Mr. Turkel, please refer to Mr. Fowler either as Mr. Fowler or as the defendant."

Reasonable, Turkel agreed. "Sure, Your Honor. Sorry again."

"Let's start again, shall we?" Hardy said. "How long have you known the defendant?"

"Your Honor? Relevance?"

Now Hardy looked to the jury. "Your Honor, I'd like to have Mr. Turkel be able to get in a word of testimony at some point during this cross-examination. His relationship with the defendant is relevant if we're to understand the context of the actual words used in their discussions together." ·

This, of course, directly related to the testimony yesterday about Andy saying he'd in effect kill Nash. But Hardy was beginning to think if he could get Pullios running she might trip on her own feet. Chomorro overruled her and Turkel got to answer.

"About four years, I've known Mr. Fowler about four years."

"In what capacity?"

"Mostly professional. Referrals, like that. But we get along okay. We played golf together a coupla times." Turkel looked at the jury again, explaining. "He saw me wear this nice green coat in court one time, figured I'd won the Masters."

This time Chomorro said nothing. Good. Hardy turned around. Fowler was smiling, some of the jury would notice that.

"All right, so the . . . defendant was rather more than a professional acquaintance but less than a friend?"

"Objection, Your Honor, leading the witness."

"You're allowed to do that on cross, Ms. Pullios. Overruled."

Hardy took a breath and held it. Here was an eccentric on the stand, clearly liked by the jury, and for some reason he was being thoroughly harassed by the D.A. "One moment, Your Honor."

Hardy went back to his table and pretended to read more notes. There really wasn't any testimony of Turkel's he believed could help his case. The bare facts were pretty damning—Andy had hired him to find out why May had left him, then Turkel had found out and told him about Owen Nash. And you didn't simply get information for the hell of it. Once you had it, at least the temptation was to do something with it . . . not, he thought, too much of a stretch for someone to believe that what Andy had done was to identify his enemy, and why would he do that if he wasn't planning on acting against him . . .

Still, at this moment, Turkel on the stand somehow had made Hardy feel—and perhaps the jury as well—that Andy was a good guy and that the powers arrayed against him were nitpickers and bureaucrats and maybe worse. Leave it at that. He turned around and spoke from the defense desk.

"I have no further questions of this witness."

As it turned out they went for Chinese. Andy said he was buying— which he always did. Hardy, Jane and her father caught a cab outside the Hall and got to Grant Street, the center of Chinatown, in about eight minutes.

All the way up, Hardy sat silently. He didn't know how long he could keep this up. The effusive, charming Andy Fowler, his client, was wearing him down.

"I had to see her," he was saying. "I was certain she'd see me, tell me why she would want to testify against me."

"What did she say?"

The answers were all there. "You know how they get you," he said in the voice of reason. "She lost sight of what the prosecution, the D.A.'s office—what they were doing."

"What were they doing?" Jane said.

"They had held back a lot of her valuables from the *Eloise* and they put things to her so that the point seemed to be that coming down to be a witness was essentially a formality so that she could get her things back. They've been inundating her with paper. I just didn't want her to be taken in, misled. She told me she did not have any-thing to say against me—she, of course, knew I hadn't killed Owen Nash, so what could be the problem? But now she'd promised them . . ." He shook his head. "So I explained to her the appearance of the connection about me knowing the gun was on the boat . . ."

The cab arrived at the restaurant and they got into a booth with a curtain. The dim sum began to arrive—pork bao, shark's fin soup, pot stickers. Hardy tasted none of it. Finally he had to say something. "You realize, Andy, that if Pullios finds out you tried to influence May's testimony, all of this will come out, making you look even worse than you do now."

Andy seemed unfazed. "May and I had a good talk. She under-stands now. Why should it come out?"

"A better question is why do you think you can keep it locked up?"

Fowler spooned up some soup and said to his daughter, "This man is too pessimistic," and then to Hardy, "Listen, Diz, she's a good woman, I don't care about her background. I know her . . . she is *not* out to get me. To the contrary, she is very upset with the prosecu-tion people." He continued popping morsels of food. "This is an eye-opener for me, you know. When I was on the bench I liked to believe that we not only had an efficient crew out there but that there were certain established rules. We differed on the propriety of what I con-sidered entrapment, which didn't make me a prosecutor's favorite, but by and large there was a community of the legal system. I'm find-ing the generally accepted rules don't apply, at least not in this case. They've misled May about the gist of her testimony, and they were pretty slipshod, too."

Hardy asked what they had done.

"You'd think that since they were trading it for her cooperation they would check the inventory and make sure she got everything back. But evidently someone with the police had stolen the most important thing to her. So even without my intervention she's not inclined to help them anymore."

"She's already talked, Andy. I read the transcript this morning."

Fowler shrugged. "She won't say the same thing on the stand—"

"She'll perjure herself to help you?"

Fowler took a sip of tea. "She'll say she was coerced at the interview, which in effect she was, and that under oath she just can't remember—"

Hardy cradled his forehead in the palm of his hand. "Lord help me."

"What did they steal?" Jane kept to the essentials.

"Her favorite coat," Fowler said. Tightening his face . . . "Nash had given it to her. She said it was like a work of art, full-length goosedown. He got it in Japan for her. Remarkable design, colors . . ."

Hardy had to get back to business. "So what's she going to say when they call her?"

"Diz, relax, it's completely understandable. Think about it. They've got to know she's potentially a hostile witness anyway. She's suing the City, for God's sake. They won't pursue it."

Hardy wasn't at all certain of that, but there was no arguing now—the deed had been done. If Fowler's scenario transpired—an enormous if—then possibly he'd helped his case. But at what risk!

"So what now? If you're going to start seeing her again, do me a favor and at least wait until after the trial."

"We didn't even discuss that."

"How did she behave with you?" Hardy asked.

Fowler looked unhappy. "Well, to tell you the truth, it wasn't very heartening, but, well, it was still good to see her, even if it seemed like the old feelings were gone, for her. As though the whole experience had just worn her down. Everything, she said, had gone wrong for her, so it shouldn't have been a great surprise that they'd stolen her coat, lied to her . . . She gave me the impression that . . . that she thought going on at all with her life was a waste of time. The whole question of her testimony didn't seem to matter much, but if I thought it would be a help she'd try."

"Maybe she's looking for something again," Jane said. "Maybe when this is all over . . ."

The judge nodded. "I suppose that's what I've got to hope for. And that's why I was late," he said, turning to Hardy. "I just couldn't leave her that way, feeling so down. I . . . we just talked. I tried to convince her, especially if her money comes through, that there *is* a future."

Hardy reached behind him and pulled the curtain, signaling for the check. "We'd better get back," he said.

Hardy thought the afternoon would have made a root canal look like a walk in the park.

In furtherance of her consciousness-of-guilt theory, Pullios called a succession of witnesses—including two Superior Court judges, several community leaders, a city supervisor and Fowler's own clerk—and all of them testified that Andy Fowler had told them after the May Shinn trial had been canceled but before his own indictment that the first he had heard of Owen Nash, other than reading about him in the newspapers from time to time, was after his death. He had told one and all that he had no idea that Nash had been seeing May Shinn.

The only one Hardy saw fit to cross-examine was a Pat Shields, the silver-haired president of the Olympic Club, who had intimated that Andy Fowler and Owen Nash, as fellow members of the Club, must have known each other.

Hardy had whispered to Fowler at the defense table. "Please tell me you really never knew Owen Nash."

Fowler said he hadn't, and Hardy, hoping at last he wasn't being lied to, stood up.

"Mr. Shields," he said, "how long has Mr. Fowler been a member of the Olympic Club?"

"I'd say forever. Certainly longer than myself. He's second generation."

"And Mr. Nash?"

"We'd been recruiting him for years. Quietly, of course, but . . . in any event, he joined about a year ago."

"So he was in the club for how long?"

"A few months."

"A few months. He died in June and he joined in, when, November or December?"

"Yes, I believe so. Around there."

"And did he come into the club every day?"

"Well, we have two locations, you know, downtown and the golf course, so I couldn't speak for both. But as to downtown, I'd say no, perhaps once a month."

"Six times?"

Shields lifted his shoulders. "Let's say between five and ten. I didn't count." He smiled affably. "It's not like we keep tabs on members."

Hardy turned friendly. "Of course not. The times Mr. Nash came in downtown, did he come in for lunch or dinner, or to work out, or what?"

"Mostly I'd say lunch, although that's just an impression."

"All right. Well, let me ask you this. Did you ever see Mr. Nash having lunch with Mr. Fowler?"

"No."

"Do you recall ever seeing Mr. Nash and Mr. Fowler in the club having lunch at the same time?"

"No, not specifically."

"Not specifically? Do you mean you might have and you don't remember? You just have an impression?"

"No . . . I mean I didn't see them together or at the same time." He glanced at the jury, showing signs of nerves. "It was just a figure of speech."

"Of course. How about sports? Squash, golf? To your knowledge, did Mr. Nash play either of these with Mr. Fowler?"

"Not to my knowledge, no."

"Well, isn't it a fact, Mr. Shields, that the prosecution here asked you to check your reservations cards for both the golf course out by the ocean and the courts at the downtown location—tennis and squash—to see if Mr. Nash and Mr. Fowler had reserved time together?"

Shields frowned. Apparently this smacked of keeping tabs on the members. Even if one of them was on trial for murder, members were presumed to be gentlemen and were not to be checked up on. "Yes, that's true."

"And did you do that?"

He nodded. "Yes. Yes, I did that."

"And did you find any record that Mr. Nash had ever played any of these sports with Mr. Fowler? Or even in an approximate time span?"

"No . . ."

"In fact, Mr. Shields, isn't it true that you have no indication whatever that Mr. Nash and Mr. Fowler knew each other or spent time in each other's company in any way at all?"

"Yes, I suppose that's true."

Hardy said he had no further questions.

Of course, it still didn't prove Fowler had not lied to Shields about when he had known Owen Nash. Or if he had known Owen Nash at all. In fact, Hardy thought, here he had danced around with this man for the better part of a half hour and hadn't really challenged his essential testimony in a substantive way. What was there to challenge? Like the other afternoon's witnesses, Shields was a good man who no doubt was telling the truth. Fowler was a man charged with murder who was known to have lied in the past. Hardy could throw up smoke, but he doubted he could obscure that fact from the jury.

54

Glitsky came up through the gallery, pushed open the swinging door and strode into the courtroom proper. He was a well-known and respected police officer and his entrance, in itself, was not unusual. That he came to the defense table was, though not unprecedented, very much out of the ordinary.

Pullios was standing in what had become counsel's spot in front of the bench. She was beginning to question Gary Smythe, Andy Fowler's golf partner, fellow Olympic Club member and stockbroker. They certainly had done their homework—witnesses were coming out of the woodwork.

Glitsky leaned over, putting a hand on Hardy's arm. Looking up at him, he thought he'd never seen the sergeant so drawn. There was a pallor underneath the pigment of his skin. His eyes seemed to have trouble focusing, and Hardy was reminded of cases of shell-shock he had witnessed in Vietnam. "Get a recess," he whispered. "We've got to talk, now."

Abe Glitsky wasn't given to histrionics. If he said "now" he had good reason. Hardy nodded. "Excuse me," he said, interrupting Pullios, who had been in the middle of a question. She turned to face him, her expression unpleasant.

"Yes, Mr. Hardy?" Chomorro said.

"Your Honor, an emergency has come up. I wonder if the court would grant a short recess."

"Your Honor," Pullios fumed, "I've just begun with this witness."

"Ten minutes, Your Honor."

Pullios gave Glitsky a questioning look.

Chomorro checked the wall clock. "If I give you ten minutes now we won't have time on direct here." He took in the jury and gave them a weary smile. "How about if we call it a day today and pick up with Mr. Smythe tomorrow?"

"No," Glitsky said sotto voce to Hardy. "Don't let them do that."

Hardy stood. "That won't be necessary, Your Honor. A couple of minutes will do."

Which annoyed Chomorro. "Well, which is it, Mr. Hardy? Do you want a recess or not?" He directed himself to Glitsky. "What's this about, Sergeant? Care to share it with the court?"

Glitsky was clearly torn. It was ingrained that cops didn't work with the defense, even if there was a personal connection, such as he and Hardy. It got to be too much. He shrugged at Hardy, as much to say he tried. Then, to Chomorro and Pullios, "With counsel?"

The judge motioned them all forward and they clustered in front of the raised bench. Glitsky still looked pale. "This is unofficial, Your Honor, and I apologize for interrupting, but I've just come down from homicide."

"Yes?"

Glitsky took a breath. "It seems May Shinn is dead."

"Jesus Christ!" from Hardy. Pullios hung as if poleaxed. "What?"

"And we got two neighbors—independently—who read the papers, watch some TV." Glitsky turned to Hardy. "Both of them say they saw your man there this morning."

"Fowler?" Pullios nearly yelled.

Glitsky turned back to her and nodded. "The same."

At that moment Peter Struler pushed open the outer doors and started up the aisle, almost running. "I think this might make it official," Glitsky said.

NASH MISTRESS FOUND DEAD
Homicide Not Ruled Out In Apparent Suicide
by Jeffrey Elliot
Chronicle Staff Writer

May Shinn, who for a short time last summer was the prime suspect in the murder of Owen Nash, was found dead in her apartment this afternoon, apparently a suicide victim. The body was discovered by Special Investigator Sergeant Peter Struler, who had had an earlier appointment with Ms. Shinn following a statement she had given yesterday in the murder trial of former Superior Court Judge Andrew Fowler.

In spite of the appearance of suicide, spokespersons for both the police department and the district attorney's office refuse to rule out homicide as the cause of death. Following the discovery that Mr. Fowler had visited Ms. Shinn in her apartment this morning, jurors in his trial have been sequestered and Mr. Fowler himself has been placed into custody. Mr. Fowler had been late to court this morning and had initially told the court he'd had car trouble.

As this paper goes to press the exact time of Ms. Shinn's death has not been determined. Her body was discovered slumped over a make-shift altar in her apartment, dressed in the ceremonial white robes of the Japanese ritual suicide known as seppuku, or more commonly, hara-kiri. Most other essential forms of that ritual were carried out as well, according to police sources (see box on back page). The altar had been strewn with papers from litigation Ms. Shinn had been involved in related to charges brought against her by the grand jury and the district attorney's office last summer.

Ms. Shinn's attorney, David Freeman, said he was "terribly shocked and saddened" by the death of his client. "May Shinn has become another victim of the lack of due process in our courts," Freeman said. "Her illegal, premature arrest following the death of the man she loved put her into a downward spiral of depression from which there was no escape. One can only hope she has now found some peace . . ."

As JEFF ELLIOT WAS TYPING THE LAST WORDS INTO HIS COMPUTER, Dismas Hardy was drinking what must have been his twentieth cup of coffee. He sat, no place to go, on a yellow bench in the windowless visitor's room at the morgue.

Strout was still inside, personally doing the autopsy on May Shinn. Locke himself had put in an appearance, as had Drysdale, Pullios and, of course, Struler. Glitsky had come in around eight-thirty and stayed to keep him company for a while. Hardy was not responsive.

He was still reliving the scene in Chomorro's chambers after Struler had come in with the official word.

They were in Andy Fowler's old office but all vestiges of Andy's old WASP effects had been decorated away. The gray Berber wall-to-wall had been lifted and hardwood shined up beneath it. Inca or Aztec rugs lay under stuffed furniture in bold Latin designs. Photographs of

Reagan, Bush, Quayle, George Deukmejian and Pete Wilson shaking hands with Leo Chomorro covered the back wall. The desk was heavy and black and, unlike Andy's, nearly bare on its surface. Chomorro sat behind it, elbows on it, hands together.

Pullios leaned, arms crossed, against the bookshelves. Struler straddled a fold-up chair, and Glitsky stood by the doorway. Drysdale sat in one of the chairs next to Hardy, who tried to appear calm.

Chomorro addressed himself to Hardy.

"Do you mean to tell me that you knew Fowler had been to Shinn's this morning when you told me he had car trouble?"

"No, judge, not then. He told me at lunch—"

"And how long were you planning to withhold this information?"

"I don't know." It was the truth.

"You don't *know*. Your client is suborning, threatening, possibly killing a prosecution witness—"

"We don't know that, Your Honor. There's no hint of that—"

"Not yet," Pullios said.

"In any event, you thought you could keep this to yourself? At the very least, Mr. Hardy, I'm going to have to report this to the State Bar."

"He did not threaten her," Hardy said, "and Struler here says she killed herself—"

"It *appeared* she killed herself," Struler said quickly.

"Fowler didn't kill her."

Pullios looked at him. "Like he didn't kill Nash, right?"

Hardy kept his voice flat. "That's right, Bets. How about, as a change of pace, we wait for the coroner's report? Get a fact or two and find out what we're dealing with before the accusations start."

Chomorro broke it up. "Regardless of what Mr. Fowler did or didn't do, you've got a defendant going to visit a prosecution witness. At the very least, her testimony's going to be no good."

"She's not giving any testimony," Pullios said. "She's dead."

Chomorro shook his head. "I don't know. I'm inclined to think we've got a mistrial here. Maybe we ought to start over fresh."

"I'd agree to that," Hardy said quickly. He could barely admit it to himself, but the thought still wouldn't go away . . . *had* Andy killed May?

But a mistrial wasn't to Pullios's liking—she thought she had the thing won now. Hardy couldn't say he blamed her.

"I'm sorry, Judge, I don't agree." She went on to argue that May

Shinn was only one witness and that her testimony hadn't, in the event, been suborned. "If Mr. Hardy will stipulate to the fact that the defendant had known the gun was on board—"

"Not a chance," he said.

"I'm sure you discussed it in his daughter's presence," Pullios said. "I'll call her."

"She'd never testify against her father."

Chomorro's black eyes glared. "She'd better or I'll hold her in contempt and put her in jail until she does . . ."

And so it had gone. Hardy couldn't have Jane get on the stand for any reason—by some incredible stretch she might mention having known—biblically—Owen Nash. What was worse? The jury knowing about Andy's pre-awareness that May's gun was on board, or another reason he might have had to want Nash dead?

In the end, Chomorro had decided on his strategy to keep Fowler in custody at least until it had been determined that May Shinn had or had not killed herself. The jury, which up to now had been allowed to return to their homes under the stricture that they not discuss the case with anyone, were to be sequestered in a hotel until that question was settled so that this development would not prejudice them against the defendant.

Glitsky finally saw fit to interject a thought—Fowler's clothes should be tested for fibers, hairs, semen and blood. He was a homicide cop—if there had been a killing he didn't want the evidence to get thrown away this time. Pullios told him that was a good idea and he told her he knew it was. Investigating murders was what he did when people let him.

55

The door to the visitor's room opened. It was after ten-thirty and Hardy looked up, half-expecting to see Strout coming in to tell him that May had in fact been murdered, that the knife wounds were inconsistent with what could be self-inflicted. Instead, he looked into the basset face of David Freeman, who asked politely if he could sit down.

"Ah, Mr. Hardy. Just came to pay my respects," he said. In the past months Hardy had had two interviews with Freeman in his office regarding the testimony he was going to give for the prosecution. Nominally adversarial, the two men both had maverick streaks, which they recognized in each other and which Hardy felt formed a bond of sorts that, at this point, was still unacknowledged. "Strout still in with her?" Freeman asked.

Hardy nodded, considered a moment, then decided to speak his mind. "You know," he said, "I wish you'd taken this case when Andy first asked you."

Freeman shook his head. "I don't think you've lost it. It's not over until the jury comes in."

Hardy raised his eyes. "That's what they say."

"Particularly if Andy didn't kill May. I think they're reaching if they think he did."

"He was there at May's this morning." Hardy was testing.

Freeman shrugged. "I was there two days ago. Does the jury know it? Do they need to know it?"

Hardy grabbed the nugget. At this point he'd take anything from any source. "Why do you think they're reaching? I mean beyond wanting a conviction."

In their previous four hours of discussions, Hardy thought he had adequately covered the trial ground with Freeman, but he was beginning to realize that Freeman tended to answer only what he had been

397

asked, and Hardy had stuck to Fowler's actions as they related to the consciousness-of-guilt theory. He had all but ignored May Shinn the person, thinking she had fallen out of the loop. Now he was no longer sure of that.

"Because May was depressed, she *was* suicidal. I spent over an hour last night trying to talk her out of killing herself."

"Why was she so depressed?"

"I think that's obvious, don't you?"

"Not just a coat."

"Coat? Oh, that? No, that just might have been the last straw, just another reminder that she couldn't hope for anything anymore. That's why she first called me, I guess—upset over it being stolen. But the depression itself—that's been going on since the summer. She was in love with Owen Nash. Believed she was. After he died she lost what she'd put her hopes in. What had kept her going. Then to be put on trial for his murder . . ."

Hardy shook his head, still testing. "I don't know what she told you, but she didn't love Owen Nash." Or so Farris had said.

"No. No, you're wrong there. Why do you say that?"

"Same as with Fowler. You don't take money from someone you love, not for sex anyway."

"She didn't take money from Nash, she never did."

That stopped Hardy cold. "What?"

"She never took money from him."

"What about the will?"

"What about it? The will was a will. I think it started out as more of a gesture, but when Owen died . . . I mean, wouldn't you pursue two million dollars?"

Hardy's head was beginning to throb again. He reached for the cup of now cold coffee on the table next to him. Why had he always assumed that Owen was paying May Shinn? Had it been Ken Farris who'd told him that early on? Had Farris been lying?

"No," Freeman was going on. "May did love Owen Nash. There's no doubt about that. And I've come to believe he loved her, too. He was wearing her ring when he was found. She was a lovable woman."

Clearly true. Look what she'd done to Andy Fowler. May obviously had more substance than he'd given her credit for. But she certainly had deceived Andy Fowler, and he reminded Freeman of this.

Freeman nodded as if this were old news. "That was before Owen Nash. Before Nash she did whatever was expedient. She told me this.

Certain clients, you can become like a confessor to them. Psychologist, devil's advocate. A dependency develops."

Hardy, remembering Celine, didn't need a reminder of that.

"In May's case she and I actually became pretty close. We were doing a lot of work together." At Hardy's glance, Freeman went on, "And no, we *weren't* sleeping together. Anyway, something very real seems to have happened with May *and* Owen, who were both pretty cynical to begin with. They changed each other, for the better."

"What does that mean?"

"May dropped her old lovers—Andy Fowler, for example. Could be she might have been able to scam Owen along like she'd done with men before, but she wanted to clear the slate."

"And Nash?"

"I gather it was pretty much the same, except of course he had a wider circle and more responsibilities. It might have taken longer to put into effect—this decision to go public with their intended marriage, for example."

Hardy remembered that Farris had said that Owen had "changed" in the last months of his life. Was that the explanation?

"You really think they were going to get married?"

"I do, yes, and I'm not too easily conned."

Hardy had never seriously considered that. And why, more than anything, was that? Because Ken Farris had told him May and Owen were definitely *breaking up*. It brought him up short, wondering what else he'd overlooked or ignored.

His good friend, and very competent investigator, Abe Glitsky, had supposedly checked the alibi of Ken Farris, but now the thought occurred that in this one area, Pullios may have been right. Abe might have been so burned by the false arrest of May that his heart wasn't into pursuing the leads in this case as he otherwise might have. He had, after all, not followed up the unidentified fingerprint on the murder weapon—while Struler had done so. He hadn't discovered the private eye, Emmet Turkel. Hardy found himself wondering if Abe had actually flown to Taos or only made a few phone calls.

Owen Nash's death had left Ken Farris in sole charge of a $150 million empire, unencumbered now by a controlling eccentric. Might not that be worth killing for?

"Something ring a bell?" Freeman asked mildly.

"Maybe."

They heard footsteps and were both standing by the time Strout opened the door. "Y'all want to come in?" he said.

The body lay covered on a gurney in the chilled room. Strout led the way and pulled back the sheet from over her face. It struck Hardy how young she had been. Her face, without makeup or expression, was one of a young girl, sleeping.

Freeman moved closer to the gurney, traced a finger along the line of May's jaw, lifted the sheet further and looked down at her body, grimacing. Strout and Hardy backed away.

"Where are her clothes?" Hardy asked.

"Bagged and gone. They're checking for fabrics, hairs, stains. SOP. A waste of time."

"Why?"

"Because there is no doubt this woman killed herself."

Hardy felt the fatigue leave in a rush. The clock up over the freezers said it was past eleven, and suddenly his client had at least been proclaimed innocent of committing this murder—because, in fact, it wasn't a murder.

Somehow he felt the case had turned. Fowler hadn't killed May. It made no rational difference in this case about Nash, and yet it seemed to matter a great deal. In everything Andy Fowler had done, Hardy saw evidence of confusion, concern for his reputation, a misdirected vision that he could somehow plug eleven holes with ten fingers.

But what he didn't see—suddenly and with clarity—was a murderer. Andy did impulsive things and then made up foolish stories to cover up how foolish he had been; he was a man out of his depth with his emotions.

What Andy had not done was plan the cold-blooded killing of another man. Somebody else had done that—someone cold, efficient and organized, with neither remorse nor emotion. In fact, the murderer of Owen Nash was close to the polar opposite of Andy Fowler.

Jeff Elliot knew that in the old days, six months ago, before he met Dorothy, he would have been waiting at the morgue until the results came in on the postmortem so he could have a chance to make the morning edition. But tonight he had written his piece, proofed and filed it and headed home.

Other stories around the Hall of Justice were getting attention now

—one concerned a cat the D.A.'s had bought to control the influx of mice that had started to show up in the building in the wake of the construction for the new jail. The cat had been named Arnold Mousenegger and had already gotten several graphs in the *Chronicle,* a "quote of the day" from Chris Locke ("Arnold is a budgetary godsend. We couldn't afford to exterminate the whole building.") and an appearance on Channel 5. Hot stuff.

And Owen Nash was still as dead as he'd ever been. Andy Fowler was in jail and wasn't about to get out to kill anybody else tonight. The trial proceeded at its own pace. Jeff's work would keep until the morning.

Dorothy had been asleep but got up to greet him when he opened the door. She poured them both glasses of domestic white wine while, sitting on the bed, he took his clothes off. The telephone rang and without thinking he picked it up.

"Jeff, this is Dismas Hardy and I'm doing you a favor."

"You still awake? Don't you have a trial in the morning?"

"Good lawyers never sleep, and I wanted you to be the first to know, on the record, that Strout has ruled May Shinn a suicide. Andy Fowler did not kill her. Nobody killed her. She killed herself."

"Department of redundancy department," Jeff said. "Suicide means she killed herself."

Hardy thanked him sincerely for the lesson in grammar. Dorothy come over and placed the wineglass on the table next to the phone. She sat next to him and rubbed his shoulders.

"Is this solid?" Jeff asked.

"Horse's mouth, the horse being Strout. I'm still at the morgue. I thought you'd like to know."

Jeff hesitated a moment—it meant he wasn't going to sleep for a few more hours. "I've already filed the first edition."

"Hey," Hardy said, "it's not even midnight. Don't you guys just stop the presses, rip out the front page?"

"Maybe if Arnold Mousenegger had four confirmed kills in one day."

Everybody knew about Arnold. "By the way," Hardy asked, "you still willing to dig a little if I can find a likely hole?"

"By the way, huh?"

"It just occurred to me."

"I'm sure it did. But yeah, I guess so. What is it?"

"I'm not sure yet. I'll let you know."

When Jeff hung up, he took a sip of his wine and kissed Dorothy. "Sorry," he said, "when news breaks . . ."

She kissed him back. "When you win the Pulitzer," she said, "I'll forgive you for this."

"Dismas, you've got to get some sleep." Frannie looked very pregnant, standing in his office doorway. "What time is it?"

Hardy stretched, afraid to check his watch. "Time is for wimps," he said.

She came behind his desk and put her arms around him, leaning into his back. "How will you be able to think tomorrow?"

"Tomorrow's Friday," he said.

"Good. Actually today is Friday. Does that mean anything?"

"It means tomorrow I can catch up on some sleep. Tonight I've got to catch up on these dailies"—he held up a thick pile of typed pages—"two days' worth. I took last night off, remember?" He rested his head back against her. "Remember?"

She messed his hair. "I remember very well. But still . . ."

"Andy Fowler didn't kill May," he said. "She killed herself, just like it looked."

Frannie straightened up. "Well, that's good, I guess."

"It's good, though why the idiot went to May's house—"

She shushed him. "Don't get going," she said. "Do your reading, come to bed. Now."

"A few more pages. Promise."

The first thing he had to do in the morning was call Ken Farris and get some answers. If he didn't like the answers he would call Jeff Elliot back, maybe even hire his own Emmet Turkel and do a number on a weekend in Taos last June.

He also had to remember the questions. They kept flitting in and out, and he found himself making a list while he tried to read the dailies from two days before, which now seemed like two months. With all that had happened since they'd testified, he barely remembered Tom Waddell and José Ochorio, much less what they'd said or why it might be relevant.

The yellow pad with his notes said: "Nash paying May? Records?" On another line, the words: "Specifics of O.N. changes? How was he different?" Then: "Breaking up? Why ring?"

The notion that May had been honest throughout put a very different light on everything that had happened. Hardy started another pad, intending to begin with the assumption that May and Owen had, in fact, loved each other. He would go through his first file folders— the ones he'd copied so long ago—over the weekend and review every word she'd said.

He wrote a few words on the May pad, then jumped to the dailies. He had to turn back to see who was talking, Tom or José. He reminded himself—Tom was the afternoon guy, the kid he'd met that first day. He grabbed the early folder, opening it to Glitsky's interrogations of them both, intending to start over, get a fresh grip on the facts. Again.

He hadn't slept in twenty hours. Now he was reading about José seeing May Shinn leaving the boat on Thursday, but Jose was the morning guy, so he couldn't have seen May on Thursday morning, it must have been Wednesday, which made no sense because May said she'd gone to the boat on Thursday, so Hardy—quick—went back to the pad with the May questions.

He looked back. Oh, it must have been Tom, after all, who'd said it. One of the folders was open to Tom.

Frannie was right—you couldn't work if you couldn't think, and Hardy's brain had just shifted to OFF. Enough. He couldn't keep it all straight.

56

What seemed like only seconds later, he was in bed, the telephone was ringing in his ear and it had gotten light.

"Wake you up?" Glitsky asked brightly.

Hardy looked at the clock: 6:10. "No," he said, "I was just sorting my socks. I like to get it done before the weekend."

"This is what time real working people get up," Glitsky said. "Besides, I thought you might have hung around downtown to find out what Strout decided."

"Strout decided May Shinn killed herself." He started to tell Abe about last night, a little of his talk with Freeman. Frannie came in with a cup of hot coffee, and Hardy, still talking, swung himself up to sit on the side of the bed. "So Freeman says they were really planning to get married," he concluded. "How does that grab you?"

Glitsky was silent a long moment. "Nash was wearing the ring, wasn't he?"

"Right there on his finger."

"And he wasn't wearing it the last time Farris saw him?"

"If Farris wasn't lying." Hardy went on to describe a few of the inconsistencies he'd come across in the last twelve hours. "So what do you think?"

"It's something to think about," Abe said, "especially if you're convinced Farris lied."

Hardy, fully awake, sipped his coffee. "This whole business has made me be not positive of anything, Abe. First, I'm not *positive* May was in love with Owen or vice-versa. The difference is, now I'm willing to consider it, and once I do that, it opens this other can of worms."

"Preconceptions are my favorite."

"Yeah, they're a good time." Hardy was still on his earlier problem.

"I guess the only thing I'm positive of is that, *if* May didn't lie, then I've got myself a passel of rethinking to do over the weekend."

"Well, you know," Abe said, "I'm busy, but I'm here."

It was an offer Hardy knew didn't come easy. But Abe had his own reasons, too. As had happened with Hardy months before, when Pullios took *his* case away, it rankled.

Hardy thought a minute. It had to be something Abe—the police—had access to and he didn't. "You could find out who took the coat," he said. "I mean, maybe they took something else. One of your guys . . ."

No response.

"Hey, Abe, you there?"

"Sure. I thought you were talking to Frannie."

"No, Abe, I was talking to you."

"You were talking to me about a *coat?*"

Hardy caught up to where Abe must be, then ran it down to him. Abe could check over the inventory on the *Eloise,* find if a member of the department had taken May's coat, apply a little pressure, find out if some evidence had been misplaced.

"Diz," Abe said, "our guys don't steal from crime scenes. I mean, if they do, we've got to go to Internal Affairs. But they don't."

Hardy drank more coffee. "It's someplace to look. See if something jumps out at you. Maybe, although of course I'd never suggest you do this, you could have an off-the-record chat with the guys who were there."

"Taking the inventory of what was on the *Eloise?*"

"Right."

"I could never do that."

"I know," Hardy said. "And as I said, I'd never ask."

Hardy had tried Farris at his home and gotten his answering machine. At his office he got another answering machine and left a message, hearing a couple of beeps as he did so. There was a concept, he thought. Recording the answering machine recording. Department of redundancy department indeed.

He felt like a receptionist. As soon as he'd finished leaving his message at Owen Industries for Farris to call him at home and leave a number where he could be reached, his telephone rang again.

"Grand Central Station," he said, picking up.

"What are we going to do about clothes?" It was Jane. She told

Hardy that they'd taken her father's suit for the lab tests, and what was he going to wear to court today? Hardy told her to swing by her father's house, get him a decent change and meet him downtown at eight-fifteen, enough time to change and try to determine where they would try to go today with what he figured would be by now the most hostile jury in the history of jurisprudence, angry at having been locked up themselves. Since Jeff Elliot's article had made the morning edition, like the rest of the world, Jane knew for certain now that her father hadn't killed May.

This time, when he hung up, Frannie poked her head in his office. "In keeping with your popularity this morning," she said, "your daughter would appreciate a short audience."

Hardy glanced at the pile on his desk—the two days' worth of dailies, the binders and notepads, the cassettes. He raised his eyes back to his wife. She was smiling but did not appear particularly amused.

The Beck appeared on her still wobbly legs next to Frannie. Seeing Hardy, she lit up like the Christmas tree, held out her hands, yelled "da da da" and started to run toward him, tripping on her own feet and pitching headlong into the front of his desk.

Hardy was up and around before Frannie could get to her. He picked her up, holding her against him, rubbing the red spot on her forehead where the bump would come up, kissing her. He hugged and rocked her. "It's okay, Beck. It's okay, honey. Daddy's here. Everything's all right."

He took the dailies with him. He'd have to find the time to review them, maybe during lunch, maybe while Andy was getting dressed. He and Jane had delivered the new suit upstairs, leaving it at the guard's desk with instructions for delivery, then he'd asked her if she could leave him to his reading until nine-fifteen, half a precious hour later.

He got settled in their little conference room, took the binders from his huge lawyer's briefcase and spread them out, intending to start where he'd left off last night, or with where he thought he'd been—Tom's testimony about May coming to the *Eloise* on Thursday.

But he couldn't find it.

After the first pass through every word Tom had said to him, Glitsky or the court, Hardy rubbed his hands over his eyes and wondered if he had finally lost his mind. Maybe he wasn't cut out for this kind of pressure. He ought to buy a boat and move to Mexico, start a fishing fleet.

Not by bread alone, he thought. No, sleep, too. Sleep ought to come into the picture. He wondered if Pullios was sleeping. Should he hire someone to call her every hour around the clock, level out the field?

He forced himself back. All right, it wasn't in Tom's testimony, where it should have been. How about José's?

Finally he found it at the end of Glitsky's initial interview with José. But that was wrong. It had to be wrong. Hardy reread the transcript, José answering when Glitsky asked if he remembered exactly what May had been doing when he'd seen her:

A: I don't know. She was out there, on the street. Walking back to her car, maybe, I don't know. I see her going away.

Q: And you're sure it was May?

A: Sí. It was her.

Q: Are you certain what day it was? It could be very important. [Pause.]

A: I think it was Thursday. Oh sure. It must have been. I remember, I got the note from Tom he'd locked the boat, which was Wednesday, right? So I go check it. It's still locked. Thursday, I'm sure, sí, Thursday.

Had May mentioned going back to the *Eloise* twice on Thursday? For some reason, because Tom and José had both seen May on Thursday, Hardy had been assuming it was the same sighting. But it couldn't have been. José was there in the morning and that's when he saw her. Later that same afternoon, Tom said that he saw her there again.

Hardy pulled another legal pad and wrote a heading on the top. "Questions for Freeman." Someone who had talked to May more frequently might be able to supply answers. Under his heading he wrote: "Number of visits—Thursday?"

It didn't even matter, or rather he couldn't figure why it might matter, but he was starting to believe that nothing here was irrelevant.

Hardy, walking next to Jane, got to the courtroom as Celine was coming up. As she had taken to doing, she looked right through him. Maybe that was the best way she could handle it. He thought probably it was best for him too. If they were going to be seeing each other on a daily basis it would be easier, better, if she avoided communication.

But here they were, face to face. He reached for her arm and stopped her.

She froze.

Hardy backed off a step and apologized. "I just wondered if you'd heard from Ken Farris lately."

She tried to gain control. "I spoke to him last night. I asked him about the Shinn woman's claim, now that she was dead." At Hardy's uncomprehending stare, she quickly, with annoyance, added, "The two million dollars."

Hardy had never had any indication that Celine gave a damn about the money. He was interested in Farris, wanted to locate him. "So he was home? He wasn't out of town?"

"I think I just said that."

"That's right, you did." She didn't want to talk to him and he wouldn't force it. He was, after all, defending the man on trial for her father's murder. "If you talk to him again would you tell him I'd like a word with him?"

She looked him over, glanced at Jane, came back to him. "Certainly," she said. "Now if you'll excuse me."

Jane, almost protectively, took Hardy's arm, holding him as they watched her walk away.

As she opened the courtroom doors, Celine turned back to look again, seeing Hardy, Jane's arm through his. From her perspective he realized that this attractive woman who had been at his side since the trial started was at least a new girlfriend. Celine knew it wasn't his wife, whom she'd seen twice at their house.

More reason for her to be hostile, he thought. Celine must believe he had lied to her, that he had decided to stop seeing her not because he was married but because he had found someone new.

When Fowler was led in, Jane squeezed Hardy's arm. "Oh my God."

He was wearing the clothes Jane had brought, but he looked more like a bum wearing a borrowed suit. Everything seemed to hang wrong. The tie wasn't tightened and his top button was undone. The pants, beltless, fell over his shoes. His hair didn't look like it had been washed or combed. His eyes were red-rimmed.

He patted his daughter's hand after the guard led him to the table. Smiling weakly, he told her and Hardy that he was all right, he would be fine. May's death had hit him hard, that was all.

Jane did her best to get him fixed up before they brought the jury in

—tie, top button, hair. When the disgruntled jury started to file in, she went back to the gallery, and everybody waited for the judge.

Chomorro's first order of business was to apologize to the jury for the need to sequester them. "At the end of the day yesterday we had an extraordinary set of circumstances develop and I determined that, having put all of you through as much of this as we've already done, we would try our best to keep those efforts from being wasted in a mistrial. In brief I will tell you that a central prosecution witness in this case—May Shinn—committed suicide yesterday."

This was not news to anyone in the gallery so there wasn't the expected buzz, but Hardy could see the effect it had on the jury. Each of them—some more obviously than others—scanned the defense table.

"At the time there was considerable media conjecture, as you might imagine, as to how this development related to the case we are hearing now, and my purpose in having you sequestered was to keep you from that exposure. I apologize for the need to have done that, but in my view it was essential to keep this trial on track.

"That stricture has now been eased and I will be letting you go to your homes for the weekend. However, let me admonish each and every one of you again, do not discuss this case or the evidence you are considering with anyone while we are still in this proceeding." Chomorro took a sip from a glass of water. "You are probably going to be unable to avoid hearing opinions about the defendant's relationship with Ms. Shinn. You may also hear that Mr. Fowler visited Ms. Shinn yesterday morning. I must make it clear to you, however, that these two events—Mr. Fowler's visit and Ms. Shinn's death—are causally unrelated and, for the purposes of this trial, not relevant.

"The coroner has issued an unequivocal verdict of death by suicide for Ms. Shinn. The police department has already determined from their investigations that there is no evidence linking Mr. Fowler to Ms. Shinn's death. In light of that I instruct you to disregard any rumors or opinions you might come across that purport to establish that link —there is no factual basis for it."

Chomorro stopped again. Hardy patted the back of Fowler's hand and got a wan smile in return.

The judge took another sip of water. "Now, moving along, counsel for both parties here have stipulated to the facts Ms. Shinn was to present in her testimony." Chomorro stopped reading and made eye contact with the jury. "You may want to take notes, as the facts you are about to hear may possibly not make the impression they would if you heard them recited by a witness on the stand." He adjusted his glasses and again looked down at the desk in front of him. "One, you are to take as an established fact that Ms. Shinn spoke to Mr. Fowler in March and told him that she had removed the murder weapon, People's Exhibit One, from her apartment and kept it stored in the desk next to Mr. Nash's bed aboard the *Eloise*."

From the reaction, the jury understood the significance of this fact. Even without ornamentation, it was a compelling point, but Hardy had decided there was nothing he could do about it. Those points were on the board; Hardy put them behind him. He had fought for the phrasing of the rest of the stipulation and sat forward in his chair waiting for it.

"Two," Chomorro continued, "it is also a fact that, during that same conversation, Mr. Fowler asked Ms. Shinn if she would consider reestablishing their relationship—Fowler's and Shinn's—if she stopped seeing Mr. Nash."

Hardy let out the breath he'd been holding. That was better than "if something happened to Mr. Nash."

Chomorro kept reading. "Ms. Shinn answered that she did not know and could not say. She did say she loved Owen Nash and that Mr. Fowler *had been* someone she felt very close to."

Hardy winced inwardly at the emphasis.

Pullios, speaking in a relaxed tone, was nonetheless teeing off on Gary Smythe. Fowler's broker and sometimes golf partner was clearly reluctant to give what he thought was testimony damaging to his friend. Ironically, this worked in Pullios's favor. If he were openly excoriating Fowler the jury might have reason to think there was a grudge against Andy, something personal he was paying back and enjoying. But to the contrary, every word was wrung out of him, which provided strong credibility to what he said.

Pullios was enjoying herself, as well she might, Hardy thought, after the events that had begun with Andy showing up late in the courtroom, May's death, the sequestering of the jury, Chomorro's admonition to the jury this morning and finally the stipulations about May's testimony.

Freeman may have told him the previous night that he thought he still could win it, and with the new questions he had for Farris and the

Marina guards Hardy was the most convinced he'd been of Fowler's innocence, but right now he knew he was losing the jury while Pullios had the floor.

"Mr. Smythe, I show you here the May sixteenth page from the desk calendar of the defendant, showing the initials 'O.N.' and the word '*Eloise.*'" She entered the page into evidence as People's Exhibit 18, then went back to the witness. "On or about May sixteenth, did you have a discussion with Mr. Fowler about Mr. Nash?"

"Yes." Smythe didn't like it.

"Tell us the substance of that discussion."

"Well, it wasn't much . . ."

Chomorro leaned over from the bench. "Try not to characterize what it was, Mr. Smythe. Just tell us what was said."

Smythe nodded, was silent for a minute, then tried again. "Judge Fowler and I have been active in fund-raising for a long time. I mentioned to him I had received an invitation to a charity event that Owen Nash was sponsoring aboard his boat and he asked me if I could get him an invitation. We could double-team him."

"And how did you respond?"

"I thought it was a good idea."

"And you got him an invitation?"

"Yes."

"So did both of you go?"

"No. As it turned out, neither of us did. I became sick and Andy decided not to."

"Did he say why he so decided, after going out of his way to get the invitation?"

Smythe looked at Fowler, then down at his lap. "He was having a hard time back then, he didn't feel like going out."

"A hard time? Personally?"

Hardy got up, objecting, and was sustained.

"So what happened to your fund-raising plans with Mr. Nash?"

"You have to understand, these things go on continuously. They're fluid in their timing. But I was a little disappointed that neither Andy —Judge Fowler—that neither of us had taken advantage of such an opportunity, and I said as much to Andy." He paused, looking again at his friend at the defense table. "Andy said he had other reasons to talk with Owen Nash anyway and he promised he'd get to him within a month."

Pullios hung on him for a beat, then turned to the jury. "He promised he'd get to him within a month," she repeated. Then, to Hardy, "Your witness."

"Mr. Smythe," Hardy said. "To your knowledge, did Mr. Fowler ever meet Mr. Nash face to face?"

"No."

"Did Mr. Fowler ever tell you he had made an appointment with Mr. Nash to discuss anything, aboard the *Eloise* or anywhere else?"

"No, he did not."

"Did you have occasion to talk to Mr. Fowler between May sixteenth and June twentieth, the day Owen Nash died?"

"Oh, yes. We talked almost every day."

"You talked almost every day. Do you recall if Mr. Nash's name came up between May sixteenth and June twentieth?"

"Well, the one discussion I told Ms. Pullios about."

"And after that?"

"No."

"No, you don't recall, or no, it didn't come up?"

"I don't recall it coming up."

"If he had made an appointment with Mr. Nash, don't you think he would have told you—?"

"Objection!" Pullios said. "Speculation."

It was sustained as Hardy had known it would be, but that was okay with him.

He continued. "I'd like to clarify this. On May sixteenth Mr. Fowler —despite having an invitation—did *not* go to the *Eloise?*"

"That's true."

"At no time during the following month did he mention either making an appointment with Owen Nash or going to the *Eloise?*"

"Right."

"So if I may summarize the *facts* elicited in your testimony, Mr. Smythe, to your personal knowledge, Mr. Fowler never met Mr. Nash and never boarded the *Eloise.*"

"That's correct. Not to my knowledge."

"Is it a *fact,* Mr. Smythe, that Mr. Fowler promised, as you said, that he would 'get to' Owen Nash within a month of May sixteenth?"

Smythe frowned. "Yes, he did say that."

"So the *fact* is that he told you he was going to do it. It is not a fact that he actually did it? In fact, you are aware of no evidence at all that he did do it. Isn't that true?"

"Yes, that's correct."

Pullios had narrowed down her witness list to David Freeman and Maury Carter, the bail bondsman. After lunch she was obviously going to close things up for the prosecution with the character issue, leaving the jury with the impression that Andy's consciousness of his guilt over the murder was the only possible explanation for his actions. Chomorro had made it clear he was going to allow all the testimony in this vein.

Hardy looked forward to having Freeman on the stand. Although his testimony would get into evidence the bare facts of Andy's unethical behavior, as a lifetime defense lawyer he would be instinctively opposed to Pullios. Hardy had, of course, talked with him several times during the two months he had been preparing for the trial and in those discussions Freeman had seemed genuinely distressed by his upcoming role as a prosecution witness.

But facts were facts—Andy Fowler had hired him to defend May Shinn. Freeman had told Andy flat out, in Fowler's own chambers, that in his opinion he had no option but to recuse himself from the case now that it had turned up in his courtroom. He had arranged with Maury Carter for the bail.

In Freeman's long career, he had told Hardy, he had never seen a judge do anything like what Andy Fowler had done. Of course, he wasn't going to put it like that on the stand, but Fowler's actions had been so incredible to Freeman that they beggared description.

However, last night he had also indicated to Hardy that Hardy hadn't lost the case yet. And that had been before they'd been certain May had killed herself, when things had looked even worse. Was he perhaps planning some emphasis in his testimony to make it less damning than it seemed on the face of it?

Chomorro decided that Andy Fowler could be readmitted to bail, and now the subdued ex-judge and his daughter made clear they did not want to be with his attorney and went off to lunch by themselves. Which at the moment suited Hardy just fine.

57

"Did you get a chronology of May for the whole week?" Hardy asked Freeman.

"Of course."

Hardy and Freeman were talking in the hallway. It would not do for the two of them to spend an hour lunching at Lou's just before Freeman went on the stand for Pullios, so Hardy took advantage of what camouflage there might be out in the open halls.

"Do you remember her going to the *Eloise*?"

Freeman looked like he had slept in the clothes he had worn at the morgue the previous night. "Yes. Not a smart move."

"Why did she tell you she did it?"

"They're not going to ask me about this, you know. Pullios is going to want to know about Judge Fowler hiring me, not about May Shinn."

Hardy didn't want to push, but neither did he intend to back down. "It's for me, not Pullios. I want to know about May Shinn," he said.

"All right, but I'm not sure why it matters when, if or why May Shinn went to the *Eloise*. I'll tell you what she told me, okay?" His eyes searched the hallway, perhaps looking for members of the prosecution team, then he came back to Hardy. "She read about herself, linked to Nash, in the *Chronicle* on Thursday morning—the first day it was speculated that the mystery hand might be Nash's. She was afraid that they'd try to find something to tie her to him—a very justified fear, as it turned out. She knew her gun was on the *Eloise* and she decided she'd come down and remove it before the investigation heated up. But when she went there it was the middle of the day and she realized she'd be recognized, even worse, somehow be connected to what had happened. So she would come back later when it was dark or no one was around, but by that time the police had closed it off."

414

Hardy stood with his arms folded, filtering, thinking. "How did she know she could get aboard? Did she have a key?"

"Good." It was as though Freeman had been through all of this before, was checking Hardy on his thought processes. "No. She did not have a key. That was one of the other things that stopped her. Aside from the recognition factor."

"We're assuming everything she said was true, now, isn't that right?"

"I believed her. Two things. One, it wasn't unknown for Nash to forget to lock up. And two, if he'd been killed on board—which in fact he had been—perhaps the killer didn't have a key or forgot to lock up. May thought that was likely."

More than that, Hardy thought, it was true. The *Eloise* had not been locked on Wednesday night when he had gotten to it. "All right," Hardy said, "so here is my question. Did May tell you she *also* came down early Thursday morning?"

"No. Why would she have done that?"

"Same reasons."

"Well, then why would she have come back?"

"I don't know."

Freeman paced away a step or two. He recalled something else. "How early? That whole week she was a wreck. Once she finally got to sleep, she sometimes slept until noon."

Hardy shook his head. "No, it was way before then. Right about when the morning guard was coming on. Say seven-thirty."

"He said he saw somebody?"

"More than that, he said he saw *May*."

"On the *Eloise*?"

"No. Walking away."

"Close up? Positive ID?"

"Neither." Hardy, saying it, realized what it meant.

Freeman said, "Well, to answer your original question, May told me she went down to the *Eloise* one time, Thursday afternoon, to see if she could get the gun."

A thought occurred to Hardy. "Maybe she knew Fowler's prints were on it and she was going down to protect him."

Freeman shook his head impatiently. "She wasn't protecting Fowler. He didn't matter to her anymore, much as it might pain him to hear it . . . I wouldn't bring up that particular point on cross . . . You got something here, don't you?"

"If I do, I don't know what it is. Yesterday, when I hadn't believed May, everything seemed tight. Today"—Hardy lifted his shoulders—"I don't know. The board tilted and I've got a new angle and now some of the pieces don't fit. I'm trying to decide which angle's the right one."

"The right one is the one that gets your client off."

"That May wasn't lying?"

But to Freeman, that had already been asked and answered. He moved closer to Hardy. "In any event, I hope you've written your eleven-eighteen?"

He was referring to Section 1118.1 of the California Penal Code, a motion for directed verdict of acquittal, by which the judge directed the jury to return a verdict to acquit. True, this section was almost automatically invoked by defense attorneys after the prosecution rested in every trial, but especially in cases such as this one in which the evidence might be deemed insufficient to sustain a conviction. Just as automatically, the motion was nearly always denied, but Freeman was making it clear that in this case he believed it had a chance.

Hardy said he was filing the motion but didn't hold out much hope for it.

Neither did Freeman, it seemed. "Chomorro doesn't have the experience. This is his first big trial, he's *got* to leave it for the jury." Having said that, he raised his hands palms up. "But the law is a wonderful thing, and you just never know."

Hardy had another twenty minutes before court reconvened. He went upstairs to the fourth floor, found Glitsky alone in the Homicide room chewing on his damned ice and hunched over his desk reading. He looked up now. "You were wrong," he said.

Hardy pulled a chair up against his desk. "I'm listening."

"There was no coat." Glitsky shoved the paper he was reading at Hardy. "Check it out. Anybody comes in while you're looking, be smart, right? This sheet here," he said, putting a finger on it, "is the inventory—down to the rubberbands in the desk, Diz, it's complete—of the master suite on the *Eloise*. This other one is the list Struler got from May, all of her stuff. What she wanted returned to her in exchange for testifying."

"Why didn't they just subpoena her?"

Glitsky chewed some ice, swallowed. "I guess they thought this would make her more agreeable." He shook his head. "But guess what?"

Hardy was scanning the list. "Yeah?" he said absently.

"Hey, you know this happens all the time. You get somebody suing the City and thinks they can get an extra fur coat or something out of the deal. Put it on the list, say we stole it, it was there. But"—he hit the sheet again—"surprise. It wasn't there. It's why we make our Day One inventories."

This was going backward again. Hardy wasn't going to entertain it. "May didn't lie, Abe, that's where we're at." He understood Glitsky being upset with May Shinn. She had, after all, named him personally in her suit for false arrest. And hadn't she lied to him about not going to Japan? Hadn't that been what moved him to arrest her?

"Okay, all of the above," Hardy said, "but she thought this coat was there. She called David Freeman about it, mentioned it to Fowler when he came by. She jumped all over Struler."

"Wouldn't you?"

"Wouldn't I what?"

"If you had a scam like this, wouldn't you play it up?"

Hardy couldn't agree. He was going to run with the idea of May telling the truth until he got to a wall. This might not make sense in the face of it, but it wasn't yet a wall. Still, Glitsky was on his side and he wanted to keep him there. "Maybe," he conceded, "but either way this helps—"

"It doesn't help me. Everywhere I look there's more of nothing. You find anything about Farris?"

"No. I got a call in. Speaking of which . . ." He grabbed Glitsky's telephone and pushed some buttons. "Lunch break," he told Frannie. "Any calls?" When he hung up he shook his head. "Nothing."

"He out of town or what?"

Hardy shrugged. "Probably just busy. Plus I'm not on his side anymore, remember? I'm defending Nash's killer. Now if you wanted—"

"No way. I've already done him up and down. If you get a line on some physical evidence I'll see what I can do, but . . . Now you've got Shinn telling the truth and Farris lying for no apparent reason, neither of which I think I buy. I *know* Farris didn't kill Nash. He was in Taos. You're barking up the wrong tree."

Hardy didn't argue—he knew better than to push any further. "All right, maybe he'll call me back. If something pops, though, I'm going to call you."

Glitsky finished chewing his ice, loudly. "That knowledge gives meaning to my life," he said.

"Can I have these?" Hardy asked, gathering the inventories.

"Not only can you have them," Glitsky replied, "you must have them. I had to wait all morning for the office to empty out so I could make you some copies."

Hardy tapped his palm against Glitsky's cheek. "You're such a sweet guy," he said. "Don't ever change."

Glitsky growled. "I wasn't planning to."

Fowler and Jane were sitting at the defense table when Hardy entered the courtroom at one-twenty. Celine was already at her spot on the aisle in the second bench. He found himself slowing down coming abreast of her, then forced himself along through the swinging doors.

Fowler didn't look much better. Hardy pulled up his chair and placed a hand on his back. "You holding up?" Jane, on the other side of her father, gave Hardy a worried look. He forced a show of enthusiasm. "We've got a couple of interesting developments."

"I'm a fool, Diz, been one all along." Physically, Andy's eyes looked better. The redness had gone down, the black bagginess under them had receded. But the expression in them—or rather the lack of it—was almost more unsettling. "She never cared a damn at all, did she?"

Why beat around about it? "No," Hardy said. "No, I guess she didn't, Andy." Jane frosted him from across her father but he ignored it. "Now how about you stop having to suffer for what she's done to you? She's gone. Didn't you tell Jane once you just had to treat it as though it was a friend that died? Well, now that's what it is."

"She lied to me."

Hardy was getting tired of the explanation—to himself as well—that May lied as the answer for everything. "Did she? Or did you lie to yourself?"

Jane fairly hissed at him. "Dismas!"

"You know, Andy," he pressed on, "maybe you just needed more, that was all. She gave you what you were paying for, which was a fantasy. And you're a guy, Judge, who can make things happen, maybe even make your fantasy come true. You weren't like the other guys, the lesser types whose lives passed through your hands every day—"

"Dismas, *stop it.*"

Jane said it loud enough this time that several jury members looked their way. Hardy saw the reaction and gave a controlled nod in that direction. He lowered his voice. "The fantasy's over, Judge. You're reduced to being a mortal. I can't say I blame you for crying over it, but at least it's a real place to start."

Fowler's eyes had gotten something back in them—anger or hatred or both. Either, Hardy thought, was better than nothing.

"You're a big help, Dismas, thanks a lot." At least Jane had modulated her voice.

Fowler straightened up. "Don't tell me I don't want her back. You don't know . . ."

Hardy nodded. "You're right, Andy, I don't know. What I do know. is that you never had a chance to get her back because you never had her in the first place."

"What do you suppose this is doing, Dismas?" Jane asked.

"It's all right, hon," Fowler told her.

Hardy kept at it. "Damn straight, it's all right. You ask what it's doing, Jane? I don't know. Maybe I'm getting a little tired of wading through all of this while the ol' judge here sails on overhead." He spoke to his client. "Andy, I'm sorry, but you're not some tragic hero. I can't just sit here and watch you waste away over some fairy tale you've concocted that's pretty well destroyed everything you've worked for." Hardy softened his voice, put his hand on Fowler's back. "The woman's *dead*, Andy. She's not coming back. It's time to wake up and this is your wake-up call."

David Freeman, famed defense counsel, was the centerpiece of the prosecution's case, and Elizabeth Pullios knew it. Thus far they had established beyond any doubt, reasonable or otherwise, that Andy Fowler had been devastated by May, had hired a private investigator to find out why she had stopped seeing him, had found out it was because she had fallen in love with Owen Nash, or acted like she did, and had kept a surveillance on the movements of Nash for the next several months, until the man's murder.

To nearly everyone he knew—except for Gary Smythe—he had told less than the truth, had indeed lied, about Owen Nash. He knew the location of the gun on the boat and his fingerprints were on it. He was an expert sailor in his own right and could easily have taken the *Eloise* in and tied it up after dark, even in rough water.

All that established, however, Hardy still thought the jury would have a difficult time bringing in a murder verdict, especially after Fowler testified for himself (assuming Hardy could move him to do so). So far everything the judge had done—a couple of white lies, a more or less natural curiosity to understand more about why a lover, as perceived by him, had tired of him, a plausible explanation of how fingerprints came to be on the murder weapon—could be explained, Hardy hoped, by the overriding fact that he had merely wanted to keep an illicit and embarrassing relationship secret.

Up to now, Hardy believed, none of this showed sufficient consciousness-of-guilt to prove anything to secure a conviction. When David Freeman took the stand, however, all that would change. In spite of Freeman's private support, it was going to get ugly, Hardy thought. He was prepared to object to every question if need be, and if the jury didn't like him for it, so be it. The bare facts of Freeman's testimony would be damning enough—he at least wanted to try to contain any interpretation of them.

Pullios, playing affable and deferential, began to walk Freeman gently through some establishing testimony, then commenced zeroing in on the events of the previous June.

"Mr. Freeman, do you know the defendant?"

"Yes."

"For how long?"

"I've known the judge for many years." He didn't so much as glance at Hardy.

"Would you say you were friends?"

"We've had a courteous professional relationship. We don't see each other socially. Sort of like me and you."

He smiled. She smiled. The jury seemed to like it.

"Last June, did your relationship change?"

"Yes."

"How?"

"The judge hired me."

Chomorro: "Mr. Freeman, we're all aware that the defendant was a judge in this court. For accuracy's sake, please refer to Mr. Fowler either by his name or as the defendant."

Freeman said it was a habit, he was sorry.

"And what did Mr. Fowler hire you to do?"

"To defend May Shinn, who had been charged with killing Owen Nash—"

Chomorro's gavel came down with a crash. Hardy suppressed a smile. Nice, Dave, he thought.

"Mr. Freeman, restrict your answers to the questions asked."

"I'm sorry, Your Honor, I thought that was what was asked."

But there it was in the record. Pullios could not very well object since she had asked the question. There was nothing to do but press on. "Mr. Fowler hired you to defend May Shinn, who, as you say, was charged with murder?"

"That's right."

"Were you surprised by his request?"

"Not at first."

This was a wrinkle Hardy had not expected. In his deposition Freeman had said he was stunned by it. Now he was not surprised "at first."

Pullios went with it. "Why not 'at first'?"

"Sometimes the court will want to check out a couple of defense firms before giving a criminal assignment. See if they might be overloaded, that type of thing."

"But that wasn't the case here?"

"No."

"What was the case here?"

"Well, the judge—excuse me, the defendant—wanted to hire me as a private person."

"To defend Ms. Shinn?"

"Yes."

"And was that unusual?"

"I'd say, yes, it was."

"Was there anything else unusual about the arrangements?"

Hardy stood at his table. "Objection. Overbroad."

"Sustained."

Pullios tried again. "Was Ms. Shinn to know about this arrangement?"

Hardy was up again. Conclusion from the witness and hearsay. Pullios might be getting it out, but it was going to be pulling teeth. She smiled tightly. "Can you describe to us the conversation you had with the defendant regarding her defense?"

"Up to a point, yes," Freeman said. He spoke directly to the jury. "After I accepted the job, of course Mr. Fowler became my client and our conversations were privileged."

Freeman wasn't giving up a thing. Hardy had been planning on drawing him out on cross, going into the false arrest of May Shinn, all of that. But it seemed Freeman was doing his work for him.

Pullios, however, could read the signs, too—this one said "Ambush

Ahead." Freeman was, in prosecutor's lingo, going sideways. Witnesses did it all the time. Pullios had seen it before. She got a little less friendly.

"Mr. Freeman, is it a fact that Mr. Fowler asked you to keep your relationship with him a secret from Ms. Shinn?"

"Yes."

"Is it a fact that bail of five hundred thousand dollars was set for Ms. Shinn?"

The facts continued to come out: that Fowler had put up his apartment building as collateral; that Ms. Shinn was indicted by the grand jury for murder, putting the case in Superior Court; that Shinn's trial was assigned to Fowler's courtroom . . .

Now Pullios was on a roll and there wasn't much to do about it. "Now, Mr. Freeman, knowing as you did the relationship between the defendant and Ms. Shinn, what was your reaction to the assignment of Ms. Shinn's trial to Mr. Fowler's courtroom?"

Freeman thought about his answer for a moment. "Well, I had mixed feelings. I thought it would be good for my client if the trial went on in Mr. Fowler's court, but I thought there was no chance that would happen."

An answer Pullios wanted. "You expected Mr. Fowler to recuse himself?"

Hardy objected, citing relevance. "Who cares what Mr. Freeman expected?"

Chomorro thought, I do, and said, "Overruled."

Pullios repeated the questions, asking whether Freeman expected Fowler to recuse himself.

"Of course."

"But he did not?"

Freeman gave it a second, but there was really no avoiding it. "No, he did not."

Hardy thought he could make a few points.

"Mr. Freeman, Ms. Shinn was charged with killing Owen Nash, the same individual the defendant is now charged with killing?"

"That's right."

"Before you had agreed to defend Ms. Shinn on that charge, and hence before you had established an attorney-client relationship with Mr. Fowler, did the defendant tell you why he wanted you to defend Ms. Shinn?"

"He wanted an attorney he knew would present a strong defense."

"Did he say Ms. Shinn would need a strong defense?"

"Yes."

"In your opinion, Mr. Freeman, did Mr. Fowler think Ms. Shinn was guilty?"

"Objection!"

Hardy rephrased it. "Did Mr. Fowler tell you he thought Ms. Shinn was guilty of murdering Owen Nash?"

"Yes, he did. He thought so."

"You have won acquittals in several murder cases, have you not, Mr. Freeman?"

"Objection, Your Honor. This isn't relevant here."

Hardy was matter-of-fact. "Your Honor, the prosecution went over Mr. Freeman's credentials at the beginning of his testimony. I want the jury to be aware of Mr. Freeman's reputation not just as a defense attorney but as an *excellent* defense attorney."

"All right." Chomorro, as he often did later in the day, was getting surly. "But let's move it along." He had the recorder reread the question, and Freeman answered that yes, he had won several acquittals.

"In fact, wasn't it through your efforts that the charges against Ms. Shinn were dropped?"

"Yes. Largely."

"Now let's see if we can get this straight. Mr. Fowler, knowing your reputation, hired you to represent Ms. Shinn, who was subsequently cleared of the murder charge through your efforts?"

"Yes, true."

"And that reopened the investigation, leading to Mr. Fowler's own arrest for the same crime?"

"Objection," Pullios said. "Calls for a conclusion."

"What's your question, Mr. Hardy?"

Hardy thought he had made his point by inference, at least. Would a man who was guilty of murder hire an attorney whose past record of successes made it likely he could get the case reopened? The most reasonable explanation for hiring Freeman was that, in fact, Fowler did believe May had been guilty. And, of course, if he thought that, then *he* wasn't.

"I'll leave it, Your Honor," he said. Turning back to Freeman, Hardy asked if, at the time he had been hired, he thought there was any chance that May Shinn's trial would go to Fowler's courtroom.

"No, none at all. If I had thought there was at that time, I would not have taken it. But there wasn't."

"Why not?"

"Well, she was in Department Twenty-two. There were seven trial judges available and I was sure that if Andy got the case he'd recuse himself."

Pullios was up like a shot, but these were relevant facts and Hardy was able to get Freeman to tell most of the story—how judges were picked for trials, the circuitous route May's proceedings took before it came before Fowler. It could not have been foreseen . . .

Finally, Hardy came to the end of it. "On the day charges were dropped against Ms. Shinn, how many days had she already been on trial? I mean, for example, had you picked a jury? Had the prosecution begun its case?"

"No. None of that."

"Were you aware of any other developments in that case on that day?"

"Yes. Judge Fowler resigned."

"Do you mean he recused himself from the case?"

"I mean he resigned as a judge, he quit the bench."

"And this was how long after the trial had come to his courtroom?"

"One day."

Hardy turned to the jury. "One day," he repeated.

Pullios did not have any redirect on Freeman, and neither did she call Maury Carter, the bail bondsman, since facts relating to the bail had been substantially nailed down in Freeman's testimony. Instead, after Hardy had finished with Freeman, the prosecution rested.

Hardy had to feel better. Freeman's testimony, which he had feared would be disastrous, had not been anything of the sort, it seemed. The jury knew the worst of what Andy had done, but at least, Hardy felt, they had gotten it in the least damaging light possible.

During the recess Hardy argued his 1118.1 motion in Chomorro's chambers. The judge, to his surprise, seemed to be giving him his full attention and proved it by telling counsel he was going to take the weekend to consider the motion. He would render his decision on the motion for a directed verdict of acquittal on Monday. Meanwhile, however, Hardy should be prepared to begin calling his defense witnesses.

His client had not said a word to him the entire afternoon. When the judge came out and adjourned court for the week, he only muttered, "See you Monday," and went back to join his daughter.

Hardy gathered his papers.

58

At ten past five it was already dark as he went out toward the parking lot. A storm was coming in and a wind had risen, steady and cold, Alaska written all over it.

Hardy put down his heavy briefcase and stood by the entrance to the morgue, looking through a hole in the plywood into the construction site where the new jail was slowly rising. A steady trickle of workers getting off passed behind him, and he envied their snatches of conversation, of laughter, plans for the night, for the weekend. He turned up his suit collar against the wind, feeling alone and desolate.

"Hey, Hardy! Dismas! Is that you? Knocking off early? Glad I caught up with you." It was Ken Farris, walking against the tide flowing from the building. "I got your messages but couldn't get away, thought I'd try to catch you after court. You adjourned already? Is it over?"

What Farris had said was true—he normally could have expected to find Hardy in the courtroom at this time, but his arrival just now struck Hardy as a little convenient. He could just have called back. Hardy said as much.

"Ah, you know the office. You get to the end of the week, any excuse to get out early. This is on my way home anyway. So how's it going? What can I do for you? This about May Shinn?"

Hardy looked at him levelly. "I guess it's about a lot if you've got some time. You feel like a drink?"

Farris seemed to rein himself in. "Sure," he said. "Something wrong?"

"Well, let's say all's not right."

They walked back through the Hall and crossed the street. Lou's, crowded and noisy, was hung with yards of red and green tinsel, lit by Christmas bulbs. With all the seats taken, they stood at the bar. Hardy called for a Bass Ale, Farris ordered a Beefeater martini extra dry. Lou, behind the bar, caught Hardy's eye. "He new?"

Hardy introduced them, and Lou said, dryly, that all their martinis were extra dry—no vermouth. Farris said he'd take whatever Lou poured, which was the right answer—he got some ice, several ounces of gin, a couple of olives.

"Hell of a place," he said, taking it in. He clinked his glass against Hardy's. "Okay, what's happening?"

"The prosecution's rested. I start calling my defense witnesses on Monday."

"You're not asking me to be a witness for Andy Fowler, are you?"

"No. Why do you ask? You think he killed Owen?"

Farris sipped his gin. "Tell you the truth, I wouldn't be surprised if he killed May too. I don't care what they say."

"No, Mr. Farris. May killed herself. If they had found anything that connected to Fowler he'd have been long since charged with it. And they were looking." But Hardy didn't like it, because if Farris still genuinely entertained the thought, maybe the jury did, too, in spite of Chomorro's instructions. He'd better not forget that. "About May . . . when we first talked, you told me Owen had been paying her?"

"Right. He paid all of them. So?"

"Do you know for a fact that he was paying her? Did he specifically tell you he was?" Farris appeared to be giving it thought. Hardy continued, "You told me Nash had changed the last few months. I was wondering, might that have been one of the changes."

Farris seemed somewhere inside himself. Finally he said, scarcely loud enough to be heard over the din, "Owen went with call girls, prostitutes, call them what you will. It was just his nature. It was who he was. And that's who, what, May was."

"Well, maybe not," Hardy said, "that's what I'm getting at."

Which seemed to anger Farris. "Goddamn it, that's never been in dispute."

Hardy sipped his ale. "It's in dispute now. May's lawyer—you've met him, Freeman—he says the two of them actually loved each other."

Farris was shaking his head. "That's got to be bullshit."

"Why?"

"Because he just didn't, that's why. This is Owen Nash we're talking about. He wasn't going to go marry some whore. Why are you digging all this up?"

"Because I don't believe Andy Fowler killed anybody. Why is it so upsetting to you if Owen loved May Shinn?"

"Because I knew Owen and that wasn't him!"

Hardy stepped back, taking a beat. Both men went to their drinks. Hardy leaned forward again. "Listen, Ken, you've just spent six months contesting the validity of the will. It's no wonder you're committed to your position. I'm just asking if you've got any *proof* Owen was paying her—his own admission to you, canceled checks, whatever. You're the one who'd told me he'd changed with her. Was a for-hire deal with a whore going to change him? Wasn't he wearing her ring when he was shot?"

"We don't know that. Someone could have put it on him."

"Why?"

"I don't know."

Hardy kept at it. "It doesn't make any sense. He put it on himself. He was planning on telling you sometime, possibly soon. I think he had decided to marry the woman, just as she had said."

Ken Farris was down to an olive. "Jesus," he said, "I just . . ." He shook his head.

"You just assumed, didn't you?"

"Why wouldn't he have told me? He told me everything."

"Maybe he didn't know. Maybe it snuck up on him. But it's all pretty consistent if you put it together—we've got the change in behavior, the settling down, leaving her number with you for emergencies, the will, the ring. If you buy the premise, then May wasn't lying about anything. Which is why I called you. I needed to verify that."

Lou, unasked, had slid another round under their elbows. Farris didn't seem to notice. He picked up the new drink and knocked off a third of it. "There were no *checks*," he said finally. "Of course, cash . . . You know, I don't think we ever talked about whether he paid her—it never came up." A retreat? A cover?

The bad news, Hardy thought, was that Farris maybe, probably hadn't been lying . . . maybe he'd honestly believed an untruth and passed it along as a fact, which wasn't nearly the same thing, and it left a hole where there had at least been the chance of another suspect besides Hardy's client.

Large drops of rain fell in sheets, splattering on his windshield. He found a parking place half a block down the street from his house and turned off the engine, thinking he would wait for a break in the storm.

Could this be the beginning of the end of the drought? Now in its seventh year, and Hardy knew a lot of people in San Francisco who believed it would never end, that this was the new California of the greenhouse effect, the precursor of a future world of ozone depletion, skin cancers, AIDS and acid rain.

This cleansing Pacific downpour soothed him somehow. He sat back in his seat, eyes closed, listening to the steady tattoo of the drops on the roof.

There was still an unanswered question with May—the coat—maybe it would lead somewhere. And then on Monday Chomorro *might* decide to grant his 1118.1 motion and that would be the end of the trial, and he felt sure, the end of his relationship with both his ex-wife and her father. He wasn't sure how he felt about that.

Whatever, if he got Andy off on the murder charge, which is what he'd been hired to do, he'd take whatever fallout developed.

But he also knew the trial coming to an early end was a very long shot. And it still nagged that the truth, if there was a truth, continued to elude him. He could get Andy off, he could flap his arms and fly to the moon if he wanted, but until he found out who did put two bullets into Owen Nash, he knew he wouldn't feel he'd accomplished what he'd really set out to do.

If nothing else, he would still have to live with the fact that he was only ninety-seven-percent certain that Nash's killer had not been the man he had labored to set free.

59

It had rained hard all night, awakening Hardy and Frannie several times with peals of thunder, a sound almost unknown in San Francisco. Sometime in the middle of the night Hardy got up to Rebecca's cries and brought her to sleep between them in their bed.

Up alone at dawn, he put on his running shoes, shorts and a t-shirt, and headed out around the park in the rain. After a shower he made himself a breakfast of hash, eggs, toast and coffee, and ate reading the paper, occasionally looking up into the gray clouds through the kitchen skylight.

Jeff Elliot was not featured on the front page or anywhere else. The day-to-day workings of the trial were not exactly grist for the media mill. He knew Jeff would be around when the jury retired to deliberate, maybe sit in for the closing arguments, but that the mundane world of the courtroom was no match for the exploits of Arnold Mousenegger. Journalistic priorities. Mice over men.

After breakfast he leaned over to kiss his wife and baby. He wore jeans and work boots, his old Greek sailor's hat over a heavy white fisherman's sweater. He hoped that this day, of all days, José decided to get to work on time.

It was still steadily pouring as Hardy turned into the Marina parking lot on a day possibly much like the one on which Owen Nash had gone out for the last time. There were only two other cars in the lot; Hardy got within fifty feet of the guard station, opened his car door, grabbed his smaller briefcase and sprinted.

José, at the desk beyond the counter, put down his issue of Sports Illustrated and stood up. He recognized Hardy right away.

"I bet you're getting a little bored with this, but I've got a couple of questions for you," Hardy said. He took off his hat and put it on the counter next to the briefcase.

José seemed to be an easygoing guy. It was a miserable morning with no one else around. He was happy with the interruption.

"I was going over your statement yesterday, José." Hardy snapped open the briefcase and was getting out some of the paper. "And there's something I didn't understand."

José nodded, leaning over the counter, looking at the inch-thick pile of type. He grinned. "I say all that?"

"Well, between your interview with Sergeant Glitsky and your trial testimony—"

"My girlfriend, she say I'm too quiet, I never talk. I should show her these."

"I could make you a copy if you want," Hardy said. "Meanwhile, let me ask you, see here, when you were first talking to Sergeant Glitsky . . ." Hardy opened the transcript to the page he had highlighted and turned it around for José to see. "At the end of the interview you said you'd seen May Shinn here at the Marina on Thursday morning."

José was frowning, looking at the page. "Sí," he said uncertainly. "Tom and me, we talk about that after we see she kill herself, right?"

"What did you talk about?"

"Well, you know after the trial, we talk about that day."

"The Thursday?"

"Sí. Only I see her in the morning, you know?"

"I know, José. That's what I'm trying to figure out." He pointed down to the transcript. "You see this part? Where you say she was going away from you?"

"Sí."

"So how could you be sure it was May?"

"Well, I see her a lot. También, that thing she wear on her head, and that coat. Nobody else with a coat like that one."

Hardy tried to keep his voice flat. "What was the thing she was wearing on her head?"

"I don't know how you call it. Like a fur hat."

"And the coat?"

"Well, you know, the coat like some," he searched for the word, "like some painting. Muchos colores."

"Okay, José, let me ask you this, and I've got all day if you want to think about it—did you at any time see May's face?"

"No. I don't have to think. She was, like, way down there." He gestured down the street. "She don't have a car, I think. Least I never see her drive a car. She always before come down with Señor Nash."

"She never came down alone, maybe a little early to wait for him, let herself aboard?"

He shook his head. "No. Not that I remember. Maybe Tom, he know something else."

"Maybe." Hardy, trying different combinations, had to look back down at the questions he had prepared. This time he did not want to leave anything out. "José, do you remember what time you got into work that morning, that Thursday?"

José straightened up nervously. "The shift begin at six-thirty."

Hardy gave him a conspiratorial look. "I know that, José. But I'm talking about that specific day. I won't tell a soul, I promise." He was hoping he wouldn't have to make José himself tell the world on the stand, but he wasn't promising that.

José shrugged. "I think a little late. Tom talk to me about it that day, I remember. Somebody come by the day before, asking about it, too. So I stop after that."

Hardy smiled at him. "You were safe," he said, "that was me. But that day . . . ?"

José grinned back. "Pretty bad," he said. "Maybe eight, eight-thirty." The rain pounded at the glass all around them. "But I really stop being *tarde* back then, you know? This morning, even, no one going out, I'm here."

He was close to Green's, a place he favored for lunch for their breads and coffees and the sculpted wood and the view of the water. He had never been there this early in the morning, and they weren't yet open for business, but they took pity on him standing out in the rain and let him sit at the bar and have a cup of coffee.

Okay, it wasn't certain that it hadn't been May. Remember that. Keeping up about the trial on her own, May could have realized the implications of José's testimony—she'd been seen in her coat—and then gotten rid of it, trying to scam with Struler to cover where it had gone.

He didn't think so.

What he thought, was at least beginning to consider, to realize it had been perking for a while, was that someone else—the person who had really killed Owen Nash—had returned to the *Eloise* on Thursday morning. Maybe she—it had to be a she now, even in May's coat José wasn't going to mistake Andy Fowler for May Shinn—maybe she had left something incriminating on the boat, and seeing the *Eloise* in the morning paper, realized she'd have to work fast. Helped by José's tardiness, she had gone aboard, taken out whatever it was, stolen May's coat so that in case she was seen (which she was), identification would be confusing.

But wait . . . she couldn't have gotten aboard. Tom had locked up the boat in Hardy's presence the night before, and José had rechecked it on his shift the next day.

Unless, of course, the person had a key to the *Eloise*.

Or how about if she wasn't going to remove something from the boat but was going to put something back in? For the twentieth time, Hardy tried to picture that drawer in the rolltop desk—the drawer where Abe had discovered the murder weapon, the same drawer he'd looked in on Wednesday night and seen nothing.

Maybe, as they were so fond of saying about baseball, it was a game of inches.

"This is ridiculous."

Abe hadn't been thrilled to get his call before nine on a Saturday morning, but Hardy sweetly reminded him of his own call at six the day before. Besides, Glitsky was a cop first, and he was dressed and going out for another interview anyway. He might grumble, but Hardy knew that the murder of Owen Nash would get Abe's attention until it was solved. As it was, Abe made it down to the Marina in less than a half hour and he, Hardy and José walked together in the steady rain out to where the *Eloise* still rested at her slip.

"I know it is." Hardy agreed, but the implications of his what-ifs were staggering. He wouldn't have to consider them—in fact he couldn't—if he didn't get this fact nailed down.

The police tape had been removed, and José unlocked the door and stepped aside so Glitsky could lead the way down.

The generators were off. It was dark inside. The rain thrummed above as the three of them stood a minute, letting their eyes adjust.

"Looks about the same," Hardy said.

Glitsky wasn't here to take inventory. "All right, what?"

Hardy went forward through the galley, the short hall, the master suite. The police might have removed May's belongings but the room seemed eerily the same—the exercycle, desks, as though someone still lived aboard. Glitsky pulled back one of the curtains to let in a little more light, and Hardy walked to the rolltop desk. He opened the drawer.

"Okay, humor me, would you? Take your time, close your eyes and visualize it. Show me exactly where you found the gun."

Glitsky came around the bed and looked in at the open drawer. He took a small knife out of his pocket—"This is about the same length, right?"—and placed it on top of the maps that were still in the drawer, back maybe three inches from the front.

Hardy nodded. "Did you jerk the drawer open?" Which would have caused the gun to slip forward or backward on the maps.

Glitsky was patient. "No. I was my usual wonderful methodical self. You want to tell me what this is about?"

Hardy looked down again at the knife in the drawer, doing his own visualizing, making sure. He picked up the knife and gave it back to Glitsky. "The gun wasn't there Wednesday night, Abe. I looked in this drawer."

A new onslaught of rain raked the boat. In the room, it sounded like they were inside a tin drum. Hardy stood there in his hat and pea coat; Glitsky and José wore slickers. All the men had their hands in their pockets. The boat bumped the slip.

Glitsky thought on it. "So May came and brought the gun back Thursday morning."

"Making her the stupidest person in America."

"Maybe not. Maybe she saw her name in the paper and didn't want it in her house."

"The gun hadn't been in her house. It was here, remember. Besides, she didn't have a key."

"You know, that's probably worth double-checking at her apartment." Abe wrote himself a note. "Let me get this straight. You're saying the shooter took the gun off this boat on Saturday. So who's going to bring the gun *back*?"

"Someone who wants to, and almost did, frame May."

Glitsky looked around another minute. "You'd swear on this, about the gun?"

Hardy nodded. "It wasn't here, Abe. Somebody came by here Thursday morning, unlocked the boat and put it in this drawer. Then they took May's fancy coat from the closet along with a babushka or something like that, locked up and waltzed away."

"Why?"

"Because they hated May." Hardy felt like he was on a roll. "Owen dumped somebody for May. So this person, the perp, killed Owen out of jealousy, then when they saw May linked to the *Eloise,* figured this was a good chance to get her too."

Glitsky sucked at his teeth. "What time was this, when this person came back?"

Hardy glanced at José, making a little face. "It must have been pretty early."

"Then it doesn't really let off your man Fowler, does it?"

"Well, I was thinking it couldn't very well have been a man at all. José here recognized the coat—"

The guard piped in, "It was a woman, sir. There's no doubt of that."

"It was a woman wearing the coat, okay. It could have been a man who let himself onto the boat. It could have been two separate incidents."

"Andy didn't have a key."

"You can't prove a negative."

Hardy was getting frustrated that Glitsky didn't see this. "Abe, the coat was aboard here."

"How do we know that, Diz?"

"May said it was here," he said. "Our perp took it, which was why it wasn't in your inventory."

Glitsky patiently answered. "I'm not saying it didn't happen your way, Diz. I'm saying it also very well could have happened at least one other way. May could have worn the coat down here, seen Andy—hell, if he was framing her he could've invited her down for just that reason, so she'd be seen in her unique coat. After she realized what was happening she dumped the coat, then saw her chance to get it back by hassling us."

"That just didn't happen, Abe."

"So prove it."

"It was a woman, Abe—"

Glitsky was not convinced. "I'd make pretty sure what your client was doing that morning before I brought it up to the jury. Besides, the only woman alive related to this case is Celine Nash. Aside from having no motive, she was in Santa Cruz. I checked."

Hardy stood his ground. "I still think it was a woman."

Glitsky shrugged. "Well, neither of us think May did it, so who . . . ?"

Hardy's mind was wrestling with the incomprehensible—Jane, his ex-wife, Andy Fowler's daughter. She hadn't told him the whole truth about her relationship with Owen Nash. It was understandable, why should she have, a one-time thing, he'd told himself. But what if . . . ? All right, what if. Get tough, face the possible, however impossible. Jane had continued seeing Nash, he had dumped her for May Shinn . . . he had totally worked her, and she had killed him and either confided in her father or, somehow, he had found out on his own. No wonder he was acting genial, passive. Cover for his daughter . . . Would he have done everything he'd done with that motivation? Sure, he would have hated Nash. And this torch he was supposedly carrying for Shinn—didn't it make more sense that he'd be angry at *her* for dropping him? There would be a sweetness in making her pay for his daughter's crime. As pay she certainly had.

He parked in front of Jane's house—once it had belonged to both of them—on Jackson in Pacific Heights. He had heard on the radio coming over that more than two inches of rain had already fallen since midnight. Going up the steps, he knocked at the custom door with its molded glass inlay. He saw a man's form appear through the door. "Perfect," he thought, thinking he was about to meet Chuck Chuck Bo-Buck or whoever else was the man of the month.

The door opened and he was looking at his client.

"Andy, we've got to talk," he said.

"You are such a bastard." Jane was crying, her legs curled up under her on her bed.

"Jane, I'm trying to save your father's life here. It's not been the best time I've ever had either."

Hardy felt terrible seeing his ex-wife in tears. He could be glib—or pretend to be—about the men in her life after him, but he wasn't blind to the fact that she was looking for the right one, that what she wanted was a man steady and strong who would love her and stay true and she wasn't finding him. He supposed, perhaps wrongly, that he'd at least come the closest to that ideal, but something—their own history?—had made the commitment impossible.

He could see her every day and not think about it, but now, confronted by it, it was very hard.

"How can you even *think* that, Dismas? What kind of person do you really think I am? I *told* you it was nothing. *It was just a night.*"

Andy was waiting in the living room. Hardy would get to him if he had to, but first he had to know about Jane and Owen Nash. "Just *one* night? And you never saw him again?"

"That's *right*. It happens. What do you want me to say?"

"I don't want you to say anything if that's the truth."

She hit the bed with a balled-up fist. "I *told* you it's the truth. I saw Owen Nash one day, one night. One."

"Okay, okay, Jane."

"What are you saying? *I* killed him?" Reading his expression, she brought her hand to her mouth. "Oh, my God, you really think that." She jumped up, sniffling, and went to her bureau, opening a wide black book and turning the pages. She turned to him, holding the book open for him to see. "June eighteenth to twenty-second. The I. Magnin Summer Fashions Exposition. All day every day I'm giving seminars and hosting teas. Check on it."

Hardy looked down, hating this. "I believe you, Jane, I said I believed you."

She pulled the bureau chair out and sat back down, crying again, silently, wiping at her eyes with a Kleenex. Hardy got up off the bed and left the room.

60

He told Andy they had to get together the next day to go over his testimony. They made an appointment for noon, and then Hardy left him to comfort his daughter.

He had written Frannie a note saying he would probably be gone all day and she had left one for him—she was at her late ex-husband's mother's, Rebecca's grandmother's, house, and would be back by six. She hoped to see him then.

He went to his office and threw darts for twenty minutes, now and then glancing at the window to watch the rain drop out of the gray.

This was the time he was supposed to be gearing up for his defense, for the legal battle between him and Pullios on the interpretation of the evidence that Andy Fowler had allegedly killed Owen Nash. But Hardy felt that somehow the essence was being lost. It reminded him of his high-school debates where he would argue both sides of something, sometimes three or four times, in the same afternoon. As though there was no correct answer.

Oh, and he knew it was the fashion, had been since he had gone to college—don't make value judgments. Relativity was king. There was no absolute truth. But, like it or not, he had grown up to believe that there was truth, that right differed fundamentally from wrong.

And what he was supposed to do on Monday was continue the debate. He knew that. He would call Abe Glitsky and Art Drysdale, and possibly José, as witnesses, and wind up with Andy testifying in his own behalf. He had been preparing his summation almost since the trial had begun.

The problem was that now, so far as he could sort it out, little of what really had happened had found its way into this trial, the supposed crucible of truth.

On the one hand he didn't want to divert his attention away from his defense of Andy—he knew he should be sitting at his desk, outlining, writing key phrases and arguments to win over the jury. But the other side of him felt that now that he was satisfied that he knew what had happened he should pursue that truth singlemindedly. Only that pursuit could take Andy Fowler's fate out of the hands of the jury, remove it from debate.

The only thing that would ultimately clear his client was an alternate explanation of events. But the time he spent on that took away from his formal defense at trial.

He threw darts.

The inventories were no help. They listed sweatbands taken from the drawers in the desks next to the bed, some weight-lifting gloves, leg warmers. Switching back to his formal trial preparation, Hardy pulled his legal pad in front of him. Should he call José as a witness and introduce everything he had found this morning? He wrote it down, looked at it and realized that nothing he had found out proved that Andy had not been on the boat Thursday morning. Prove a negative . . .

What about the significance and believability of the gun in the drawer? He could call Pullios and Chomorro right now and say that he, personally, had discovered a crucial bit of evidence that would demand a retrial because he could not be a witness for his own client. He would testify that the gun had not been in the drawer on Wednesday night. But proving it to a new jury would, again, be difficult. It was still possible, he had to admit, that the gun had slid forward or backward with every opening of the drawer. He *could* simply have overlooked it—missed it in his haste. And even if he did establish the gun's absence, did that *necessarily* mean the prosecution would have the burden of proving that Andy Fowler had somehow acquired a key to the *Eloise*? Playing Glitsky, he came up with five reasons in five minutes why they wouldn't.

He got up and fed his fish. He knew what he knew—the gun had been brought back to the *Eloise* on Thursday morning by the jealous woman who had killed her past lover, Owen Nash. She had done it to get it out of her own possession and to shift the blame to May, and on both counts the strategy had worked.

He had to hit and hit again the fact that the burden of proof was *always* on the prosecution. *They* had to prove Fowler had killed Nash —it wasn't Hardy's job to prove he hadn't. What he had to do was keep the jury clear on that point. Pullios had to *prove* Andy's guilt. Even if the jury thought Andy was guilty of something to some degree, he had to make the point to the jury that they weren't to determine whether or not Andy was *innocent,* but rather whether the prosecution, by the evidence presented, had proved him guilty. And if not, then—although he might not be innocent—he was legally *not guilty.*

Innocent did not mean exactly the same thing as not guilty. It was, in this case, a crucial distinction.

Back at his desk, he pushed some buttons, then exchanged a few words with Ken Farris about the terrible weather. "You still at it?" Farris asked.

"No rest for the weary," Hardy said. "A point occurs to me, if you don't mind helping the defense."

"I can go half a yard," Farris said, "though I'd prefer not to think of it as assisting the defense." He paused briefly. "Dismas, let me ask you something—I get a feeling this is more than just a job for you. You don't think Fowler did it, do you? You wouldn't do this as an exercise in the law."

Hardy had been through it all before. "Fowler didn't do it," he said. "I'm also trying to find out who did."

A pause, then, "Why do they keep putting us through this? Getting the wrong people?"

Hardy knew it was a long story—Nash's fame, Pullios's ambition, Fowler's duplicity. Suspicion and prejudice and all of the above. But Farris had asked it rhetorically and Hardy passed it by. "Did Owen give the key to the *Eloise* to any of his girlfriends?" he asked.

"I doubt it. The *Eloise* was his baby, you know. He'd have people aboard, but not without him."

"Did he have any other long-standing girlfriends, mistresses, whatever—besides May?" He had to, Hardy was thinking.

"A few weeks, once in a while a month, that was about it. He paid them off, they went their way."

"Do you remember him talking about any of them being bitter, angry, rejected, anything at all like that?"

"No. I'm sorry, but there just wasn't that much made of it, or, I should say, them. They came and went like the seasons." He laughed dryly. "No, scratch that, more like the courses of a meal. That was the big difference with May—she was around awhile."

"And no one else was?"

"No. Except Celine, of course."

Hardy sat riveted to his chair. He felt the blood draining out of his face. The rain beat on his window. Darkness was settling in. "Did Celine have a key to the *Eloise?*" he asked, keeping his voice calm.

"Hey, I was kidding about that. Really, a bad joke."

"Does she have a key?"

"Well, I think she does, she used to. But she didn't—"

"I know that." Hardy forced himself to slow down, to speak calmly. "Just another something to think about. Keeping track of these keys, that's all. But do me a favor, would you?"

"Sure."

"She's mad enough at me about all this, defending the man on trial for her father's murder. Would you try not to mention this key business to her if you see her?"

"Yeah, okay, no problem."

When he hung up, he didn't move for several minutes. The house wasn't there, nor was his office, nor the rain, nor the darkness outside.

The night Celine had come by for the first time she had quickly left after seeing him in his green jogging suit, the same kind Owen Nash had been wearing on the day he had been shot. Was seeing him like seeing her father's ghost? She'd reacted, at least for a moment, as though she had . . . "You just suddenly reminded me so much of my father . . ."

So rethink that visit. How could he have reminded her of her father, with that intensity, if she hadn't seen him in the same outfit, *if she hadn't been with him on that last day?* Of course, she might have seen him other times in his jogging clothes . . . except that wasn't very likely. They didn't live together, they didn't jog together.

Strout . . . he had mentioned in the case of May Shinn—though Hardy knew it was true anyway—that standard operating procedure at the morgue was to bag the victim's clothes. Celine had seen Nash at the coroner's . . . but he'd been naked.

Certainly the jogging suit was a better explanation of her extreme reaction than just seeing him in domestic bliss with wife and child. If he hadn't been so convinced she was in love with him, would he have ever believed her explanation for her reaction? Dismas, the lady-killer. He shook his head in disgust.

*   *   *

But *why?*

Money? Greed? Well, it was true she stood to benefit with May gone, more than anyone except perhaps Ken Farris, but since she already had more than she needed he'd quickly discounted that potential motive, not to mention that he never considered her a suspect anyway.

He wasn't happy with it. The more you got, the more you wanted? Money, the alleged root of all evil? Including murder? What about her reaction to May's death—"At least she won't get the money." Greed—one of the seven deadly sins. And greed didn't presuppose poverty or exclude the wealthy.

There had to be more.

It was rocking him. He was aware, sitting back now in his chair, that his stomach had tightened. He consciously unclenched his fists. He knew he was right, but wasn't sure why. One thing was sure, as the killer she had acted plausibly, smartly—played on his male ego, let him think she was fixed on him in his role as her father's avenger while May was a suspect. How better keep him from suspecting her than to fabricate and build their own illicit relationship, to use his libido, as insurance? He was such a fool.

But Glitsky had looked into this. Celine had been in Santa Cruz, she couldn't have been out on the *Eloise.*

Hardy thought he had read and reread each of the binders on his desk, but he hadn't—Abe's reports following up on alibis for Ken and Celine sat there within their tabs. He had listened to Abe telling him about the two weight lifters who lived with one of their mothers, about Celine spending the weekend remodeling their Victorian house. Now he read Abe's synopsis of the telephone interview he had conducted.

The telephone rang on his desk and he grabbed at it.

"Mr. Hardy. This is Judge Chomorro."

And I'm the Queen of Spain, Hardy thought.

But it was the judge's voice, no mistake. What was he doing calling Hardy at home over the weekend during a trial? This being his first murder trial, Hardy wasn't certain what to make of it—was a call from a judge to a defense attorney a relatively common practice, or another example of Chomorro's own inexperience? There was nothing to do but hear him out.

He said hello and listened while the judge told him that he had called to give him fair and decent warning that he had decided to deny Hardy's 1118.1 motion, that the evidence was going to the jury for their verdict. Pullios had also been informed.

"By the way," Chomorro said, "again in the interests of total fairness for the defense"—or covering your ass in an appeal, Hardy thought—"I want you to be prepared for the prosecution to object to your argument on the investigation procedure leading to the indictment of Mr. Fowler." He paused a moment. "And I am of a mind to sustain those objections."

Hardy tried to get out an objection now. "I understand we'd covered that in pretrial, Your Honor."

"Well, I've given it a lot of thought since then, especially since yesterday, going over your eleven-eighteen, and I fail to see any direct relevance to the evidence that's been presented. Ms. Pullios may have moved too quickly on Ms. Shinn, but there was ample evidence to indict Mr. Fowler in the first place, and certainly enough for a jury to decide to convict. We'll leave it up to them."

"Your Honor, you realize that was the main thrust of my defense."

"Frankly, that's one of the reasons for this courtesy call. I wanted to give you some time to prepare. Talk to your client—he can tell you there was nothing technically improper about his indictment. A trial is supposed to weigh evidence. If you want to impugn the system, you're of course free to appeal, as I presume you will if you lose."

Hardy could imagine Drysdale or Locke or both of them having had a chat with Chomorro the previous night or this morning, reminding him "a trial is supposed to weigh evidence." Right out of the textbook.

Here was the reason for Chomorro's unorthodox call. He'd talked to somebody and been told that his ruling on the law regarding Hardy's defense would—perhaps—provide grounds for a prosecutorial appeal. No, Chomorro wasn't going to screw up his first murder trial. It was a straightforward procedure. Evidence was presented and the jury decided. That was how he was going to play it.

No way he felt he could ask Glitsky. It was a fishing expedition, and Hardy knew it, and Abe had his own work to do. He wouldn't run off on what he'd consider a hunch of Hardy's to double-check his own work. Hardy couldn't blame him.

Frannie called at six-thirty, a half hour late. He hadn't noticed and swore at himself. "How are you?" he asked. "How's the Beck?"

Her voice seemed small and far away. He told her he was still working and she said that she'd known that. Erin, Rebecca's grand-mother, had invited her to stay for dinner, maybe even overnight if the rain didn't let up. He'd be at it until the wee hours anyway. She didn't think he'd mind. Did he?

He didn't mind, he said. How could he? This had been his doing and he was going to have to fix it.

He told her he loved her, would miss her but understood. He was getting to the end of it.

Jeff Elliot owed him one. He was an investigative reporter, and if there was something to discover in Santa Cruz, Hardy hoped he was the guy to find it. He only had to sell him on the idea.

"In this weather? Are you kidding me?"

"It's probably going to be beautiful there tomorrow."

"Hardy, read the papers, will you? This is supposed to go on all weekend."

"Jeff, it'll be an adventure. Take your girlfriend, go down there and have a little vacation, on me. What's a little rain among lovers?"

He got himself a large can of Foster's Lager and a handful of nuts and walked through the long and suddenly lonely house. Wind howled between the buildings, the rain fell without letup, the worst storm in years.

He turned on the Christmas-tree lights, planted his beer and nuts on the reading table next to his reclining chair and put a match under the kindling in the fire.

Sam Cooke played in his mind—Saturday night and I ain't got no-body. Forget that. He had brought up his binders and was going to go through them again.

His own notes. He'd taken so many notes he thought his wrist was going to fall off. Every time he had spoken to Pullios, Drysdale, Glit-sky, Farris, Celine (while it had still been strictly professional), he had jotted down at least the gist of the conversations if they concerned this case. Random thoughts, theories of Moses and Frannie, of Pico and his old officemates.

At a little after ten-thirty he got up for another beer, after which he was going to hang it up for the night and get some sleep. He had just gotten to the time Ken Farris had come downtown, ostensibly to verify Owen's handwriting on the will. Hardy remembered that they had gotten into how the system worked too slowly—Farris *knew* May had been on the *Eloise* . . . Celine had told him. Hardy had dutifully noted it, then written "hearsay" in the margin and had, if not forgotten it, at least dropped it from his active consideration.

Celine had also told Hardy that May had planned to go out on the *Eloise* with Owen. They'd been walking back from their first meeting; he remembered it, now, distinctly.

May, however, had denied it, and May, it turned out, was telling the truth.

So Celine had lied . . . except he still couldn't prove it. Opening the refrigerator, he stopped. He slammed the door closed and nearly ran back up through the house to his binders.

It took only a minute. It had been when Pullios had him question Celine in front of the grand jury, trying for the indictment on May Shinn. Celine had testified that on Tuesday morning, June 16, she had called her father at his office, wanting to make sure he hadn't made any plans for that weekend that included her. He had said no, that he and May were going out alone on the *Eloise*.

Okay, Celine's version was in the record. But it was still hearsay. It was also a lie, but how to prove—?

Farris's office.

Where there was a beep every twenty seconds and everything was on tape?

61

Hardy slept fitfully, waking before dawn.

Rain continued to fall, but more gently now, in a thick drizzle. He showered and dressed and sat drinking coffee, staring at the clock on the wall, wondering what would be a reasonable time to call Ken Farris again. Reasonable or not, he wanted to call him before he had time to leave the house.

He went back to the binders and read over the testimony, wanting to make sure—although he knew it—that it hadn't been fatigue. He had asked Celine when she had called her father.

"Sometime in the morning. It was the Tuesday, I believe."

"The sixteenth?"

"If that was the Tuesday, yes. He was at his office down in South San Francisco . . ."

He held out until seven-fifteen, about the longest ninety minutes of his life. Farris didn't appear to appreciate his restraint.

"What the hell, Hardy? What time is it?"

He told him, apologizing, explaining, keeping him on the line. "I've got a real lead," he concluded. "I don't want to put you through all this again, give you another suspect to worry about, but I think I've found a place to finally get some physical evidence." He told him his conjecture about the tapes. "Please tell me you've still got them."

"We should," he said, "we keep them for six months."

"So you've still got the ones for June?"

"I don't know. Is that six months? I'm not really awake yet, you know."

"What I'd like to do is review the last two weeks of June, all the calls Nash made or took at his office."

Farris sounded like he yawned. At least he was waking up. "That's all? How about a full-scale audit while you're at it?"

446

Hardy could take a little abuse if he was going to get what he wanted. He waited.

"Shit, why not? You looking for anything in particular?"

"Something, yeah, but I'd rather not say exactly what just now."

"I mention it because we keep logs. You won't have to listen to all the tapes if you know who you want." He went on, sounding more like himself now. "I know all this taping seems like excessive security, but we're in a high-tech field. There really is espionage. People have claimed oral contracts with me or Owen on some things. We like to protect ourselves."

"You don't have to justify a thing to me. Where do you keep the logs?"

"They're in South City at the plant. We've got a vault." Farris sighed. "I don't imagine this is going to wait until, say, business hours tomorrow morning, is it?"

Dorothy took the exit and headed the car up the hill away from the ocean. The wipers clickety-clacked on the flat windshield of the old VW bug. The windows on both sides were down an inch to act as defrosters. Both she and Jeff wore parkas for warmth. The heater didn't work. The drive to Santa Cruz down Highway 1 from San Francisco had taken them a little over an hour, and they probably should have been in sour moods. Dorothy rolled down her window further and put her hand out, catching raindrops.

"I don't think I'll ever hate the rain again."

"Maybe we should move to Oregon."

"Tierra del Fuego," she said. "It rains all the time there, I hear." They had used yesterday's storm as an excuse to stay inside for the whole day, nothing to do but curl up, stay warm, enjoy each other. When Hardy had called they were ready to go outside. Not dying for it, but it had some appeal. "I've got to meet this friend of yours, Hardy. What a great idea!"

"Well, he's not exactly a friend. He's a source."

"If you remember, I was a source for your bail story."

"You're prettier than he is. A little bit, anyway."

She slapped at him. The car swerved and she straightened it. They were driving through a heavily wooded pine section back up behind the UC campus. A brown slick of water ran down the center of the street. There was a house about every two hundred yards.

"I think that was our street you just passed," Jeff said. "Plus you said you'd have an idea by now."

She pulled the car over and stopped, looking behind her at the street sign. She started making a U-turn. "I do have an idea," she said, "although I don't know why I have to think of everything."

Jeff put his hand on her leg. "I think of some things."

She smiled, looked down, and covered his hand with her own, driving now with one hand. She squeezed it. "Yes, you do."

The idea was to get them talking.

Len and Karl weren't home—they were down at the gym, pumping iron together. They did it every morning, Karl's mother explained. They were religious about it. Both were very disciplined boys, very structured. Len was currently runner-up Mr. Northern California and Karl was going down to Santa Monica right after New Year's for the Gold's Gym prelims.

The three of them, Jeff, Dorothy, Mrs. Franck, sat in the kitchen nook—brand new hardwood floors, a custom oak table, curved glass in the windows. They were drinking herb tea and Mrs. Franck had cut up some fiber bars into cookielike things. The old Victorian house was large, newly painted, immaculate. Everywhere there were new rugs, framed prints on the walls, antiques.

"But look at me, chattering on. You didn't come here to talk about my sons—I call them both my sons. Len's my son-in-law really, but he's like a son. They were legally married last summer, you know."

"I think that's wonderful," Dorothy said.

Mrs. Franck beamed. "I'm so glad. A lot of people don't understand, you know. They see two men . . . and you know. I admit I had a difficult time accepting it at first. But if you could see them—and then offering to take me in—I mean they're just wonderful boys, and they do love one another. And then having all this . . ."

Looking around, Jeff took the opening. "Somebody must be doing very well already."

Mrs. Franck beamed. "I know," she said. "This place now. It's a dream come true."

"It is beautiful," Dorothy said.

"I don't think even Celine did it justice," Jeff said, almost as an aside to Dorothy. "I'm glad we came down."

"Are you really going to feature it in the *Chronicle?*"

Jeff nodded. "It's why we're here. Celine told me I couldn't do a complete feature on restored Victorians if I didn't see this place. But I still think she sold it short—I don't think there's one in San Francisco that's this nice."

"Well, if the boys come home, don't even breathe a bad word about Celine. They won't hear of it."

"You're all pretty close, huh?" Jeff had his notepad out.

Mrs. Franck nodded. "She must be the most generous person God ever put on this earth."

"She was a help, was she?"

Karl's mother rolled her eyes to the heavens. "You can't imagine! Anything we needed. You should have seen the place before, and now . . ." She gestured to take it all in.

"So, is Celine like a sponsor, or what?" Jeff asked.

"You know, that's the funny thing. I think she just took a liking to Karl. He had been up in the city, trying to work out some things—they have a coach up there who's really marvelous—and he met her at her club. She's in fine shape herself, you know."

"And what happened?"

"Well, you have to know Karl. But he is the sweetest man. Everyone loves him. The two of them—he and Celine—just got to be friends. I think he was a little lonely for Len, up there all alone in the city like he was. He needed someone to talk to, and you know he's so faithful —he didn't want to lead on any other men—so I guess he and Celine just clicked and he started telling her about his dreams, you know, his life, his career, this house he and Len wanted to fix up." Mrs. Franck lowered her voice and leaned toward them across the table. "Celine's very rich, you know. Her father was Owen Nash."

Jeff and Dorothy both nodded.

"It's a terrible shame about her father, isn't it, that poor man. Has that judge been found guilty yet?"

Jeff told her the trial was still going on.

"Well, it's just so awful, the whole thing. Especially for Celine." She sighed. "And on top of everything else."

Dorothy spoke up. "Are other things hard for her too?"

"Oh, you know, even the rich. Sometimes I think it's almost harder for them."

"Why?" Jeff asked.

"Oh, you know. All the people after their money. You never know if anyone's sincere. I think that why she cares so much about Karl. I mean, before he even knew about the money, that she had money

. . . well, he's just always been there for her. He'd do anything for her. We all would. I think she just needs some friends she can count on, who don't pester her. She needs a place to stay where it's not a hotel, where she's not Celine Nash, just a normal person."

"That's nice," Dorothy said, "everybody needs that."

Mrs. Franck nodded. "We just let her come and go. She's got her own room—well, I guess you'll see it when we go on up—Karl fixed it up for her especially. Lord knows, one thing this house has is enough rooms. But that's Karl. He says this house is her house. She's welcome even if we're not here."

"Is that often?" Jeff asked.

"Oh, you know, with the boys competing, sometimes she'll come down on a Thursday or Friday and we'll all be going off for the weekend someplace—Long Beach or Las Vegas. We come back Sunday or Monday and she'll have a dinner or something waiting for us. She's really so great."

The Monterey Bay Club had a listing of all the sanctioned weight-lifting events of 1992. On June 20–21, Saturday and Sunday, the Mr. California regionals had been held in San Diego at the Mission Bay Inn.

Dorothy sat in a booth at the Pelican's Nest just off the Santa Cruz boardwalk, sipping a Bloody Mary, checking the shine on her new diamond. The rain had picked up again, slanting sheets of water across the bay. Jeff was coming back from the pay telephones. He walked easily with the crutches, barely seeming to need them when he was hot on a lead like this one.

He slid into the booth and kissed her. "Karl Franck and his mother checked in with Len Hoeffner on Friday evening, June nineteenth. Both were listed as entrants in the pageant."

"So Celine wasn't here?"

"She might have been. She might have come down on Friday night to see them off. I'm sure there are plane records somewhere, but I don't think Hardy's going to need them."

"And she was back by Sunday." It wasn't a question.

Jeff nodded. "And so far as the Francks knew or assumed, she was there all weekend. They weren't even lying, as far as they knew, when they said so. She probably had a nice meal waiting for them when they got home and a story about a relaxed weekend doing nothing."

"Except for killing her father."

Jeff stared out the window at the rain. "Except, maybe, for that."

Hardy had gone down to pick up Frannie and Rebecca. He took them out to breakfast and then swung by their house again for another day's clothes and baby supplies before dropping them back at her former mother-in-law's. He probably wasn't going to be back home all day anyway and he had some nagging notion that things could get dangerous. Maybe that was ridiculous, but he'd play it safe anyway. He'd feel more comfortable if his wife and child were out of harm's way.

The other thing he had done was call Andy Fowler, still at Jane's, and cancel their noon appointment to go over his trial testimony. He told him about Chomorro's decision not to allow his line of questioning on the "backward" collection of evidence.

Fowler had been low-key. "Listen, Diz, when you get me on the stand I'll simply tell the truth. I did not kill Owen Nash and they haven't proved I did. Their burden, remember. I think it's a good idea to take the day off, get a little rest." . . . Take the day off. Sure.

Now he was closing the Owen Industries security logbook. It hadn't taken much time. He had reviewed the calls to and from Nash's office for the two weeks prior to his death. There was one call to Celine, though it was on Monday, not Tuesday, hardly by itself a critical flaw in Celine's testimony.

He was sitting at Ken's desk at his office—the one so much like his own—at Owen Industries in South San Francisco. Farris had come down with his security supervisor—Gary Simpson—at eleven-thirty, then left the two men to find whatever it was Hardy was looking for.

Simpson sat, legs crossed and bored, across the desk from him. "Okay," Hardy said, "we've got one hit. You mind if we give it a listen."

Simpson shrugged and stood up, stretching theatrically. He was a tall man in jeans and a flannel shirt. "That's what I'm here for." He motioned with his head. "Back this way."

They walked, Hardy following, down the red-tiled hallways and around a couple of corners. The door marked "Security" was oversized, double-locked with deadbolts. Simpson's office was to the right inside, and there was a small anteroom with two waiting chairs, an end table and a coffee table, and, in contrast to the rest of the building, no plants anywhere. These rooms were much colder than the others. Simpson gestured for Hardy to follow him back.

Behind his desk was a walk-in vault, and Hardy waited while Simpson unlocked and opened the desk, pushed a series of buttons inside a drawer, then did the same thing on a panel next to the door to the vault.

"High-tech," Hardy said.

Simpson half turned. "Well, we're in the business. We ought to keep up on state of the art."

The door opened inward. Hardy had envisioned a bunch of drawers filled with tapes, but again was confronted with an array of buttons and lights—more state of the art. Simpson sat at a console featuring innumerable LEDs and three computer terminals.

"What's your number, there, on the left column, for the call you want?"

Hardy, still carrying the thin logbook, opened to the page. He read out the six-digit number and Simpson entered it on the board. There was a brief wait, then a click.

"You're lucky," Simpson said. "This date gets automatically erased in two days."

"You want to override it so it doesn't do that?"

"Sure, no sweat." He pushed a few buttons. "Okay," he said, "you ready?"

Hardy was surprised at the sound of Owen Nash's voice—somehow less authoritarian than Hardy had imagined—raspy but consciously softened, Hardy thought, as though he were speaking to a child.

"I know you're unhappy with me," he said, "but don't hang up, please."

A longish pause. The digital sound reproduction was superb—Hardy could hear Celine's breathing become more rapid.

"All right," she said evenly, "I won't hang up."

"We have to see each other," Nash said. "We need to talk about this."

"No. I don't want to see you about this. I want you back—"

"It's happening, Celine. It's going to happen."

A breathy silence.

"It *can't*, Daddy, it just can't. What about me?"

"You'll be fine, honey. I still love you."

"You don't."

Now it was Owen's turn to take a beat. "I'll always love you, honey.

We just can't go on . . . the way we have. I've changed. It's different—"

"Because of her."

"No, not just her. Because of me. Maybe she's made me see it, but the change is mine, it's my decision—"

"I won't let you make it."

"Celine . . ."

"I won't, Daddy, she can't do this, she can't have you—"

"It's *not* her," he repeated, "it's me. And I have made the decision."

"I'll change your mind. I know I can." Suddenly there was a deeper, insinuating tone. It was unusual enough that Simpson turned around to look at Hardy. *"You* know I can."

Nash did not answer immediately. When he did, his voice was a whisper, as though wrung from the depths of him. "No, you can't anymore, Celine. That's done. That's over. It's come terribly close to ruining both of our lives. It can't go on—"

A strident laugh. "I suppose you won't see me, your own daughter."

"I'll always see you, Celine. Whenever you want. Just not, not that way . . ."

"I want one chance, Daddy."

"Hon—"

Almost screaming now, somehow without raising her voice. Then the throbbing voice again. "Please. Please, Daddy, I just need to see you."

"It won't—" Nash began.

"If it doesn't, I'll leave it. I promise."

Resigned. "When?"

"Whenever you want. Wherever you want."

A final pause, then Nash's voice, thick. "I'll call you."

Jeff Elliot's call was on Hardy's answering machine at his office at home. Celine may have been in Santa Cruz at some point during the weekend, but neither Len nor Karl nor his mother could verify she'd been there on Saturday, since regardless of what they had told or implied to Glitsky, they hadn't been home themselves.

The assistant district attorney in charge of sexual crimes was a woman named Alyson Skrwlewski. Hardy had barely known her, though he guessed that by now she'd have heard of him.

"I just have a quick general question if you don't mind."

She considered a moment. Like most of the D.A.'s staff, she wasn't disposed to do any favors that would hurt a prosecution case. And even if she was inclined to be helpful, the situation—Hardy calling her this way on a Sunday afternoon—made her uncomfortable. "Let's hear the question first," she said, "then I'll tell you whether I can answer it."

"I guess I want to know is what are the most common manifestations of father-daughter incest?"

"Well, I guess that's general enough. I can talk about that. What do you want to know?"

"Everything I can, but specifically, when the victim grows up, is she likely to do anything differently than other women who haven't had that experience?"

"Not when, *if* she grows up, you mean. Suicide would be high on the list." Hardy let her think. "Her relationships are going to stink, probably. She'll be an enabler, maybe let her husband abuse her own daughter. That's if she wants a husband."

"They don't marry often?"

"Oh, no, not that so much. I mean, this is almost too general. Every case is different. It's just such an all-encompassing, terrible situation —they might marry five times, finding the so-called right mix of somebody who abuses them and babies them. It sucks."

Hardy agreed, but she wasn't telling him anything that might help him. "What about backgrounds?"

"What about them?"

"Anything you might expect to see more than in someone else?"

"You mean with the victim, or the father?"

"Both, I guess."

"Well, there's some evidence that if the father didn't interact immediately, normally, with the victim in the first years of her life, he's *more* likely to be sexually attracted to her. If he never changed a diaper, never burped her, and so forth, the incest taboo doesn't kick in." She sounded apologetic. "Hey, that's a fairly new theory and pretty unprovable. With the women, at least there's more data."

"What do they do?"

"Well, a surprising number of them try to burn down their houses. No one really seems to know why, besides some obvious symbolic stuff, but arson is often in the profile."

Hardy felt the hairs rise on his arms.

Skrwlewski continued. "And then, of course, there's the prostitution, but everyone knows that."

"They all go into prostitution?"

"No, no. Not so much go into that life—although, of course, many do—but more have some isolated experiences. Their self-image is so low, they don't feel attractive, you know. Yet they know men want them, daddy did, and they can take out their hostility by making them pay. It all gets pretty twisted around."

"Sounds like it."

"I guess some people don't react as badly. But you'll almost always get the manipulation, using sex for something else, the love substitute."

Hardy's stomach was a knot. He sat at his desk with his arms folded across his chest. Outside his window, the wind had died down and there were a few breaks in the clouds.

He had all the proof he needed for himself. But there was the same problem that had dogged the murder of Owen Nash from the outset— the lack of physical evidence.

Celine's conversation with her father, provocative and revealing as it had been, never named a date, didn't so much as mention the *Eloise*. It also hadn't mentioned May, but Celine could argue with absolute credibility that she had simply been mistaken as to the day when she'd talked with her father about him meeting May on the boat. She had the one talk with him at his office, then another one later in the week—he said he'd call her, didn't he?—and she'd gotten the two mixed up.

The Santa Cruz people being away didn't necessarily mean she *hadn't* been there. It meant her alibi was weaker—almost undoubtedly false—but by itself it still didn't put her on the *Eloise* on Saturday.

Other hints came back to him. He remembered Celine telling him she'd only been a member of Hardbodies! for six months—in other words, from about the time she'd stopped working out on the *Eloise* when Owen had started seeing May regularly. Surely the headbands on the boat—never claimed by May—had been Celine's. So had the lifting gloves, one pair of which she'd no doubt worn when she had fired May's Beretta.

As with Andy Fowler and May Shinn before him, there was no apparent physical link tying Celine Nash to the murder of her father.

He had been right, though he took little satisfaction from it—Owen Nash had been killed by a jealous woman. But the woman had been his own daughter. And if he had been sexually abusing his own daughter since—he supposed—their trip around the world together when she'd been six years old, or even earlier, he certainly deserved whatever punishment she could give him. He knew she had done it, and now he knew why. More accurately, he knew she had done it *because* he knew why.

He thought of his own adopted baby girl, then tried to imagine the immense physical and psychological damage Owen Nash's abuse had visited on his own daughter, and suddenly he found he had lost any desire to see Celine punished—she had been punished enough, hadn't she? She'd never get out from under the private stigma, never away from the pain.

Deep down, he didn't even blame her.

But, though punishment might not be his motive, he still had to prove it to clear Andy Fowler, and Celine was nobody to underestimate. Earlier in the morning he had sent Frannie and Rebecca away, deriding himself for considering that Celine might be dangerous. Now he was glad that he had.

She had shot and killed her father. She hadn't blinked at, and had in fact done her best to bring about, the false accusation of May Shinn. From the gallery she had daily watched the slow skewering of Andy Fowler, his once-distinguished career in ruins. She had clearly been prepared to take Hardy's marriage down with her to get him off her scent.

Hardy still had Andy Fowler to defend.

The trial would have to go on. Pullios couldn't let it go now and without a smoking gun, Hardy's accusations of Celine at this stage would come across as rank courtroom shenanigans—it might at last get him the long-promised contempt citation from Chomorro.

"The key is my only hope, Abe. She's got to have the key."

Glitsky had listened patiently, for him. He interrupted only about every ten seconds, tired of Hardy's meddling, not liking to hear that Celine's alibi—the one *he* had provided—was suspect.

"Now it's Celine?" he asked at last. "Too bad Nash didn't have a dog. After Celine's trial we could indict the dog."

"Come on, Abe, I've run it all down for you. We need a warrant. If she's got the key, if it's at her house . . ."

Glitsky stopped him. "Big deal."

"It proves she could have gone to the *Eloise* on Thursday morning."

"Proves she *could have*. Please, this one time, give me a break, Diz. It doesn't prove anything. It's just another theory. You know that's how they're going to see it."

"That's why we need the physical evidence. The key. With my testimony—"

"*If* anybody believes you."

"Why wouldn't they?"

"Because, my friend, it is in your own best interests to make up something like this. Like the gun not having been there when you looked on Wednesday night."

"It wasn't there, Abe."

"I'm not saying it was. The issue here, as always, is proof. And I'm telling you how it's going to look. Can you think of any judge in the city who would issue a search warrant on this?"

Hardy was silent.

"Okay, how about in all of America?"

"All right, all right, I understand, Abe. But I'm telling you, Celine did it. I'm telling you why. What am I supposed to do about that? There's no way Andy Fowler's going down for this."

"I hate to tell you this, ol' buddy, but you want my opinion—he is unless you get him off."

62

Coming in a little after nine, the size of the crowd in the gallery was daunting. Hardy wondered if someone had leaked the news that his witnesses might not be appearing, that they'd be moving right along to Andy's testimony, then closing arguments and jury instructions. The verdict might even come in today, and the media wanted to be there.

His witnesses had been subpoenaed, though, and they were on hand: Glitsky in a coat and tie; Glitsky's lieutenant, Frank Batiste; Ron Reynolds, his polygraph expert; Art Drysdale sitting next to Chris Locke himself. Hardy wasn't too surprised to see David Freeman, down for the show. Celine was sitting in her usual spot by the aisle.

Abe, he realized, had been right. His job had never varied. He had to convince the jury that the evidence did not warrant a conviction. He had come up with an idea to get to Celine if he had to—he might have to prove that she was guilty in order to get Andy off—but he didn't want to confuse the two issues.

Andy, in a dark blue suit, entered with Jane. Still hurt and angry at Hardy for the grilling he'd given her on Saturday about her relationship with Owen Nash, she didn't come through the rail as she usually did.

Fowler, however, seemed to have forgotten Hardy's outburst at him on Friday about his stance, the transparency of his attachment to May —and sat down calmly at the defense table.

From his vantage now, certain that his client had not killed anyone, Hardy was more equable about the judge's attitude and appearance, much of which was, he decided, a brave front. This was an innocent man. He could seem to remain above it all if he wanted, if it made him feel better.

Hardy was also beginning to understand a little of what was behind Andy's apparent sangfroid. The man had, after all, spent thirty years on the bench, and it was in his blood to believe in the jury system—

there would not be a miscarriage of justice here, he didn't kill Owen Nash, the jury would come up with the right decision. If he didn't believe that, what had he been doing presiding over the system for three decades?

If Hardy wanted the jury to believe that Andy was more of a regular Joe, it was because he thought it would make him appear more sympathetic. Now he was realizing that the jury's empathy with Andy wasn't the issue either. In reality, there was only one issue: did the evidence prove he had killed Owen Nash?

The judge entered and everyone stood. Hardy went to the center of the courtroom and nodded at the members of the jury, then at the judge. Chomorro had given fair enough notice. "The defense calls Inspector Sergeant Abraham Glitsky."

He turned to watch Abe come forward, catching a raised eye from Pullios at the prosecution table. Well, object all day, Betsy, he thought to himself. This is relevant and I'm going to bring it up.

Glitsky was sworn in, and Hardy, after establishing Abe's credentials as an experienced homicide investigator, began.

"For the jury's benefit, Sergeant, would you tell us how an inspector such as yourself gets assigned to a homicide investigation?"

Glitsky sat comfortably in the witness chair, having been there many times. Forthcoming, competent, with nothing to hide, he looked directly from Hardy to the jury. "It's more or less random," he said. "There are twelve inspectors and typically we each handle between three and six cases, rotating them as they come in. If it gets a little unbalanced, Lieutenant Batiste might shuffle one or two around."

"All right. Now in this random manner, did you happen to get the Owen Nash homicide?"

"Yes, I did."

"In that capacity, what was your role in collecting evidence?"

Glitsky gave it a minute's thought. "I am in charge of coordinating all the physical evidence that we eventually turn over to the district attorney's office if the matter is going to be charged. I also check on the alibis of suspects, potential motives. We look into paper records, bank accounts, telephone logs, anything we feel relates to the homicide. In this case I also supervised the forensics team that went aboard the *Eloise,* Mr. Nash's boat."

Glitsky and Hardy had been over all this many times.

"Did you go aboard the *Eloise* yourself?"

"Yes, I did."

"And what did you find there?"

Glitsky went over the inventory—the bloodstains, the slug in the baseboard, the exercise equipment, the murder weapon.

"When you got to the *Eloise,* was it locked up?"

"Yes, the attendant there had to open the cabin for us."

"This was Thursday afternoon, June twenty-fifth, is that right?"

"Right."

"Now, Sergeant, as your investigation proceeded, did it eventually center on one suspect?"

"Yes, it did."

"Because of the physical evidence?"

"To some extent. There were fingerprints on the murder weapon, a lack of an alibi, an apparent motive."

Hardy had decided he might be able to introduce all of this testimony if he avoided having Glitsky draw any conclusions and if he kept May Shinn's name out of it. So far, he was talking about the formal police investigation into the murder of Owen Nash—relevant testimony.

"And based on that evidence, those suspicions, did you make an arrest?"

"No, not right then. There wasn't enough to justify it."

"But eventually you did make an arrest. Did you find more evidence?"

"No more physical evidence, but I came to the conclusion that the suspect was about to flee."

Hardy turned to the jury. "In other words, your suspect was exhibiting consciousness-of-guilt, and you felt justified making an arrest because of that."

"That's correct."

Hardy turned back to Glitsky. "Sergeant, this person with fingerprints on the gun, no alibi, an apparent motive, the one acting so guilty—was that suspect Andy Fowler?"

"No, it was not."

Hardy nodded and turned to Pullios. He had gotten through it without an objection. "Your witness."

"Sergeant Glitsky, when you did make the initial arrest in his case, the one Mr. Hardy has just referred to, were you coerced in any way by any member of your department or by the district attorney's staff?"

Hardy couldn't believe it—Pullios was inadvertently introducing the very argument he had been trying to avoid because of Chomorro's decision.

"No. At that time it was a fairly standard investigation. Although we do try to move quickly." He looked at the jury. "The trail of a homicide gets cold in a hurry."

"Before making your arrest, did you wait for the complete fingerprint analysis on the murder weapon, People's Exhibit One?"

"Yes."

"And didn't Mr. Fowler's prints turn up?"

"Well, at the time, they were unidentified."

"You don't deny that Mr. Fowler's fingerprints were on the gun, do you?"

"No."

"But before you knew whose they were, you arrested another person? You told Mr. Hardy your suspect had an 'apparent' motive and alibi. Did you get an opportunity—before the arrest—to check that alibi?"

"No, but—"

"And isn't it true that, in fact, your suspect had two eyewitnesses to where she was on the day of the murder—eyewitnesses you failed to locate?"

"I wouldn't characterize it as—"

"Please just answer the question, Sergeant. It's very straightforward."

Glitsky looked down for the first time. Hardy thought it wasn't a good sign. "Yes, that's true. I didn't locate them."

Pullios walked back to her table, took a sip of water and read some notes, shifting gears. "Now, Sergeant," she began again, "how many homicides were you handling at this time, back in June?"

Hardy stood up, objecting. "The sergeant's caseload isn't relevant here."

"On the contrary," Pullios said, "Mr. Hardy went to some lengths to establish Sergeant Glitsky's professional routine under normal conditions. If these were not normal conditions, if the sergeant was under unusual stress, for example, the rigor of his investigations might suffer for it."

Glitsky's lips were tight. "The suspect was leaving the country," he said.

Chomorro tapped his gavel. "Please confine yourself to answering the questions, Sergeant. Ms. Pullios, I'm going to sustain Mr. Hardy here. No one is questioning the sergeant's handling of his case."

But, of course, Pullios had done just that: trying to discredit a prosecution witness who consorted with the defense.

As soon as Glitsky stepped down, Chomorro asked to see counsel in his chambers and called a ten-minute recess.

He stood in front of his desk. "Now look," he began as soon as Pullios and Hardy were inside, "I've warned you both about opening this can of worms and I'm not going to have it. This isn't a conspiracy case on either side. Mr. Hardy, that was some pretty nice navigating through some difficult shoals, but we're not going on in this direction. I notice you've got Lieutenant Batiste up soon. Do I take it he's going to say Sergeant Glitsky is a good cop who always follows established procedures?"

"More or less."

Chomorro shook his head. "Well, he's not going to. I've also got some real concerns about how you intend to handle Art Drysdale. I think it's all getting pretty irrelevant here." He held up a hand. "I'm not trying to cramp your style, Mr. Hardy, but unless you've got something a little more substantive I think you might reconsider your direction. I know you'll have the defendant up there half the day. I'll let you summarize your procedure questions in the closing argument— up to a point. But I'm not inclined to let this thing degenerate into character assassinations of everyone in this building. Clear?"

"Yes, Your Honor. But in that case, I do have a request. I'd like to add a witness."

"At this point?" Pullios asked.

"You've just asked me to cut out half of my witnesses. It doesn't seem unreasonable to take another tack. It's a small point anyway."

"Judge—"

Chomorro cut Pullios off. "Who is it?"

"Celine Nash, the victim's daughter."

"You're calling her for the *defense?*"

Hardy shrugged. "I'm calling her to get at the truth, Your Honor. The substance of her testimony will be access to the *Eloise,* Nash's habits on board."

"How is that relevant to Andy Fowler?" Pullios asked.

"Come on, Elizabeth, I don't want to give everything away. I'll get to it when she's on the stand." That wasn't strictly true, but it was a small enough point, and Chomorro, having taken away, ought to give him one back.

"All right," the judge said. "All right, Elizabeth?"

Pullios thought about it, then nodded. "Okay," she said, "why not?"

Testimony before lunch was taken up by Ron Reynolds, the polygraph expert. Hardy kept him on the stand longer than he thought really necessary, since the only important point he had to make was that Andy had *volunteered* to take the lie detector test. If Andy Fowler had been guilty, or even acting with a consciousness-of-guilt, he would not have done that, was Hardy's point.

Of course, polygraph evidence of this sort was only admissible by stipulation. But Pullios had agreed to the testimony, provided she could make the point that Fowler hadn't actually passed the test. Hardy didn't need Reynolds's point, but Pullios couldn't do much with hers, either, and Hardy needed Reynolds to take up most of the rest of the morning on the stand—he had to take the good with the bad.

So he ran Reynolds around with how the polygraph worked in general, why people did well or poorly on it, margin for error and so on. On cross, Pullios, as expected, leaned on the fact that Fowler, with his vast experience, would conceivably know how to beat the test and therefore could have volunteered to take it knowing he could throw off the results.

But for Hardy, it accomplished his ultimate goal. He did not want to call Celine Nash before lunch. Suddenly, after the recess in Chomorro's office, the course of the trial lay clearly charted before him. He would take Celine, the witness, baiting the trap, after lunch. Afterward, Fowler would testify on his own behalf, then perhaps Hardy would get to his closing argument.

Tomorrow, Chomorro would give the jury their instructions and leave it in their hands.

But today, after she testified, Celine would remain in the courtroom, as she had every day, until that day's business was done. He was counting on the fact that she would not risk altering her routine, not when she was so close to winning.

"Celine Nash."

She reacted almost as though she'd been hit, turning in her seat abruptly to look around her. Recovering her composure, she stood in

the gallery and walked up through the railing, looking questioningly at
Hardy.

She settled herself into the witness box. She wore charcoal pinstripes over a magenta silk blouse, the effect of which was, somehow,
both severe and demure. Her hair was pulled back, accenting the
chiseled face, the aristocratic lines. Hardy steeled himself and moved
to his spot as she was being sworn in.

"Ms. Nash, I've just a few questions, if you feel up to them."

She nodded, wary, looking to the jury, then to Pullios. When she
came back to Hardy she seemed to relax, getting into the role. "Go
ahead, Mr. Hardy, I'm fine."

"Thank you. You and your father, Owen Nash, were very close, were
you not?"

"Yes, we were."

"And you spoke often, saw each other often?"

"Yes. At least once a week, often more."

"Going sailing, having dinner, that type of thing?"

"Yes."

"Now in the last few weeks of your father's life, did this pattern
continue?"

"Well, yes. I know I talked to him the week—" she lowered her eyes
—"the week he died, for example. It had been normal."

"And did you talk about any particular subject most of the time?"

"No, not really. We talked about a lot of things. We were very close,
like old friends."

"I see. You talked about a lot of things—business associates, sports,
gossip, personal matters?"

"Pretty much, yes . . ."

"Now, during these last weeks, did he ever mention the name of
Andy Fowler, either to you or in your presence?"

She considered. "No, not that I remember."

Hardy walked back to the defense table and picked up some papers.
"I have here," he said, "a copy of the transcript of your testimony
before the grand jury in which you said that your father had told you
he was planning on going out on the *Eloise* with May Shinn on the
day he was killed. Do you remember that testimony?"

"Yes, of course."

"And yet we know that May Shinn did not go out with your father
that day."

It wasn't a question, and Chomorro took the opportunity to lean down from the bench. "I trust you're going somewhere here, Mr. Hardy."

He really wasn't. He was telling Celine he hadn't forgotten about that testimony. He apologized to the judge and went back to his table, replacing the transcript.

Turning, he started over in a mellower tone. "Ms. Nash, your father took a great deal of pride in his boat, did he not?"

Easier ground. "He loved it," she said, sitting back. "It was like a home to him. His real home."

"You were familiar with it, then? You spent a lot of time on board?" Casual.

"Well, yes. But not so much recently . . . He was taking May out on it a good deal."

"Do you know, did your father tell you, if May Shinn had a key to the *Eloise?*"

Pullios stood up. "Your Honor, I know we're on boats here, but this is a little too much fishing for my taste."

"Mr. Hardy, do you have a point?"

"Your Honor, sometime between Wednesday night, June twenty-fourth, and the next afternoon the person who killed Owen Nash brought the murder weapon back onto the *Eloise*. That person would need a key."

"Your Honor! This is outrageous. How does this unsubstantiated claim relate to this proceeding, to Mr. Fowler, to anything? No evidence has been entered, even hinted at, on this point."

Hardy knew this would be the response, but he had to get the message to Celine that he knew. He kept calm. Her face, he noticed, had gone pale, although at the moment no one else was looking at her. He was at the center of the storm.

"Mr. Hardy," Chomorro said, "we've heard Sergeant Glitsky testify that he found the gun on Thursday aboard the *Eloise*. Do you have a witness with a different version of events?"

"No, Your Honor, not yet."

"Well, this is neither the time nor the place to find it. Is there anything *relevant* you'd like to ask Ms. Nash? Otherwise . . ." He leaned over toward Celine as Hardy said no. "The court apologizes, Ms. Nash. If Ms. Pullios has no objection . . . ?"

"No, pass the witness," Pullios said.

When Hardy sat down, Fowler whispered to him. "What the hell was all that about? If that's the best we got, then let me up there."

*   *   *

Celine was cool, but he'd always known that. She walked by his table without a glance at him. He turned to watch her go back to her seat on the aisle. Thank God, he thought. As he'd assumed, she wasn't leaving.

Finally Andy Fowler took the stand, and Hardy led him through the testimony they had rehearsed fifty times. He did look good up there, Hardy thought. Self-assured, confident, speaking clearly, giving the jury his attention and respect.

They went through it all from the beginning, taking the good with the bad. There were a few rough moments, such as when Hardy asked him, as they had decided he would, just why it was he had hired Emmet Turkel.

"I didn't hire him to find out about Owen Nash," Fowler said. "I don't deny that was what he found, but I just wanted to know why May would not see me anymore. I thought she might even be in some trouble. I just wanted to know, and she had made it clear she didn't want to talk to me about it."

They went over how the fingerprints came to be on the clip of the gun, the tortuous and unlikely route that May's proceeding had traveled to wind up in Andy's courtroom.

"And once it was there," Fowler said, "I felt it was too late. It was a mistake, a terrible mistake, but it wasn't something I had contrived. It just happened—it fell in my lap."

He admitted the lies to his colleagues, portraying himself—accurately, Hardy thought—as a man torn between his private needs and his professional position. "I should have asked her to marry me months before and taken whatever came from that," he said. "But I never thought about losing her until she was gone. And then, again, it was too late." Flat out.

As to his weekend in the Sierras, what could he say? He had gone up to clear his head, with the express purpose of seeing no one. He had succeeded only too well. He wished he hadn't. "It would have saved the state"—he took in the jurors—"and the jury much time, trouble and expense."

In all, it took less than two hours of relaxed if meticulous testimony. Fowler remained composed, saying what needed to be said.

Pullios was obliged to charge not like a bull but like a terrier, holding onto his trouser leg, hoping to pull him off balance. Watching her

work, Hardy was struck once again by her passion. Here was no act—
every ounce of her dripped with the conviction that Andy Fowler lied
with every breath he drew and had cold-bloodedly murdered Owen
Nash.

"Would you say, Mr. Fowler, that you are an avid camper?"

The judge smiled. "No, not particularly."

"How many times, roughly, have you been camping in, say, the past
year?"

"Just the once, I'm sure of that."

"How about in the past couple of years?"

"No."

"No what?"

"No, I've only gone that once in the last few years. I'm a pretty busy
man. Or have been . . ."

"And yet last June, out of the blue, you suddenly decided to take a
weekend off and go backpacking in the high Sierras?"

"That's right."

"Would you mind telling us where you ate on Friday night? Friday
night was the night you left town, wasn't it?"

"Yes. It was one of those spots up Highway Fifty above Placerville. I
don't remember the exact name."

"Do you recall what town it was near?"

Fowler shook his head. "No, I'm really not too familiar with the
area."

"Do you remember what you ate?"

His frown grew pronounced. "I believe I ate a steak." He tried some
levity. "But since I'm under oath I won't swear to it."

She kept at it. Was it dark when he had finished dinner? Where had
he spent the night exactly? When did he hit the trailhead? What was
his destination? How had he found it? What did he bring with him to
eat on Saturday night?

It was getting to him. "You know," he said, "I didn't give a great
deal of thought to that weekend until after I was charged with this
crime. It was simply a weekend away, not one to remember."

"Yes," Pullios said, turning to the jury, "we can see that."

She moved along, as Hardy feared she would, to the stipulation
about Fowler knowing not only that the gun was on the boat but
exactly where it had been kept.

"And this was after you had broken up, you found this out?"

"Yes."

"When May Shinn wasn't talking to you to the extent that you had to hire a private investigator to find out why she wouldn't see you?"

"Well, she talked to me that once."

"Why did she do that?"

"I don't really know. I called and she happened to answer the phone. Usually it was set to her machine. But she picked up, so we talked."

"And just casually talking, she happened to mention that her Beretta was in the desk at the side of Owen Nash's bed on board the *Eloise?*"

"No, it wasn't quite like that."

"Would you tell us, please, what it was quite like?"

Hardy looked at the clock. She had at least another hour today and she was, to his regret, hammering at the evidence they did have, avoiding for the moment the entire consciousness-of-guilt issue, although he knew that too would come. Also, and perhaps worse, Andy seemed to be losing it a little, beginning to come across peevish.

"Let's talk about Mr. Turkel again. You've testified that you were curious about why Ms. Shinn was breaking up with you?"

"That's right."

"And so you hired Mr. Turkel?"

Short questions, little tugs on the trousers. But they were doing the job.

Fowler nodded wearily. "Yes, I hired Mr. Turkel."

"How much did he charge you?"

"I think it was about a hundred and thirty-five dollars a day, plus expenses."

Pullios brought in the jury again. "One hundred thirty-five dollars a day. And did you pay for his plane fare out here?"

"Yes."

"And back?"

She brought out that he had spent over $1500 to obtain detailed information on Owen Nash and May Shinn. "And now, having spent all this money, what did you intend to do with this information?"

"Why, nothing. I just wanted to know, as I've explained."

"You paid fifteen hundred dollars to find out something about which you intended to do nothing?"

"That's right."

Hardy was nervous. Confidence eroding, his client, now into his third hour on the stand, eyes shifting from Pullios to Hardy to the judge, was coming across, body language and all, like a pathological liar.

Pullios saw that, of course, and it led her naturally into all the real lies—to his friends, associates, to anyone who would listen.

And then, finally, the litany of his admitted transgressions designed to show Andy's consciousness-of-guilt. How long have you been on the bench? Did you swear a sacred oath never to subvert the judicial process? Have you ever previously recused yourself from a case? Oh? Several times? Were the grounds as strong as they were here? Had he ever even *heard* of another judge putting up bail for a defendant?

On and on and on.

Hardy took a page of notes, then gave up on it. Pullios wasn't twisting the facts—she was *using* them very effectively to create a character and a circumstance that made murder not only seem consistent but inevitable.

At a quarter to five she finished at last and turned Fowler back to Hardy for redirect. He only had one area to which he wanted to return, where he thought he might be able to repair some of the damage.

"Mr. Fowler, was your conduct regarding the May Shinn matter investigated by the Ethics Committee of the Bar Association of California?"

"Objection." Pullios was sounding a little weary.

Chomorro knew the end was in sight and cut Hardy a little slack. "Overruled."

Hardy repeated the question and Fowler, on the stand, nodded. "Yes, it was."

"And were you, in fact, disbarred for what Ms. Pullios has been calling your egregious misconduct?"

Hardy knew that Andy had been reprimanded, but not otherwise disciplined on the Shinn trial issue. And even after Andy was indicted for murder, the Bar Association wasn't going to disbar—or do anything—to a fellow attorney until he had been convicted.

"No, I was not."

"Are you, in fact, as we sit here now, a member in good standing of the state bar?"

"I am."

"All right, thank you."

63

Fowler had wanted to talk. Jane wanted to argue. Frannie, he was sure, wanted him to come home. Jeff Elliot had arrived in the gallery and wanted an interview.

But Celine had been leaving the courtroom and there wasn't time for any of that. He had stuffed his papers into his briefcase earlier and now, making excuses, pushed his way through the gallery and out into the hallway. She was fifty feet ahead of him as she left the building through the back door by the morgue.

A cold night had fallen. The air still felt damp from the storm, although it had stopped raining. Hardy jogged to keep close. He too was parked in the back lot and got to his car about when Celine reached hers. He left the lot three cars behind her and followed her uptown across Market to Van Ness, then north to Lombard, always keeping at least one vehicle between them. He had to run only two red lights.

On Lombard, as she turned west, he ventured closer in the lane next to her. She drove a little over the speed limit but not recklessly. For a moment as they approached the Golden Gate Bridge turnoff, he felt a moment of panic—he was wrong and she was going to Sausalito or somewhere, maybe to visit Ken Farris.

But she took the turnoff, avoiding the bridge, and swung out through the swaying eucalyptus of the Presidio. He had never been to her house. He didn't know where she lived. But he was certain she was going home.

He might have guessed. Her house was less than three blocks from her late father's palace in the Seacliff section, really not so far from his own house in distance, although light years away in other respects. Celine's place, however, was not a palace—it didn't appear much bigger than Hardy's.

She turned into the driveway and he pulled up to the curb across the street and killed his lights.

This, he knew, was a long shot, but it had come to him last night as the only possibility left to break the evidence deadlock. If Celine still had her key to the *Eloise*, it would be over. It was the only explanation of the missing gun, how it had come back into the drawer after he had seen it empty on Wednesday night. What he had to do was get it, find it on her, in her possession.

Ring the bell, knock her down, tie her up and search the house— but he couldn't do that. He had to wait. She could be flushing it down the toilet, throwing it into the garbage. But he didn't think she'd do anything like that. She'd want it out of the house, away from the area entirely. If she had it, her nature would make her get rid of it dramatically. He hoped.

So he waited.

A light went on in the upstairs window, her shadow moving across it. Even in the cold, he realized his palms were sweating. What was he doing this for? He should have somehow cajoled or forced Abe to come along. But here he was.

He waited.

The light went out, then another one downstairs. He heard a door slam, then a car door open and close, and he turned on his own ignition.

With his lights off, he swung a U-turn and followed her back the way she had come on the El Camino del Mar. But she only drove for about three minutes before pulling into the darkened parking lot at Phelan Beach.

The night was eerily still after the rain. Eucalyptus leaves scratched and clacked overhead; a foghorn bellowed from far away.

Hardy had let her get into the trees before he parked by the entrance and started to jog, again, through the light forest.

She had driven to the front of the lot, turned off her engine, doused her lights. The Golden Gate Bridge loomed spectacularly overhead in the clear night air. The door opened and she got out and, without turning or hesitating, started for the beach.

A three-quarter moon reflected off the water, casting a light shadow as she walked unhurriedly across the sand. Hardy got to the edge of the beach and pulled off his shoes. She was halfway to the water when he broke into a run toward her.

She heard. As he closed the distance, she turned.

"Celine."

It was almost as if she had been expecting him. This was no gener-alized fear—she knew who he was, and seeing him she nodded as if to herself, then whirled with her right hand in the air.

Hardy lunged for her wrist, caught it and closed his other hand around hers. God, he'd forgotten how strong she was! She pulled against him, kicking at his legs, his groin.

He held her, never relaxing his grip on her hands, forcing himself to kick back, catching her at the side of the knee, sending her twisting down, falling on top of her.

Still struggling, she bit into his arm near the shoulder. Spinning around, he forced his weight down on top of her. Her legs came up, trying to knee him, throwing sand over them both, into faces and eyes.

He rolled over onto her hand, holding it clenched tight beneath him, and began to pry at the fingers. With her other hand she reached up, digging her nails into his scalp. He felt the skin tear down into his neck.

She was getting weaker. The vise grip of her hand slowly opened enough for him to feel what she held there, to grab it and roll away.

He didn't know if that would end it so he kept rolling until he got a little distance, maybe six feet, then came to his knees facing her, panting from the exertion. Celine still lay there in her tailored char-coal suit, now torn to rags.

Gasping for breath, he didn't take his eyes from her. He looked down at the key in his hand—attached to a little ring and a small block of wood. He knew without being able to see it that the wood would have written on it, either burned or indelibly marked, the word "Eloise."

Gradually he became aware of the lapping of the water against the beach. Celine turned onto her side and curled up in a fetal position. Her sobbing ignored him . . . it was totally private, and chilling. A keening for all she had lost, for all she never had.

Owen Nash grinned into the wind as he brought the boom around. His cigar was out, half-consumed in his mouth. They had been out on the water for two hours and it was going to be all right. He had told Celine he was going to marry May. She would see, she'd eventually accept it. And now she could be free of him and the thing they'd begun so long ago that had bound them in guilt and lust for so long he couldn't remember when it hadn't been there.

They had not talked much yet but he had always been able to control her, and now it was just a matter of waiting for the right moment.

The door to the cabin opened and she came out, wind whipping that fine wet hair. He had started telling her as they were going through the Gate, together fighting the current and the wind. Afterward— okay, it shook her when she saw he meant it—she said she needed to be alone. Even with the rough seas, she wanted to go below and do some aerobics, let it all settle. Get loose. She had apparently taken a shower, and stood now in the doorway to the cabin wrapped in a turkish robe.

Barefoot, she came up another step onto the deck. The robe swung open and he caught a glimpse of the front of her, breasts and belly, her shaved pubis. She did not pull the robe closed, but came toward him unsteadily in the rocking boat, her eyes glazed, he presumed, from the exertion.

Coming around the wheel, she pressed herself up against him, opening the robe. "Come below, Daddy."

He had to fight for his breath, for the control he swore he would have. "Honey, I've told you . . ."

Her hand went down to him, caressing. "I know what you've said. I don't care if you have her, but you've got to keep me. You've got to keep us."

She found him under the green jogging pants, and against his will, he began to respond. As he always did. Suddenly the boat heeled and pushed him up against her, both of them against the wheel. "Come below," she whispered, holding him.

But this could not go on—he would never let it happen again—he had promised himself and he had promised May. He had found something real for the first time since his marriage to Eloise. It was his last chance, and his selfish, beautiful daughter was not going to take it from him, as she'd taken Eloise years before, because of his weakness for her flesh.

Hating himself, and hating her for what they'd both become, he pushed back against her. "No! No!" He shoved her hard. "I said it's over, Celine! Goddammit, over, leave me alone."

She went down on the slippery deck, the robe spilling open around her. And then he saw it in her eyes: the hate he knew had to be there— you didn't live this way without hate.

Glazed but dry-eyed, she stared at him as if he were an alien force, then she gathered herself up, wrapped the robe around her and went below without a word.

He had lost the wind, goddammit. His cigar was gone, too.

The drizzle increased—visibility was about a hundred yards. He squinted through the mist, checked his compass, making sure he was on a south or southwest heading. He didn't want to beach her. He listened for the telltale sound of breakers.

She'd be all right, he thought again. It was the kind of thing that would take some time. He ought to have factored that in instead of just laying it on her. She'd get used to the idea eventually. He was sure.

She emerged again a couple of minutes later, still in the robe, but more under control now. There—see?—he was right. She'd work it out. You couldn't expect a woman not to try some histrionics.

He was surprised to see her wearing her lifting gloves—she must have wanted to work off some of it. He thought it was getting to be time to head the Eloise *back in.*

"Daddy."

He wasn't cruel. He didn't want to hurt her. If she were ready to talk again, he'd talk. Gently. He understood her. He came around the wheel and started walking toward her.

She took the gun from the pocket of the terry robe and leveled it at him. He stopped, tried to smile, as he might with an errant child, reaching out one hand. "Honey . . ."

She lowered her aim and fired. He felt a punch, then a pain deep in his groin. His legs went dead and he dropped to his knees, looking up at her with a surprised expression, at the tiny muzzle of May's tiny gun. "My God, Celine, you've killed your father . . ."

She shook her head. "Not yet, Daddy." He saw the muzzle come up and settle on his heart.

64

FOWLER DIDN'T DO IT
Not-Guilty Verdict Returned in Nash Murder Trial
by Jeffrey Elliot
Chronicle Staff Writer

Former Superior Court Judge Andrew B. Fowler yesterday was found not guilty of the murder of financier Owen Nash. The jury deliberated less than two full days in returning the verdict in favor of the former judge, who had been a fixture on the San Francisco bench for over three decades.

The trial marked a personal victory both for Fowler and for his attorney, Dismas Hardy, an ex-prosecutor for whom this trial marked a defense debut. Hardy insisted that he had never doubted his client's innocence, that Judge Fowler had himself been a victim of infighting within the city's judiciary.

"There was never any physical evidence tying the judge to the crime," Hardy said. "Of course that doesn't mean the jury might not have found him guilty. But this verdict is a wonderful vindication of the system."

"We weren't happy from the beginning," said jury foreman Shane Pollett. "They'd already arrested someone else on pretty much the same evidence. It wasn't that Fowler hadn't done some bad things, but nobody proved he'd killed Nash. The prosecution had to prove Fowler killed Nash, and they didn't do it."

This verdict marks the second defeat for the district attorney's office surrounding the death of Owen Nash. Last summer the office charged Nash's mistress, May Shinn, of the murder, but subsequently was forced to drop the charge when her alibi was corroborated by two witnesses.

District Attorney Christopher Locke denied there was any "witch-

475

hunt" of Judge Fowler. "The evidence," he said, "and we looked at it very closely for several months, strongly implicated the judge. But the jury has spoken. That's how it works. That's the end of it."

Asked if he was going to pursue another investigation into the death of Owen Nash, Locke said that that was up to the police department. "If they bring us another suspect and new evidence, of course we'll move on it immediately." There are, however, no new suspects at this time.

Judge Fowler plans to spend the next few weeks in Hawaii and then resume his position as a partner in the firm of Strand, Worke & Luzinski.

HARDY SAT ACROSS FROM JEFF ELLIOT'S DESK in the *Chronicle* Building. "What do you mean Celine didn't do it? What about everything I found out in Santa Cruz?"

"Speaking of which, I trust you had a good time," Hardy said. "You should have, for four hundred dollars. What costs four hundred dollars in Santa Cruz?"

Elliot said, straight-faced, "I think we rode the Roller Coaster a hundred and forty times each. But listen, getting back to this thing, my story—"

Hardy stopped him. "All you found out was she might not have been there, right?"

Elliot nodded.

"You got anything anywhere that puts her on the boat?"

"No."

"Ask yourself why this sounds familiar." Hardy hated to take Jeff's story away, but he wasn't in the prosecution business anymore. "Look, Jeff, you can try to get some police action on this, but they won't thank you for it. I've tried, I know. Owen Nash gives everybody downtown a bad headache. You got any reason why you think Celine might have done it, other than I told you she might have?"

Jeff shrugged. "Somebody lies about their alibi—"

"*Everybody* has lied about their alibi in this case. Or looked like they have." He put a hand on Jeff's shoulder. "You're welcome to it, Jeff, but it's a dry well. It's just another maybe."

Elliot turned to his computer, squinted at something, came back to Hardy. "What made you change your mind? I got the impression you honestly thought she'd done it."

Hardy crossed a leg over another one. "That was before my client was cleared, Jeff. If I'd needed to find out who killed Nash to get Fowler off, I suppose I would have kept on it. But now . . . Andy didn't do it. That was my main interest."

"You're not curious?"

Hardy got cryptic. "No. I know everything I need to."

"Keeping life simple, right?"

Hardy nodded. "Something like that."

On December 21, Hardy stood holding Rebecca in one arm and a package in the other at the Clement Street post office. With the Christmas rush, he had waited for almost twenty minutes by the time he got to the window.

The clerk took the package, a box about two-by-three inches. "No way," he said.

"No way what?" Hardy asked.

"Christmas, man. There's no way." The clerk looked at the address. "I were you, I'd just deliver it. It's only half a mile, if that. Be there in fifteen minutes. Nice houses up there. I love it when it's lit up."

"It's not a Christmas present," Hardy said, "it doesn't have to get there any time."

"Probably won't make it till New Years."

"That's okay. It doesn't matter."

The clerk shook the box. "It's not fragile, is it? Sounds like keys or something."

"That's what it is," Hardy said. "Somebody lost some keys."

He read about it on the day his son, Vincent, was born. He was still in St. Mary's hospital, on the top of the world. He had spent the night coaching Frannie, breathing and yelling and pushing with her until nearly dawn when the head had come through and then, five minutes later, the doctor told them they had a boy.

Frannie had pulled Hardy into the bed with her and the doctor lay the baby between them. The two of them looked in wonder at the life they'd produced. Vincent cuddled into both of them.

That afternoon Uncle Moses brought Rebecca by. He also brought the day's newspaper. After Moses had gone, Frannie had gone to sleep with Rebecca on the bed. Hardy started reading the *Chronicle*. On page 3, Jeff Elliot had written a brief story outlining the stabbing death of Celine Nash, "the daughter of the late financier Owen

Nash," at a rough trade hotel in the Tenderloin District. There were no suspects yet in connection with the slaying and it was presumed that the victim, who had a past history of occasional prostitution, had simply gotten unlucky with a john.

Hardy closed the paper. Out the window of the hospital room, the day was fading into an overcast dusk.

A while later, they brought Vincent in for feeding. Hardy gave Frannie a distracted smile, then looked back out at the falling night.

"Are you all right?" Frannie was nursing the baby, studying him. "What is it?"

Hardy shook himself away from his thoughts. He got up from his chair and came over to her bed. Lifting the sleeping Beck onto him, squeezing in next to Frannie, he said, "Nothing. Just the world out there, I guess."

"You know what," she said. "That's not the world. The world is on this bed right now."

Frannie laced her fingers in his hand. Hardy felt his daughter stir against him and his son made some contented sounds. He tried to blink the room back into focus, but it didn't work, so he brought his hand up to his eyes.